"I had a look at part of th[e] [...] "I know you didn't ask me t[o] [...] was one detail in there th[at] [...] recall coming out in the trial."

"What?" I asked, intrigued.

""Well, there was blood splatter, blowback from the head wound Tiffany had. But there were some voids in the splatter. One area was on the driver's side door. There was blood on the outside of Benjamin Middleton's jacket sleeves but none on the inside. That doesn't make sense to me if he was facing Tiffany down, aiming the gun at her. There was also splatter on the right side of the bodice part of his jacket, but none on the left. That suggests that Middleton was facing forward in the car. And there was also a long space running down the inside of the driver door, near the middle, where there was no blood splatter. This was in front of where Ben's body would have been, and there was splatter on either side of it. To me, that suggests that something blocked the splatter."

"Like another person's arm reaching in through the window?" I asked, playing out the scene in my mind.

"Exactly," Tyrese said.

"You said voids, plural," Mal noted. "What were the others?"

"There was only one other area I noted, and it was on the gun itself. There was a void around the trigger, which you'd expect to find if someone had a finger wrapped around it, but there was also a void along the top of the barrel. In fact, most of the barrel was clean. And Benjamin Middleton had blood on the backs of both of his hands."

Mal said, "If someone had a hand wrapped around that gun barrel wrestling for it, it might explain the void."

Books by Allyson K. Abbott

Murder on the Rocks

Murder with a Twist

In the Drink

Shots in the Dark

Published by Kensington Publishing Corp.

Shots in the Dark

ALLYSON K. ABBOTT

KENSINGTON BOOKS

http://www.kensingtonbooks.com

KENSINGTON BOOKS are published by

Kensington Publishing Corp.
119 West 40th Street
New York, NY 10018

All Kensington titles, imprints and distributed lines are available at special quantity discounts for bulk purchases for sales promotion, premiums, fund-raising, educational or institutional use. Special book excerpts or customized printings can also be created to fit specific needs. For details, write or phone the office of the Kensington Special Sales Manager: Kensington Publishing Corp., 119 West 40th Street, New York, NY 10018. Attn. Special Sales Department. Phone: 1-800-221-2647.

Kensington and the K logo Reg. U.S. Pat. & TM Off.

ISBN-13: 978-1-4967-0170-1
ISBN-10: 1-4967-0170-4
First Kensington Mass Market Edition: August 2016

eISBN-13: 978-1-4967-0171-8
eISBN-10: 1-4967-0171-2
First Kensington Electronic Edition: August 2016

10 9 8 7 6 5 4 3 2 1

Printed in the United States of America

For Ashley, James, Rowan, and Anna

Acknowledgments

While writing is a solitary endeavor (but not a lonely one, as there are so many imaginary people in my head!), I couldn't do it without all the people who have been a part of my life, people who have influenced not only the way I think but also the way I feel and who I am today. There are bits and pieces of every one of you in my books.

Of course, there are some who exert more influence than others, and some who are an integral part of this whole process. Special mention goes to Scott, the love of my life and the man who patiently gives me the time and space to write when I know he'd rather we were doing other things; to my sisters, Cathy, Laurie, and Amy, who have shaped so much of my outlook on life and honed my warped sense of humor; to my son, Ryan, and my daughter-in-law, Jennifer, whose love, wit, and humor keep me going; to my editor, Peter Senftleben, whose guidance and wisdom have always been spot-on and much appreciated; to my agent, Adam Chromy, whose tireless efforts on my behalf make the business part of this writing stuff nearly painless; and to Morgan Elwell, the sharpest, most effective marketing person I've met yet in this business.

My appreciation also goes to the many coworkers I've had throughout my nursing career, people whose humor, support, and input have been invaluable in so many ways. There are too many of you to mention individually, so please know that I have been honored to work beside every one of you. Thanks also go to the friends and acquaintances who have supported me with word-of-mouth advertising, laughter breaks, and the occasional funny bon mot or plot idea, some of which I have shamelessly stolen (Callie and Bree, thanks for the great ones you gave me today, right before I wrote this!).

Finally, I wish to express my gratitude to my readers, the people who are the very reason I do this. I can't thank all of you enough for letting me into your lives and allowing me to entertain you for a short while. It would all be pointless without you. Happy reading!

Chapter 1

The winter streets of Milwaukee could be tough to negotiate on the best of days, but this was the one time of year when no one seemed to mind. Bright lights reflected off crisp white snow in a kaleidoscope of color and holiday cheer. The air smelled of pine, cinnamon, and a buttery goodness, which helped to ease the bite of the bitter cold air that stung my nose when I breathed. Varying strands of music— some close, some from afar, some secular, some holy, some vocal, and some instrumental—mixed and mingled in my ears. Christmas was right around the corner, and the city streets were filled with happy-looking people, their cheeks flushed red by the cold winter air, their eyes alight with warmth and anticipation, their souls filled with holiday spirit.

My name is Mackenzie Dalton, though most everyone calls me Mack, and as I walked amid the holiday throng, I couldn't help but feel like an alien, an impostor, a hypocrite. I had no interest in holiday shopping, sharing a wassail, or singing a carol. I wasn't feeling the holiday spirit. And at that moment I hated the cold, because it reminded me of things frozen, unmoving, and dead. I'd never been a big fan of Christmas, and I was dreading this one in particular, not because I was a bah-humbuggy Scrooge type, but because all those noises, sights, and smells had an overwhelming physical effect on me. I have synesthesia, a neurological disorder that results in my sensory input getting cross-wired. Because of this, I experience every sense in at least two ways. For instance, I may taste something I hear, or see something I smell. Even my emotions come as a two-for-one sale.

My emotions during this holiday season were more intense than usual because I had recently lost someone close to me—several someones, in fact—and hanging over my head was the threat of more to come. It began with my father's murder back in January, and then his girlfriend, Ginny, was murdered in August. Both deaths occurred in or near my bar, and the Grim Reaper had been a rather persistent companion of mine ever since, so much so that my planned Christmas gift to everyone was to try to prevent any more murders among my circle of friends. It wouldn't be easy, for reasons I'll explain in a moment.

Mack's Bar was my father's legacy to me. He opened it right before I was born and named it after himself. Then he named me Mackenzie, with the assumption that I would one day carry on the business. I grew up in the bar with my father; my mother died right after I was born, due to a traumatic head injury she sustained in a car accident. She was left brain dead from the accident, but the doctors were able to keep her alive long enough for me to grow inside her and make my entrance into the world. My father and I lived in an apartment on the floor above the bar, and now I live there alone. As a result, my childhood days were spent mingling with any number of strangers and "regulars" who patronized the place, and I knew how to mix a slew of drinks before I knew basic math. Up until my father's death, my life was tidy, predictable and, some might say, boring. I liked it that way.

My father's death put an end to my comfortable, complacent lifestyle, and Ginny's death compounded the problem. A lot of new people came into my life, the most noteworthy being Duncan Albright, a homicide detective who was relatively new to Milwaukee at the time. As part of his investigation into Ginny's murder, he worked undercover in my bar and ended up under the covers on my bed. He discovered my disorder could be useful in helping him solve crimes, and he dragged me into a few cases. I resisted at first because my synesthesia was something I felt a need to hide; it embarrassed me and made me feel like a freak. But when Duncan showed me how I could use it to do something good, my attitude began to change. I opened up my mind to the idea of my synesthesia being something both helpful and useful. And I opened up my heart to Duncan.

Neither change came easily. It seemed the general public and Duncan's bosses weren't as open-minded about my synesthesia as Duncan was. When the local press got wind of my involvement in a high-profile case involving a missing child, news pieces about how the local police were using witchcraft, ESP, and voodoo hit the papers and the airwaves. This didn't go over well with the brass at the Milwaukee Police Department, and Duncan ended up getting suspended. We spent some time apart, hoping the furor would die down, but it didn't. If anything, it got worse. My life was turned upside down to the point that it became the antithesis of that dull, predictable life I'd had while growing up. This was due in part to other deaths associated with my bar. One of those deaths was that of my bouncer and fill-in bartender, Gary Gunderson, who was murdered just two days ago. And in a way it was my fault.

I was being stalked, taunted, and tormented by a diabolical killer. This person kept sending me letters with puzzles I had to figure out by a deadline in order to prevent the death of someone I knew. And just in case I doubted the veracity of that claim, the writer killed one of my customers, Lewis Carmichael, a nurse who worked at a nearby hospital. Lewis was not only a customer but also a member of the Capone Club, a group of crime solvers from a variety of backgrounds who came to my bar on a regular basis.

The first couple of letters that arrived after Lewis's death I managed to interpret and solve in time, but I stumbled over the last one. My initial interpretation was wrong, and by the time I figured out what it was supposed to be, it was too late. Gary died because of my mistake.

On the heels of Gary's death, my fear and frustration with the letter writer morphed into a white-hot anger. I became mad as hell and determined to find the person behind it all. I wasn't alone in my efforts, because I had the help of some of the members of the Capone Club. A handful of them—those I was closest to, those I considered my family now that I had none of my own—knew about the letter writer. Cora Kingsley, a forty-something, redheaded man hunter and computer geek, was like a sister to me. Her skills with computers had proved invaluable, both in interpreting the clues and in logging my synesthetic reactions so I could better use and understand them. And Joe and Frank Signoriello, two retired, seventy-something brothers who were ex–insurance salesmen, were also in the loop. These two men have known me my entire life, and when my father died, they took on the role of advisers, becoming the closest thing to family I had.

These three people and Duncan knew about the letter writer. The others in the Capone Club did not, and this created a dilemma for me since the letter writer had said the victims would be among those I knew. The deaths thus far had proven the truth of this claim, and every hour I debated the wisdom of keeping the others in the dark. But I was afraid that if the news got out about the letters, the writer might seek revenge by going on a killing spree.

While the letter writer hadn't specifically said I couldn't use the Capone Club to help me solve the puzzles, I was wary of pushing that envelope. And the instructions did make it clear that I wasn't allowed to use the help of any cops, with Duncan getting specific mention. This made my decision not to inform the club members about the letter writer a little easier, since some of the local cops participated.

Thus far I'd managed to skirt the no-cops edict by keeping Duncan involved on the sly while making it appear as if the two of us were on the outs. This facade was made easier by the fact that I was pretending to date someone else, a fellow named Mal O'Reilly, who happened to be both an undercover cop and a friend of Duncan's. I allowed the cops who participated in the Capone Club to help us solve other crimes we were working on, but I kept the letter writer to myself and took care not to involve them in any part of that investigation.

It was a thin wire I walked, because there were lots of cops around at the time, and not just because they liked my coffee. They were also around because they were investigating Gary's murder by questioning me, my employees, and many of my regular customers. Gary's death hadn't occurred at my bar, but the connection to it was clear. Not only had he worked for me, but his body was found with one of my cocktail napkins wadded up and stuffed in his mouth. Because of this, a trio of detectives had been more or less living at my bar since Wednesday night. Duncan was not one of them.

Gary's death hit me hard, not only because it ramped up my anger and my fear level, but also because I felt indebted to the man. He was an ex-con—a fact I discovered by accident during the investigation into Ginny's death—and this knowledge had colored my impression of him. When I realized how wrong I was, he not only forgave me, he literally took a bullet for me, saving my life. That put avenging his death high on my list, though my task wouldn't be an easy one. Not only did I have no clue who the letter writer was, but I was also laid up with a broken leg I'd sustained in a car accident while rushing to get to the correct location indicated in the most recent letter before the deadline. That accident had cost me time and as a result, it had cost Gary his life. Though I was determined not to make the same mistake again, my confidence had flagged. And my investigative efforts had been further hampered by the reporters who were hounding me. Still, I was determined to find a way, to figure it out before another one of my friends, employees, or customers ended up dead.

It was this need that brought me out into the colorful holiday mayhem: I needed to visit the location indicated in the last letter, the location I hadn't made it to on time. I was heading for the Milwaukee Public Market.

Chapter 2

Winter was well established, with a foot or more of snow on the ground and the threat of more to come. For the time being, the snow and cold were welcomed by most as part of the holiday experience, but I knew that once Christmas was done, the real depression of winter would set in: two to three months of cold dreariness with little to break the monotony.

I generally don't mind the winter weather, but negotiating slippery sidewalks and streets on crutches, with one leg in a cast, had given me new insight. I nearly fell twice on the way to my car, and getting into it proved a nearly equal challenge as I fumbled with the crutches. Fortunately, the leg I broke was my left one, and I was still able to drive, but I was forced to position my legs awkwardly to make room for my plaster encasement.

The Public Market was less than a mile from my bar as the crow flies, but it took me fifteen minutes to get there, thanks to heavy holiday traffic, slippery roads, and bad stoplight karma. It was a Saturday, a busy day for the market, and the closest parking space I could find was two blocks away, forcing me to negotiate the slippery terrain again. In retrospect, I realized I probably should have had someone tag along, if for no other reason than to drop me off and drive around until I was done so I wouldn't have to deal with parking and the treacherous walk.

The Public Market is a vast, high-ceilinged warehouse-type building filled with a variety of shops. Floor-to-ceiling windows keep the place well lit during the day, and at night the overhead lighting, combined with the individual shops' lighting, creates a cozy ambience. It was mid-afternoon, and despite the bitter cold, the day was bright, with a blue, cloudless sky.

The onslaught of sights, sounds, and smells as I entered the place triggered a synesthetic frenzy of reactions that nearly overwhelmed me. But I was used to it—it happened every time I came here—and I knew what to do. Just inside the door I stopped, closed my eyes, and took a minute to suppress all the ancillary sensory experiences I was having, including the visuals, which didn't stop simply because I had my eyes closed. Images flashed across the backs of my eyelids like a movie in a darkened theater. Over the years I had learned how to deal with these situations, and after a minute or so of suppressive efforts, I felt comfortable enough to open my eyes and venture deeper into the building.

The synesthetic reactions I had to the smells proved the hardest to ignore because there were so many different aromas mingling and mixing together, many of them quite strong. The salty smell of fish mixed with the fragrant aroma of freshly ground coffee, and the sugary smell of just-baked cookies mingled with the perfumed scent of hothouse flowers. Since all the shops were basically open stalls of some sort, all the smells were free to infiltrate the building. On top of that, there were the people smells: perfumes, shampoos, aftershaves, laundry detergents, even the occasional whiff of body odor. Given that each of these smells triggered either a sound or a physical sensation in me, it was a constant struggle to dampen my senses and stay focused.

The last letter I received, the one that led to Gary's death, had contained a number of small items—a tiny portion of a map, magazine clippings with pictures of a faucet and a Broadway marquee, fish scales, a single flower petal, some ground cinnamon, a piece of coffee-soaked filter paper, a tiny piece of green terry cloth that had been soaked in wine, and a small piece of bread—multiple clues that, when put together, pointed to the Public Market. But Cora and I had put them together in a way that seemed to point to another location, a local church. By the time we realized our mistake and I headed for the market, time had run out.

Even though it was too late to save Gary, I desperately wanted to get my hands on the next clue. Over the past two days I'd been thinking about how to go about this task, and I knew I needed to start with the market vendors. I had no way of knowing if any of them were the target the letter writer had singled out, but based on past experience with the clues and the fact that the vendors were the one constant during the window of time I'd been given in the letter, I assumed one of them would prove to be key. Several specific vendors had been referenced in the clues, and I figured I'd start with them first. Duncan's surreptitious analysis of those clues using the police lab had uncovered some flower pollen mixed in with the cinnamon, something that might have been intentional or accidental. If it was intentional, it meant the florist shop was referenced more than the other shops, so I decided to start there. Granted, it was little more than a hunch, but I had to start somewhere, and it made as much sense as anything else.

The florist shop was located near the spice store, so my olfactory senses were working overtime as I approached. A white-haired, grandmotherly type woman was standing behind the counter, and she smiled warmly at me as I hobbled up.

"You look like you could use a little something to brighten up your day," she said, no doubt in preparation for her sales pitch. Her voice triggered a citrusy taste in my mouth.

I smiled back and gave her a half nod of agreement. I had a backstory I'd used when I'd approached others about the clues, and since it had worked before, I decided to stick to it. "I do need something, but I'm not sure exactly where it is, and I may be too late. There's this scavenger hunt game I participate in online. Well, you sign up for it online, but the hunt part is in the real world. Anyway, you get these clues that are delivered to people and places out and about, and you have to decipher the clues in a limited amount of time in order to get the next clue. My last clue led me here, but on the way I was hit by another car, which ran a stop sign, and I ended up with this." I waved a hand toward my leg. "Because of that, I missed my deadline, but I'm hoping someone might still have my next clue. Any chance you had a package delivered here to your shop with instructions to give it to someone who looked like me or to someone with the name Macken-zie Dalton?"

The woman gave me a bemused smile. "Are you saying someone bought you flowers that you're sup-posed to pick up here?"

"No. I don't think so. It would be an envelope of some sort." I wasn't certain of this, but that was the format used with the previous connections, so I was inclined to believe this one would be the same.

"Sorry, honey, but I don't have anything like that."

"You didn't receive a package or an envelope of some sort with instructions to destroy it if it wasn't picked up by a certain time?"

Her smile never wavered, but there was a wary look in her eye, which told me she was beginning to think I might not be firing on all cylinders. "Sorry," she said with an apologetic smile and a shrug.

One of the perks of my synesthesia—though some might call it a quirk—is that I can often tell if people are lying. My synesthetic reaction to the sound of their voice changes in some way. But in order to use it, I have to have a baseline lie for comparison, something I know is an untruth. I thought about asking the woman to lie to me on purpose, but I couldn't think of a way to broach the subject without her thinking I was a lunatic. Momentarily stymied, I decided to let it pass for now and to come back to her later if I struck out with the other vendors.

I thanked her and moved on to the neighboring spice shop. A woman who looked to be in her late forties was standing behind a small desk.

"Can I help you find something?" she asked with a sales-friendly smile. Her voice triggered the taste of coffee with an underlay of cinnamon, although the cinnamon taste might have come from a real smell. Sometimes I can't tell my synesthetic experiences from the real ones.

"Perhaps, Trudy," I said, reading her name tag. I repeated my story about the scavenger hunt, my accident, and how I'd missed my deadline. As I talked, her demeanor shifted 180 degrees. Her smile faded, her body language screamed wariness, and the way she chewed on her lip told me she was nervous. I feared she recognized me from some of the recent news coverage.

"Any chance you received an envelope or a package with instructions to destroy it after a certain time if no one claimed it?" I asked.

Trudy crossed her arms over her chest and narrowed her eyes at me. She was chewing on a piece of gum, and her cheek muscles twitched and popped as she chomped on it. "I didn't get any unusual package," she said, and the taste of her voice turned burnt and bitter, like coffee that's been left on the heat too long. Even without this synesthetic cue, I knew she was lying just from her body language. What I didn't know was why, but what she said next gave me a good idea. "I told those cops who came around Thursday the same thing."

I cursed under my breath but continued to smile warmly, hoping to put her at ease. Duncan was part of the investigative team looking into Gary's death, and since Gary's body had been found in his car, which had been parked in the Public Market lot, Duncan had volunteered to do the market queries, hoping he might get a lead on the letter writer.

"Cops?" I said, looking and sounding amused and befuddled. "They don't have anything to do with this. It's just a game I play."

"I don't know anything about any game," she said, tight-lipped.

"Are there other employees who work here? Maybe someone else got it."

She didn't respond right away, and when she finally did, it wasn't an answer to my question. It was verification of my earlier fear. "You're that bar owner who's been on the news," she said. "That man they found here the other night, the one that was killed, he worked for you, didn't he?"

I knew at that point there was little to be gained by continuing my ruse, so I bowed my head and sighed. "Yes, I'm that woman," I said. "And yes, Gary worked for me."

"Sorry for your loss," she said, not sounding sorry at all. Her face was set and determined. "Now, if you don't mind, I have work to do."

She turned and started to move away from me, but I grabbed her sleeve to stop her. "Please," I said in my best pleading tone. She glared pointedly at my hand on her sleeve, and I let it go. "Look, I'm sorry I lied to you about my reason for inquiring. All I can tell you is that I'm not working for or with the police, and any package that might have come here for me is private, personal, and extremely important."

Something in how I looked or sounded must have broken through her determination, because her stony expression softened a tad. But she wasn't softened enough. She slowly shook her head, her arms still crossed over her chest. "Sorry. I can't help you."

Feeling frustrated, I shifted gears. "I know you got a letter," I said. "And I know you're lying to me about it. I don't want to play hardball with you, but you have to understand how important this is. It's literally a matter of life and death." At that point, the pain and guilt I felt over Gary's death overwhelmed me, and tears flooded my eyes. I glanced around to see if anyone was in earshot, and then leaned in closer. "Gary died because I didn't get here in time to get that letter. I need to get to the bottom of this. Please, help me, Trudy."

A standoff ensued as Trudy eyed me with indecision. "You swear you're not working with the cops?" she said after several long seconds.

"I swear." I held up one hand to affirm my words. Then I positioned both hands so that it looked like I was praying, feeling a glimmer of hope. "Please," I begged.

She sighed, looked around the same way I had a moment ago, and then in a low voice she said, "I did get something. A large envelope was propped up against my door when I went to leave for work last Sunday." The taste of her voice at this point was smooth and mellow, like a light-roast coffee. I felt certain she was being honest with me now.

"You mean at your home?"

She nodded.

"What did it look like?"

"It was a plain manila envelope with my name written on it in big block letters. No address or anything. Inside the outer envelope was a note and another, smaller envelope, one of those number ten business-size things. The second envelope didn't have anything written on it."

"The note was instructions to you, yes?"

She nodded, and something about her expression told me she was holding something back. I took a stab at what it might be.

"There was money in the envelope, too, right? Money for you?"

She hesitated a second or two before nodding.

"That's fine," I said, smiling. "I have no interest in the money."

Her shoulders relaxed.

"What were your instructions?"

"The note said I was supposed to hand the envelope over to a woman named Mackenzie Dalton if she came asking for it. If you didn't show by eight o'clock Wednesday night, I was supposed to take the envelope home and burn it in my fireplace without opening it."

"And did you do that?" I asked, praying she hadn't.

To my chagrin, she nodded. "I was curious about it," she admitted. "I thought maybe it was some kind of secret note between lovers involved in a tryst or something." She scoffed and shook her head. "I'm a hopeless romantic at times. But then I started thinking it might be something darker, like drugs, or even a poison of some sort. What a perfect way to murder someone, right?" she said with a half grin. Then she seemed to realize how inappropriate that comment might be, and she winced. "Sorry. I didn't mean . . ."

"It's okay," I said with a little smile. I reached over and patted her arm as extra reassurance. "Can you tell me anything else about the outer envelope? Or the handwriting? Was there anything distinctive about any of it?"

She thought a moment but shook her head. "The envelopes were the same kind you can buy at any grocery or office supply store. And the writing was block printing . . . with a felt-tipped marker, I think. My name was on the outer envelope, and the instructions in the note were written out in the same block letters."

"Did it have both your first and last name on it?"

She nodded, looking a little worried. I assumed she was just now realizing the implications this had. Someone was dead because of that letter, and whoever had written it and sent it knew her full name and address.

"Anything else?" I asked.

She shook her head, still looking concerned. Her gaze cast anxiously about, as if she thought someone might be lurking nearby, ready to kill us both. When she finally looked back at me, she said, "I'm sorry about your friend." Her voice tasted sincere.

"Thank you."

Then she finally voiced her fears. "Am I in any kind of trouble or danger with this thing?"

I didn't know if she was worried about legal trouble or something more sinister, but it didn't matter either way. I shook my head and gave her a reassuring smile. "Other people before you have received packages. The person sending them has been picking people more or less at random, I think. You were nothing more than a conduit."

As I said this, I started wondering about how the letter writer chose those conduits and knew so much about the recipients. That gave me an idea that imbued me with a renewed sense of hope. I thanked Trudy for her honesty, promised again that our conversation would go no further, and then bought a bottle of seafood seasoning as both a gesture of goodwill and a way to explain why we'd just spent several minutes in conversation.

I don't think it did much to reassure her because as I left, I felt her worried stare following me down the aisle.

Chapter 3

I stopped at another shop to buy some cheeses I could use in my bar kitchen before I made my way back to my car. The return drive was as slow as the drive to the market, and my trek from my parking place to the bar—two blocks away was the closest I could get—was just as treacherous, and complicated by the bag of purchases I had to carry as I crutched my way along. The warmth of the bar was a welcome relief, and after briefly greeting the staff on duty out front, I headed into the kitchen to drop off my cheeses and spices. During the week my main full-time cook was Jon, a new hire I'd brought on when my longtime cook, Helmut, quit after his wife threatened to leave him if he didn't. She felt two murders in less than a year's time made my bar a dangerous workplace, the likes of which OSHA was unable to fix. I couldn't blame her for her concerns, and to be honest, Helmut had been well past retirement age and kind of set in his ways. Every time I made any changes to the menu, it seemed to overwhelm him. So while I missed the old curmudgeon at times, I wasn't sorry to see him go. So far Jon had proven to be a good fit.

On the weekends and some evenings, I had another new hire working part-time as cook: Rich Zeigler, a UW grad student who was studying sociology and had a flair for creating dishes that lived up to his first name. At the moment, Rich was on duty, whipping up a couple of pizzas.

"Hey, Rich," I said, showing him the cheeses I'd bought. I had the seafood seasoning in my pocket, intending to keep it for myself. "I thought you might like to experiment with these."

"Sweet," he said, eyeing the goods with a smile. "I bet that horseradish cheddar would be kick-ass on a burger, maybe even on a pizza. Stick them in the fridge, and I'll see what I can do with them later."

"It's busy today," I said, putting away the cheeses. "Are you managing okay?"

"I'm doing fine," he said.

"Holler at me if you need any help."

He waved me away with a wink and a *pshaw*.

I went into my office, shed my coat, and called Duncan. He didn't answer, so I left a voice message for him to call me and headed back out to the bar.

It was early afternoon, but because it was a Saturday and lots of people were out and about doing their holiday errands, the place was hopping. My evening and weekend bartender, Billy Hughes, was behind the bar, working his drink-mixing magic. Billy was a law student at the U of W in Milwaukee, and with his dark skin, green eyes, and charming personality, he was also a chick magnet and good for drawing in business. He and Debra Landers, my full-time day waitress, were my most reliable and trusted employees.

"Sorry I had to slip out for a bit," I said to Billy. "How's it going?"

"It's a bit crazy without Gary here," he said. "But I'm managing. Debra has stepped behind the bar a few times to help. And that new waitress you hired, Linda, is doing better."

"Good." Linda had been a slow starter, but I'd asked the other staff members to give her more time to see if she could get up to speed. Each day she seemed to do a little better. "I hope Linda continues to do well. I get the sense she really wants and needs this job."

"Speaking of needing a job," Billy said, "I don't suppose you've had time to start interviewing replacements for Gary? I know it seems a little crude to be asking so soon after. . . ."

He didn't finish his comment. He didn't need to. "No, I haven't," I said with an apologetic smile. "But I'm on it. I looked over some applications this morning."

"I know someone who might be a good fit," Billy said. "He's a friend of mine, an art student whose parents are cutting off their financial support because they want him to pursue a career with more potential." He made little air quotes around the word *potential*. "He's a big guy, like six-six and three hundred pounds, and he worked for a time as a waiter and bartender at a country club when he was right out of high school."

"Tell him to come in and talk to me. What's his name?"

"Theodore Berenson. We all call him Teddy or, if we're giving him a hard time, Teddy Bear."

"Berenson? Is he related to Harley Berenson, the shipping magnate?"

"One and the same," Billy said. "Harley is his father. But Teddy's not stuck up like the rest of the family.

He's just a regular guy, a hard worker, and desperate to make some money."

"Okay, then. Let me know when he can come in and talk."

"I'll call him right now," Billy said, taking out his cell phone. "Can you cover for me for a minute or two?"

"Of course."

I took over behind the bar as Billy stepped away to make his call. He returned a few minutes later, still on the phone, though he put his hand over the speaker.

"Teddy says he can come in anytime. Today even."

"Wow. He is desperate," I said with a smile. Desperate was good. It meant he could likely start right away. "Can he be here in an hour?"

Billy asked the question and a moment later nodded at me. "He says he can be here by two thirty. Will that do?"

"It will."

Billy relayed the info, disconnected his call, and resumed his duties behind the bar. I stayed with him for the next hour to help out with the crowd. When two thirty rolled around, Teddy Berenson came walking through the front door. I knew him right away based on Billy's description. He was a huge hulk of a guy in his late twenties, with big, soft brown eyes, a full head of dark hair, and a neatly trimmed beard and mustache. It was easy to see how he'd earned the nickname Teddy Bear.

After Billy introduced us, I led Teddy into my office and directed him to sit in the chair across from mine at the desk. He handed me a piece of paper, which, I was surprised to see, was a neatly typed résumé—you don't see many of those from job applicants in this business—and settled into the chair. It was a tight fit.

As I interviewed him, I noticed Teddy's voice fitted him. It was deep and rumbling, and it made me taste walnuts. His upbringing showed; he was polite, charming, and cultured. But there was also a comfortable easiness about him that made me believe Billy's claim that the guy had no pretentions. I liked him and wanted to hire him on the spot. According to his résumé, he already had a bartender's license, and he certainly had the physical characteristics I needed for a bouncer, but I had to do some basic checking to make sure everything was on the up-and-up.

"When would you be able to start?" I asked him after I'd finished with my standard interview questions and a rundown of the job requirements.

"Tonight," he said with a shrug and a smile.

I started to tell him I needed to check his references first, but given the family he came from and Billy's personal recommendation, I wondered if that was necessary. Still, with everything that had gone on lately, it was better to be safe than sorry. "Tell you what, Teddy," I said. "I need to check on a few things. Why don't you go out to the bar and hang with Billy for a bit to get the lay of the land. I'll get back to you shortly."

He flashed me a big smile and said, "Will do!" Then he popped out of his chair with amazing grace and headed back out to the bar.

As soon as he was gone, I got on my cell phone and called Cora, who I knew was upstairs in the room used by the Capone Club. Cora was a daily fixture in my bar, and more often than not, she could be found in the Capone Club room.

"What's up?" she answered. Cora rarely mentioned

me by name when she answered one of my calls, knowing I sometimes needed to meet with her on the sly.

"I need a favor. I just interviewed a young man I'm considering as a replacement for Gary, and I'm wondering if you can do a license and background check on him. Run his name through whatever databases you have access to and check to see if he has any criminal record. And verify that he is who he says he is." I then gave her his name.

Cora let out a low whistle. "Is he related to Harley Berenson?"

"Yep. He's his son."

"What the hell is he doing looking for a job with you, then? His family is filthy rich."

"And he's apparently the black sheep in that family. See what you can dig up."

"I'm on it."

"I'll be up in a little bit."

I disconnected the call and then headed out to the main bar area. Teddy was behind the bar, shadowing Billy, and he looked comfortable and eager. I walked up to them and smiled.

"Show Teddy here the ropes," I said to Billy. Then, with a wink, I added, "Give him a trial by fire."

"Can do," Billy said.

"Any sign of today's mail yet?" My mail delivery typically came mid-afternoon, and the mailman brought it inside and handed it off to whoever was behind the bar. But for the last week or so, the delivery had been later than usual due to the extra holiday mail.

"Not yet," Billy said. "I'll put it in your office when it comes." Billy and Debra were the only employees who had a key to my office.

I left the two of them and made rounds on the rest of my staff. Debra was her usual hustling self, and I was glad to see that Linda was moving faster than the snail's pace she'd had when she first started the job.

I walked up to Debra after she finished taking a drink order. "Billy said Linda is doing better. Is that true?"

Debra nodded. "It is, thank goodness." She blew a strand of hair out of her face.

"Good. Are you managing okay?"

She nodded and then gestured toward the bar. "Who's the big teddy bear behind the bar with Billy?"

"Funny you worded it that way," I said with a smile. Then I filled her in. "Keep an eye on him and let me know what you think."

I left Debra and made my way to Linda, who was working tables in the new section of my bar, an area that had been open only for a few weeks. When the building that adjoined mine had become available, I snatched it up and did some renovations to expand the bar, a project that wouldn't have been possible if not for Ginny leaving me a surprise inheritance. Eventually, I was hoping to have some live music in the new area, where Linda was working, but for now I wanted to see if I had enough business to sustain the expansion.

I caught up with Linda in between tables and asked her how everything was going.

"I'm feeling much better about things," she said cheerfully. "I finally have a system worked out, and I'm getting a better feel for all the drink names."

"I'm happy to hear that. I've gotten some great feedback from the rest of the staff, so keep up the good work and let me know if there's anything I can do to help you."

I started to turn away but paused when her face screwed up and her eyes began to tear. The girl was rather plain looking, bordering on mousy, but at the moment her cheeks were rosy, her eyes sparkled, and her mouth had a hint of a smile. "Thank you so much for your patience with me," she said. "For not giving up on me."

"You're very welcome." I gave her shoulder a squeeze, and then, in a tone of faux sternness, I added, "Now, get back to work, woman."

Her smile broadened, and she scurried off.

I headed upstairs to check in with the Capone Club group. Most of the participants were customers and friends who became involved in solving Ginny's murder and, in the process, discovered a connection between my bar and Al Capone. Hence the name. And when I expanded the bar, I created a special room on the second floor for the group to meet in, replete with a gas fireplace, comfy chairs, and an assortment of crime-related books on built-in shelves. The unofficial leaders and founders of the group were Cora, the Signoriello brothers, and Tad Amundsen, a local investor and a tax adviser to some of the area's wealthiest residents. Tad used to be a run-of-the-mill CPA, but his good looks and charm had won him the role of trophy husband to Suzanne Collier, one of the richest women in Wisconsin. In turn, Suzanne diverted many of her friends to Tad for financial and investment advice, and he eventually opened up his own business, the offices of which were located around the corner from my bar.

The original Capone Club members had enjoyed their sleuthing attempts enough that they decided to continue with them. They progressed from playing with made-up practice cases to assisting me on some real ones, and the number of participants had grown, thanks to word of mouth and some of the press attention garnered by the cases I'd worked with Duncan. There were always some members present on a daily basis, though their number waxed and waned throughout the day. It was a varied group, with folks from many different walks of life, and that brought a lot of expertise and ideas to the process.

Some of the core regulars were Sam Warner, a graduate student in psychology; Carter Fitzpatrick, a writer and part-time waiter; Holly Martinson, a bank teller and Carter's girlfriend; Alicia Maldonado, also a bank teller and Holly's friend and coworker; Kevin Baldwin, a local trash collector, though he preferred the title sanitation engineer; Karen Tannenbaum, or Dr. T, as we called her, an ER physician; and Tiny Gruber, a construction worker and Cora's current paramour. Several members of my staff also participated in the group when they could. Billy considered it a good prep for his future career as a criminal defense lawyer, while the others did it more for entertainment.

The most recent case the group had worked on was the twelve-year-old unsolved murders of Tiny's sister, Lori Gruber, and her friend Anna Hermann. The group and I had been able to solve the crime, and it generated a lot of publicity—most of it centered on me, because of the earlier media fiasco with me and Duncan. While the publicity had been a nightmare for me personally, it was great for business, drawing in lots of curious people who wanted to gawk and a few who wanted to participate in the Capone Club.

Because it was the weekend, most of the core regulars in the group were present, but I saw a few new faces, too. I was greeted with a chorus of cheery hellos as Cora pulled up a chair for me next to her. As soon as I settled in and propped my crutches against the wall behind me, she leaned over and whispered in my ear.

"Your boy checks out. He is who he says he is, and I can't find any bad stuff about him."

"Good," I said with a smile. "Because I think I'm putting him on the payroll as of tonight."

Cora gave me a cautionary look. "Is the rest of the staff going to be okay with that, you think? I mean, so soon after Gary and all."

I shrugged. "They're going to have to be. I need the help."

Cora switched gears, nodding toward the unfamiliar faces in the room. "We have two new folks here today," she said, her voice still low. "I got their names and checked them out. I'm pretty sure they aren't reporters, but be careful with what you talk about."

I nodded my understanding and prepared for introductions, but before that happened, yet another new face entered the room. Nothing about her looked extraordinary—she was pretty, but in an everyday kind of way—yet I sensed something as I watched her walk in. It didn't take long for my instincts to prove reliable, because within a matter of minutes our newest arrival introduced us to our next case, which would turn out to be the most interesting one yet.

Chapter 4

The weekends were when the Capone Club was at its fullest, and they were also when we got the most new people wandering in. Most of the newcomers expressed an interest in participating, and they were treated with polite wariness by the others initially. Local reporters had tried to infiltrate the group several times, so whenever anyone new showed up, they were asked to provide an introduction and to say why they were there. Until Cora, with her computer sleuthing skills, could do a background check, the group would stick to posing test scenarios or discussing crime solving in general, never offering up information on any of the real crimes we were or had been working on. This had a tendency to weed out the vast majority of the newcomers, most of whom were curiosity seekers or lookie-loos who never came back again.

So far, the only person who had come back after the initial visit, and after he passed Cora's muster, was Stephen McGregor, a physics teacher at a local high school. He was present on the day in question, and I later learned who the two first timers in the group were: a man in his forties named Greg Nash, who worked as a local Realtor and who had known Ginny, and Sonja West, who said she was the owner of an upscale hair salon named Aphrodite's, located a few blocks away.

The latest newcomer—the one who had entered the room shortly after I had—introduced herself as Sandra Middleton but offered up nothing more. That was enough for Cora, who started typing away on her laptop. I invited Sandra to have a seat, and she took an empty chair next to Sam, setting the large purse she was carrying—though actually it looked more like a messenger bag—on the floor beside her. As soon as she was settled, Holly asked her what she did for a living.

"I'm between jobs at the moment," Sandra said with a sad little smile. "I love mysteries, and I heard about your group, so I thought I'd check it out."

Cora's quick machinations on the computer revealed that Sandra's interest in the group was likely due to more than a love of mysteries. "You're related to Benjamin Middleton," she said.

Sandra nodded, looking sheepish. "I am," she said in a very soft voice that triggered a faint herbal taste in my mouth. She sighed and flashed an apologetic smile, shifting in her chair. "Okay, the real reason I'm here is that I'm hoping your group can help me. Benjamin is my brother, and he's in prison, convicted of the murder of his wife, Tiffany."

"How do you want us to help you?" I asked.

"He didn't do it," Sandra said with absolute conviction. "He's innocent. I know he is, but I need someone to help me prove it."

I and the group were typically skeptical of innocence

claims—an all too common theme among criminals—
and Sandra wasn't the first person to come to us with
such a plea. But I learned the hard way that sometimes
those claims were true, because it turned out that
Gary Gunderson had done time for a crime he didn't
commit.

Because of the publicity surrounding me and the
Capone Club, the core group had a discussion not
long ago during which we agreed not to take on any
active, ongoing investigations and to consider only cold
or concluded ones. My relationship with the police was
dicey enough as it was. I didn't want to antagonize
them further by interfering in an active investigation,
and the cops who participated in the group from time
to time had warned us that if we interfered in an active
investigation, it could get us into some serious trouble.

The group's decision hadn't come easily. The members were desperate to look into the deaths of both
Gary and Lewis Carmichael, since they had known
both of them. Lewis, in fact, had been a part-time participant in the Capone Club. On the surface, Lewis's
death appeared to be a mugging gone wrong, an un-
fortunate case of being in the wrong place at the
wrong time. Aside from Duncan and Mal O'Reilly, my
purported new paramour, only Cora, Frank, Joe, and
I knew otherwise. I feared other group members
might become targets of the letter writer if they dug
too deeply into either Gary's or Lewis's death, so with
the secret help of Duncan, and some in-your-face
advice from the local police, it was made clear to the
group that current, ongoing investigations were off
the table.

I did my best to reinforce this as subtly as I could,
and in a way, Sandra's arrival and plea aided me in that

endeavor. The case fit our initial parameters since it was closed, with the presumed culprit sentenced and behind bars. I hoped that the distraction of a new case would get everyone's minds off of Gary and Lewis for a while and keep the group from doing anything stupid. But I also was wary of giving Sandra Middleton any false hope.

To Sandra, I said, "We'll be happy to hear you out regarding your brother's case, and perhaps even look into it. But you need to understand that we don't offer any promises. If at any time we feel like we should drop the case, we will." I paused and looked around at the others in the room, hoping I was playing it right and didn't seem overeager. "Does everyone agree?"

There were a bunch of nods and a couple of murmured assents.

Sandra smiled meekly. "I understand," she said. "Thank you for even considering it. I don't know who else to turn to, and when I heard on the news about how your group managed to solve a couple of other cases recently, I thought you might be able to help."

"Let's start by hearing your thoughts on the case," I said. "Convince us it's worth pursuing."

Sandra looked perplexed. "My brother is innocent, and I need help proving it," she said with a shrug.

"I understand that," I said, giving her a patient smile. "But we need a little more than your admittedly biased opinion on the matter."

Cora, hands poised over her laptop, prompted Sandra for more information. "Tell us the details of the case as you know them," she said. "Start with some background information about your brother and his wife, and then tell us what your brother says happened on the night in question."

Sandra sucked in a deep, bracing breath before she spoke. As she began to talk, Cora typed away, taking notes so we could review the details later. "Ben met Tiffany four years ago, when they were both students at Northwestern," she began. Her voice was lilting, rhythmic, even, and its soft tones threatened to lull me to sleep. "Ben and I come from a middle-class family. My mother is a nurse executive, and my father is the CFO of a big trucking company. We aren't what I would call wealthy, but we never wanted for anything, either. Tiffany Gallagher, however, came from money, and lots of it. Her father owns and runs the Gallagher Shipping Company, and he's estimated to be worth several hundred million."

A few eyebrows in the room arched with this information, but no one said anything, so Sandra continued.

"When Ben first met Tiffany, he didn't think she'd give him the time of day, but something clicked between the two of them right from the get-go. Her father wasn't happy about it. He did everything he could to try to break them up, but Ben and Tiff were meant to be together. They loved one another. There's no way my brother would have killed her."

She paused and looked at the faces in the room, her expression begging us to believe her.

Sam said, "I don't mean to discount the fact that you know your brother better than we do, but you have to admit that your opinion is bound to be biased. So why don't you tell us what you know about the facts of the case, things like when, where, and how the crime occurred."

Sandra nodded. "It happened almost a year ago, on February fifteenth. Ben and Tiff were coming back from Door County, where they'd gone for a weeklong getaway to celebrate Valentine's Day and their second wedding anniversary. They'd stayed in an isolated rental house along the shore of Lake Michigan, and on the day Tiff was killed, they were headed back home. It was late in the day. They had originally planned to stay another day, but a snowstorm had come through the night before, and there was another, bigger one coming in the next morning. So they'd decided to leave around five or so, because they wanted to get home before the roads became impassable.

"Ben said they headed out along a narrow back road that led to one of the more main roads, but it was slow going because it was dark already and there was a brisk wind that stirred up the snow, whiting things out at times and creating big drifts on the road. After crawling along for about ten minutes, they came upon some guy standing in the middle of the road, flagging them down. Ben stopped and rolled his window down, thinking the guy might be hurt or in need of help in some way, but the next thing he knew, the guy was sticking a gun in his face and yelling at him to get out of the car.

"Ben grabbed at the gun without thinking, and after he grappled with the guy for several seconds, the gun fired twice. Ben said he continued to wrestle for the gun for several seconds after that, and then the man suddenly let go and ran off." She paused and grimaced. "That was when Ben realized Tiffany had been shot. She was hit in the head and died instantly."

"What did this guy with the gun look like?" Cora asked.

"Ben said he was wearing a hooded parka and had a knit cap on beneath that. He also had a scarf wrapped around his lower face, so Ben wasn't able to provide much of a description. He said the guy was white and his eyes were brown. Ben thought he was tall, around six feet or so, because of how far the guy had to bend down to stick the gun in the window."

"Not much to go on," Joe Signoriello said. "What did your brother say happened next?"

Sandra leaned forward in her seat, her elbows resting on her knees, her hands laced together. "Ben said he tried to call for help, but there was no cell service there. So he drove on as fast as he dared given the conditions. It was ten, maybe fifteen minutes later before he reached a part of the road where he had some kind of cell signal. He called nine-one-one, and an officer was dispatched out to the scene. Ben said they told him to wait where he was. He did, but he didn't want to, because he realized the cops weren't going to get to him very fast given the road conditions, and he didn't know where the guy with the gun had gone. He worried the guy might try to come after them again. He wanted to keep driving along the road, thinking that would get him to the cops sooner, and get Tiffany help quicker."

She paused again and looked down at her hands with a sad expression. "He said that's what he was thinking, but he admitted that some part of him knew at that point that Tiffany was beyond help. So he stayed where he was but remained watchful and vigilant, ready to bolt if he had to."

She straightened up, placing her hands on the arms of her chair and taking in a slow, bracing breath. "The cops met up with him some ten or fifteen minutes later, and an ambulance arrived shortly after that. The paramedics pronounced Tiffany dead there in the car, and the cops put Ben in one of their cars to get his story. I don't know how long they were there, but at some point the cops drove down the road with Ben to try to find the spot where the guy with the gun had first appeared. But Ben was unable to pinpoint the exact spot because the wind had drifted the snow, changing the terrain and covering up any tracks."

She gave a wan smile then. "The rest you can more or less figure out. The cops took Ben to a local station and questioned him into the night. They released him the next morning, and he rented a car to drive home. One week later he was arrested for Tiffany's murder. The cops said they didn't believe there was an attempted carjacking. They thought Ben killed Tiffany and made up the story about the guy with the gun."

She looked around the room, gauging the various reactions. Several seconds of silence ensued as everyone digested the story. Some of the folks in the room—Joe, Frank, Carter, and Sam—studied Sandra Middleton. The others looked at anything but her.

Carter finally broke the silence with a new question. "What evidence was there against your brother?"

"Well, for starters, the cops said the gun was traced back to some thug here in Milwaukee, who admitted to selling it to a man two weeks before the shooting. And supposedly this guy identified Ben in a photo lineup as the man he sold it to. The cops theorized that Ben and Tiff's marriage was falling apart and the trip was a last-ditch effort to try to save it. Knowing that it might not work, Ben had a backup plan, because he realized he might lose out on the Gallagher family money if he and Tiffany divorced. So when things didn't go so well, he decided to kill Tiffany instead and make it look like a carjacking gone wrong."

Sandra paused again and studied some of the faces in the room. "That's not what happened," she insisted. "Ben loved Tiffany so much. She was his life. If you could have heard him talk about her the way I did, you'd know there's no way he killed her."

Sam shrugged. "Money is a powerful motive," he said. "And it wouldn't be the first time intense love turned to intense hate."

Sandra shook her head vehemently. "Ben wouldn't hurt a fly. And I mean that literally. When we were kids, we had this cabin up north, on Lake Superior, that my parents took us to every summer. The place had no air-conditioning, so the windows were open all the time, and despite the screens, tons of flies always made it inside. My parents hung those sticky fly strips all over the place. I can remember Ben standing beneath one of those strips, staring up at a couple of flies that were stuck to it and still alive, still moving. He looked so sad, and when I asked him what was wrong, he told me he couldn't stand seeing the flies suffer like that. It bothered him so much that he actually got a kitchen knife and tried to scrape one of the flies from the strip and set it free outside." She paused, a half smile on her face. "The fly died, anyway, and Ben cried for it."

Several people in the group looked skeptical.

"I know it isn't much," Sandra said, not missing the doubt on some of the faces. "But I know my brother. He didn't do this."

"Does he have any theories as to who did?" Frank asked.

Sandra shook her head, looking frustrated and sad. "He insists he didn't know the guy with the gun."

"So they have this money motive and a witness who

says your brother bought the gun used in the crime," Carter said. "That doesn't seem like a lot of evidence. What else do they have?"

"They found Ben's fingerprints on the gun, and gunpowder residue on his hands and sleeves. But Ben said he was holding the gun and struggling with the carjacker both times it fired. Wouldn't that explain the gunpowder residue?"

"It could," Carter said, and a few others in the room nodded in agreement.

"Ben also said that once the carjacker gave up and let go of the gun, he held it with his hand on the trigger, pointing it out the window as the carjacker ran off, in case he came back. So that explains why his fingerprints were on it."

"Were his the only ones?" Carter asked.

Sandra nodded. "It was cold and blustery outside, and Ben said the guy with the gun was wearing gloves. Ben's car had a heated steering wheel, so he had taken his off."

"What about the bullets?" Carter asked. Originally, Carter had been focused on writing novels, but once he joined the Capone Club, he shifted his interest to writing true crime. As part of this newfound career, he'd been doing some forensic homework, and now he was putting some of that newly acquired knowledge to work. "Any prints on those or the spent cartridges?"

"Not that I know of," Sandra said.

I said, "What proof did they offer that your brother's marriage was on the rocks? If he and Tiffany were celebrating their anniversary and a romantic Valentine's Day, it would seem to imply that their relationship was on good terms."

"As far as I knew, it was," Sandra said with a shrug.

"They seemed loving, and Ben told me not long before this last trip that they were talking about starting a family." She frowned and gave us a half smile. "I mean, they fought. All couples do. But they never stayed mad at one another for very long, and overall, they seemed to get along just fine. But . . ." Sandra paused, biting her lip.

"There was something that came out in the trial. During the autopsy, they found seminal fluid in Tiffany's . . . you know." She blushed, waving a hand in the air, and several people nodded. "Anyway, they said there was no sperm, just the fluid, and apparently, they weren't able to get any DNA. But they were able to determine a blood type or something like that, and they said the blood type ruled out Ben as the donor. So the assumption was that Tiffany was having an affair."

Looks were exchanged, and Sandra didn't miss them. "Look, I don't blame you for being skeptical," she said in an exasperated tone. "Clearly, there was evidence that pointed toward my brother. Otherwise he wouldn't be where he is now. But I'm telling you, he didn't do it." She hesitated, casting that pleading expression around the room yet again. "Ben loved Tiffany so much that even if Tiffany was having an affair and he found out about it, he wouldn't have killed her over it. He would have done everything he could to try to save the marriage." More looks of skepticism. "Please, all I'm asking is that you look into it."

I looked around the room at the others and sensed that they, like me, were skeptical but were also touched by Sandra's conviction. I decided to give Sandra a little test. "Sandra, I'm going to ask you to do something that might seem odd and a little unsettling. But I need you to bear with me."

"Okay," she said slowly, looking wary.

"I want you to tell me that your brother is guilty."

Sandra reared back as if I'd slapped her. "But he isn't."

"Please, just do it."

Sandra looked hurt and betrayed, and she stared back at me with barely concealed anger. I watched the emotions play over her face, curious to see what would win out. In the end she gave in to common sense or desperation, or maybe both. "My brother did it," she said with obvious distaste. "He killed Tiffany."

Her voice made the herbal taste in my mouth turn bitter, almost rancid. This suggested to me that she clearly believed in her cause, but it was no guarantee that her brother was innocent.

"Thank you," I told her with a warm smile. "I'm sorry I had to ask you to do that, and I know you don't understand why I did, but believe me when I tell you it was helpful. Would you mind giving us some time to discuss the matter among ourselves before we decide if we're going to look into your brother's case? We'll talk about it and see if we can come to some sort of consensus. Can you come back in a couple of days?"

Sandra smiled with obvious relief and a hint of hope. "Yes, of course," she said. "Thank you. Thank you so much."

"Don't thank us yet," I told her. "We haven't agreed to do anything."

"I know, but the simple fact that you're willing to even consider it gives me hope." She then reached into the messenger bag she'd brought with her, removed a folder, and held it out to me. "These are my notes regarding the trial. I quit my job and moved back home with my parents so I could attend every day."

We certainly couldn't fault her dedication to her brother.

"What kind of work did you do?" Carter asked.

"I was in pharmaceutical sales." She gave him a sheepish smile. "To be honest, I hated the job, so I was more than happy to give it up." While her altruism sank a notch with that confession, she clearly believed in her brother and was hurting over his fate. I figured the least we could do was give the case consideration.

Sandra donned her coat, grabbed her bag, and headed out, thanking us three more times as she left. Once she was gone, the group sat in silence for a minute or two. I scanned their faces, seeing doubt, skepticism, curiosity and, in Carter's case, eagerness. No doubt he was hoping the case might provide him with yet another true crime for one of his books. He was already working on a book about Tiny's sister's case and had even secured an agent who was willing to take him on and look at the work once it was done.

"What do you guys think?" I asked the group.

Carter spoke first. "She certainly seems convinced of her brother's innocence."

Everyone nodded, and then Sam offered up the first counterpoint. "But conviction from a loved one doesn't count for much."

This, too, generated several nods, and then Joe offered up a suggestion. "Mack, maybe you should talk with her brother, do that lie detector thing you do. See if his side of the story rings true."

My lie detector thing, which is just my synesthetic reaction to the subtle changes in people's voices, isn't

100 percent foolproof—I've run across some people who lie so well or mask their emotions to such an extent that there is no change for me to detect. But most people aren't good enough liars to fool me. Some of the members of the group had been skeptical of my ability at first, and they'd tested me with some games. One by one each person in the room would utter a statement that was either true or false, some tidbit about themselves or their lives. Then they would ask me to determine if it was a truth or a falsehood. I knew the members of the group and the taste of their voices well by then so the tests had been relatively easy for me. I'd been right every time, a detail that made some of them eye me nervously. I couldn't blame them for being a bit uncomfortable. I often picked up on lies among customers and with my staff, too. There were times when I'd overhear part of a conversation and know someone was fabricating a lie. As a result, my staff learned over time that if they called in sick and weren't, I'd be able to tell. So the quirk did come with some perks.

"I'm not crazy about the idea of making another prison visit," I told the group. I'd gone to the Waupun Correctional Institution recently, when we were look-ing into the Gruber-Hermann case, and it had been a disquieting experience. "But I suppose that's as good a place as any to start." I looked over at Cora, who had been tapping away on her keyboard ever since Sandra left. "Do you know where he is?"

She nodded. "Just found it," she said. "He's at Waupun. Just like Lonnie Carlisle." Carlisle had been a suspect in the Gruber investigation.

Resigned, I said, "I'll get in touch with Tyrese and see if he can arrange for me to visit him tomorrow."

Tyrese was one of the local police officers who worked with the Capone Club, and he had arranged the prior visit to the prison. I handed the folder Sandra had given me to Cora. "Make copies of this for the others in the group so everyone can look through it. Look it over and research what you can to see if you come up with anything."

Cora nodded and took the file. "Can I use the copier in your office?"

I nodded and slid my keys over to her. She gathered up her laptop, which was as much a part of her as her clothing, and headed downstairs.

Frank Signoriello said, "Mack, you made that woman tell you her brother was guilty so you could do your lie detector thing with her, didn't you?"

I nodded.

"What did you determine?"

"She seemed sincere. I can't say if her brother is innocent or not, but she definitely believes he is."

"If you believe in her, that's enough for me to commit to at least looking into it," Frank said.

"Me too," his brother said, chiming in. This was followed by a chorus of other agreements from around the room.

I looked over at the newcomers, Greg Nash and Sonja West. Normally, we tried to avoid discussing actual cases in front of new arrivals, but in this case it had been unavoidable. I could see the puzzled looks on their faces and guessed their confusion was related to the discussion of me and my lie detector abilities rather than to the case itself.

"Greg, Sonja, do the two of you have an interest in being a part of this?" I asked.

Greg nodded eagerly, but Sonja hesitated.

"You're probably wondering what this talk about my lie detector ability is all about," I said, and they both nodded. "I have a neurological disorder called synesthesia," I began, and then I explained it to them, with an occasional assist from one of the other members of the group. When I was done, I said, "Any questions?"

Greg and Sonja both shook their heads.

"Good. If the others agree, the two of you are welcome to assist us through this process." I looked around the room as the other members of the group either nodded or mumbled their assents. "Okay then. Here's how it works. We often solicit input from everyone when we discuss potential scenarios, motives, suspects, and such. Please feel free to offer up an opinion. And if you have any connections or areas of expertise that you think might be of use to us during the investigatory process, we'd appreciate any help you can provide."

Neither of them said anything, but they nodded in unison.

"One other thing," I said. "Keep in mind that anything we do needs to stay under the radar. The press has been hounding me ever since we solved our first case, and I don't want any of them to get a whiff of what we're up to. Be careful about who you talk to and who might be within earshot when you do it."

"No problem," Greg said.

"Understood," Sonja offered.

"Thanks, guys. And to show my appreciation for all the hard work you're about to do, I'm buying a round of drinks on the house." That brought smiles to everyone's faces. "In honor of the upcoming holiday, I'm treating everyone to a Santa Claus shot. I'll send someone up with them shortly." I rose from my chair and grabbed my crutches. "I've got some other business to tend to for a while, but I'll come back later."

With that, I hobbled out of the room and headed downstairs to see if the mail had come yet, because the other business I had to tend to was the letter writer. I had to make sure my little group of crime solvers stayed alive long enough to help Sandra Middleton, if her claims seemed warranted.

Chapter 5

I found Cora in my office, finishing up the copies of Sandra's file. I closed the door behind me and locked it to keep out any unwanted, spontaneous intruders. I'd spied Clay Sanders, who was one of the more persistent reporters, seated at the bar. His omnipresence of late was annoying, but I'd been rethinking things recently.

"Clay is here," I said on the off chance Cora hadn't noticed him or he hadn't been there when she came through.

"I saw him," she said with a wan smile. "He seems very determined."

"That he is."

Cora shot me a look. "I know that tone of voice, Mack," she said. "You're plotting something."

"I'm just wondering if maybe we should abide by that rule to keep your friends close and your enemies closer."

She looked at me, aghast. "You're not seriously thinking of inviting Clay to the group, are you?"

I shrugged.

"These reporters have done nothing but poke fun at you, and Clay has been among the most persistent of them. I think it would be a big mistake.."

"Let's think about it for a minute, Cora. Clay is an investigative reporter, and as such, he has a lot of resources at hand, resources we could make good use of. What if we worked out a deal with him?"

"It would be a deal with the devil."

"Maybe," I said. "But if we offer him something in return, something that would buy his loyalty, maybe we could turn him from the dark side."

"What have we got to offer him?" Her copies were finished, and she scooped them from the tray and tamped them into a pile. "And how do we know we can trust him?"

"How do we know we can trust anyone in the group?"

Cora contemplated this and acceded my point with an equivocal look and a shrug.

"What is his primary motivation?" Before she could answer, I continued. "He wants a scoop. He wants to get to the meat of a good story before anyone else does. Doing that gives him prestige, maybe even a promotion. So what if we offered him limited access, asked him to help us with some of our research, and let him participate on a trial basis, with the promise of getting that scoop?"

Cora frowned and shook her head slowly. "I don't know, Mack. It seems risky to me. Have you run this idea by Duncan?"

"I haven't run it by anyone but you," I admitted.

"I'm flattered, but I think you should run it by Duncan first to see what he thinks. There are other things at stake here. What about Mal?"

Malachi O'Reilly was a transplant to the Milwaukee

area from the state of Washington, and he worked undercover. His current assignment was with a construction company whose boss and owner was suspected of fraud. Mal's family ran a construction company back in Washington, so he had the necessary knowledge and skill set to pull off the job. He had managed to get hired by the suspect company and had been working with them for a while when he and I were set up as a blind date. We pretended he was a friend of Cora's, and ever since a couple of trial "dates," we'd been acting like a couple. Unfortunately, Duncan's plan to use Mal as a form of incognito protection for me backfired. Mal and I shared a strong attraction to one another, and our deception had trickled over into reality. The fact that my relationship with Duncan was a bit up in the air at the time hadn't helped the situation.

"I'll run it by Mal, too," I told Cora. "I don't see why he can't continue to function in his undercover role even if Clay is involved. None of the other group members know the truth about him except for you, Joe, and Frank. We can dupe Clay just as easily."

Cora's frown deepened, and I could tell she wasn't convinced. "See what Duncan and Mal have to say on the matter," she said. "I'll keep an open mind in the meantime. Speaking of which, when are you supposed to see Duncan again?"

This was a prickly question. "I'm not sure," I said. "He called yesterday and said he'd be in touch sometime this weekend. Mal is coming by later today, and we're supposed to go out to a movie and dinner. But now that we have this new case to look into, I'm not sure I want to do that."

"Is that the only reason you don't want to do it?"

Cora asked cagily. "You two are hitting it off quite well, it seems. You have feelings for him, don't you?"

I sighed and sank down onto the couch in my office, propping my crutches alongside of me. "I like him a lot," I admitted. "We get along well. I'm comfortable around him."

"And he's pretty easy on the eyes," Cora added with a wiggle of her eyebrows. "Does Duncan know?"

"He knows Mal has feelings for me, but I'm not sure if he realizes they're reciprocated to some extent. We've circled around the topic a time or two, but Duncan has avoided coming out and asking directly, and I've avoided making any claims. My feelings for Duncan are strong, stronger than what I feel for Mal at this point, but I'm not sure our relationship is going anywhere. He's not being very committal."

"You haven't known either one of them for all that long," Cora said. "Give yourself time with both of them. There's no need to rush into anything."

"No, I suppose there isn't."

"You don't sound convinced."

"It's just that ever since my dad died, I feel so alone and adrift. In the past I always had him here to share things with and to talk to about stuff. Now I don't have that."

"You have me. Anytime you want to talk, you know I'm here for you."

I gave her a grateful smile. "I know that, and I appreciate it, Cora. Believe me, I do. But there are times, like late at night, after the bar closes down, or early in the morning, when I'm having my breakfast, when I feel the loss and the loneliness so strongly. Those are the times when I can put work and crimes and all this other crap behind me. Those *were* the times when my father and I would chew the fat and discuss news stories, our futures, current events, philosophical ideas . . . whatever struck our fancy. They were relaxing, normal moments in my life, and I miss them. I miss him," I said, tears welling in my eyes.

Cora walked over and sat down beside me. She took me in her arms and gave me a hug, rocking us both gently. When she finally let me go, she sandwiched my face between her hands and looked me in the eye. "It will come with time, Mack, I promise. Of course you miss your father. He was the primary influence in your life, the one constant that was always there. And he was your only family. Now you have a temporary, makeshift family, an eclectic group of crime-solving misfits who love what they do and love you. Use us as much as you need to until you figure out where your head is at and which direction you want to go in. Once you know that, you'll be able to start your own family. Until then, I and the others are here for you."

My throat was tight with emotion, making me unable to speak. So I simply nodded instead.

Cora leaned forward and kissed me on the forehead. Then she released my face. I swiped at the tears on my cheeks and smiled at her.

"You know," she said, "I don't have any family close by, either. I have a brother who lives out in California that I haven't seen in eight years. I get one of those Christmas newsletter things every year to keep me up to date on how he and his family are doing, but otherwise I never hear from him. My father died fifteen years ago, and my mother remarried a few years later and moved to Florida. We talk on the phone from time to time, but when it comes to day-to-day stuff, I don't have anyone. I'm forty-three years old, I've never married, never had any kids, and for the most part, my business has been my life. That's probably why it's been so successful. Aside from a dozen or so romantic entanglements, I've never had anything to distract my focus. All my time and energy have gone into my business."

"Do you ever regret not marrying and having a family of your own?"

"At times," she said. "But deep down inside I know I'd make a lousy mother or wife. I bore too easily, and I value my freedom too much. And over the years I've learned that the definition of *family* stretches a lot. Between my friends and my lovers, my emotional needs are met just fine." She paused and smiled. "You've been a key part of that."

"Me? How?"

"My brother and I never got along very well, even as kids. We were so different in every way, and the five years of age difference was just enough to keep us from ever bonding well. I used to wish I had a sister, and I did what I could to fill that need with female friends. But I never got that close to any of them. I've always related better to men than women, and not just on a sexual basis. My personality just tends to mesh better with men. But you're different. With you, I feel like I've finally found the sister I never had."

"That feeling is mutual," I said, flashing a grateful smile. We hugged again, and when we were done, I changed the subject. "I went down to the Public Market earlier today. I found the vendor who got that last letter from the letter writer."

Cora's eyebrows shot up in surprise. "I thought Duncan had already talked to the vendors down there."

"He did, but he did it as part of the official investigation into Gary's murder. Since Gary's body was found in the Public Market parking lot, it allowed Duncan to talk to folks there without appearing to be involved with me or my interests in the place. He said he asked if anyone had received any unusual notes, mail, or packages, and everyone said no. But I think the fact that his inquiries were official and attached to a murder investigation made people afraid to fess up."

"Who was it? And are you going to tell the cops about it? Do you think you'll get into trouble if they find out you went down there and questioned people on your own? The cops have been giving all of us the third degree regarding Gary's murder, and it's been made pretty clear to us that we aren't supposed to try to investigate it on our own."

"It was a lady named Trudy who got the letter. She works at the spice shop. And she's petrified of getting involved with the police and the case. I promised her I wouldn't involve the authorities. As for me getting into trouble, I went to the Public Market before Gary was killed, and I'll continue to go there. Who's to say I'm not just shopping? I did buy some stuff while I was there."

"What did she tell you?"

"Nothing helpful," I said with a frown. "She got the same nondescript package the others did, and she swears she didn't open or read the contents of the inside envelope. She said she destroyed it by burning it in her fireplace."

"Do you believe her?"

"I do."

"So we're back to square one."

"It would seem so, yes."

"Are you still okay with your decision not to tell the others in the group about the letters?"

"For now. I don't want to make them paranoid. And I've got Mal and Duncan working on it with me. Hopefully, we'll come up with some answers soon."

"Okay, but be careful, Mack. Whoever this letter writer is, they are clearly not in their right mind. You need to keep a watchful eye, in case he or she is stalking you."

"I might be being watched, but I don't think I'm being stalked. I'm not sure what the endgame is, but I don't get the sense that I'm in danger, at least not yet. I think it's more about the game for now."

"You haven't gotten any new letters?"

"No, but today's mail hasn't arrived yet."

My cell phone rang then, and when I looked, I saw it was Duncan calling. "It's Duncan," I told Cora. "Hopefully, he'll have some good news."

She nodded, picked up the stack of copies, took the originals from the copier, and said, "Let me know. I'm going to head upstairs and hand these out." She dropped the originals on my desk and left the room.

With a hope and a prayer, I answered Duncan's call, eager for some good news.

Chapter 6

"Hey, Duncan," I said, trying to sound chipper, though I feared I fell short.

"Hey, gorgeous. What's up? Your message said you had some news for me."

"I do. Plus, I wanted to check in with you to see what's going on at your end of the world. I went to the Public Market this morning, and I found the person who got that last letter."

"You did? Who was it?"

"A lady named Trudy who runs the spice shop."

"I talked to her on Thursday. She told me she didn't get anything."

"I think you scared her. You're a cop, and you went there in an official capacity. That can be intimidating. I tried a friendlier approach. She lied to me at first, but eventually, she admitted to receiving it. She said she didn't open the inside letter, and she swore she destroyed it the way the instructions told her to."

"Which was?"

"She burned it in her fireplace."

"Do you believe her?"

"I do. I could tell from her body language and her voice that she was lying to me about getting anything, but eventually, she came clean. I just wish she'd been more curious or more of a procrastinator."

"You feel certain she disposed of it? Normal human curiosity would make most people either sneak a peek or hang on to it for a while."

"She seemed sincere. But it got me to thinking about something. She said the envelope was delivered to her house and left on her front porch. That's the second one that went to someone's home, and the one at the Miller brewery was at the guy's place of employment. How does the letter writer know where these people live and work? They must have something in common, some connection. Either that or the letter writer has access to such information. Couldn't that be a clue?"

"Good point," Duncan said thoughtfully. "It's something worth looking into. Any idea what the common factor might be?"

"Not yet, but give me some time to ponder it. Have you guys found any evidence related to Gary's murder that might be helpful?"

"Not much. We know the type of gun used to kill him, but we haven't been able to match the bullet to any specific weapon. The only prints we found in the car were Gary's, and we haven't come up with any other trace evidence. We looked around Gary's apartment, but nothing turned up there, either. And we also talked to his parole officer, but he said he wasn't aware of anything or anyone in Gary's life that would have set him up for this. Gary did do time, so we have to look into his prison connections to see if anything develops there, but I doubt this had anything to do with Gary personally."

"It was very personal," I said, squeezing my eyes closed. "Gary died because of me, because he knew me, because he worked for me, because he saved my life."

Duncan sighed, and the sound of his breath over the phone made me see a turbulent mix of red, orange, and yellow colors. "Mack, this is not your fault. You've got to stop thinking that any of this is your fault."

"Kind of hard to do when his death is clearly connected to this damned letter writer who's been taunting me. Why else would the killer have stuffed one of my bar napkins in his mouth? That seems like a clear message to me."

"You and I know what that napkin likely meant, but so far the rest of the investigative team is leaning toward its presence being coincidental."

"If that's true, then why were the detectives who were here asking my customers and employees if any of them had had an argument of any sort with Gary recently?"

"It's a standard line of questioning we'd do in any case like this, Mack. And so far they've come up with nothing. No one at the bar is under suspicion. The team's working theory at this point is that Gary probably had the napkin in his car, and the killer grabbed it and shoved it in his mouth to shut him up. But they haven't ruled out the idea that the killer was in your bar at some point and had the napkin on him. So they're looking into the possibility of a revenge killing, a payback from someone who might have been reprimanded, tossed out, or turned away when Gary was functioning in his bouncer role. You and I know that likely isn't the case, but given the circumstances, I'm willing to let the rest of the team think that for now."

"I don't suppose you've come up with anything new on Lewis's case?"

"Unfortunately, no. Whoever is doing this knows how to cover their tracks well."

"Perhaps that's a clue as to who it is," I suggested. "Maybe it's someone who works with evidence or in police work." I had to tread carefully on this topic because I had my own suspicions about Duncan's partner, Jimmy. The man didn't like me, didn't like what I did, and had made it clear he thought I was a charlatan leading Duncan astray. Plus, the letter writer's insistence that I wasn't to have any help from Duncan jibed with Jimmy's general opinion of me. But Duncan clearly trusted the guy, so rather than suggest Jimmy as a suspect, I was hoping to ease Duncan down the same path my own thoughts had followed.

"It doesn't take anyone with any day-to-day knowledge of investigative techniques and forensics these days," Duncan said. "All you need is someone who watches all the crime shows on TV. Much of the general public is as well educated, if not better educated, on this stuff as most of us cops are."

Not wanting to push the Jimmy idea too hard, I switched topics, though I feared my next one was just as likely to leave me discouraged. "When am I going to see you again?"

"I can't come by tonight, but tomorrow evening is looking good. Do you have any plans?"

"I have plans during the day, but the evening should be open. The Capone Club has a new case we might be looking into."

I filled him in on Sandra's visit with the group, and

when I was done, he said, "I'm not very familiar with the case, though I do remember hearing about the trial on the news. The actual crime happened before I came to town. Do you have any reason to think the guy might be innocent?"

"Nothing yet, other than his sister's conviction that he didn't do it. But I'm hoping that if I talk to Ben Middleton, it will give me a better sense."

"Are you sure you want to get involved with this, Mack? You've been complaining about all the press you and the others have been getting, and this is only likely to make that worse."

"Are you worried about my reputation or your job?"

"I'm worried about you, silly. My bosses aren't happy about the ribbing they've gotten in the media because of what you've done, but they'll get over it. And as long as they don't know I'm still working with you in any way, I should be fine."

"If it turns out this Middleton guy is innocent and we can prove that, it's not going to make the police department look any better."

"True, but maybe it will make them stand up and look at you and the group in a different light. I still think your synesthesia can be useful in helping us investigate crimes, and if you continue to show them that, maybe they'll come around."

"Or maybe they'll make life more difficult for me . . . and for you."

"Don't worry about me. I can take care of myself. And you seem to have weathered all the press quite well so far. It's even upped your business at the bar."

"That it has," I admitted. "And speaking of the press, I had an idea." I then told him my thoughts regarding Clay and the idea of bringing him into the group on a limited, need-to-know basis. "He's one of the more persistent reporters. Hell, he practically lives in my bar these days. I'm thinking if we can't beat him, we might as well join him . . . or rather invite him to join us. He could be a useful resource."

"But if he gets wind of this letter writer case, it could all blow up in our faces."

"Then we won't let him in on it. No one knows about it now except for you, Mal, Cora, and the brothers. None of them will say anything to him."

"I don't know, Mack. It's risky. We don't know if we can trust the guy."

"I'll feel him out first, see if he seems forthright. And we can test him by letting him in on the cases the Capone Club is working on and seeing if he follows the rules. I'll play it by ear."

"Is that a synesthetic thing, playing it by ear?"

"It just might be," I said, smiling.

There was a long silence, long enough that I thought our call had been dropped.

"Duncan, are you still there?"

"I'm here. I was just thinking about all this crime stuff you've gotten involved in. Maybe the bosses and Jimmy are right. Maybe it was wrong for me to bring you into it."

"It's a done deal, Duncan. No use crying over spilt vodka, as my father used to say. If I hadn't wanted to help you, I wouldn't have."

"I get that, but that was then and this is now. Maybe you should go back to being a simple bar owner. You said before that spending time dealing with the dark underbelly of the city was depressing, and I don't want you to get all melancholy again."

His use of the word *melancholy* both tickled and annoyed me. It was a quaint term to use, and that amused me, but the idea that Duncan viewed me as some emotionally handicapped woman was irritating. "The dark side of all this crime stuff *is* a little depressing to someone like me," I said, "someone who hasn't been exposed to it much until this past year. But if I can use my synesthesia to prove the innocence of someone who's been wrongly convicted, or to help put away someone who needs to be off the streets, then the upside outweighs the downside."

"You're going to continue with these cases whether I object or not, aren't you?"

"For now I am. It's a form of validation for me, Duncan. It's the first time in my life that my synesthesia has been useful in some way. I've spent all my life trying to hide it, feeling ashamed and weird because of it. This gives me a way to put it to good use."

"It also puts you in some dangerous situations. You almost got yourself killed looking into Tiny's sister's case."

"I'll be extra careful from now on. And I've got you and Mal to keep an eye on me."

"Speaking of Mal, are you seeing him anytime soon?"

"He's supposed to come by later today so we can do something together. Have to keep up appearances, you know."

"I'll give him a call and talk to him about this new case you have. I want him to stay with you as much as he can. If I can't be there with you all the time, I'll feel better knowing he's there."

I wondered if he would still feel that way if he knew that Mal's feelings for me were, to some degree, reciprocated. "Maybe it's time for Mal and me to fake a breakup," I suggested.

"Not until we get this letter writer thing figured out. Give it a little more time."

"I'm spending way more time with him than I am with you."

"I know, and I'm sorry. It won't always be that way, Mack."

"Yeah, you keep saying that, but what's going to change? This thing with Mal and me, it's starting to feel real."

"What are you saying?"

"I mean, I really like the guy, Duncan. He's funny, smart, and easy to be with."

Another silence ensued. "I know Mal is a bit sweet on you, Mack," Duncan said finally. "I can't say I blame him. But are you telling me you're developing feelings for him?"

I bit my lip, hesitating. Then I decided to take the plunge. "Yes, I think I am."

"Damn," he said. I heard an exasperated sigh and again saw a colorful maelstrom, but this time the colors were green and blue. "Mack, I know these past few weeks have been hard on us, and heaven knows our relationship hasn't gotten off to a great start. But I really care for you. Please, give us a little more time to work things out before you give up on me."

It was the most emotional thing I'd ever heard from him, and it made my heart swell, almost literally. I felt this odd heavy sensation in my chest, a pressure . . . an ache. "I haven't given up on you or on us, Duncan.

But let's face it. Our relationship is on a fast ship to nowhere at the moment."

"Give it a bit longer," he pleaded. "I know I haven't been the easiest person to be around at times, and I'll admit I'm a little gun shy when it comes to relationships, because of my past."

"What exactly happened to you, anyway? You said you were left standing at the altar, but you never gave me any details."

"It's complicated," he said, and I knew he was going to frustrate me yet again. "Please be patient. I don't want to lose you, Mack."

Irritated by his vague reply, I let out an exasperated, "Fine. I need to go tend to some bar stuff. Let me know what's what tomorrow, if you actually do come by."

"Mack, I—"

"Gotta go," I said, cutting him off. And then, before I could say something I might later regret, I disconnected the call and stuffed the phone into my pocket. I sat on my office couch and stewed for a few minutes, cursing men in general and this emotionally distant one in particular.

When I felt I had vented enough, I staggered up and crutched my way to the office door. Just as I was about to open it, there was a knock. I opened it and found Missy, one of my daytime waitresses, on the other side. Missy was in her twenties, the single mother of two young children, and living with her parents. She was blessed with dynamite good looks and a killer body, but she was overlooked in the brains department, all of which had likely led to her current living situation. But she was a hardworking and motivated employee who was good at her job and had an uncanny ability to connect a face with a drink.

"Here's today's mail," she said, handing me a thick stack of envelopes and catalogs. The holiday mail was always twice what I normally got, making me feel sorry for the mail carriers who had to hoof all that extra stuff through the cold and slush.

The stack was a large one, filled with the usual holiday catalogs and flyers, as well as my standard bunch of bills. I waded through them, tossing the catalogs and sorting the bills into a pile.

The letter was tucked in between my electric bill and a Lands' End catalog. I recognized the neat block printing right away and froze as I stared at it. After a minute or so of feeling my heart pound, which triggered a tiny pulsing red light in the periphery of my vision, I threw the catalogs in the trash and hobbled with the letter back to the couch. I stared at it for the longest time, turning it over and examining every inch of it, every nuance in the printing, the postage stamp . . . all of it. It looked so innocuous and ordinary, but I knew it wasn't. I wanted to open it but knew I shouldn't, at least not yet. I needed to preserve any evidence that might be in it, and thought about waiting until Duncan came by tomorrow. But I had no idea what deadline might be waiting for me, so time was of the essence. I thought about calling Duncan back, but he'd already said he couldn't come by tonight.

And then providence called.

Chapter 7

Providence literally called . . . on my cell phone. I dug it out of my pocket, and when I saw Mal's name come up on the screen, I felt an instant sense of relief.

"Mal, your timing is perfect."

"That's not what my last girlfriend used to say," he said with a little chuckle. There was a pause and then silence. "You didn't laugh," he said eventually. "Not a funny joke, or is something going on?"

"I just got another letter."

"Oh."

"Yeah, oh."

"Have you opened it?"

"Not yet. I'm in my office and thought I should probably carry it upstairs to my apartment." I envisioned doing just that in my mind, knowing it would be trickier than usual, thanks to my crutches and my broken leg.

"I'm on my way over there," Mal said. "I can give you a hand if you want."

"That would be great."

"How's the leg doing? Is it still pretty painful?"

"It's not bad today," I said, realizing then that Duncan hadn't bothered to inquire about my condition. I put a mental check mark in Mal's column on the little scorecard I was keeping in my head. It wasn't something I was proud of, but my mixed feelings regarding Duncan and Mal of late had me doing some oddball things.

"I'll be there in five. Meet you in your office?"

"That will work," I said with a smile. I disconnected the call and sat there, marveling at the relief I felt knowing that Mal was only minutes away. The letter sat on my lap, the block-printed address facing up, mocking me.

Time seemed to drag as I waited, but eventually, there was a knock at the door. I hobbled up and went over to open it. These days I kept it locked all the time, even when I was in the office, to prevent any nosy reporters or other thrill seekers from making an unexpected and unwanted entrance. As soon as I saw Mal on the other side, I tucked one crutch into my armpit and used that arm to give him a big hug. The return hug he gave me felt wonderful, comforting, reassuring. My eyes were closed initially, as I was relishing all the other synesthetic reactions I had to Mal's presence, but I eventually opened them and saw Clay Sanders standing about ten feet behind Mal, watching us.

"Come in," I said, finally letting Mal go. I finagled my crutch back into place and managed an awkward turn so I could head back to the couch. Mal followed me inside and shut the door behind him, blocking Clay's view.

"That reporter is certainly persistent with his nosiness," he said.

I maneuvered myself through another turn, put both crutches on one side of me, and eased myself down onto the couch. "Yes, he is," I said, tucking the crutches off to the side. "I'm thinking about bringing him on board with the Capone Club."

Mal stared at me as if I'd lost my mind. "You're not serious."

"As a heart attack," I said. Then I shared my thought processes with him on the matter. He listened, settling in next to me on the couch.

When I was done, Mal shrugged and said, "I have to admit, you're making some sense with the idea. But you're going to have to be very careful about what information he gets access to."

"I thought we could test him with some tidbits," I told him. "We have another case to look into, and we could use it to feed him information and see if he'll stick to an agreement to wait until we have something concrete, assuming we ever do, before he prints anything in the paper. If he plays fair with the test stuff, maybe I'll consider bringing him in on this case."

I picked up the letter from the arm of the couch, where I'd left it, and handed it to Mal. He hesitated, unwilling to touch it. "I don't think it makes a difference if you touch the envelope," I said. "It came through the mail, so it's been handled by any number of people already."

The cop in Mal wasn't so easily convinced. "You're probably right, but all the same, I'd rather have some gloves on before I handle it."

"Suit yourself," I said, and then I nodded toward the boxes of gloves I had on the bookshelf behind my desk. Mal got up, grabbed a pair from one of the boxes, and donned them. Then he took the letter and looked it over.

"Does Duncan know yet?"

I shook my head. "I finished talking to him on the phone right before the mail came. And you called a few minutes after that."

"We should call him and see if he can come over so we can open it."

"Don't bother. He told me he was tied up for the rest of today and wouldn't be able to come by until tomorrow."

Mal considered this, frowning. Then he said, "Let's take it upstairs so we can have some privacy, and we'll open it there. Maybe we can get Cora to come with us, and she can arrange another video hookup with Duncan on her computer."

"Good idea."

A couple of text messages and one awkward trek upstairs later, Cora, Mal, and I were settled around the dining-room table in my apartment. I had Cora go into my father's old office and grab a single sheet of white paper to put on the table, with the idea of opening the envelope above it. That way we would hopefully catch any minute trace evidence that might be inside the letter.

Mal called Duncan and was able to reach him, but we had to wait a bit for Duncan to get somewhere private before we could arrange the video chat. While we waited, Cora and I filled Mal in on the most recent case the Capone Club was considering.

"I'm hoping to make another visit to Waupun to-morrow," I told Mal. "I figure it makes sense to talk to this Middleton guy to see if I can get a feel for his innocence or lack thereof."

Mal smiled. "Do you mean that literally? When you say 'get a feel for,' do you mean you actually get a sensation or a feeling about whether or not someone is being honest?"

"Sort of, though voices trigger tastes for me rather than a feeling. Men's voices do, anyway. Sometimes women's voices manifest as a visual sensation."

Mal gave me a funny look and shook his head. "It must be very busy up there," he said, reaching over and tapping my head.

"You have no idea," I said with a roll of my eyes.

Cora's computer chimed, and she said, "There's Duncan." She tapped a key, and Duncan's face appeared on the screen.

"Hello, everyone," Duncan said. "I don't have much time, so let's make this quick if we can. Is everyone wearing gloves?"

"Mack and I are," Mal said. I had donned a pair from the boxes I'd kept on my dining-room table ever since the letters started arriving. "Cora is manning the computer."

"Then let's do it."

I let Mal have the honors this time. He picked up the letter opener I had brought to the table, and slid it beneath the flap on the envelope. Then he carefully sliced it open. He pried the two sides apart and peered inside before turning the envelope upside down over the sheet of paper. A single folded sheet of paper slid out—one that looked identical to the sheet on the table—and he gave the envelope a couple of taps to make sure it was empty. Nothing else fell out, so he set the envelope aside and picked up the letter. Carefully, he unfolded it, still holding it over the paper on the table. As he unfolded the letter, a long, narrow leaf and a single dried flower fell out.

"There's a leaf and a flower inside here," Mal said to no one in particular, though given that Cora and I could easily see them, I assumed his remark was addressed to Duncan. Mal gingerly picked up the flower and held it in front of the computer screen for Duncan to see. It was blue in color, though faded, with a circle of yellow in the middle, dozens of tiny narrow petals emanating from the center.

"That's an aster," Cora said. "It's a relatively common wildflower that blooms in the fall."

A moment of silence followed as we all contemplated the flower and tried to discern what meaning, if any, it might have.

When no one offered anything, Duncan said, "What about the leaf?"

Mal did the same thing with the leaf. "I think it's a weeping willow leaf," he said. "I have one in my yard."

Duncan said, "Let's have a look at that letter."

Mal set the leaf down and picked up the letter. I leaned in close so I could read it along with him. It was written in a calligraphic style with green ink, and I stuck my nose close to the page and took a whiff. The ink on this letter smelled essentially the same to me as that on the previous calligraphic letters, but with one subtle difference. I assumed the difference was due to whatever had been added to the ink to color it green. I said as much to the others, reminding them that the previous inks had been homemade.

Cora craned her neck, trying to read the letter, and Mal obligingly tilted it her way just enough so she could see it. For Duncan's benefit, he read the letter aloud.

> *Dear Ms. Dalton,*
>
> *It is a shame that you, with your supposed abilities, failed to interpret my last clues in a timely enough manner to save your friend Gary. Perhaps now you understand how deadly serious I am about these challenges.*
>
> *The scorecard is currently marked in my favor, and clearly, I was right in my assumption that you are a fraud. But I am willing to give you another chance. You have until 4:30 p.m. on Tuesday, December 22. I am sure you realize by now that my deadlines are carved in stone, and I sincerely hope you will be more successful than last time, before another of your friends ends up six feet under.*
>
> > *Gravely,*
> > *A skeptic*

Mal lowered the letter, and we all exchanged puzzled looks.

"This guy is really starting to piss me off," Duncan said irritably.

"I think we all feel that way," I said. "But let's not let our anger cloud our vision. What does the letter mean? Does anyone see a message in there somewhere?"

Another silence ensued, and Mal held the letter up to the computer camera so Duncan could see it.

Cora said, "Things having to do with death are mentioned several times, though that may simply be an attempt at sounding menacing. But there's a reference to six feet under, deadlines carved in stone, and the sign-off of 'gravely.' Could it be referencing a cemetery?"

It seemed as reasonable a guess as anything else at this point, but it certainly didn't narrow things down much. "That makes sense, Cora," Mal said. "It does sound like references to a cemetery, but which one? There must be dozens, maybe hundreds in the city."

"I don't think it's an accident that the ink used on this letter is green in color," I said. "Are there any cemeteries with the word *green* in the name, Cora?"

Cora started tapping away on her smartphone. After a few seconds she shook her head. "I can't find one named Green, but there is a Green Tree Meadows Cemetery and a Greenwood Cemetery."

"Well, that narrows things down with regard to the general location," Duncan said, "but it doesn't tell us which one of those it might be, or what to do and where to go once we get to them."

I said, "Based on past experience, I'm guessing I have to speak to someone in order to get the next clue. And dead people don't speak. So that means a caretaker or an office employee of some sort."

"What about the flower?" Mal asked. "It must be significant somehow."

"Maybe it's a reference to a name," I suggested. "Aster could be a last name."

"I have another idea," Cora said, still working on her phone. "When I searched for the words *green, cemetery,* and *Milwaukee,* Forest Home Cemetery also came up. It's a city landmark, and it has a special section for green burials called Prairie Rest. And Greenwood Cemetery, a Jewish cemetery, is adjacent to it. According to the Forest Home Web page, the Prairie Rest area is filled with naturally growing wildflowers, chief among them, blue asters. And the Greenwood Cemetery also has a green burial area, called Prairie Green, which contains wildflowers, prairie grasses, and trees." Cora looked up at us. "Like a weeping willow perhaps?"

"What the heck is a green burial?" Duncan asked, ignoring her suggestion for the moment.

"It's a burial involving biodegradable coffins or urns," I said. The others looked at me curiously. "I looked into it when my father died," I explained with a shrug. "The bodies are allowed to decompose naturally, so there is no embalming involved. Sort of a return-to-nature philosophy."

"Is your father buried there?" Duncan asked. "That might be why the writer targeted that cemetery."

I shook my head. "In the end I had him cremated. His ashes are in an urn in his office."

Both Mal and Cora turned to look in that direction, as if they expected my father to come strolling out of the room at any moment.

"I intend to scatter them one of these days," I said, feeling awkward. "I just haven't decided where yet."

The others refocused and turned their attention back to the letter.

"It seems we have several options to explore," Mal said. "Where should we start?"

"I think Cora is on the mark with the Forest Home and Greenwood cemeteries," I said. "It fits all the clues the best. I think we should start there."

Cora had returned to her phone, and she said, "It looks like Forest Home Cemetery handles the grounds keeping and the day-to-day business activities for Greenwood. So that's where you should probably start. But if you're hoping to hook up with any of the staff there, you're going to have to wait until Monday. According to their posted hours, they're already closed for today, and they're closed all day Sunday. On Monday they have hours from eight to four thirty. The grounds, however, are open from sunrise to sunset every day."

"The cemetery is quite large, isn't it?" I asked.

Cora nodded. "Nearly two hundred acres just for Forest Home. I don't know how much of that comprises the Prairie Rest area."

I frowned. "I can't imagine the letter writer expecting me to search the whole place. And since the time parameters give me until Tuesday, I think I'm supposed to meet with someone, like I have the other times. So I say we wait until Monday."

Mal said, "The green hint could refer to a name rather than the burial type."

"Good point," I said, looking over at him. "Any chance you can be free on Monday to go to the cemetery with me?"

"As luck would have it, I can. The boss shuts down for two weeks between Christmas and New Year's."

"Then it's a date," I said with a wan smile.

"Boy, you sure know how to show a guy a good time," he joked.

"Hey," I said with a shrug. "At least you can't say my dates are boring."

"There is nothing boring about you, Mackenzie Dalton," he said with a warm smile.

Duncan cleared his throat. I suspected that for a second there, Mal had forgotten Duncan was more or less in the room with us, because he blushed and started to squirm.

Duncan said, "I'll call you tomorrow, Mack, and let you know what time I can come by."

I got the sense he was staking his claim on me with that comment. To put his mind at ease, I said, "I'm looking forward to it."

"See you then. You guys take care." And with that, Duncan was gone.

Chapter 8

With nothing we could do about the letter until Monday, I shifted my focus back to Sandra Middleton and her brother's case. "Did you guys have any time to look over the information Sandra gave us?" I asked Cora.

"A little," she said. "But I left soon after we started looking at it, because of your text."

"Then I think we should head back to the group and see if they have come up with anything."

Mal and Cora both nodded, and after placing the letter and its contents in plastic Baggies for safe-keeping, I put them in my father's office so they'd be out of sight. I doubted we'd find any prints or trace evidence on any of it; the letter writer had been much too careful so far. But I felt it was better to be safe than sorry.

Once the evidence was taken care of, we headed down to the bar. I told Cora she should go on ahead to the Capone Club room, and that Mal and I would be there shortly to join her and the others. Cora eyed me warily—I suspected she knew I was up to something—

but she didn't ask any questions. As soon as she was gone, I hobbled my way around the bar to where Clay Sanders was sitting, Mal close on my heels. As I approached, Clay looked at me, smiled, and gave me an acknowledging nod before then looking away. Clearly, he didn't think I was coming over to him but rather merely walking by. As I sidled up beside him at the bar, he turned and gave me a quizzical look.

"Mr. Sanders," I said, balancing on my crutches, "I wonder if I might have a chat with you."

Clay looked wary and a little guilty, not surprising given that he had written several articles about me in the local paper that weren't exactly flattering. "May I ask what about?"

"I have a proposition for you." I gave him an enigmatic smile, hoping his natural curiosity would overcome any misgivings or doubts he might have about my invitation. "It's one I think you'll like," I added, further baiting the offer.

Clay narrowed his eyes at me, weighing my offer. Then he shrugged and said, "Where would you like to chat?"

"My office?"

"Lead the way."

Mal had been standing right behind me, and he moved aside so I could turn and head back the way I'd come. Clay eyed Mal with curiosity but said nothing to him. Once inside my office, I gestured toward the couch, and Clay went to it and sat. Mal remained standing by the door, a frown on his face. I settled in the chair on the back side of my desk, the one that visitors or employees typically used. I didn't want the barrier of my desk to come between me and Clay.

"Mr. Sanders, I've noticed you've been hanging out in my bar a lot lately."

"Yeah. So?" he said with a shrug of indifference. "I like your food. And it *is* a public establishment."

"True," I said with a smile. "My food is better than most bar fare. But I know you hang here for reasons other than that. You're a reporter. You're here because you're hoping to find more stories."

Clay said nothing, his expression impassive. This disappointed me. I was hoping he would deny my statement so I could see how his voice changed, assuming it did. So I decided to prompt him a bit more. "What?" I said with a questioning look. "No denials?"

"You're right," Clay said. "I'm a reporter, and I'm always looking for a new angle or a new story. But that's not the only reason I come here."

No change in his voice with this comment, I noticed.

"I really do like your food."

Again, no change.

"And frankly, you're old news," he concluded.

With this statement, I got what I wanted. Up until now, Clay's voice had tasted like a ripe, juicy orange. But as soon as he told me I was old news, the taste turned tartly bitter, as if I had bitten into the peel.

"That last statement was a lie," I said to him. "I know this because the taste of your voice changed."

From the corner of my eye, I saw Mal shift nervously where he was standing by the door. "Mack, are you sure you—"

I shushed him by holding up a hand.

Clay looked from me to Mal and back at me again, his expression curious but wary. "The *taste* of my voice changed?" he said.

I nodded. "You see, I have a disorder known as

synesthesia. It's a situation where one's senses get cross-wired, mixed up in a way. And my senses are . . . well . . . hypersensitive. I can often see, smell, taste, hear, or feel things others can't. And I experience each sense in multiple ways. For instance, everything I see triggers a smell or a physical sensation of some sort. Smells have an accompanying sound or physical sensation. Many of these secondary senses are minimal and brief, but they're there. Sounds always trigger tastes or visual manifestations, and voices, at least men's voices, always have a taste to them. When people lie, it changes their voice in subtle ways that most people can't detect. But I can because the taste of the voice changes. Do you get what I'm saying?"

Clay nodded, but he looked skeptical.

"I see you have your doubts. Perhaps a small test would help convince you?"

Now he looked intrigued. "What sort of test?"

I leaned back in my chair and laced my fingers together, my hands in my lap. "I'd like you to make a series of statements to me. Let's start with three of them at a time. Say three things to me, but have only one of them be a lie, an untruth, if you like. And then I will tell you which of the statements are true and which one is false."

"Okay," Clay said. He leaned forward, his elbows on his knees, hands fisted, chin on his hands. He looked me straight in the eye and said, "My name isn't really Clay Sanders. I'm thirty-six years old. I have two brothers and three sisters."

I looked back at him and smiled. "You're not playing fair, Mr. Sanders. I specifically said that two statements should be true and only one should be false. Everything you just told me is a lie."

Clay's eyes narrowed at me, and he cocked his head to the side.

"Therefore," I continued, "your name really is Clay Sanders, you are not thirty-six years old, and while I can't tell you how many siblings you have, you don't have two brothers and three sisters."

"Okay," Clay said with a grudging smile. "Let's try it again." He paused, looking as if he was thinking. "Give me a second," he said. "I'm trying to think of things you wouldn't have been able to find out about me by doing some basic research."

"Take your time," I said, my smile still in place.

He did. Whether he was stalling to try to unnerve me or because he really was thinking hard, I couldn't tell. After a minute or two of silence, he said, "I hate the taste of mushrooms. When I was a kid, I saw a dead body and never told anyone about it. The name of my first dog was Sunny."

"Interesting," I said with an arch of my brows. "You'll have to tell me the story about the body one of these days. And I promise never to put any mushrooms in your food. What *was* the name of your first dog?"

Clay leaned back into the couch, one hand in front of his mouth, as if to hold back whatever he was about to say next. After a few seconds he said, "Okay. I'll admit that's a cute little parlor trick."

"It's not a parlor trick," I told him. "I can do it with almost anyone."

"Almost?"

"There have been some rare exceptions."

Clay digested this, nodding slowly, never taking his eyes off me. "Is this what you were doing for the cops? Acting as some sort of human lie detector?"

"In part, yes. But all my senses are affected. I can do other things."

"Other things?"

My smile switched to a cautionary one. "Not so fast," I said. "I'm sharing this information with you because I have a deal for you. I'm trusting you to keep my . . . abilities to yourself for now."

"And why should I?"

"Because I think they can be of some use to you."

Again, Clay narrowed his eyes and studied me, contemplating. "How?"

"You are aware of the group that has formed here at my bar called the Capone Club?"

Clay nodded.

"The group has an interest in solving crimes that have already been adjudicated or are unsolved. That was how we got involved with the Gruber-Hermann case."

"You got involved with that one because the brother of one of the victims is a member of this club," Clay said.

"True," I acknowledged. "And I'm glad to see you do your homework. However, there are other cases on our radar, one in particular that we are looking at now. The group is interested in pursuing this case, and it may or may not turn out to be a case in which someone was wrongly convicted. But either way, we are going to look into it. And it occurs to me that you are a valuable resource we can take advantage of."

"You want me to help your group investigate old crimes?" His skepticism came through loud and clear, and with the tiniest hint of that bitterness. The flavor change made me think he was interested, despite his tone of indifference.

"Yes, I do. And in exchange for your help, you will get an exclusive on anything we uncover."

Clay steepled his hands and tapped at his chin. "You're saying I'd be a member of this Capone Club and privy to any information they dig up?"

I nodded. "And you'll also be privy to some more of my secrets. But those can't be printed."

"You're referring to this disorder you have?"

"More or less. There are other things, too, but first you'll need to earn my trust."

Clay seemed amused by this. "Anything to do with the recent death of your employee?"

"I'm not going to discuss that with you, at least not yet. I can't. It's an ongoing investigation, and I don't want to color it or interfere with it by giving you any information I might have."

That was it. I had successfully dangled all the bait I had, and now it was up to Clay to bite on it. I hoped I wasn't making a big mistake by bringing him in. I figured the others would be wary enough of him, at least in the beginning, to keep him on a leash. But I would have to be extra careful around him, watching everything I did and everything I said.

Clay glanced over at Mal with a scrutinizing look. "I know about you," he said.

Mal and I exchanged looks.

"I know you're a cop," Clay went on, eliminating my hope that he had meant something else. "You're working undercover. My guess is that you're investigating that construction company boss you work for."

"How did you—" I began.

Clay looked back at me. "I *am* an investigative reporter, and I'm damned good at my job. I got interested in your boy here when you started parading him around as your new boyfriend, and I did a little digging. I thought he looked familiar, and sure enough, when I looked at some old case photos from a drug bust that happened a few months back, I saw your guy here lurking in the background. The hair was longer, and he looked like a druggie, but I could tell the face was the same."

Mal sighed loudly and raked a hand through his hair. "Mr. Sanders, you can't—"

This time it was Clay's turn to do the shushing. He held up a hand and said, "Your secret is safe with me. I'm all in favor of beating crime, and in general, I support the police."

"I never would have guessed that based on the articles you've written so far," I said. "You were a bit harsh with the department."

"I was just rattling their cage a little, curious to see what might fall out."

"What fell out was Duncan Albright. You nearly cost him his job."

Clay shook his head. "He did that to himself by dragging you into it."

"He didn't drag me. I went willingly. And your stories didn't make *my* life any easier, either."

He waved away my complaint. "You have to admit, my stories have been good for your business."

He had me there. What he didn't know was that his stories had also been the impetus that brought me to the attention of the letter writer. And I wasn't about to tell him. Not yet, anyway.

"Look, I'm interested in your proposal," Clay said, leaning forward again, arms on his thighs, hands interlaced. "But I can't let you dictate what I do or don't write about."

I shook my head. "My disorder and I are off the table for now. And Mal's identity has to remain a secret."

"If I wanted to out your new boyfriend here, I would have done it already," Clay grumbled.

"What about my part in it?"

Clay chewed on his lip, thinking. "I'll tell you what," he said. "I'll give you a week to show me what you and the group can do. Consider it a freebie. I won't write about any of it unless you come up with something juicy. But if this Middleton case you're looking at doesn't pan out, then all bets are off."

The shock hit me too fast, and I knew it showed on my face. "How did you know that was the case?" I asked him. "I haven't mentioned it."

"I sat in on the entire trial. And I recognized his sister when she came into the bar earlier and headed upstairs to your group. It didn't take a rocket scientist to make the connection." He paused and flashed a guileful smile. "Plus, I happen to know the Gallagher family. I went to Penn State with one of Tiffany Gallagher's brothers."

I realized how crafty and clever Clay Sanders was, how he had manipulated me by withholding information, even as I'd thought I was manipulating him. My reservations resurfaced, and once again I wondered if I was making a huge mistake. But his revelation about his connection to the Gallagher family convinced me to continue.

"We don't know yet if there's any merit to the case," I asserted. "We haven't had a chance to look into it at all. What's your take on it?"

"I have my doubts. Benjamin Middleton seemed sincere to me, and there were some questions raised by the evidence that weren't adequately answered. I've thought all along that Middleton might have gotten a bum rap. To be honest, I thought he was going to be acquitted."

"Fair enough," I said. "So do we have a deal?"

"Not yet. You know something about Gary Gunderson's death that you're not telling me. Why?"

"I know he didn't deserve to die. And I also know that the last prison sentence he served was for a crime he didn't commit. Beyond that, I don't have anything else I can tell you." I pursed my lips, metaphorically locking away anything else I had to say on the matter. I hoped he would interpret this as me saying I knew nothing else, rather than as me saying I wasn't willing to share. In the end, I couldn't tell. Clay Sanders might have been easy to read when it came to lies and truth, but beyond that the man was an enigma.

"Okay then," he said. He got up, walked over to me, and extended his hand.

I took it and gave it a little shake, sealing the deal. His touch made me see a brief bright orange flash, like an explosion of flames, and I wondered if Cora was right.

Was I making a deal with the devil?

Chapter 9

The three of us ventured upstairs to the Capone Club room. To say that Clay's entrance made an impression would be an understatement. Everyone in the room fell silent and gaped at the man, most with suspicious, angry expressions.

"What's up, Mack?" Frank Signoriello said finally, breaking the silence.

"I've invited Mr. Sanders to join us and help out with the Middleton crime," I said. "He has some resources that might be useful to us, and in return he has agreed to play fair with regard to what he publishes. Are all of you okay with that?"

Judging from the looks on their faces, they weren't, but no one spoke up.

After waiting for what I considered a reasonable amount of time, I added, "For what it's worth, Clay is up to speed on the case, and he shared with me that he thinks Benjamin Middleton might have been innocent. So let's welcome him and see what we can find out, shall we?"

To the group's credit, they all nodded and smiled at Clay, though many of those nods were tentative.

Sam patted an empty chair beside him and said, "Come and join us."

Clay returned the smile and took the seat Sam had indicated. "Thanks for having me," he said. "As I'm sure you're all aware, I've known about your group for some time now, and I'm very curious to see what you do and how you do it."

I settled in a chair at Cora's table, ignoring the questioning look she shot me, and Mal grabbed an empty chair against the wall and brought it over next to mine. I looked at Clay and said, "Everyone here knows who you are, but you may not know everyone here. Part of the reason I think our group has been successful is because of the varied backgrounds represented by the membership." I looked at the Signoriello brothers. "Frank, why don't you start the introductions. Everyone, give your name and say a little about the background you bring to the group."

Frank complied without missing a beat, and his brother Joe went next. From there, everyone in the group stated their name and offered up a bit of information about themselves—their jobs, their interests, how long they'd been with the group, that sort of thing.

Once the intros were done, I looked over at Cora and said, "Now that that's out of the way, tell me what you guys have gleaned from the file Sandra Middleton gave us."

Cora shuffled some of the papers she had next to her computer. "It's mostly Sandra's thoughts and observations," she said. "There are some questions she raised about some of the testimony, mostly things she mentioned to us earlier, like why finding gunpowder residue on her brother's hands, and his fingerprints on the gun, didn't necessarily prove his guilt. She also has some background information on the man who claimed he sold the gun to Middleton two weeks before the incident, information I've verified myself. His name is John Harrington, and not surprisingly, he has a record, mostly drunk and disorderly types of things, although he also got caught shoplifting once. Given that, I'd say his reliability as a witness is questionable."

Carter spoke up then and filled in some more blanks. "Sandra also wrote down some comments about the victim and her family. She thought the father-in-law's testimony was pompous and one-sided, an obvious attempt to make Ben look like a money-grubbing wannabe. Apparently, Mr. Gallagher testified about some arguments Ben and Tiffany had had, and he made it sound like Ben was a selfish, abrasive jerk. Not surprisingly, Sandra noted that this wasn't true. She also witnessed at least one of the arguments Gallagher mentioned and stated that it didn't go down the way Gallagher claimed. According to her notes, she mentioned this to the defense attorney and asked to testify as to Ben's true nature and what really happened, but the lawyer didn't use her. According to the lawyer, anything Sandra said would be considered biased by the jury and would be dismissed because of her relationship to Ben."

I looked over at Clay. "You said you sat in on the trial?"

"All of it," he confirmed with a nod.

"What's your take on Sandra's claims?"

He thought a moment before he answered. "She's right about one thing. Colin Gallagher can be a pompous ass, and I think the jury saw that. Unfortunately, they also saw him break down and cry over the loss of his little girl, and I think showing that human side of himself helped the jury to forget the rest. A lot of people expect the very rich to act a bit pompous and entitled, so I don't think that aspect of Gallagher's personality played against him the way it could have."

I turned back to the group. "Anything else?"

"Yes," Carter said. "She has some information about the seminal fluid found in Tiffany during the autopsy. If her notes are correct, the presence of the seminal fluid indicates Tiffany had sex not long before she was killed, but there were no sperm found, and apparently, that's what contains the DNA."

"No sperm?" I said with a puzzled look. "What does that mean?"

Clay answered. "According to the expert who testified, it means the person Tiffany had sex with was either sterile or had had a vasectomy."

"Right," Carter said, verifying this. "The lack of sperm means there was no DNA, but apparently, there were blood-typing antibodies found in the seminal fluid that ruled Ben out as the donor."

Clay nodded and said, "The prosecution used that to establish a motive for Ben, claiming he found out about the affair and was afraid Tiffany was going to leave him for someone else and take all her money with her."

Cora arched her eyebrows. "As motives go, it's a good one."

I looked back at Clay. "What was your take on it?"

He pursed his lips and frowned. "It certainly was

damning, but Ben Middleton seemed genuinely upset and surprised by the revelation that his wife had been unfaithful."

"How long were they away on their trip?" Joe asked.

"Five days," Carter answered.

Joe arched his eyebrows. "And she was killed when they were on their way home. Does anyone know how long seminal fluid can remain?"

"The expert said up to three days, assuming Tiffany hadn't bathed," Clay said. "But Ben testified that Tiffany had taken a bath the night before and the two of them didn't have sex after that."

"So that means her tryst must have happened during the last day they were there," Joe said.

Again, Clay filled in some of the blanks. "Ben testified that he drove to a convenience store that morning to pick up some provisions because there had been a snowstorm during the night and there was a second, bigger one coming later that day. Because of the earlier storm, he said it took him nearly two hours to make a trip that should have taken half that long."

"I'm guessing that's our window of time, then," I said.

Carter said, "It would be helpful to have access to the ME's report. I wonder if Dr. T can pull her magic with their office again."

When we were investigating the Lori Gruber case, Dr. T had contacted a friend of hers in the ME's office to get copies of the autopsy reports on both Lori and Anna Hermann, the friend who was also killed. Though the summary reports were available to the public, the request process was time consuming, and it often took weeks to get the actual documents. Dr. T not only managed to expedite the process for us, but she also got her hands on more detailed information than was typically available.

Unfortunately, Dr. T wasn't present at the moment. Unlike most of the others in the group, her schedule wasn't a Monday through Friday thing. She was working twelve-hour shifts, from eleven in the morning until eleven in the evening on the weekend, which meant we likely wouldn't see her until Monday.

I said this to the group, mostly for the benefit of Clay and the newcomers, since the regulars already knew Dr. T's schedule. And once again Clay proved his value to the group.

"I can get you the ME's report. I have a copy of the one that was presented at the trial. I'll bring it tomorrow, if that helps."

"It would," I said, and others in the room nodded their agreement. While he would still have to prove his trustworthiness to the group over time, I could tell his resourcefulness was starting to win several of them over.

"Do we know who the other man was?" I asked.

Clay shook his head. "No one was presented as such, so I can only assume that neither the prosecution nor the defense knew who it was. I suppose it's possible the prosecution knew and didn't want to put the name forth, because it would only muddy the waters by providing another viable suspect and creating reasonable doubt, but if that's the case, they'll never admit to it. It would land them in a lot of hot water if they got caught hiding or suppressing evidence."

"Well, figuring out who the mystery man might be is a starting point," Holly said. "Though I'm not sure how we can go about it. If the legal teams, with all their resources, couldn't come up with it, I don't know how we can."

I nudged Cora. "If we could find a way to get ahold of Tiffany's computer or phone, do you think you could dig something up?"

"It's possible," she said with a halfhearted nod. "But how are you going to get them? I imagine they're logged in as evidence somewhere."

"I'm sure the defense team is working on appeals," I said. "They'd be able to request the evidence, wouldn't they? Maybe we should talk with them and let them know we're trying to exonerate their client."

Clay shook his head. "Except anything Cora found would not only be inadmissible, but it would likely also be considered evidence tampering. And that would jeopardize the appeals process." He paused and shook his head again. "They'll never go for it."

I looked around at the group members. All of them were wearing thoughtful expressions as they pondered the problem, and I had faith in their brainstorming abilities. Then Alicia proved me right.

"You know, we women tend to have confidantes," she said, looking over at Holly and smiling. "We need to find out who Tiffany's confidantes were and talk to them. If she was having an affair, a confidante would know."

"Good idea," Joe said, slapping his thigh.

Cora started tapping on her keyboard. "Maybe I can get some ideas by taking a look at Tiffany's social media. I'll see what I can find."

"Did she work anywhere?" Carter asked. "Coworkers often become confidantes."

"They sometimes become secret lovers, too," Sam added, bringing his psychological knowledge to the mix.

Clay said, "She didn't need to work. Her family money saw to that. She did do some volunteer work, though she dropped it several months before she was killed. Maybe she met someone there."

"It's worth looking into," Carter said. "Do you know where it was?"

Clay nodded. "She volunteered at a local animal shelter." He then provided the name of the place.

"So how should we divvy up the duties?" Carter asked of no one in particular.

One of the newer members, high school physics teacher Stephen McGregor, said, "If someone can get me any information about the car and the bullet trajectories, I can take a look at them to see if the physics fit with Middleton's story."

I glanced over at Clay with a questioning look. "Did they present any information along those lines at the trial?"

He nodded. "They did, and the trial was televised. There should be footage showing the original evidence and displays. I know someone who worked on it. I'll see if I can get a copy."

"Thanks, Clay," I said, thinking the devil might prove to be a valuable team member, after all. "I plan on heading up to the Waupun Correctional Institution tomorrow to have a chat with Ben Middleton, if it can be arranged, but I haven't spoken to Tyrese yet, so I'm not sure if that plan will fall into place. If I can't do it tomorrow, I'll get to it as soon as I can."

"Who is Tyrese?" Clay asked.

"He's a local cop and a member of this group," I said. "He helps us out when he can with stuff he feels comfortable doing."

Clay nodded thoughtfully. A silence fell over the group as the conversation stalled.

Joe Signoriello finally broke it by asking, "Did our victim have any life insurance?"

"She did," Clay said. "She and Ben were both insured for two hundred grand apiece, and that alone would be motive enough for most people. But Tiffany had access to a lot more money than that between her trust fund and the family money."

"Did Ben have ready access to any of that money?" Carter asked.

"Not sure," Clay said.

I made a mental note to ask Tad Amundsen if he could shed any light on this question. Given that the vast majority of his clients were Milwaukee's rich and elite, there was a chance he might have access to information about the Gallagher family finances.

"What did Ben do for a living?" I asked.

"He was a lawyer," Clay said with an ironic smile. "But he specialized in contract and business law, not criminal law."

Sam said, "Someone should chat with his coworkers and see if he ever talked to anyone about his marital issues."

Holly volunteered. "I know the group he worked for," she said. "In fact, I met Ben Middleton once. His firm does work for our bank. If you want, I can try to contact some of the other lawyers in the group to see if they know anything."

"You're on," I told her. I glanced at my watch and saw that it was nearly five already. "I need to call Tyrese to see if I can get to the prison tomorrow. You guys keep looking over the info we have and see if there are any other avenues of investigation we can look into."

With that, I got up and commandeered my crutches to leave the room. Mal followed behind me. So did Clay Sanders.

"Mack," Clay said in the hallway outside the room. "Any chance I can come with you when you go to Waupun?"

I frowned at this, uncomfortable with his request. I came up with the first excuse I could think of. "The fewer distractions I have, the easier it is for me to assess someone I'm talking to."

"I promise to sit on the sidelines and stay quiet. I won't say a thing."

Mal stood off to one side, behind Clay. He caught my eye and shook his head.

"Even so, Clay," I went on, "you'll be a distraction for me, and that may interfere with things." I didn't think this was true—at least from my end—but it was the only excuse I could come up with on the fly. "Besides, Middleton might not be comfortable speaking to me if he knows there is a reporter in the room."

"You don't have to tell him I'm a reporter. And I'll keep the whole thing strictly off the record. I promise." Clay was nothing if not persistent, a trait I figured was useful for an investigative reporter but was irritating for me. "I just want to see you do this thing you do with someone other than me."

I looked at him, weighing both his words and his conviction. He seemed sincere, both in his statement of why he wanted to come along and his promise to keep it off the record. I felt myself caving but then thought of one last possible escape, something to at least buy me a little time to think about the potential consequences. "I need to run it by Tyrese," I told him. "He has to be comfortable with it."

Clay nodded. "Fair enough. And in exchange, I can help you get a chat with the Gallagher family, if you want."

"That would be helpful," I admitted.

"Let me know?"

"I will."

"I'll be with the group," Clay said, gesturing toward the Capone Club room. Then with an intrigued smile, he added, "They're quite fascinating."

Chapter 10

By the time we got back to my office, I was exhausted from negotiating with my crutches both the stairs and the tortuous path between tables on the crowded floor. I fell onto my couch, took a moment to catch my breath, and looked at Mal.

"What's your take on Sanders?" I asked him.

"He's definitely a valuable asset," he said. "But I'm going to hold out on any final judgment until we've spent more time with him. I'm hoping he'll be trustworthy, but some of these reporter types have no ethics or morals when it comes to getting a scoop. Time will tell, I suppose."

I nodded, agreeing with his assessment. "I'm not sure why I don't want him along for the trip to Waupun, but I don't."

"Too much too soon," Mal said. "I get it. Sanders needs to prove himself a little more before you give him access to the inner circle. I'm sure Tyrese will happily put the kibosh on him coming along if you want him to."

"Except Clay's offer of an in with the Gallagher

family might be useful. And something tells me he won't expedite that unless I let him come along. He strikes me as a tit-for-tat kind of guy."

"Don't let him coerce you," Mal cautioned.

I gave it a moment's thought. "I think it's a risk we'll have to take. I'll set some ground rules and see if Clay obeys them. We can consider it a trial run."

Mal shrugged his acquiescence, but he didn't look happy.

I took out my cell phone and dialed Tyrese's number. He answered after four rings, sounding groggy.

"Tyrese, it's Mack. Did I wake you?"

"You did," he said. To anyone else, he might have been less blunt, or he might have tried to make the caller feel better by lying, but he knew it was a wasted effort with me.

"I'm sorry. Should I call back later?"

"No. I was planning on getting up in half an hour, anyway. Nick and I have been pulling night shifts all week. Our last one is tonight." Nick was Nicodemus Kavinsky, Tyrese's partner on the police force and someone else who participated in the Capone Club when he had the time.

"Oh. I don't suppose you'd be willing or able to arrange another trip to Waupun for me tomorrow, then," I said, my hopeful tone belying my words.

"Why? Does the group have another case?"

"We do. It's the Benjamin Middleton case."

Tyrese let out a low whistle. "How did that one end up on your radar?"

"His sister came to see the group today," I explained, and then I summarized her claims for him. "Before we get too involved in the case, I'd like to have a chat with

Mr. Middleton to get a feel for whether or not he's telling the truth."

"Understood," Tyrese said. "Let me make some phone calls, and I'll see what I can do. I have the next three days off after tonight, so I should be fine to take you up there tomorrow."

"There's something else you should know," I told him. Then I filled him in on my invitation to Clay Sanders, his participation in the group, and his request to go along to Waupun with me. I decided to wait for Tyrese to comment and express his own feelings on the matter before I gave him mine.

"Inviting Sanders to join the group is a bold move," he said. "What if he learns more about you and your ability?"

"He already has. I told him myself. I even gave him a little demonstration."

"Is that wise, Mack?"

"I don't know if it's wise, but I'm tired of hiding. I'm tired of keeping secrets."

Tyrese sighed and said nothing for a few seconds. When he finally spoke, I sensed some lingering reservation in his voice. "If you want him to come along for the ride, that's okay with me, but if you need a no man, I'm your guy."

It was an easy out, and I was tempted to take it. But my gut kept telling me to give Clay a chance. "Sanders did offer up something in exchange," I said. "Apparently, he's friends with one of the Gallagher sons, and he offered to get me an intro to the family so I can talk to them. I'm thinking we might need that. They're a rich family and very protective of their privacy. I'm not sure they'd talk to me otherwise, particularly if they know I'm looking into exonerating their son-in-law."

"That's assuming you decide to pursue the case," Tyrese said.

"True. But I like to keep my options open."

"I'll leave the decision up to you, Mack. But feel free to make me out as the bad guy if you want to tell him no. I'll call you later and let you know if I can get us up to Waupun tomorrow. Give me some time to get fully awake and have a little coffee."

"Take all the time you need. It's not like we're on any sort of tight timeline here. If we can't get there tomorrow, set it up for whenever."

"Will do."

I disconnected the call and looked up at Mal, who was leaning against the wall beside my office door. "I'm in hold-and-wait mode," I said. "Any ideas?"

"You look tired."

"I am," I admitted. "I haven't slept well since the accident. This thing"—I gestured toward my cast—"interferes with me on several different levels. It's hard to move around in bed, it makes me itch, and it smells funny. And all those sensations trigger a bunch of others. Then there's all the mental and emotional baggage associated with Gary's death and this damned letter writer. I keep looking at all the happy, celebratory people milling about, getting ready for the Christmas holiday, and I feel like it's all a facade, an elaborate display or act being put on for my benefit." I paused and sighed. "I'm having a hard time with Christmas this year. It's the first one I'll be spending alone, without my dad."

"I noticed you hadn't done any decorating upstairs,

but I wasn't sure if that was a change from your normal routine or the way you always do it."

"My dad always went all out for Christmas," I told him. "There are tons of decorations upstairs, in the attic space, but I haven't had the heart to do any of it this year. I miss him so much already. Getting those decorations out will only make it worse."

"You know you don't need to spend the holiday alone, right? What's Duncan doing?"

I shrugged. "I have no idea. We haven't planned that far ahead. We schedule things on a day-to-day basis these days."

"I assume the bar will be closed for Christmas Day?"

I shook my head. "I'll open later in the day, at five, like I do on Sundays."

"Well, as luck would have it, I'm totally free for the day. I decided not to travel for the holiday, and since all my family members are back in Washington, I'm kind of on my own, too. So if you and Duncan don't have anything planned, I'd be happy to spend the day with you."

I realized how selfish I was being by mourning my possible alone status for the holiday when there were plenty of other people in the same boat. "If you're alone for the holiday, then you are definitely spending it with me regardless of what Duncan and I end up doing."

"I don't want to be a fifth wheel."

"You are not a fifth wheel, Mal. And of all the people I know who I might spend the holiday with, you're at the top of my list."

Mal arched a brow at me. "Isn't Duncan at the top of your list?"

"At the moment, the two of you are both up there, vying for first place."

Mal looked at me, his expression questioning, curious, intrigued. I held his gaze, saying nothing more, and the moment sizzled.

"I'm sorry, Mal," I said, breaking the tension between us. "I shouldn't have said that. I don't want to mislead you. My focus for now is on my relationship with Duncan, but I like you a lot. I hope you'll always be a part of my life in some way."

"I hope so, too," he said, and while his tone sounded chipper, his face showed a hint of disappointment. "And since we are supposed to be dating, we should do something together. How about dinner? My treat."

"Do we need to keep up the facade now that Clay Sanders is in on things?"

"He doesn't know that you and I are faking it. At least he didn't let on that he knows. Nor does he seem to know that Duncan isn't really on the outs. And there are lots of other reporters out there. So yes, I think we need to keep up the facade."

He winked at me, and I wondered if he was simply arguing the point so he could continue to see me, or if he really felt it was important to continue our game play. After thinking about it for a few seconds, I realized I didn't care what his motivations were. I enjoyed his company just as he enjoyed mine, so for the time being, we might as well keep the status quo.

My cell phone rang, and I thought it might be Tyrese already, but then I saw it was Duncan instead. It was as if the guy had some special ESP or something. Every time Mal and I had one of these discussions, Duncan managed to put in an appearance somehow.

"Hey, Duncan," I answered, and I saw Mal's shoulders sag ever so slightly. "What's up?"

"I've been thinking about this latest letter, and I still think this Apostle Mike guy might be behind it. I want to take another run at him and wanted to know if you would like to observe again."

Apostle Mike, aka Michael Treat, was the leader of a semireligious extremist group that targeted non-Christians with rhetoric, philosophizing, and possibly violence. The cops hadn't been able to pin anything on him as of yet, but there had been several crimes that they felt might be connected to him. Unfortunately, Apostle Mike had enough minions blindly following him and willing to do his bidding that even if he was behind the crimes, it was likely he had someone else do his dirty work for him. That made it doubly hard to pin anything on him. He had targeted me with his rhetoric, sending me a letter in which he called me an abomination against God and hinted that I was evil. Duncan had zeroed in on it when he read through all the fan mail I had received, letters, notes, and cards that started coming shortly after the first news reports about my involvement with the police. Many of these missives had been kind, encouraging, and supportive. But a few, like Apostle Mike's, had been just the opposite.

Duncan had arranged for me to observe an interview with Apostle Mike once before. The guy was smug, condescending, and arrogant, but during that brief interview, I hadn't been able to detect any lies coming from him. Still, he wasn't questioned about me directly, because the letter writer had made it clear that I wasn't to involve Duncan at all. So the pretext used to get the man down to the police station for an interview was regarding another matter. If Apostle Mike was the letter writer, questioning him about me might have triggered another killing. In the end, though, our worries had been pointless, because someone ended up dead, anyway.

"I don't know how much good it will do," I said. "We can't ask him outright if he's the letter writer and risk his wrath if he is."

"We won't ask him about the letters directly," Duncan said. "But we *are* going to ask him about Gary's murder. It's common knowledge that Gary's murder is being investigated by the police, so it shouldn't tip him off if I'm not the one doing the questioning. We can do it like we did before, have some other guys do the actual interview, while you and I listen in from the observation room."

"But don't you need a reason to question him about Gary's murder? What connection does Gary's death have to Apostle Mike other than me?"

"None, but Treat doesn't have to know that. I can make something up . . . tell him that we discovered Gary participated in a Wiccan ceremony or something like that. Given his outspoken feelings regarding the Wiccans, it would seem logical to question him as a suspect if that was true."

"I suppose," I said. I still wasn't convinced it was a good idea, but I was out of objections. "When are you thinking of doing it?"

"Tonight. Treat is a hard guy to find at times, but we know where he is this evening. He is holding one of his *gatherings*, as he calls them, at the home of one of his followers tonight, at seven. We intend to drop in and invite him down to the station instead."

I glanced at my watch. It was nearly six already, and

that didn't leave me much time to get to the station. And the last time I'd gone there, I'd been in disguise, just in case the letter writer happened to be watching me. Duncan had arranged for a family friend of his who was a makeup artist to come by and do me over. That makeover had taken a lot of time, more time than I had tonight.

As if he was reading my mind, Duncan said, "If you're worrying about how to get here and what to do for a disguise, I have a different idea. I'm going to send a couple of detectives to your bar and have them escort you to the station, with the explanation that I want you to observe a suspect to see if you recognize him as someone who has been in the bar before or had any sort of altercation with Gary. It makes sense that you'd be asked to do that, given your relationship with Gary. I'll make it clear to the other detectives that you don't want the guy to know you're here watching him. They'll escort you in through a back entrance, and I'll take it from there."

"I suppose that's as good a plan as any," I said finally. "Even with a disguise, this cast and these crutches are a dead giveaway. But won't the other detectives know that bringing Treat in for questioning is a ruse?"

"No. I plan to use the same guys who questioned him last time. They're aware of Treat's leanings, and if I tell them I learned about a connection between Gary and the Wiccans, they'll buy into it."

"Okay," I said, surrendering.

"Atta girl. I like the guy for this, given his history. You fit right into the mold he's so against, with your supposed *voodoo magic,* as one reporter called it."

"Speaking of reporters . . ." I filled him in on what I had done with Clay Sanders.

"I'm not sure that was a smart thing to do," Duncan said, "but what's done is done. Just watch your back."

"I will."

"I'll have Arthur Cook and Doug Farrell pick you up in about forty-five minutes, if that's okay."

"Sure. Mal and I were just about to have a bite to eat, and that will give us enough time to grab something here."

"Sorry to mess up your plans, but it might work out well in the end. If you and Mal are eating somewhere in the bar where others can see you when the guys show up, it will lend credence to the scene. Fill Mal in, and he can act surprised and worried when Arty and Doug escort you away."

"Okay. See you soon, then."

I disconnected the call and gave Mal an apologetic look.

"I take it our dinner plans have changed," he said.

I nodded and filled him in.

"Let's get to it, then," he said. "The clock is ticking, and if you really want to get some food into your stomach, we need to get moving."

I was hoisting myself up from the couch when my phone rang again. I half expected it to be Duncan calling to change or cancel the plan, but it was Tyrese.

"We're good for tomorrow at Waupun," he said. "I've arranged for us to get there at one. Will that work for you?"

"It does. Can you pick me up here at the bar?"

"Sure. I'll be there around eleven thirty. Are you going to let Sanders come along?"

"I think so," I said. "Hopefully, I won't regret it. Is it okay if Mal comes along, too?"

Tyrese hesitated a few seconds, long enough to let

me know that he was pondering the rationale behind my requests to have Mal along on each of these treks.

"He's my moral support," I said. "I feel more comfortable when he's around."

"Okay then," Tyrese said, sounding resigned. "I'll see all of you in the morning."

As soon as I hung up, I filled Mal in on the plan. "I hope you don't mind that I included you," I told him when I was done. "What I told Tyrese is true. You really are my moral support. I feel better having you with me."

"I'm happy to go along," he said. "I'm curious about the case and would like to get a feel for Middleton myself. In fact, I wouldn't mind going along with you tonight to check out this Apostle Mike character."

I thought about this, knowing that bringing Mal along might upset Duncan. I'd like to get Mal's take on Apostle Mike, but I was also eager to have a little alone time with Duncan, even if it was only for a brief period in less than ideal circumstances.

"Let's not rock the boat any more than we have to," I said. "Besides, I don't want you to risk your cover."

Mal shrugged and smiled at me. "It won't be a big risk. I can play the role of your concerned boyfriend quite convincingly, I think."

"Yes, you can, but for now I'd rather keep things the way Duncan planned them."

Though he nodded his understanding, I could tell he was disappointed.

Oddly enough, so was I.

Chapter 11

We ordered a pizza at the bar and then headed up to the Capone Club room. Mal and I agreed it would be best to be seated with the rest of the group when the detectives arrived. That way everyone in the group would hear the reason why they wanted me to come down to the station, lending the story more credence.

I filled the others in on the status of my trip to Waupun the following day. "Clay has asked to come along, and I've decided to let him," I told the group. This announcement was met with mixed reactions: some slyly exchanged looks, a few worried expressions, and several people shifting uncomfortably in their seats.

"Thank you," Clay said. I gathered he hadn't missed the reactions of the others when he then addressed the group with, "I promise you I will do my best to earn the trust of all of you."

He had his work cut out for him.

I barely had time to inhale two slices of pizza before the detectives arrived. I recognized them both from my last visit to the station, and one of them I knew because he was a patron of my bar. Arthur Cook, who went by Arty, was newly single on the heels of a divorce, and he typically stopped in at the bar one or two times during the week to flirt with any available women he could find. Since he was balding and overweight, and had a tendency to reek of desperation, he never had much luck. As far as I knew, he'd always gone home alone. The second detective, Doug Farrell, was tall and slender, with muscular arms. He wasn't a bad-looking guy, but he had a scar on his face that ran from his right eyebrow up to his hairline. His haircut and posture screamed a military background, and I wondered if he acquired the scar while in the service, while working as a cop, or some other way.

Billy escorted the two men upstairs to find me, and as planned, they explained to me why they were there and that they wanted me to come with them to the station. They kept their story somewhat vague, simply saying that they had a potential suspect in Gary's case whom they wanted to question. They wanted me to observe the man to see if I recognized him as a patron of the bar or anyone who had ever had a run-in with Gary.

I excused myself from the group and hobbled my way to my office to get my coat, then followed the two men out of the bar and into a waiting double-parked car. Once I was inside the vehicle, a task made somewhat difficult by my need to drag along the cursed crutches, Doug Farrell, who was in the front passenger seat, turned to me.

"Thanks for coming with us, Ms. Dalton," he said. "I'm sure you'd like to see this case solved as much and as quickly as we would."

He had that right. "No problem," I told him. "Does this suspect you have look good for it?"

Doug frowned. "I don't want to say too much, but there are some possible connections. Right now we want to see if we can establish a connection between this guy and Mr. Gunderson. All we need you to do is observe him and tell us if he looks familiar to you. We want to know if you can recall ever seeing him in your bar, or if you can recall him having any dealings of any sort with Mr. Gunderson."

"I understand."

"You'll be in a room where you can see him, but he won't be able to see you. Detective Albright will be with you. I hope that won't make you uncomfortable with the process."

It was a leading question, one no doubt intended to solicit some information about the status of my relationship with Duncan, a relationship that had been mentioned in some of the news articles, though the romantic side of things had only been hinted and guessed at.

"Detective Albright and I will be fine," I assured him. "There are no hard feelings between us."

"That's good," Doug said, and then he turned back to face front. The remainder of our ride was made in silence, though Arty did sneak a few peeks at me in his rearview mirror.

When we arrived at the police station, Doug and Arty took me in through a back entrance and escorted me to where the interview rooms were located. Duncan was waiting outside the observation room, and I made sure to act curious about the place so as not to let on that I had been there before. I greeted Duncan with polite friendliness.

Doug said, "Detective Albright will take you into the observation room. It's set up for listening, as well as viewing, but all we want you to do for now is look. A simple look-see might not be enough, so we'll give you plenty of time to watch him while we talk to him, but you won't be able to hear what we're saying. If you're not sure about his face, maybe some of his mannerisms will strike a familiar chord."

I nodded my understanding, and with no further ado, I followed Duncan into the observation room. As soon as the door closed behind us, Duncan pulled me into his arms and gave me a very nice kiss.

"I've missed you, Mack," he said.

"I've missed you, too," I said. "Though this isn't the greatest of circumstances, I'm glad to have this chance to see you."

"Sometimes we have to take what we can get," he said with a wry smile.

When he finally released me, I looked around at the observation windows and saw that Michael Treat, aka Apostle Mike, was already in one of the interview rooms. He looked much the same as he had the last time I saw him, which was only days ago. Once again I marveled at how ordinary he looked, how little he resembled the crazy-eyed, fervent heathen I had imagined him to be. He was tall, lean, bald, and handsome, and he looked like any other business worker one might pass on the streets of downtown Milwaukee. He was wearing the same gray parka he'd worn the last time, and the same two mismatched knit gloves—one blue, one green—were on the table in front of him, one stacked neatly atop the other.

As I watched him, he shrugged off his parka and hung it on the back of his chair. He spent a moment or two adjusting the coat so that it hung just so, and then he stood back from the chair and eyed it a moment before taking his seat. His clothing was plain but very neat. His shirt, a light blue button-down, was pressed, and though his pants were blue jeans, there was a crease down the front of each leg. He crossed one leg over the other, and I saw that his feet were clad in brown low-top boots over a pair of dark blue socks.

Arty and Doug entered the room, and Treat barely acknowledged their presence.

"Am I really forbidden to hear what they're saying?" I asked Duncan.

"No, but we need to be very careful. Saturday nights are typically busy around here, and while the other rooms are empty for the moment, someone could come in here at any time. I can't let anyone see you wearing the headphones."

"Then what do you suggest?"

"Just listen through one of the earpieces for now," he said, handing me a headset. "I'm going to stand guard by the door, and if I see anyone heading this way, I'll tell you so you can drop them."

I put one of the earpieces up to my head and listened. Arty was asking Treat about his whereabouts on the night of Gary's murder. Treat eyed him with weary impatience and said nothing. Arty asked again, and when Treat still didn't answer, Arty slid a notepad he'd carried into the room across the table, toward Treat.

"Perhaps you'd prefer to write down your answers?" Arty said with a hint of irritation.

The notepad knocked Treat's gloves askew, and the man calmly gathered them up and laid one atop the other again, aligning them perfectly. Then he squared the notepad with the edge of the table, the pen with the edge of the notepad, and sat back, giving Arty a smug smile.

Something about this scene bothered me, but I couldn't put a finger on it. I studied Treat, his clothing, his jacket, the items on the table . . . and then it hit me.

"Duncan," I said, setting the headset down, "Treat strikes me as being a very organized and orderly person, to the point of compulsiveness. Look at how neatly he arranged those gloves and that notepad, and look at how sharp his clothing is, even though it's casual wear."

Duncan glanced at Treat, then back at me. "Yeah. So?"

"So why would a man that obsessed with his appearance and the items around him wear two different-colored gloves?"

Duncan looked back at the room, presumably at the gloves, with a quizzical expression. "I don't follow," he said after a few seconds.

"Can you talk to Arty or Doug?"

He nodded. "Arty is wearing an earpiece."

"Tell him to ask Treat what color his gloves are."

"What's that going to accomplish? Besides, Treat doesn't seem to want to talk."

He had a point. "Okay, have Arty talk about those gloves. . . . Have him admire them or say he likes them or something like that. And then have him point out that the gloves are two different colors and ask Treat if he did that on purpose to match his two different-colored socks."

Duncan looked through the window at Treat's legs. "His socks are both blue," he said in a confused tone.

"I know. Trust me on this one."

Duncan gave me a puzzled look for a few seconds, shrugged, and walked over to pick up a headset. After turning some dials on one of the wall knobs, he talked into the headset, saying what I'd told him to.

Arty looked as puzzled as Duncan had, but after a bit of a pause, he did what was asked of him.

I picked up my headset and again held an earpiece to my ear, listening.

"Those gloves you have are nice," Arty said. He reached across the table and pulled the gloves toward him. "I'll bet they're real warm. They look handmade. Someone make them for you?"

Treat stayed silent, staring at Arty with a whimsical expression.

"I'm curious as to why you wear two different colors, though," Arty then said. "One blue one and one green one. Why is that? Is it so they will match your socks?"

Treat's expression morphed into one of confusion, then doubt, and finally irritation. He leaned forward and pulled both of his pant legs up and stared at his socks. His gaze shifted from one sock to the other, his expression a mix of irritation and befuddlement.

Arty, sensing that he'd somehow hit a nerve, though I suspected he didn't fully understand why, pushed on. "A guy like you, dressed all natty and pressed and neat . . . It seems odd that you'd wear mismatched gloves and socks," he said.

Treat let go of his pant legs and glared at Arty. "Give me back my gloves," he said, tight-lipped. He stood up, pushed his chair back, and held out a hand. "Now please. I'm done here. If you have something to hold me on, do it. Otherwise I'm leaving."

Arty handed him back the gloves, and after Treat put his parka back on, he started to do the same with the gloves. But after getting the first one halfway on, he pulled it off and stuffed both of the gloves into a pocket of his coat. He spun around and headed for the door, with Arty and Doug on his tail.

I set down my headset and looked at Duncan. "Treat is not the letter writer," I told him.

"How do you know?"

"He's color blind. Didn't you see how upset he was when Arty pointed out the two different colors to him? The most common type of color blindness is red-green, meaning that the people who have it can't distinguish those two colors. Treat had no idea that his gloves didn't match, and he couldn't tell that Arty was lying about the socks. Once he found out the gloves didn't match, he couldn't wear them. It was too incongruent for him. So he stuffed them in his pocket instead."

"How does that rule him out?"

"Think about the most recent letter, Duncan. The ink was green. And except for the color, it was the same homemade ink that was used in that earlier letter, the very first one. There's no way Treat could mix up green ink."

A dawning came over Duncan's face. "I see what you're getting at, but it doesn't rule him out completely. He could have had someone else make the ink. Or maybe the green color was a mistake."

I shook my head. "Treat is all about control. He wouldn't hand that job off to someone else, and he'd be precise with his ink recipe. It's not him."

Duncan sighed.

"I'm sorry," I said. "Believe me, I want this thing solved as much as you do. But Treat isn't our guy."

Duncan nodded, and I could tell from the expression on his face how disappointed he was.

"At least we managed to rattle him," I said. "He's a little less smug now. That's something, isn't it?"

Duncan gave me a weak smile. "I suppose it is." He leaned down, gave me a quick kiss, and then said, "Thanks for coming down here. I'll have the guys drive you back to the bar."

"You can't get away for a bit?"

"Wish I could, but I can't. Not tonight. I'm working several cases, and like I said before, Saturdays are busy around here. But I promise we'll do something tomorrow evening."

The door to the room opened, and both Arty and Doug walked in. Arty looked at Duncan as if he was crazy.

"What the hell was that thing with the gloves all about?" he asked, sounding a little miffed.

"I was trying to think of a way to get Treat to talk," Duncan said. He shot me a quick glance. "Mack here picked up on the fact that, despite the man's otherwise neat, orderly appearance, he was wearing two different-colored gloves. She wondered if maybe he's color blind. Given what seems to be an OCD type of personality, I thought pointing that faux pas out to him might rattle him enough to get him talking. Apparently, it rattled him enough to make him leave instead. Sorry."

Arty's expression softened a bit. "Don't think it mattered. He wasn't going to talk to us, anyway. And it did rattle him." He looked over at me with an expression of grudging admiration. "Nice observation," he said. "Any chance you recognized the guy?"

I shook my head. "No. I'm certain he's never been in my bar before, at least not when I've been there.

I'm really good at remembering faces, and I've never seen his."

Arty looked at Duncan. "I guess we're back to square one," he said. "Do you want us to try to take a different run at this Apostle Mike guy?"

Duncan shook his head. "No. Let it go for now. I suspect it's a dead end. Let's go back and take another look at the evidence."

That was my cue to do the same. Back to the latest letter and a pending trip to a cemetery. I hoped it wasn't a sign of things to come.

Chapter 12

Arty and Doug drove me back to the bar, and our return trip was as silent as the first one. Arty muttered a "Sorry, Mack," as they pulled up in front of the bar.

"Me too," I said. "I had hoped we might finally have a resolution to this thing."

"We'll keep at it," Doug said. "Have faith."

His words struck a chord with me. It was a similar expression uttered by an Episcopalian minister, and a bit of intuition, that had led to the solving of the last case, albeit a little too late. As I dragged myself and my crutches from the car and made my way back into the bar, I felt defeated and exhausted. I had no faith in my ability to figure this thing out, and I prayed—while I'm not a religious person per se, I'm not above hedging my bets—that an answer would come soon.

Back inside, I headed up to the Capone Club room. Navigating the steps with my crutches made me feel even more tired than I had before, and I cursed myself for not putting in an elevator when I did the new construction. By the time I got upstairs, I knew I would be of little use to anyone for the rest of the night. The group greeted me with expectant looks and enthusiasm, no doubt hoping I'd be delivering news of a break in Gary's case. Cora, Joe, Frank, and Mal knew just how involved that case was, but the others simply thought Gary's death had been a bad bit of luck. At least I thought they did.

"Any news?" Cora asked as I settled into a chair next to Mal. He laid a hand on my arm and gave me a quick kiss on the cheek. His touch was reassuring.

"I'm afraid not," I told them. "They had a suspect who they thought might have had a connection to the bar or to Gary, but I didn't recognize him at all."

"Just because he hasn't been in the bar doesn't mean he didn't do it," Carter said.

"I suppose," I said with a shrug. "But I don't think they have any other connections between this man and Gary. Sorry, guys, but it looks like it's a no go."

The disappointment on their faces made me want to cry. For the hundredth time, I debated telling them all the truth about the case, letting them know that their lives might be in danger. Was I doing the right thing by keeping it to myself? Every time I considered revealing all, I imagined what the group would do. They'd tackle the case with everything they had, and I feared that would only escalate the letter writer's actions. But didn't they have a right to know? I looked over at Clay Sanders and wondered what he would do with the information if he knew about it. Could I trust him not to print a story about it? Not yet, I decided. But then Carter threw me a curveball.

"We were discussing Gary's case while you were gone," he said. "His and Lewis's. And we all agreed that it's too much of a coincidence that two people from your bar, from this group, have been killed by someone. We're starting to wonder if we're the target."

I felt Mal's grip on my arm tighten ever so slightly. "Why would you be a target?" I said, trying to sound more nonchalant than I felt.

"Well, we *have* solved several crimes recently," Carter said, "although the main impetus behind those solutions was you." He paused and gave me an apologetic look. "We also considered that you alone may be the target."

I looked around the room at the faces of everyone, their concern for me ramping up my guilt over my seeming lack of concern for them.

I pointed toward my crutches, which I had leaned against the side of my chair. "Well, if I'm a target, I'm an easy one," I said lightheartedly. "But your theory about the group being a target is an interesting one. Maybe we should disband."

"Or maybe we should just be extra alert," Holly said.

Several people nodded their agreement with this sentiment.

"That's always a good idea," I said. "But just in case you're onto something with this theory of yours, any of you who want to drop out of the group for now would be perfectly justified to do so."

Everyone in the room exchanged looks, waiting for someone to be the first to speak up. It was Sam who finally did.

"I'm staying put," he said. "I agree that we should perhaps be more alert and wary of who and what's around us, but this work we're doing here is too important to me to drop it." He paused and gave everyone a sheepish smile. "Besides, I rather enjoy it."

"Me too," Holly said, and Alicia echoed the sentiment.

"I'm in," Carter said.

Tad, Frank, and Joe echoed his remark. The newcomers—Greg Nash, Sonja West, and Stephen McGregor—nodded, too, but they looked less determined.

Clay Sanders said, "If the police thought any of us were in danger, they'd say something, wouldn't they?"

He shot a knowing glance at Mal when he said this, and I felt Mal's grip on my arm tighten again almost imperceptibly.

"I'm sure they would," I said quickly. "But it's still a good idea to keep your ears and eyes open, just in case."

Clay narrowed his eyes at me, and I could tell he suspected I knew something I wasn't sharing. The mental strain of it all was wearing on me, and I wanted some time alone to think. So I grabbed my crutches and pushed myself up from my chair. "I need to go downstairs and check on some things," I said to no one in particular. "I'm not sure if I'll be back up here tonight. If I'm not, I'll see all of you tomorrow, assuming you choose to come back." I looked over at Clay. "You need to be here tomorrow morning by eleven thirty. Knock on the front door, and I'll let you in."

"I'll be here with bells on," he said with a smile.

I didn't smile back. I was too tired even to muster up basic social politeness. I simply nodded and left the room. Mal got up and followed me.

"Are you okay?" he asked as I tackled the stairs.

"I'm fine. Just tired. Everything is a bit over-whelming."

"Did this Apostle Mike really turn out to be a bust?" he asked in a low voice.

I nodded. "It turns out he's color blind, and I'm

certain there's no way he could have written the most recent letter, given the green ink and all."

"Interesting," Mal said. "So where does that leave us?"

"With a trip to a cemetery come Monday. In the meantime, I want to stay focused on the Middleton case."

When we reached the main floor, I turned to him and said, "Why don't you head home. I'm going to check on some things at the bar, and then I'm going to go upstairs for the night. Billy can close up for me. I want to rest so my mind is fresh tomorrow, when we go to the prison."

"Are you sure? I can stay if you want, sleep on your couch again."

I smiled at him. "Thanks, but I really do want to be alone. I need to sort my head out."

"Okay then. I'll see you in the morning. Want me to bring breakfast?"

"Sure."

"What would you like?"

"Surprise me."

"Okay." He gave me another one of those chaste kisses on the cheek, and then he was gone.

I headed behind the bar, where Billy and Teddy were both working. "How's it going?" I asked Billy.

"Teddy is a natural at this."

Teddy looked over at me with a hopeful smile.

"You're hired," I said. "Can you work tomorrow?"

"I can work seven days a week if you need me to," he said excitedly. "Thanks!"

I turned back to Billy. "Would you mind doing the closing stuff for me tonight? I'm feeling a little puny, and I'm going to head upstairs."

His smile faded into a look of concern. "Sure. Are you okay?"

"I'm fine," I said with a dismissive wave of my hand. "Or at least I will be once I get some rest. This darned leg is a heavy thing to haul around. Between that and the pain pills, I'm just tired."

"No problem," Billy said. "You know you can count on me."

I did, and it was a nice feeling. "Thanks, Billy. See you tomorrow. I'm not sure if I'll be here when you open up at five. I'm planning a trip up to Waupun."

"The prison?" Teddy said, and I nodded. "Who do you know there?"

"You have another case," Billy said before I could answer. "I heard Missy talking about it. What is it?"

"It's that Middleton carjacking and murder case that happened last year," I said, knowing Billy was up to speed on all the crimes in the area, particularly one as high profile as the Middleton case had been. "I'm not sure if we're going to look full into it yet. I'm going to have a chat with the accused tomorrow to see how it shakes out."

Teddy looked back and forth between me and Billy with a curious expression. "What's this all about?"

Billy said, "I'll fill you in later. Suffice it to say that Mack and some of the other patrons here are fervent crime solvers."

"Speaking of which, you might be able to help us out, Teddy," I said. "Did you know Tiffany Gallagher?"

"I knew of her," he said. "I can't say we were friends or anything like that, but up until recently we ran in a lot of the same circles. I know her brothers, Aidan and Rory."

"Any chance you heard any gossip about her having an affair?"

Teddy thought a moment before slowly shaking his head. "Can't say that I have. But I know some folks I could ask, people who are more in the know with that crowd these days than I am."

"If you don't mind," I said. "It could be helpful."

"Happy to help," he said. "I'll let you know."

With that, I said good night and headed upstairs to my apartment. I ran a hot bath and threw some bubbles in for good measure, feeling a need to pamper myself. When the tub was ready, I carefully lowered myself in, while keeping my casted leg out of the water. Once I was settled in, with my bad leg resting on the side of the tub, I closed my eyes and let my brain go into free thought. Doing this sometimes helped me to figure out problems, but tonight the only thing my mind would focus on was the dead. I kept seeing a parade of people who were gone: my father, Ginny, Lewis, Gary. . . .

I wondered if these visual manifestations were a synesthetic reaction or just a product of my exhausted mind and the events of the day. Whatever it was, it ruined any chance I had of relaxing, so after ten minutes of soaking, I gave up and got out of the tub . . . an Olympic feat with the damned cast.

Half an hour later I was in bed with the TV on, but I had no clue what was airing. Within seconds of my head hitting the pillow, I was sound asleep.

Chapter 13

I awoke on Sunday morning just before nine o'clock, feeling rested and eager to tackle the day. I made a pot of coffee and sat down at my kitchen table with the morning news online. After an hour of reading, I tackled the crossword puzzle but had barely gotten started when my phone rang. I saw it was Mal and answered with a chipper "Good morning, Malachi. When are you bringing me my breakfast?"

"I have it here now," he said. "I'm downstairs, by the front door."

"I'll be there in a sec. Make that a minute or two. I'm not a fast mover these days."

I disconnected the call and made my way downstairs. Mal stood outside, bearing a bag filled with something that smelled awesome and triggered a warm, soothing feeling on my skin, not unlike the sensation I'd had last night, as I'd sunk into the tub.

"You brought doughnuts," I said, licking my lips.

"Man, it's hard to surprise you," Mal said with a smile. He came inside, and I shut and locked the door behind him. He followed me upstairs, where I poured him a cup of coffee and took out plates for the goodies. After eyeing the choices for several seconds, I finally opted for an apple cider doughnut covered with caramel frosting. My first bite triggered a sound like wind chimes, and I closed my eyes to relish both the flavors and the music.

"Yummy," I said. "Thanks for this. It's the perfect way to start the day."

"Are you feeling better?"

"I am. I really needed the rest last night. Life has been a bit . . . overwhelming of late."

We spent the next hour or so sampling the wares and chatting about life in general. At one point Mal gave me an update on the status of his undercover job, stating that he felt like he was finally making some progress and would hopefully garner an invite into the boss's inner circle soon.

At a little after eleven we headed downstairs to the bar to await the arrival of Clay and Tyrese, taking the remaining doughnuts with us. Clay showed up at eleven fifteen, knocked on the front door, and then peered in through the window at the top of it. Mal went over and let him in. locking the door behind him.

"Thanks again for letting me come along," Clay said, settling down at our table. He had a to-go cup of something from a nearby coffee shop. "I know you have some reservations about me, and to be honest, I have a few about you still, too. But if today plays out the way I think it will, we might have a bright future working together."

"We shall see," I said noncommittally, a little put off by his presumptuousness. I offered him a doughnut, and he surveyed the selection much as I had before finally settling on a plain glazed one. His choice surprised me; I had him pegged as more of a fruit-filling kind of guy.

My phone dinged with a text message just before eleven thirty. "It's Tyrese," I said, reading the message. "He says he's five minutes away."

"Then we best get a move on," Clay said.

Mal helped me get my coat on and then grabbed up the bag with the remaining doughnuts. Tyrese was out front in his car, waiting for us, by the time we got to the door.

Clay took the front passenger seat, while Mal and I climbed into the backseat, dragging my crutches along with me. I did the introductions between Clay and Tyrese, who both regarded one another with polite reservation.

Once that was done, Tyrese inhaled deeply, eyed the bag in Mal's lap, and said, "Whatcha got in there? Whatever it is smells yummy."

Mal handed him the bag. "Help yourself. Mack insisted we share."

"It's the least we can do since you're playing chauffeur," I said.

Tyrese peeked in the bag, stuck his hand in, and pulled out the sugared, jelly-filled doughnut I had thought Clay was going to take. "Thanks, Mack," he said, handing the bag back to Mal. "You're okay in my book. I don't care what the other guys say about you."

Though I suspected he meant the comment as a joke, I didn't smile. "Are they talking about me?"

He gave Clay a nervous glance and then looked at me in the rearview mirror. "I was just kidding," he said with a dismissive expression, and I knew from the taste of his voice that he was lying. He smiled, trying to look innocent, but the smile faded fast. "Well, mostly kidding, anyway."

"What are they saying?" I asked.

Still looking at me in the rearview mirror, Tyrese shot his eyes toward Clay and raised his eyebrows in question. I gave him a subtle nod as he stalled for time by taking a big bite of his pastry. A large dribble of raspberry jelly oozed out the bottom and onto his jacket. "Damn," he said, scraping the jelly up with his finger and eating it. Then he proceeded to make the small reddish stain larger by swiping at it with a napkin.

I waited, prepared to repeat my question if necessary, but I didn't have to.

"There was some talk last night among some of the guys. Those detectives who brought you in to observe that Apostle Mike guy said you really do have a knack when it comes to sizing up people. They said you picked up on something no one else had."

"Did they say it in a good way or in a 'she's spooky, crazy, weird, and we better stay away from her' way?"

"Neither," Tyrese said, dabbing at some sugar on the corner of his mouth. "It was more of a 'let's not dismiss her too quickly' kind of tone." He took another bite and pulled out into traffic. "Despite what the brass feels about you, Mack, you have a lot of fans within the department."

This surprised me some, and it also made me feel better.

Clay, who so far had sat quietly through all of this, finally spoke up. "Why were you at the police station?"

"They had a suspect they wanted me to look at, to see if I recognized him at all. It was regarding Gary's murder."

Clay nodded, and I could tell his wheels were spinning as he tried to discern if there was more to the story than what I was telling him. I half expected him to grill me more on the topic, but he surprised me with his next comment. "You just need a spin doctor, Mack."

"A spin doctor?"

"Yeah. You know, someone who will spin you in a more positive light."

"I don't want to be spun at all."

"Well, it's going to happen if your group keeps solving crimes," he said. "The problem isn't with you per se. It's with the way the press has portrayed the police."

"Pot, kettle," I said.

Clay smiled and shrugged. "I wasn't as harsh as some, and all I did was report the facts. Those facts made the cops look a bit foolish and incompetent. They'll get over it." Tyrese shot Clay a look of irritation, which Clay either didn't see or chose to ignore. "And if the right reporter writes you and your group up in a way that makes the police and the DA look smart, it could lead to some future working relationships that would benefit everyone involved."

"And are you offering to do that?" I asked.

"Maybe. Let's wait and see how this visit turns out, and we can talk some more about it later."

I was relieved that he hadn't immediately jumped on the idea. If he had, I would have suspected him of trying to butter me up simply to gain my trust. The fact that he was still on the fence reassured me some. But judging from the frowns on the faces of the other two men in the car, I was alone in this judgment.

Our ride took just short of an hour and a half, and by some unspoken agreement, we switched the topic of conversation to miscellaneous stuff for a while—safe, innocuous topics. But as we drew closer to Waupun, talk inevitably shifted to the Middleton case.

"I had a look at part of the police file," Tyrese said. "I know you didn't ask me to, but I got curious. There wasn't much there of interest that I could see, at least nothing more than what was in the news about the case. But there was one detail in there that struck me, one I don't recall coming out in the trial."

"What?" I asked, intrigued.

"Well, there was blood splatter, blowback from the head wound Tiffany had. But there were some voids in the splatter. One area was on the driver's side door. There was blood on the outside of Benjamin Middleton's jacket sleeves but none on the inside. That doesn't make sense to me if he was facing Tiffany down, aiming the gun at her. There was also splatter on the right side of the bodice part of his jacket, but none on the left. That suggests that Middleton was facing forward in the car. And there was also a long space running down the inside of the driver door, near the middle, where there was no blood splatter. This was in front of where Ben's body would have been, and there was splatter on either side of it. To me, that suggests that something blocked the splatter."

"Like another person's arm reaching in through the window?" I asked, playing out the scene in my mind.

"Exactly," Tyrese said.

"You said 'voids.' Plural," Mal noted. "What were the others?"

"There was only one other area I noted, and it was on the gun itself. There was a void around the trigger, which you'd expect to find if someone had a finger wrapped around it, but there was also a void along the top of the barrel. In fact, most of the barrel was clean. And Benjamin Middleton had blood on the backs of both of his hands."

Mal said, "If someone had a hand wrapped around that gun barrel, wrestling for it, it might explain the void."

"It might," Tyrese agreed, giving Mal a curious look. "And if Middleton did shoot his wife, why would he have a hand wrapped over the top of the barrel?"

"Maybe Tiffany saw what he was about to do, and she wrestled him for the gun," I said.

"Perhaps," Tyrese said, sounding unconvinced. "But I saw no mention of the presence of gunpowder residue on Tiffany's hands, and there would have been if she'd had a hold on the gun."

"When we talk to Middleton, we should have him reenact the crime for us," I said. "See if his story jibes with this blood splatter evidence."

Our arrival at the Waupun prison went almost exactly like it had during our previous visit. We checked in at an outer gate, drove inside the compound, and parked. Tyrese led the way to the front entrance, where we had to pass through another guarded gate—this one with a metal detector—before we were allowed inside the main building. Then we checked in at a third gated station, where we all had to hand over our IDs to a guard sitting behind a glass enclosure that ran along a barred floor-to-ceiling wall with a gate. On our previous visit there had been two guards inside the enclosure; today there were three. Seated at the check-in spot was a man whose name tag said R. DINKLE—the

same guard we'd encountered on our first visit here—
and behind him sat a second guard, one I didn't
recognize, who was watching a series of monitors that
showed various areas in and around the prison. Standing beside Dinkle was a third guard named Karl Hous-
ton, someone else I recognized from our previous trip.

"Back again so soon?" Dinkle asked, eyeing us dubi-
ously. "Your entourage is growing. Planning a party?"
No one answered him, so he looked at a clipboard he
had in front of him and started flipping sheets. "Here
to talk to the same prisoner?"

Tyrese shook his head. "No. We're here to see Benjamin Middleton."

"Ah, Mr. Fancy Pants," Dinkle said. He apparently
had arrived at the proper sheet, because he stopped
flipping and read the page in front of him. "His lawyer
isn't here yet, so you'll have to wait. Karl can take you
to the meeting room, and you can wait there."

After handing us back our IDs, Dinkle slid a clipboard toward us through a slot in the glass and had
us all sign in. Once that was done, Karl pressed a
button and the gate slid open. We followed him down
the same short hallway we'd been in before, and the
barred gate we'd just come through banged closed
behind us. At the end of the hallway we stopped in
front of a large metal door, which Karl unlocked, and
we all stepped through into a second, bigger hallway.
There were five windowed doors—two on each side
and one at the opposite end—and at this point our
trip changed. The last time we had entered the room
behind the last door on the left, and this time we were
led to the first door on the left.

The room might have been a different one, but

you'd never know it. It looked exactly the same: a bare-walled, windowless cinder-block structure with a scarred wooden table at the center. Karl locked us inside, and we made our way to the table, which once again had only two chairs on the side closest to us and one on the opposite side. On our last visit, the men had remained standing, and I had taken one of the closer seats. The other had been occupied by the prisoner's lawyer, who had arrived ahead of us. For now, we all stood on our side of the table, waiting. I could tell the men in the room felt as uncomfortable as I did, locked inside the barren, cold room. They shifted nervously, Tyrese with his hands shoved in his jacket pockets, Mal with his arms folded over his chest, Clay looking around the room, taking it all in. I wondered if Clay was composing a story in his head and gathering details so he could adequately set the scene.

"I hope we don't have to wait too long," I said, an attempt at idle conversation. I had hoped it would help everyone to relax, but my voice echoed coldly inside the room, making our isolation seem even more pronounced.

The minutes ticked by, and I swore I felt each one as a tiny drip of water on my arms. Finally, the door behind us was unlocked, and a woman who looked about my age walked in. She was wearing slacks, ankle-high boots, and a red wool car-length coat. Her hair was black and cut short; her eyes were a brown so dark, it looked like her pupils were fully dilated. Over one shoulder she had a leather messenger bag. She approached us with a warm smile and addressed me before the men.

"You must be this crime-solving savant I've been hearing about," she said, extending a hand.

I took it, shook it, and said, "Something like that. I'm Mack Dalton."

"And I'm Christine Powell, Ben Middleton's attorney." She turned her attention to the three men.

"I'm Tyrese Washington, the cop who set this up." He extended a hand.

Christine shook it and then shifted her attention to Mal. "What is your interest in this case?" She sounded merely curious, not challenging, but I felt uncomfortable nonetheless.

"This is Mal O'Reilly," I said. "He's with me, my moral support." I smiled, hoping this would be enough. Apparently it was. Christine moved on to Clay.

"Clay Sanders," he said, also extending his hand. "I'm a reporter for the *Milwaukee Journal Sentinel.*"

This time Christine ignored the extended hand. She eyed Clay with suspicion. "A reporter? Why?" She looked to me for the answer.

"He's a member of our group," I said vaguely. "He's here solely to observe and help us decide on the veracity of your client's story. He's not going to write up anything about it, at least not yet. Right, Clay?" I said pointedly, giving him a challenging look.

"That's right," Clay said. "If it turns out that your client really is innocent and that can be proven, then I will write something for the paper. But until then I'm just here to observe."

This explanation seemed to satisfy Christine, though she still ignored Clay's outstretched hand. She headed for one of the chairs, set her bag on the table, and went about removing her coat, which she folded over the back of the chair.

Clay let his arm drop to his side.

"I should probably tell you that Ben didn't want to talk to you," Christine said. "His sister and I convinced him to give you a chance, but I can't promise how co-operative he'll be. He swears he's been set up and framed, and that has left him very suspicious of everyone along about now. I have to confess, I was a bit wary at first, too, when Sandra approached me with the idea, but I've done some digging into Ms. Dalton and her reputation, and I'm comfortable with hearing what you have to offer."

I gave her an apologetic smile. "I don't know that we have anything to offer yet. We have uncovered some inconsistencies that have our curiosity piqued, so we're willing to hear Ben out and take a look at things to see what we can come up with. But at this point we aren't making any promises."

"Understood," Christine said. "Ben should be here any sec—"

With that, the door on the opposite side of the room opened, and Benjamin Middleton was brought in. He and his sister looked a lot alike, the same coloring, the same facial features, and the same chagrined expression. He was cuffed—both his wrists and his ankles—and the noise made by his shuffling gait made my vision go grainy for a few seconds. He settled into the chair on his side of the table, and the guard who had brought him in asked if we wanted him to stay in the room or wait outside the door.

"You can wait outside," I said, and I saw Middleton shoot me a look.

Once the guard had retreated, Christine said, "Ben, these folks are here at the request of your sister. They're part of a group of people who look at old crimes to see if there is any new evidence they can find. They've had some success with other cases, and they are willing to look into your case. If they find anything significant, anything that points to your innocence, they will do what they can to exonerate you." Christine paused and looked over at me. "Did I get that right?"

"Essentially," I said with a smile. I looked at Middleton. "We've already run across some items of evidence that don't seem to jibe with the prosecution's theory of events, but before we decide whether or not to take on your case, we need to ask you some questions. Are you willing to help us help you?"

Middleton eyed me for a moment and then shifted his gaze to Mal, Clay, and Tyrese. His expression was flat, devoid of emotion. He looked like a man resigned to his fate. An air of defeat lay over him like a heavy, wet blanket. His shoulders sagged, his neck muscles bulged, as if it was an effort to hold his head up, and his eyes looked vacant and tired.

After a long silence, he said, "I suppose I've got nothing to lose." He raised his cuffed hands as far as he could and gave us a grim smile. "Have at me," he said. "Maybe someone can finally get this right." And then his hands dropped heavily into his lap.

Chapter 14

We did some basic introductions—names only, no occupations—and then I asked Ben Middleton to tell us what happened on the night his wife was killed. "Be as detailed as you can," I told him. "And be honest, even if you think the truth will make you look bad. If you lie to us, it isn't going to help anyone."

"So far the truth hasn't done much for me, either," he said. His voice was a little raspy, and it tasted like peanut butter.

"Try it, anyway," I said with a smile.

He sighed, put his cuffed hands on the table, and idly twiddled his fingers, staring at them as he began to speak. "Tiffany and I were heading home after a romantic retreat to celebrate our anniversary and Valentine's Day. We had rented a small house on the shores of Lake Michigan, up in Door County, and we'd been there for four days so far. A storm had come in overnight, dropping six inches or so of snow, and they were calling for a second storm that evening and throughout the night, with high winds and lots of lake-effect snow. At first we thought we would just ride the storm out, since we still had a couple of days left on our rental. I headed into town around noon that day to pick up some provisions to see us through. The nearest place to shop was about ten miles away, and the road to our place was narrow and it hadn't been plowed, so the driving was slow. It took me almost two hours to make the trip. When I got back to the house, Tiffany was in a mood."

"What do you mean by that?" I asked him.

"She would get that way sometimes, quiet, withdrawn, distant. It didn't happen often, but when it did, it always seemed to come on fast and without warning. When she got like that, she sometimes had panic attacks or crying binges, so I'd learned to leave her be unless she asked me for something. When I got back from the store, I saw that she was pacing and biting her nails, a sure sign that one of her moods had settled in. She kept looking out the windows of the house, like she expected to see a goblin out there or something. I asked her what was wrong, and at first she said nothing. But I persisted, and eventually, she told me that she didn't want to stay in the house with the big storm coming. She said it made her feel claustrophobic and isolated."

He paused, still staring at his fingers, but now they were still. "I should have agreed to leave right then. It was obvious from her behavior that she was close to a panic attack already. But our time together up until then had been so great, and she'd been so happy and calm and affectionate. I desperately wanted that version of Tiffany back, so I tried to convince her that we would be fine, that we had plenty of stuff on hand to keep us warm and fed, and that it would be cozy and romantic. But I couldn't sway her, and when her voice turned shrill and she started looking like a trapped animal, I knew it was pointless to try any longer. So we packed up our stuff and headed out."

He leaned back in his chair and closed his eyes, letting his hands drop to his lap. "It was after five and getting dark out by the time we left. The storm had already begun, coming earlier than predicted. It was snowing heavily, and the road still hadn't been plowed from the night before, because it's a narrow back road that doesn't see much traffic. The wind had picked up, gusting and drifting and making for whiteout conditions at times. It was a slow, white-knuckle drive, and after about ten minutes we'd gone only a couple of miles down the road."

He paused, licked his lips, and his breathing sped up a hair. "All of a sudden I see this guy up ahead, standing in the middle of the road, waving us down. I thought he might need help or be in trouble of some kind, so I stopped and rolled down my window." Middleton paused again and swallowed hard, his eyes still closed. "I started to ask the guy if he needed some help, and the next thing I know, he's sticking a gun in my face and telling me to get out of the car. I . . . I tried to reason with him. I told him he could have the car and begged him not to hurt anyone. But he just repeated his demand for me to get out of the car, and I could tell from the look in his eyes that he meant business. So I—"

Mal stopped him and asked, "Was your car in park or in drive when this happened?"

Middleton opened his eyes and looked at Mal with a puzzled and slightly impatient expression. "I don't know," he said after several seconds. "I don't remember shifting into park."

"Was your foot on the brake?" Mal asked.

Middleton thought about it and grimaced. "I don't know. I'm sorry. I can't remember. All I remember is grabbing for the gun, wanting to push it away from me and Tiffany." He looked at Mal, and his expression turned sad. "If the car *had been* in drive, I could have hit the gas and gunned it, right?"

Mal said nothing, did nothing. Neither did any of the rest of us.

Middleton closed his eyes again, looking sad and remorseful. "I think the car must have been in park, or it would have lurched forward at some point. I can't imagine that I managed to keep my foot on the brake during the struggle. The idea of hitting the gas never occurred to me at the time, though given the road conditions, I doubt it would have done any good. The wheels would have just spun. And all I could think about was that gun."

"Tell us about the struggle," I said. "Give us as much detail as you can remember regarding where your hands and body were, anything you said or did, any movements you made."

Middleton opened his eyes and zeroed in on me. Then he nodded slowly. "I reached up and shoved the man's arm with my left hand, and then I grabbed the barrel of the gun with my right. It fired, and I remember the sound was deafening and the barrel felt hot. The man tried to swing the gun back toward me, but I had the advantage, I think, because I was pushing straight out and he was trying to move his arms sideways. When he realized his efforts weren't working, he started pulling back on the gun." He shifted his gaze to the tabletop, and his face scrunched up with pain. "That's when the gun fired for the second time."

"Where inside the car was the gun when it fired the second time?" Tyrese asked.

Middleton furrowed his brow and held his cuffed hands in front of his face, about eighteen inches away. "About here," he said. He stared at his hands for a moment and then readjusted their positions slightly. The right hand closed tighter, as if it was gripping something, and he bent the left one back at the wrist. "Like this, I think," he said.

It was easy for me to imagine his left hand wrapped around a man's forearm and the right one gripping the barrel of a gun. That jibed with the blood splatter evidence Tyrese had mentioned.

Middleton began to move his hands up and down, back and forth, covering an area about a foot square. "I can't be sure of the exact positions, but we struggled something like this. And then the guy just let go of the gun, turned, and ran off. That's when I looked over and saw that Tiffany was . . . that she'd been . . ." He swallowed hard and seemed unable to finish his sentence.

"Which way did the man run?" I asked.

"Toward the back of the car," he said without hesitation. "I had my finger on the gun's trigger, ready to fire, and I kept craning my neck around to see if he was coming at us from the back window or going around to Tiff's side of the car. But he didn't. He just disappeared into the night." He hesitated and stared at all of us, his gaze moving from one face to another. His expression was expectant, querying, and a little suspicious, as if he was waiting for us to call a foul on his version of the events.

"What did you do next?" I asked after a period of silence.

Middleton looked away from us then and stared down at the tabletop. He winced and said, "I hollered at Tiffany, asking her if she was okay. There was blood and . . . other stuff all over the side of her head and neck and shoulder. I grabbed her arm and tried to find a pulse and couldn't. . . . She had this empty, vacant stare. . . . I knew she was gone."

Tears welled up in his eyes as he spoke, and the expression on his face was one of pure agony and despair. I had no doubt then that the man had loved his wife. But that didn't mean he didn't kill her.

"Where was the gun at this point?" Mal asked.

"In my lap," Middleton said without hesitation. He leaned forward and swiped at his nose with one hand, the other one dangling below it within the cuffs. "I tried to call for help, but I couldn't get a signal on my phone. So I started driving. I'm not sure how far I drove or for how long. It seemed like an eternity. When I reached a main road and finally got a signal, I called nine-one-one. I wanted to keep driving, but they told me to stay put. So I did. . . . I knew Tiff was gone," he said with an expression of hopelessness.

"Did the cops find any prints in the snow?" I asked.

Middleton shook his head. "By the time they reached me and checked Tiffany, some time had passed. Eventually, one of the cops put me in his car, and we drove back the way I'd come, trying to find the spot where it all happened. But the wind and the snowdrifts had covered everything up. We couldn't even see my tire tracks on the road." He hung his head, and I saw a tear roll down his cheek.

"Mr. Middleton," I said, "the evidence presented at your trial suggests that your wife was having an affair at the time."

Middleton looked up at me, his face a thundercloud of emotion.

"Did you know about it?" I asked.

He shook his head. "I had no idea. I thought everything between us was fine."

The taste of his voice changed with this statement. It went from its prior peanut butter to something more like a rancid nut. I narrowed my eyes at him. "You just lied to me."

Middleton stared at me, eyes wide.

"I told you in the beginning that you had to be totally honest with us. No lying. Now that you've lied to us, it makes everything else you said seem suspect."

"But I didn't lie," he insisted. "I didn't know anything about Tiffany having an affair."

With this, his voice returned to the peanut butter taste, momentarily making me doubt my reaction and interpretation. Then a lightbulb turned on in my head—both figuratively and literally, since I had a vision of an actual lightbulb coming on.

"You lied when you said you thought everything was fine between the two of you," I said.

He looked startled and then chagrined. "How did you . . ." He left the question hanging, but I knew what he meant to ask.

"I have an ability to tell when people are lying to me," I explained.

He stared at me, looking bemused. "Are you a mind reader or something?"

"Something like that."

He weighed my proclamation for a few seconds and then said, "Okay then. Yes, things had been strained between me and Tiffany for a while, but we were getting it back on track. This trip was supposed to be a chance to reconnect." He paused and frowned. "If I'd known she was seeing someone else, I probably wouldn't have arranged the trip. But I didn't know, I swear."

As far as I could tell, this was the truth. "Were there specific issues between you and Tiffany that were causing problems?" I asked. "I apologize for getting personal, but how were things in the bedroom?"

"They hadn't been good for some time. Several months, in fact. I knew something was bothering her, but like I said before, she sometimes had these moods. I knew my schedule was an issue for her a lot of the time. I worked long hours, and that didn't leave us much in the way of together time. But I felt like I had to pull my weight financially, you know?" He gave me an appealing look, begging me to understand, and I nodded. Marrying into a rich family couldn't have been easy. "If I had it all to do over again, I'd let the work stuff go and pay more attention to my marriage. In retrospect, I don't think the money mattered all that much to her."

I couldn't help but draw comparisons between Ben and Tiffany's relationship and mine with Duncan. Duncan's long work hours often frustrated me. My expectations were pretty simple and basic, but the opportunity to share time together was important in any relationship. I wondered how the lack of it would impact Duncan and me.

"So you don't have any idea who the other man was?" Mal asked.

Middleton shook his head. "I've thought about it, believe me." He flashed his attorney a mirthless smile. "Christine nagged me on the subject, saying it would give us another suspect and the reasonable doubt we needed, but I didn't have a clue. I still don't."

Christine nodded, verifying Middleton's statement.

"You didn't find anything in Tiffany's e-mails or text messages or phone records that might have provided a clue?" Tyrese asked Christine.

She shook her head. "All her contacts were friends or family members. And the friends were largely female. There were a few men she knew as friends, but she hadn't had contact with any of them in the month before her death and only minimal contact with one or two prior to that. If I remember right, the most recent one was around five weeks before, a guy who has been a friend of the Gallagher family for years and is now married, with kids."

"That doesn't mean he can't have an affair," Mal said. "And these days, maybe folks are smart enough not to leave an electronic trail. If you watch any crime TV at all, it doesn't take a rocket scientist to see that that kind of stuff is the downfall for many people."

Christine smiled, with a hint of smugness. "Valid points," she said. "But the fact that this guy and his family were in London at the time of the murder and several months before that kind of ruled him out."

"Oh," Mal said.

Oh, indeed. "What about girlfriends Tiffany was close to?" I asked Middleton, remembering Alicia's idea about confidantes. "Was there anyone she might have shared something like this with?"

"Melanie Smithson was her closest friend," he said. "The two of them grew up together, and they've been best buds since before kindergarten. Melanie was the maid of honor at our wedding, and she and Tiffany get together—" He stopped abruptly and winced. "She and Tiff *got* together at least once a week for drinks or lunch or dinner. I imagine if anyone knew Tiff's secrets, it would be her."

Tyrese wrote down the name, and as he did so, Christine said, "I talked to Melanie already, months ago. She said she wasn't aware of Tiffany having any affairs." She shrugged and added, "I suppose she could have been lying."

"Maybe I can figure that out if I have a chat with her," I said.

Mal had been frowning for the past minute or so, and when he posed the next question, I got an idea as to why. "Mr. Middleton, if we assume that your version of the events is true, and this man approached you, stuck a gun in your face, and said to get out of the car, why didn't Tiffany do just that? Why did she stay in the car?"

"I have no idea," Middleton said, raising his cuffed hands and rubbing at his forehead with the sides of his thumbs. "I've often asked myself that same question. The only thing I can think of is that she was so scared, she froze."

It was a good question. Most people under those circumstances would have hightailed it out of the vehicle. "You said Tiffany was prone to panic attacks," I said. "Do you think she had one during all of this?"

Middleton gave me a sad smile. "I suppose it's possible. To be honest, I wasn't focused on Tiffany when it all went down. I was focused on the man and that damned gun. But like I said before, Tiffany had these moods where she'd often become withdrawn . . . closed off. There were times when she looked frightened . . . not of me, but rather of some ethereal thing. She would stare out the window or at the door with a panicky expression, as if she expected someone or *something* to be lurking out there. And she'd had that look when she said she wanted to leave the rental house and head home." He hesitated, his eyes staring off into space. "I asked her father about it once, and he told me Tiffany had always been that way. He told me Tiffany needed someone who was strong, someone who could keep her safe and secure." He scoffed and shook his head.

"You sound a little resentful," I said.

"I am," he admitted. "Not of Tiffany per se, but of her father, Colin Gallagher. That man put me through the wringer when Tiff and I got engaged. He kept questioning me about how I was going to give Tiff the kind of lifestyle she deserved. And he came right out and asked me if I was marrying her for her money. Several times he told me that I wasn't good enough for her, that she deserved someone better. And to top it off, I found out that he hired a private detective to do an extensive background check on me."

"How did you figure that out?"

"The bastard told me," Middleton said irritably. "But not until after I accused him of it." He smiled bitterly. "This PI he hired wasn't very good, and he's also rather distinctive looking. He's quite tall, like six-six or something, and has a ruddy, pockmarked face and a big beak of a nose. That combo made him stand out in any crowd. At first I thought he might have been one of Tiffany's exes or someone who was fixated on her, because when I first noticed him, it was always when the two of us were together. But then I started seeing him when I was on my own. It didn't take me long to figure out the guy was stalking me, and since I'm not a very stalk-worthy person otherwise, I guessed that Colin had to be behind it. So I asked him about it, and he admitted it. He acted like it was no big deal and like he couldn't understand why I was so upset over it. He said it was SOP for a guy like him with a daughter like Tiffany."

"So you and your father-in-law didn't get along," Mal said.

"That's an understatement," Middleton said with a sardonic chuckle. "Though in fairness to the guy, I suspect he would have done the same thing to anyone who showed an interest in Tiffany."

"When did things start to go bad between you and Tiffany?" I asked. "Was there a sudden increase in the frequency or the number of these mood swings she had?"

Middleton furrowed his brow. "Things were really good with us in the beginning. Yes, Tiff sometimes had one of her moods, but I figured out early on how to deal with them. And whenever she'd get scared, I could often reassure her. But that started to change about six months before . . . well, before the night in question. We went to this family gathering the Gallaghers had for Tiffany's brother Rory when he finished grad school. When we went home that night, she seemed distant, distracted, upset about something. I tried to ask her what was wrong, but she just kept blowing me off and saying everything was fine, that she was just tired. I figured it was one of her moods and gave her the space she needed to get through it, letting her know I was there if she needed me. In the past her moods had never lasted more than a day or two, but this time it hung on for weeks. I kept asking her if something was bothering her, but she gave me the same brush-off and feeble reassurances every time."

He sighed. "I didn't buy it. I could tell something was different with this episode. She never wanted to go anywhere or do anything with me, and she gave up her volunteer work at the animal shelter. She started spending nights in our guest room instead of in our bed, and our sex life dried up. Hell, our entire life dried up. Before this happened, we used to talk all the time, sharing our days with one another or indulging in long, friendly debates about current topics. But all that stopped." He gave me a forlorn, miserable look. "That was what the anniversary trip was for, to bring us back together without any other distractions . . . to give us some quality time together. And at first, it seemed to be working. The first few days we spent in that house were like old times."

"You said this change occurred after a family gathering," I said. "Are you aware of any dealings or exchanges she had with anyone during the event that might have triggered it?"

Middleton shook his head. "No. It was a fun event. Tiffany seemed to be enjoying herself. I didn't see her argue with anyone, and she didn't mention anything to me that would indicate she was having a problem with anyone."

"I take it the two of you didn't stay together the whole time?" I said.

"No, maybe half of the time. There were a lot of old friends present that Tiffany hadn't seen in a while, so she kept wandering off to chat. I didn't know anyone there other than the Gallagher family, so I kind of stayed to myself for most of it."

"Did any of Tiffany's other family members seem to have a dislike for you?" Mal asked.

"I don't think so. If they did, they hid it well. But then the rest of that family is a lot more polite and tactful than Colin is." He paused and then amended his statement. "At least her mother and her brother Aidan are. Rory's kind of quiet. I never got to know him very well."

I was out of questions, but I had a lot of new ideas about where we could go from here. I looked over at Mal, Clay, and Tyrese. "Do you guys have anything you want to ask?"

They all shook their heads, so I turned to Middleton. "Do you have any questions for us?"

"Yeah . . . one. Why?"

"Why what?"

"Why are you doing this? What are you getting out of it? And what is it going to cost me?"

"That's three questions," I said in a light, joking tone, but Middleton didn't smile, so I continued on a more sobering note. "As for cost, there is none, at least not in any monetary sense." I paused to see if he would ask for further clarification on this point, but he remained silent. "As for what we get out of it, we get the satisfaction of finding the truth, and if that truth exonerates you, we get the satisfaction of knowing we righted a wrong. If that does turn out to be the case and we can figure out who really did it, we also get to see justice properly served. That's compensation enough."

This wasn't the whole story, of course. I suspect many of the Capone Club members did what they did for these reasons, but also because their lives were less boring and ordinary thanks to their involvement. For me, the motivation was a bit different. My synesthesia was something I'd always considered a quirk, a flaw, a handicap. It was something that made me stand out, and not in a good way. But once I saw how my synesthesia could be useful . . . valuable even . . . I was hooked. The intrinsic reward for me was validation and the feeling that I was unique in a good, special way, as opposed to a weird, creepy way. I was shrugging off the mantle of a lifelong stigma, and I found the process not only highly satisfying but also addictive.

Middleton took a few seconds to weigh my answer. "Fair enough," he said finally. "Are you going to continue to look into my case?"

"I am," I said. "And I imagine the rest of the group will follow suit. But I have to reiterate that we can't make any promises."

"I understand."

There was one more thing I wanted to do. I hesitated because I knew it might upset Middleton, but it had to be done, so I pushed on. "I do have one last question for you. Did you kill your wife?"

Ben Middleton didn't blink. He didn't move. He didn't look away. Without hesitation, maintaining eye contact with me the entire time, he said, "I did not."

Peanut butter all the way.

I looked at the others. "Does anyone else have anything to say?"

Everyone shook their heads.

"Then let's get to it," I said.

Chapter 15

We left the prison after telling Christine we would keep her posted on our progress.

Once we were inside the car, Mal asked me, "What was your take on Middleton?"

"The guy was being truthful, as far as I could tell, other than that one time. It was fortunate that he did lie at least once to give me a comparison. I'm inclined to believe him when he says he didn't do it."

"I agree," Tyrese said. "He seemed sincere."

Clay said nothing, and after a moment I asked him for his opinion.

"I'm on the fence," he said. "I agree the guy seemed sincere, but I've dealt with killers before who were able to do the same thing convincingly, even though it was obvious they were guilty." He turned and looked over his shoulder at me. "While your judgment about whether or not he was telling the truth is interesting, I'm going to need something more than just your say-so before I'm convinced. Though I'm willing to keep an open mind."

"Fair enough."

"So what do we do next?" Clay asked.

"I want to talk to this friend of Tiffany's," I said. "And, Clay, I'd love to take you up on your offer of arranging a chat with Tiffany's family."

He nodded. "I'll see what I can do."

"There's something that bothers me about the prosecution's theory," Mal said. "If Middleton really did want to kill his wife, why do it in the confines of the car like that? Why stop on a road where there might be witnesses and risk the whole thing being observed by someone? Why not just kill her somewhere else, somewhere private, and come up with a different story, like a home invasion?"

"It sounds like it was plenty private," Tyrese said. "And killing her at the house still would have pointed the finger right at him. So maybe the carjacking thing was the best he could come up with."

"I don't know," Mal said. "Middleton seems like an intelligent guy. I think he could have come up with something better."

At that point we dropped the topic of the Middleton case and went back to discussing mundane topics, like the weather and current events. Clay listened but said nothing more for the entire ride.

Tyrese dropped us off outside the bar and said he'd be back later that evening, after he took a nap. Clay said he would get right on trying to set up a meet and greet with the Gallaghers and get back to me with the details once it was arranged. With that, he parted our company and walked down the block to his car. Mal and I watched him leave before we headed inside.

Once we were in the bar, with the door securely locked behind us, I said, "Mind if we switch gears and talk about the other case?"

I didn't need to specify what the other case was. The letter writer was foremost in my mind, and I felt certain it was in the upper echelons of Mal's, too.

"What about it?"

"I've been thinking about all the people who have been involved, the ones who received the packages. Those packages were delivered to their places of employment and their home addresses. That implies to me that the letter writer knows these people somehow or has access to their information. They must have something in common."

Mal nodded thoughtfully, following me into the bar kitchen. I switched on the lights and fired up the deep fryer.

"Want something to eat?" I asked.

"Sure. What do you have in mind?"

"I'm in the mood for a burger and fries myself, but I can make you anything you like."

"I'll have what you're having. It sounds good." He leaned back against the sink and watched me work as I went about preparing the food. "Do you have any ideas about what these people might have in common?" he asked at one point.

"Not yet, but I thought I might get Cora working on it, to see what she can dig up."

"That's a good idea. I have to say, that woman is quite resourceful."

I had the burgers on the grill and the fries in the fryer, so I handed Mal a package of buns and pointed him toward the fridge. "I'll take lettuce, tomato, and onion on mine, with a little mayo. Fix yours the way you want. Do you want cheese?"

He nodded.

"What kind? I have cheddar, American, pepper jack,

provolone, and Swiss. Oh, and I also have a kick-ass horseradish cheddar."

"I'll go with the horseradish cheddar."

While he got the buns and condiments ready, I sent a text message to Cora, asking her if she could come by and offering her a free lunch in exchange for her time. She answered me less than a minute later, texting back that she would be at my front door in five minutes. Since I was cooking, I had Mal go meet her at the door.

Ten minutes later we were all seated at a table near the bar, Mal and I with our burgers, Cora with her standard glass of chardonnay. She wasn't hungry and said she'd take a rain check on the free meal. After summarizing our trip to Waupun and our chat with Ben Middleton, we explained to Cora what we wanted with regard to background information on the people who had received the packages from the letter writer. After reviewing the information we already knew, she went to work, tapping away on her laptop.

While Cora worked, Mal and I shared some theories about Ben Middleton's case.

"An obvious alternative suspect is whoever Tiffany had her affair with," Mal said.

Cora looked up from her laptop long enough to comment. "I did look into Tiffany's social media, and I didn't come up with much other than some contacts you might want to talk to. But since it's been almost a year since her death, it might not be very fruitful."

Mal said," You never know what people may remember. It's worth a shot if we run out of other ideas."

Cora nodded. "I'll give you a list of names later today." Then she went back to her research.

"I don't think we can rule out Middleton's version

of the events," I said. "His carjacking scenario seems feasible, and I haven't seen any evidence yet that suggests otherwise."

"Occam's razor," Mal said.

I gave him a puzzled look, and he explained.

"It's a scientific principle. Essentially, it means that the least complicated, most obvious answer is the most likely one."

"Perhaps that works in science," I said, "but we're dealing with humans, in all their frailty and complexity. In my experience, that tends to complicate things."

"True," Mal admitted. "And along those lines, we should consider the possibility that Ben Middleton was the intended victim. If Tiffany was having an affair, her new paramour might have arranged the carjacking scenario, hoping to kill Ben."

"If that was the case, why didn't the guy just shoot Ben outright, then?" I posed.

"Maybe Tiffany didn't want to risk getting hit," Mal said with a shrug. Then his eyes widened, and I could tell another idea had come to him. "Or maybe the carjacker didn't want to get blood all over the inside of his newly acquired car. Or maybe the killer needed the car for a getaway and intended to fake a kidnapping. In fact, we should look at Tiffany's financials closely. Given the acrimonious nature of the relationship between Ben Middleton and Colin Gallagher, it's possible that he threatened to cut his daughter off from the family money. A staged kidnapping might have been a way to get some of that money back."

"Good idea," I said, scribbling notes on a cocktail napkin. "We should probably check into Ben Middleton's life more thoroughly, too. Maybe *he* was having an affair or had an admirer he didn't know about, who wanted Tiffany out of the way. Someone needs to track down this PI who was following him and see what he knows."

Cora said, "While looking into Tiffany's online life, I also checked out Ben's. He kept a pretty low profile prior to the murder, but ever since, there have been a number of Web sites that have popped up both for and against him. He has a lot of admirers now, those crazy women who seem attracted to bad boys and go after prisoners who swear their innocence."

"What prisoner doesn't swear innocence?" Mal said with no small amount of sarcasm, asking what was clearly a rhetorical question.

"I'll never understand those women," I said, shaking my head.

After a few seconds of silence, during which we all pondered the enigma of women who went after convicted felons, Mal asked me, "Which theory do you like the best?"

"I'm not sure," I said after giving it a few seconds' thought. "If we consider this to be a planned event involving a third party of any sort, there's something about Middleton's scenario that's bothering me. How would a third party have known where they would be at any given time? And how did the carjacker get out there? We should talk to Christine and see if she looked into that. He had to have come from a house out there somewhere or had a vehicle of some sort."

"Good question," Mal acknowledged with a frown.

Cora looked up from her laptop and said, "Middleton's lawyer did look into it, but she didn't find any likely suspects who might have been in the vicinity. And if the carjacker had transportation of some sort, the snow obliterated any tracks it might have left."

"So that's a dead end," Mal said, his frown deepening. "Frankly, it makes the whole idea of a carjacker seem less feasible."

"But there is the blood-splatter evidence that suggests a third party was involved," I reminded him. "And I think Middleton was telling us the truth."

"Bingo!" Cora said. Mal and I both jumped as she sat back in her chair and gave us a self-satisfied smile. "I found a commonality among our letter writer's recipients. I don't know how good a one it is, but at least it's something."

"Well, don't keep us in suspense," I said.

"Everyone has some sort of connection to the university. Your art store guy, Adam, is the go-to person for art students at the university. The girl at the zoo and the boy who worked at the Miller Brewing Company plant are both students there. And that spice shop in the Public Market is a vendor for several eateries and dorms on campus."

I considered this and gave Cora a doubtful look. "I don't know, Cora. The UW campus is probably less than six degrees of separation from half the people in this city. It seems too broad, too vague."

Mal said, "I have to agree. Those connections don't seem strong enough, common enough. If they were all students who were in a class together, or all professors of some sort, then maybe you'd have something. But I'd wager Mack is right. We could poll people on the street, and I bet more than half of them would have some sort of connection to the university."

"Heck, most of the Capone Club members have

connections to the university," I added. "Plus, there's this latest letter. If we're right in our interpretation of it and it has something to do with the cemetery, how does that fit in?"

Cora looked wounded, which made me feel bad.

"I'm sorry, Cora. I didn't mean to burst your bubble."

"You haven't. The connection is there, however feeble it may be. Maybe it's a coincidence that they all have connections to the school. Maybe we're wrong about the cemetery. Or maybe we just don't see the connection between it and the school yet."

Mal said, "I generally don't believe in coincidences."

"Neither do I," Cora said. "So I'm not going to toss the idea just yet. But in the meantime, I'll keep looking for anything else they all share in common."

My cell rang then. I checked the caller ID, but no name came up, and I didn't recognize the number. For a moment, I considered not answering it, but in the end curiosity got the better of me. "Hello?"

"Mack, it's Clay Sanders. How soon can you be free to meet with the Gallaghers?"

"Anytime," I said. "Why? What have you got in mind?"

"I just finished talking to Aidan, and he informed me that the family is having a get-together this afternoon at Colin Gallagher's place. I told Aidan what we're doing and why we want to talk to the family, and he's willing to take us out there as his guest. But he said that once we're there, we're on our own, and not to expect a lot of cooperation, particularly if the rest of the family finds out what we're up to."

"It's worth a shot," I said.

"If you're game, we need to go now. Aidan said he

can meet us at the base of the driveway to the property in half an hour."

"I'm ready when you are."

"I'm only a couple of blocks away from your bar now. Can you meet me out front?"

"Can do. Would it be okay if I bring Mal along?"

Clay didn't answer right away, and I knew he was trying to find a polite way to tell me no. In the end he opted for simple bluntness. "Let's not complicate this by bringing a whole crowd out there. This is going to be hard enough as it is."

"You're right," I said, and while I truly believed he was, I still felt ill at ease about going with him and no one else. My trust of him wasn't on solid ground yet. "See you in a couple of minutes."

I disconnected the call, then explained to Cora and Mal what I was doing as I fetched my coat and put it on—with Mal's help as I balanced with my crutches. Before either of them could ask any questions or make any objections, I gimped my way to the door.

"I'll be back as soon as I can," I said. Mal followed me to the door, and I could tell he had a million questions he wanted to ask, but before he could, I smiled at him and said, "You're welcome to wait here. My staff should be arriving soon to open up. Lock the door behind me, would you?"

With that I headed out the door, pulling it closed behind me.

Chapter 16

Clay was already waiting for me, idling in the street. His car was an older model Toyota sedan, navy blue, rusted in spots from the salt of too many winters in Wisconsin. For some reason, I envisioned a cluttered, messy interior, yet the inside was neat, clean, and new looking. Clay was a hard guy to peg.

He drove off as soon as I was settled, and headed for the interstate. "I hope you don't intimidate easily," he said as soon as we were under way. "The Gallaghers live on the lakeshore in Whitefish Bay, and the place is quite impressive. Worth around two and half million or so, I'd guess. I've been to the house a couple of times, when Aidan had parties, and every time I go there, I'm awestruck."

"I'll be fine," I said, though I heard the doubt in my voice.

"I cooked up a bit of a story for the two of us," Clay said, shooting me a sidelong glance. "Aidan is going to tell his family that he ran into us downtown and invited us out. He's going to introduce you as my girlfriend. Are you okay with that?"

I nodded. Lately, I seemed to be everyone's girl-friend except Duncan's.

"Do you think we should come up with a fake name for you? You've been on the news a lot recently, and if the family makes the connection between why you were on the news and any conversations you try to start about Tiffany, I suspect they'll clamp down pretty fast."

"They may recognize me regardless of what name I use," I said. "You can introduce me as Mackenzie rather than Mack, if you like. Most of the TV and news cover-age referred to me as Mack, because that's the name of the bar, so with Mackenzie, they might not make the connection. We're already lying to them about my relationship to you and our reason for coming to their house. Let's not complicate it even more. Besides, if they do recognize me, it might make it easier to segue to the topic of Tiffany. They don't need to know that we're looking into the case."

"If there's any of the usual small talk, they're going to ask what you do for a living. How should we answer that?"

I thought about it for a minute. "Why don't we give them a vague truth? We can say I work in sales in the food and beverage industry. If they ask for a company, I'll toss out the name of one of my suppliers."

"Okay. Should we come up with a story about how the two of us met?"

I looked over at him with a wry smile. "You're very thorough."

"I like things that are well planned."

"I'm more of a seat-of-my-pants kind of gal." I let

out an exaggerated sigh and gave him a sad look. "Given our obvious differences, I don't think this fling of ours is going to last, Clay."

He let out a hearty laugh, the first one I'd heard from him. "Seat of the pants, it is," he said. "Everybody should live on the edge once in a while."

We met Aidan Gallagher at the base of the driveway. After climbing out of his car, he leaned in Clay's rolled-down window, letting in the cold, blustery air. It chilled me, and my casted foot, which I was able to cover only with socks, since no shoes or boots would fit over it, felt like it was immersed in icy water. Aidan looked and smelled like money. His hands were manicured, his clothes were high-end, his jaw was square, and his voice was cultured and smooth. He was tall and on the slender side, with blue eyes and dark blond hair that hung down over his forehead in a rakish manner. It all worked together to create a handsome package, and I sensed an air of confidence about him.

After a quick introduction, he looked over at me and said, "I've heard about you. You're some kind of mind reader or something, right?"

"Not exactly," I said with a wince. "I just have a strong second sense. And sometimes a third," I added with a wink.

He looked intrigued but asked no more questions. He simply said, "Good luck."

Clay briefly filled him in on the details we'd discussed during our drive, and with that out of the way, Aidan got back in his car and headed up the long drive. We followed and eventually parked in a massive concrete area in front of the house that was bordered by a three-car garage.

Clay hadn't exaggerated. The house, built on the shore of Lake Michigan, was a sprawling white stone structure with huge windows and a blue roof. The entryway was intimidating enough based solely on its size, but once we went inside, I was awestruck. We entered a high-ceilinged foyer topped off with a massive chandelier. The coat closet was bigger than my bathroom. After shucking our winter outerwear, we walked on gleaming hardwood floors into the living room portion of a large open area. Here there was a high cathedral ceiling and a sweeping wall of floor-to-ceiling windows that tied the living and dining areas together and offered a magnificent view of the lake. Those windows would keep the great room area brightly lit during the day, but it was dusk now, and the setting sun cast the water with a reddish-gold glow that warmed the room. A Persian rug centered the living room furniture, which was plush and covered in a soft material done in a red and brown Moroccan pattern. Large beams crossed the ceiling, and to our right was a fireplace with a stone facade that went all the way up to the peak. Christmas decorations—a tasteful green garland adorned with silver and red glass ornaments and tapered candles—covered the mantel. In the area of the room where the living room flowed into the dining room was a ten-foot-high Christmas tree decorated with the same silver and red ornaments.

The dining area flowed into a pristine, stunning kitchen. Here there were tall white cabinets, high-end stainless-steel appliances, beige granite countertops with veins of gold and black, and a huge island topped with the same granite and surrounded by six high pub-style chairs. The windows here were smaller but they had the same breathtaking view of the lake. Cooling on one of the kitchen counters was an assortment of Christmas cookies, which scented the air with hints of vanilla and almond. But a much stronger aroma, something spicy, emanated from the area around the stove. Beyond the kitchen I could see a combination mudroom and laundry room that was bigger than my kitchen. It, too, had windows overlooking the lake.

Seated at the island were two people: a tall, well-built, brown-haired man who looked to be in his fifties and a tall, slender blond woman who, I assumed, was Mrs. Gallagher. Based on the ages of their children, Mrs. Gallagher had to be around the same age as her husband, but she looked ten years younger. Standing in front of the six-burner stove, which would give any chef a case of envy, was a man who looked to be in his early thirties. I saw the family resemblance at once: he had Aidan's build, eyes, nose, and blond hair, a shock of which hung down over his forehead, but the face was longer, the chin weak and narrow rather than square. His features came together just shy of the handsome, patrician look Aidan possessed.

"Mom, Dad, you remember Clay Sanders, right?" Aidan said as we walked in.

Colin Gallagher rose from his chair and walked over to Clay. "Of course we do," he said in a deep baritone voice. "How is our ace reporter doing these days?"

"Doing as well as can be expected," Clay said, shaking Colin's hand.

Colin Gallagher then shifted his attention to me. He was a handsome man, with graying temples, a square jaw, and brilliant blue eyes, which sparkled when he smiled at me. "And who is this?" he asked, extending his hand to me.

"This is my girlfriend, Mackenzie," Clay said. I noticed that he didn't offer up my last name, and I figured this was intentional.

I took Colin Gallagher's hand, expecting to shake

it, but instead he gripped my hand, brought it to his face, and placed a butterfly kiss on the back of it. "You have excellent taste, Clay," he said.

Aidan said, "I ran into Clay downtown, and we were catching up on old times. I hope it's okay that I invited him and Mackenzie to stop by."

"Of course it is," Mrs. Gallagher said with a warm smile. She slid off her seat, walked over to Clay, and gave him a hug. "Good to see you again, Clay."

She was a beautiful woman with a perfect tan—sprayed or from a bed, I couldn't tell—and bright, lively blue eyes. Her face was heart-shaped; her lips were full; her nose was tiny and slightly upturned. At first I thought she might have had some work done, but I saw a strong resemblance to the pictures I'd seen of Tiffany, which made me think she had come by her attributes naturally.

When she finally released Clay, she turned to me. "And it's a pleasure to meet you, Mackenzie. I'm Kelly Gallagher, Aidan's mom."

"Nice to meet you," I said.

I saw the man at the stove shoot a perturbed look our way. I assumed this was the other brother, Rory, and wondered if his annoyance was due to our presence or the fact that his mother had claimed only Aidan as her son. He saw me looking at him and quickly turned back to tend to what was cooking on the stove.

"What happened to your leg?" Kelly asked, eyeing my cast.

"Car accident," I said, dismissing her concern with a wave of my hand. "It's nothing serious. More of a nuisance than anything."

Kelly studied my face with a curious expression as I

talked, and when I was done, she said, "Have we met before? You look vaguely familiar."

"I don't think so," I said with a smile. "In fact, I'm certain we haven't. I'd remember meeting someone as lovely as you." Eager to change the subject, I added, "I apologize for dropping in on you this way, but I'm glad I had a chance to see your house." I turned and looked out the windows at the lake. "It is stunningly beautiful. Your view is amazing."

"Thank you," she said with a proud smile, and Colin Gallagher beamed, as well.

I glanced back at the man by the stove and saw he was again watching us. He didn't frown, nor did he smile, but the narrowing of his eyes told me he was observing the goings-on with an intense scrutiny.

Aidan saw the direction of my gaze and in a teasing tone said, "That useless hunk of flesh over there by the stove is my brother, Rory. Rory, this is Clay and Mackenzie."

"Yeah, I heard," Rory said, still not smiling. He turned back to the stove and said over his shoulder, "Your timing is impeccable, as usual, Aidan. I'm whipping up a pot of my famous chili with the usual fixings, and it will all be ready in about one minute."

"I don't want to impose," I said, even though I kind of did. Not only did I want to dig into this family's history and dynamic, but I also wanted to dig into Rory's chili. It smelled delicious.

"Don't be ridiculous," Kelly said. "We have plenty. Please join us."

We settled in around the island, and Rory brought over the chili and set it atop the island, still in the pot he had cooked it in. He dropped a ladle into the pot and said, "Help yourselves. I'll get the corn bread."

Kelly grabbed bowls from one of the cabinets, and then she went to the fridge and brought out some shredded cheddar cheese and a dish of sour cream. A moment later Rory set the corn bread on the table— cut up into squares on a plate, rather than in a pan—and then he grabbed a crystal butter dish from another counter and set this on the island, as well.

We all dug in. The Gallaghers insisted that Clay and I serve ourselves first, and I gave myself a generous helping. The chili was delicious: hot, spicy, flavorful, and the perfect accompaniment to the cold winter afternoon.

Anxious to keep the conversation focused on any- thing but me, I asked the Gallaghers about their house, guessing correctly that they would expound on this topic for quite some time. At one point, Kelly gave me the perfect lead-in for the topic I really wanted to discuss.

"Our daughter, Tiffany, made those stained-glass lamp shades you see in the dining and living rooms," she said. "Tiff was a talented artist, and she loved painting and crafting glass. She had a workshop of sorts down in the basement."

"Had?" I said, swallowing a yummy bite of buttery corn bread. "She doesn't do it anymore?"

There was an awkward silence around the table, and I saw Kelly and Colin exchange looks. Rory kept his face down and focused on his bowl of chili. Aidan was the one who finally answered.

"My sister was killed nearly a year ago. Her husband, Ben Middleton, was convicted of her murder. Perhaps you heard about it in the news?"

I looked properly aghast. "Oh no. That carjacking thing?" I said.

Kelly nodded, looking sad. Colin simply looked angry.

"I'm so sorry for your loss," I said, hating the rote sound of this trite phrase. I looked at the lamp shades again and added, "She must have been very talented. Tell me about her."

It was a bold request, one I wasn't sure would work. The men all frowned, Clay included, though I wasn't sure if he genuinely disapproved of my request or was merely putting on a show. Kelly, however, was eager to talk.

"Tiffany was beautiful, smart, and a very talented artist," she said. "Some of her paintings hung in a gallery downtown, and several sold for quite a bit of money. One critic labeled her a bright star with a dark center." Kelly paused and flashed a timid smile. "Her paintings were rather dark, kind of creepy. Not my style at all, but she definitely had her fans."

"Do you have any of her paintings here?" I asked.

Kelly nodded. "There are several down in the basement, in her workshop. We pulled them all out of the gallery after she died, even though the owners said they would probably sell better and for more money now that she's gone. But we wanted to keep every bit of her we could, and we didn't want a bunch of vultures picking over her remains."

"Kelly," Colin chastised with a frown. He shook his head. He and Aidan then exchanged a look I couldn't quite interpret; Rory kept his head down, focusing on his bowl of chili. Clay sat with a spoonful of chili poised between his bowl and his mouth, studying the various expressions on everyone's faces.

In an effort to keep things moving in the desired direction, I said, "I'd love to see her works if it wouldn't be too painful for you to show them to me."

Kelly weighed my request, and after a few seconds, during which she ignored her husband's cautionary looks, she smiled and said, "Perhaps once we're done eating."

Sensing that pushing it any harder at this point would only antagonize the situation, I let the topic drop. The conversation switched to lighter topics, like the weather, local politics, and the upcoming holiday. The expected question of how Clay and I met arose, and I listened, amused, as Clay invented a story, which I embellished a time or two. Everyone joined in the conversation except for Rory, who continued to sit silently, brooding the entire time.

When we were finished eating, Kelly slid off her chair and beckoned me to follow her. "Come with me, Mackenzie, and I'll show you some of Tiffany's works."

"Do you really think that's wise?" Rory said, finally finding his voice. "You don't want to dredge up a bunch of bad memories."

"Your sister is not a bad memory," Kelly snapped. Her expression was one of cold anger and frustration, and Rory shied away from the look she gave him. Then her face morphed back into that of the pleasant, smiling woman I'd met initially. Without another word, she turned and left the room.

I followed, feeling the curious stares of the men behind me.

Chapter 17

Kelly led me back across the great room and past a hallway to our left that seemed to go on forever. Off this hallway was a series of doors—bedrooms, I guessed—all of which no doubt had the same spectacular windows and views of the lake. Kelly entered the front foyer and headed for a door opposite the coat closet. This led into another, smaller foyer. Straight ahead was the entrance to the garage, and to our left was a door that led downstairs.

The basement boasted a family room, this one decorated with the same holiday decor as the living room—including a second tree—but furnished much less formally. There was a large flat-screen TV on one wall and a sectional sofa covered in buttery-soft brown leather. A wet bar was built into one corner, and there was a computer desk—very modern, with black surfaces and chrome legs—in another corner. The wall facing the back of the house was wall-to-ceiling glass, with a sliding door in the middle. A huge, snow-covered yard led down to the water's edge with enough of a slope that I couldn't see the shore but had an expansive view of the lake beyond.

I stood and admired the rising moon over the lake, its pale white light glimmering off the snow and the water. "I envy you this view," I told Kelly. "It must be magical to see this every day and night."

"I do enjoy it," she said, "though sometimes I feel a little selfish having it all to myself and not sharing it. I used to entertain a lot, but that kind of fell by the wayside."

"Losing your daughter . . . What an awful thing for you to go through," I said. "No parent should have to lose a child, and to have it happen with such suddenness and violence . . ." My throat closed up on me as memories of my father's death swarmed over me. I felt Kelly's eyes on me and tore my gaze away from the view to look at her.

"You lost someone to violence, too, didn't you?" she said.

I nodded. "My father," I managed to say. "I found him . . . shot . . . dying." I couldn't get any more words out, and I turned back to look at the lake as I felt tears well in my eyes. Kelly placed a hand on my shoulder, and the two of us stood there like that for several minutes, staring out at that spectacular view, trying to suppress the emotions that tore at us.

Eventually, Kelly said, "Come on," and she took her hand from my shoulder. She headed for a hallway off the family room, and I followed along behind her. She opened up the first door on the right and led me into Tiffany's workshop.

Like every other room I'd seen so far, this one had big windows and a knockout view. On the wall opposite the windows was a row of easels, positioned so that anyone standing in front of them would have their back to the view. At first this puzzled me, but then I realized that the light coming in through the windows would be ideal for painting. At the opposite end of the room was a large wooden table with an exhaust fan above it. Scattered over the top of the table were various pieces of glass in a variety of colors and textures. In the center of it all was a half-finished project that depicted a rocky shoreline, a blue expanse of water made out of rippled glass, and a lighthouse with a red base, a white top, and gold-colored glass making up the windows in the lantern. The sky above was unfinished.

"That's the last thing she was working on," Kelly said, seeing the direction of my gaze. "It was supposed to be a gift for me for my fiftieth birthday. At least that's what Aidan said."

"You should have someone finish it so you can display it. It would look beautiful hanging in one of your windows."

"Maybe someday," she said wistfully. "But not yet." She turned and looked at the four easels behind us. "These are the paintings that were left at the gallery," she said.

It was easy to see why Tiffany's work had been called dark. The painting on the first easel featured a woman's face, the mouth open in a silent scream, her hair wild around her, her eyes shedding tears of blood. The background was a maelstrom of black and dark red colors.

The second painting depicted an expanse of flowers beneath a brilliant blue sky. There were trees off in the distance, the leaves painted in varying shades of green, the trunks in brown and black. This part of the painting was serene and beautiful, but the flowers in the foreground were painted in shades of brown, black, and gray, and they hung over, wilted and limp. The ground they grew from looked scorched and desolate.

I moved on to the third painting, a seascape done beneath a stormy sky. The waves peaked and splashed, breaking in curds of white foam, and dark, menacing clouds hovered in a gray and black sky. In the midst of the sea was a single flower, a bright red poppy adrift on a wave. Beneath the flower, and heading up toward it, was the vague outline of a shark—gray, menacing, its mouth gaping open, its teeth visible just beneath the flower. The clearest thing on the shark was its eye, which was open, black, and dead looking.

I suppressed a shudder and moved on to the fourth and final easel. This one was the most disturbing of all. At its center, on a sandy shore, was a small rowboat tipped up on its side. Behind it the lake glimmered and shimmered beneath a bright yellow sun. Half buried in the sand beneath the boat was the rotting skeleton of a woman, with the torn remnants of a flowery dress hanging on the bones, and long blond hair matted and splayed out from the skull. The red poppy put in an appearance again, this time resting by the skeleton's half-buried hip bone. And off to the left, in the calm shimmer of the water, was an eye, the same dead-looking eye that had been painted on the shark.

"Wow," I said in a low voice. "I see what you mean."

Kelly stared at the paintings, one elbow nestled in a palm, a hand cupped over her mouth.

"When did she paint these?"

Kelly dropped her hand from her mouth. "She did these two"—she pointed at the ones with the poppies—"right after she finished high school. It was her first year of college. The others she did during the years that followed. I also have some unfinished canvases in a closet, ones that she did later. Those have . . ." She hesitated. "They have a happier feel about them."

"Forgive me for asking this," I said in as gentle a voice as I could muster, "but was your daughter troubled in any way? These paintings seem to suggest there was a darkness inside her."

Kelly dropped her hand from her face and turned to look at me. Tears glistened in her eyes as she spoke. "When Tiff was little, she was a bright, beautiful kid with an infectious laugh and a sunny outlook on life. But when she hit her teen years, something changed. She would get these moods where she'd be weepy and irritable and sullen. . . ." Her voice drifted off, and she swallowed hard, looking past me to the other end of the room. Her eyes were unfocused, as if she was seeing something that was only in her mind or her memory.

She went on. "I suggested she go see a counselor, but she refused. I made her go, anyway, when she was fifteen, but all she did was sit in the woman's office in stony silence. After four sessions of that, I gave up. It seemed to get better during her junior year in high school, but the summer after that, her demons resurfaced." She shot me a teary-eyed, shameful look and then quickly glanced away again. "Once I caught her in her bedroom with a razor. She was cutting herself on her legs, not bad, not deep, but enough to draw blood."

I stepped closer to her and draped an arm over her shoulder. "I'm sorry," I said, and I meant it. Her pain was palpable. It seeped from her pores. I felt her shudder beneath my arm, and it made a scene of jagged, sharp rocks flash before my eyes. I blinked it away and gave her a small sideways hug.

Her next words made my body go rigid.

"You're not really dating Clay, are you?" she said just above a whisper.

Chapter 18

"It's okay," Kelly said, and then she looked at me with that expression of raw pain. "I know who you are. You're that barkeep who was on the news, the one who solves crimes with ESP or something, right?"

"Not exactly," I said. "Yes, I'm that person. And yes, I do look into crimes from time to time. But I don't have ESP."

"Are you looking into Tiffany's?"

I couldn't lie to her. "I am." I waited for her to get angry, to demand that I leave her house at once and to chastise me for my impudence. But she did none of those things. Instead, she looked back at the paintings again and continued her story.

"After I caught Tiffany cutting on herself, I threatened to send her away somewhere for inpatient treatment. She cried and begged me not to and promised me she wouldn't do it again. I relented, only because I figured it wouldn't do any more good than the therapy sessions had, and might even do her more harm. A month or two went by, and her mood worsened to the point that I made her strip down and show me her body, to prove to me that she wasn't cutting on herself anymore. She wasn't, but around the start of her senior year in high school, something happened." She paused, staring at the paintings.

I didn't move or say a word, unsure if she was going to continue but hoping she would.

"I found a pregnancy test in her bathroom trash," Kelly said finally. "It was positive."

She sighed, a long shuddering exhalation that seemed to brace her. "Colin and I grilled her and drilled her to try to determine who the boy was, but she refused to say. And then she started with the morning sickness, only she had it at all times throughout the day. She missed the whole first week of school. Colin and I spent that week debating what to do about the pregnancy. We both come from strict Irish Catholic families, and the idea of an abortion was out of the question with him. I was a little more open to the idea because I knew having a child would only complicate things for Tiffany, and I'm not as devout as Colin is." She glanced over at me, I assumed to gauge my judgment of her.

I shrugged and gave her a small nod of understanding, which seemed to satisfy her.

"In the end we decided to send her to a special school overseas, a private boarding school designed for girls who . . . girls in trouble." Again, she looked over at me, this time with an apologetic smile. "I probably shouldn't be telling you any of this, and you can't tell any of it to Clay. Promise me."

I hesitated a split second before answering. The raw pain on her face helped me make the decision. "I promise."

She weighed my sincerity and must have found me

passing, because eventually she nodded. "It's just that I haven't had anyone to talk to since . . . well, since forever, it seems. I'm always surrounded by the men in my family—Colin and my sons—and they never want to talk about anything . . . any of it. They still don't." She sighed again, turned back to the paintings, and began to pick at one of her fingernails.

"When we sent Tiffany away, I didn't dare tell any of my friends, because I knew it would get out. That didn't stop them from prying and gossiping, though, and eventually, I kind of withdrew from the social circle. Over time the curiosity waned, and I was just starting to get involved socially again when Tiffany died. After that, everyone avoided me. I guess what happened to her was just too difficult for them to deal with."

"What happened to the baby?"

Her face contorted into a sad smile. "It was stillborn, which was probably for the best. At first I thought it might push Tiffany over the edge. When she came back that next summer, she was her old happy self at first. But her mood quickly grew dark and sullen. That's when she did those paintings. Then in the fall she went off to college, and things got better. During her junior year she met Ben, and she seemed so happy and content and in love. It was the first time in a long time I felt truly hopeful about her future."

"But he killed her," I said softly. I watched her closely as I said the words, gauging her reaction.

For the longest time, she didn't move, didn't even blink. Her face was blank; I couldn't tell what she was thinking.

"Mrs. Gallagher, do you think Ben killed Tiffany?"

She finally looked at me with a sad expression. "The

evidence said so. And he *was* convicted. So I guess he did."

Up until now, her voice had tasted like apples: sweet, ripe, with an occasional hint of tartness. But with this last statement, the taste turned rotten, as if I'd bitten into an apple that was brown and mushy in the middle.

"You don't think he did it, do you?" I said.

She eyed me curiously, her brows drawing down for a few seconds. "Why would you say that?"

"It's your voice. It changed when you answered my question about his guilt."

She looked away for a second or two, staring at the floor, her brows drawn down into a consternated V. When she looked back at me, she gave me a fleeting smile. "Are you reading my mind now? Is that it?"

I shook my head. "I don't read minds, Mrs. Gallagher. I have a neurological disorder that cross-wires my senses so that I experience each one in multiple ways. For instance, I typically experience a taste with people's voices and can tell when they're lying to me because the taste changes. It's some subtle difference in the voice. I think it's the knowledge that one is lying, or perhaps a lack of conviction, that causes it. Your voice, the taste of it, has been consistent all evening, up until the statement you just made about Ben's guilt. That tells me that you don't believe what you're saying."

She stared at me, wordless.

"I'm right, aren't I? You think he's innocent."

A host of emotions flitted across her face: fear, doubt, anger, confusion.

I closed the gap between us and took one of her

hands, then sandwiched it between mine. "Tell me why you think he's innocent," I urged.

Kelly blinked several times. Her mouth opened and closed, opened and closed . . . the proverbial fish out of water. But she didn't pull her hand away. Finally, she said, "Because he truly loved her. He made her happy, happier than I'd seen her in years. The way he talked to her, and about her, the way they touched one another . . . secret little love pats and holding hands under the table when they didn't think we would notice."

"How do you know it wasn't all just an act on Ben's part?"

She thought a moment before shaking her head. "I just do," she said. "They came by the house the day they left for their trip, and Ben was so happy, so full of hope, you know?" Her eyes appealed to me, begging me to tell her that her read of the situation had been correct.

"You say Ben seemed happy. What about Tiffany?"

A cloud crossed over her face, and I knew there was more to the story. She pulled her hand loose and turned away from me, chewing on the side of her thumb. She began rocking back and forth on her feet, chewing, staring, and agonizing.

"Kelly, all I'm interested in here is the truth. If Ben did kill Tiffany, then I hope he rots in prison forever. But if he didn't, not only do I want to see him exonerated, but I also want real justice for Tiffany. If Ben didn't do it, the real killer is still out there somewhere, walking around free. We owe it to Tiffany to get to the truth."

It was the best speech I could drum up for the moment, and as I watched Kelly continue to chew and rock, I grew more certain with every passing second that it wasn't enough. So I tossed out the last thing I had.

"The evidence revealed that Tiffany had sex with someone other than Ben not long before she was killed," I said. "Any idea who the other man was?"

This time I got a reaction. Kelly whirled on me, glaring, angry, ready to defend her daughter's honor. But a split second before she released that anger balloon on me, it deflated. Her shoulders sagged, her face fell, and she let out a long, choppy sigh. She was a woman defeated, and I felt for her.

"I don't know," she said, barely above a whisper. She was staring at the floor when she said this, but she finally raised her head and looked me in the eye. "I didn't believe it when I heard it, but the evidence doesn't lie. Tiff talked to me about her and Ben several times. They were . . . They had some problems, but she was determined to work them out. I just can't make myself believe that she had some sort of fling. It wasn't like her. In fact, she once told me that she didn't like sex all that much."

This didn't sway me one way or the other. It was possible that Tiff simply didn't like sex with Ben, and when she found another lover, she changed her way of thinking. But I didn't voice this to Kelly.

"Was there anyone she was close to? A male friend or confidante?"

Kelly shook her head.

"And you never figured out who the guy was from her senior year?"

"No. She refused to tell us. Although . . ."

Whatever she was about to say next was lost because Colin Gallagher walked into the room.

"Clay is ready to leave," he said. I was pretty sure it was Colin who was ready for us to leave. This was confirmed when he glanced over at the paintings and then quickly looked away. "Enough of this, Kelly," he said.

She turned to me, putting her back to him, and her pleading look begged me to keep her secret. I smiled and gave her a little nod. Then I took her hands in mine and gave them a gentle squeeze. Colin watched us with a scowl on his face as Kelly mouthed the words "Thank you" to me. Then she pulled her hands from mine and pushed past her husband, exiting the room. I smiled at Colin—it wasn't returned—and followed Kelly out of the room. As I crossed the family room and headed toward the stairs, I heard Colin close the door to the workshop firmly behind him. By the time I was halfway up the stairs—slow going, thanks to my crutches—he was hot on my heels.

I found Clay standing in the foyer, his coat already on, mine draped over his arm. Kelly was nowhere to be seen.

"Ready?" Clay said, holding my coat out for me.

As I balanced on my crutches and shrugged into my coat, Colin Gallagher stood there, watching me intently. His stare made me uncomfortable, and I sensed a deep anger in him. I wondered if it was because he had also figured out who I was and why I was here, or if it was simply because he was upset with his wife.

"Thank you for being so gracious as to invite us into your home at the last minute and to feed us," I said to him. "It was a pleasure to meet you and see your lovely home. And tell Rory I want the recipe for his chili. It was delicious."

Colin smiled, but it looked forced, and all he said was, "Nice to meet you."

As Clay and I stepped out into the cold winter night, the front door of the Gallagher home closed behind us with a solid *thunk*.

Chapter 19

Once we were inside Clay's car and heading down the driveway, he said, "Boy, Colin Gallagher sure didn't like the idea of you and his wife going to look at those paintings."

"I gathered that."

"How did it go?"

"It was interesting, sad, and a little creepy. And for what it's worth, Kelly doesn't think Ben killed Tiffany."

"She said that?"

"She didn't deny it."

"Not the same thing," Clay said.

"You'll just have to trust me on this one."

"What was the creepy part?"

"Tiffany's paintings." I described them to him the best I could, but my words seemed inadequate.

"So Tiffany had some dark thoughts," he said with a shrug. "Lots of young folks these days do."

"Maybe," I said, unconvinced. "What were you boys doing while we were downstairs?"

"Aidan and I were catching up on old times. Rory

and his dad disappeared for a bit. When they came back, Colin seemed eager to have us leave."

"Do you think any of them recognized me?" I said. "I caught Rory staring at me a couple of times, and he didn't look happy."

"If he did, he didn't say anything. And Rory always looks unhappy. That's the price you pay for being the younger sibling of the golden boy."

"Is Rory older or younger than Tiffany?"

"Tiffany was the baby. According to Aidan, she was the light of Kelly's eye."

"Kelly recognized me."

Clay shot me a look, nearly driving off the road. "She did?" he said, struggling to get back on the road. "Was she mad?"

"Surprisingly, no. I think she was desperate for someone to talk to."

"Wouldn't surprise me," Clay said. "Colin is a tight-lipped, private, stern sort of guy, if you can believe what Aidan says. And apparently, Rory takes after his father."

My cell phone rang then, and when I saw it was Duncan calling, I told Clay I had to take the call.

"Hey," I said, holding the phone tight to my ear so Clay couldn't eavesdrop. "What's up?"

I just woke up," he said in a bleary voice that made me taste rich, dark chocolate. "It was a long night."

"Sorry."

"Where are you? It doesn't sound like the typical bar background noise."

"I'm in a car with Clay Sanders, the reporter." I hoped that would refresh his memory and make him understand that I couldn't say much on my end.

"Ah, then I'll be quick. I have something in mind I

want you to do. I want to sneak you into our impound lot and let you have a go at Gary's car."

"Have a go at it?"

"Yeah, have a look at it, smell it . . . like you did on that other case. See if you can pick up any clues. They're done processing it for evidence, so it won't affect anything."

"Okay," I said slowly. "How?"

"I'm going to involve Isabel again."

Isabel was a friend of Duncan's who worked in the theater business as a makeup artist. When I went to the police station to see Apostle Mike the first time, Duncan had her come by my bar and fix me up so that anyone watching wouldn't recognize me and figure out I was working with the police and Duncan. She did a stellar job, making me unrecognizable even to myself. But even her magical ministrations couldn't hide my cast and crutches. Or so I thought. But Duncan was anticipating this objection.

"I know you're worried about being recognized because of the crutches, but I have an idea on how to get around that." He then filled me in on his plan.

"Interesting idea," I said when he was done.

"I want you to meet Isabel at her house."

"Are you sure?"

"I am. Have Mal drive you. He knows how to spot a tail, and he can drive evasively if he has to."

I thought about what he was suggesting, and though I had some misgivings about the plan, I was eager to do anything I could to help avenge Gary's death and find this damned letter writer. Then I realized I could use Isabel in another way.

I was keenly aware of Clay listening to my end of the conversation and decided that if he asked who had called, and I felt certain he would, I'd tell him it was Isabel. When she'd come to my bar that first time, I'd passed her off as an interior decorator who was going to help me redo my apartment. I figured sticking to that story now would be easiest, and I tried to gear my remarks to Duncan to fit in with that scenario.

"Okay, but don't get your hopes up too high," I said. "It's been a long time since anything was done there." I was trying to relay to Duncan how the amount of time that had passed would likely affect my ability to pick up on anything in Gary's car. Not to mention the fact that the evidence technicians had probably added their own brand of contamination, things like finger-print powder.

"I understand," Duncan said, "but on the off chance that there is something, I think it's worth a shot."

"Okay. Where and when?"

"Tonight," he said. Then he gave me Isabel's address, which I committed to memory. One thing about my synesthesia that comes in handy is it makes it easy for me to memorize things. "She's waiting there for you now," Duncan went on. "The sooner you can get there, the better."

I glanced at my watch and saw that it was nearly seven in the evening. "I'd like to include Mal in this, get his input into the plan. But I'm not sure where he is right now."

It turned out Duncan had this covered, too. "I already called him," he said. "He'll meet you at the bar. In fact, he might be there already."

"Okay. I'm about ten minutes from the bar. Once I hook up with Mal, we'll head your way and look over the samples. See you soon."

I disconnected the call, looked over at Clay with a

smile, and decided to beat him to the punch. "That was my interior designer. She's going to be redoing my apartment, and she has some furniture and fabric samples she wants me to look at."

"On a Sunday night?" he said, the skepticism clear in his voice.

"She works odd hours. And that works well for me since I tend to keep odd hours, too."

"What furniture stores are open this time on a Sunday night?"

It was a good question, one that made me see what made Clay such a good journalist. He had an analytical—and suspicious—mind.

Thinking quickly, I said, "She has her own warehouse where she stores stuff. She does staging for real estate agents, too, so she keeps a stock of furniture on hand for that."

This seemed to satisfy Clay, though I half expected him to ask me for her name and trump up some story about how he wanted to have his place redone, too. Fortunately, he didn't.

When we arrived back at the bar, he dropped me off out front. "I have some research I need to do for another story I'm working on," he said. "I'll come by tomorrow and check in with the group."

I thanked him for his help and staggered out of the car on my crutches. When I got inside, I saw Mal seated at the bar, chatting with Billy. The place was busy for a Sunday night; all the tables in the main area were full.

"Hey, Mal," I said, crutching up behind him. I would have put a hand on his arm if I'd had one free, but the crutches prevented that.

"There's my girl," he said with a warm smile. He

snaked an arm around my waist and nudged me toward him, nearly making me lose my balance. I fell into him, and he kissed me briefly on the lips. It was what anyone watching us would expect him to do.

I looked over at Billy. "How's everything going?"

"It's been a good night," he said. "Busier than usual."

"Are you managing everything okay?"

He cocked his head to one side and flashed me a cheesy grin. "Of course, boss. When do I not?"

"Never," I said with a grateful smile. "And since you've got it all under control, I'm going to steal Mal here and head out for another appointment. I have to meet with my interior designer to look at some stuff for the apartment."

"I got it covered," Billy said, waving me away.

"I imagine I'll be back before closing, but if I'm not . . ." I winked at Billy, implying that Mal and I might stop somewhere for a little romantic fun.

"I'll close up," Billy said. "You kids go and have a good time." He winked back at me and then walked down the bar to tend to a customer.

Mal donned his coat and gloves, and we headed out. Once we were outside, Mal looked around to make sure no one was within hearing distance, and said, "I'm not sure what it is we're doing, but Duncan gave me Isabel's address and said to take you there, making sure no one tails us."

"I'll explain it to you once we're under way."

This satisfied him for the time being, and we walked the rest of the way to his car in silence. As soon as we were under way, he headed the wrong way initially and made several unnecessary turns. He kept an eye on the rearview mirror, and after ten minutes of this maneuvering, he declared us tail free and got back on track.

During the drive, I filled Mal in on the previous case I'd worked with Duncan, explaining how sitting inside the victim's car had led me to some helpful insights. Despite my newfound pride in my ability—or disability, depending on one's perspective—I still felt uncomfortable talking about my synesthesia. I'd spent so many years hiding it that it was hard for me to talk about it now, so I glossed over some of the details.

When I was done, he said, "With all that sensory input, how do you keep from getting overwhelmed? How do you know what's real and what's a secondary reaction?"

"I'm not sure," I said with a shrug. "Most of the time, I just know. My synesthetic reactions are often fleeting, and I learned when I was a kid how to shut out a lot of the extraneous stuff. I listened hard to what other people said about their experiences and figured out pretty quickly which of my experiences were primary senses and which ones were secondary. Then I just tuned out the extra stuff, the same way people tune out white noise."

"Things must be very busy inside your head. It's a wonder you're not crazy."

"Who says I'm not?" I said with a sly smile. "But I'm not sure it will help this time," I added, my smile fading. "A lot of time has passed since Gary . . . since it happened. I'm not sure how much I'll be able to pick up this late in the game. Plus, I'm sure I'll have some contamination to deal with, since the evidence techs probably messed with stuff inside the car."

"All you can do is try. You never know."

Fifteen minutes later we arrived at Isabel's house, a cute Craftsman in a suburban neighborhood on the southern outskirts of the city. A tall, thin man who looked to be in his fifties answered the door.

"Hi," he said with a warm smile. "I'm Eddie, Isabel's husband. And you must be Mack. Come on in. Isabel is waiting for you."

We stepped inside and followed him to a room at the back of the house that had windows on two sides. One look told me it was a studio of sorts for Isabel; it reminded me of Tiffany's workshop. There was a collage of pictures covering one of the windowless walls, some of them photos, others drawings. A half dozen mannequin heads on stands were atop a large center island, each one made up differently. Isabel was sitting on a stool in front of one of these, her back to the window, facing us.

"Mack, Mal," she said with a smile. "Come on in and have a seat."

She patted a stool next to her, and I crutched my way over there and settled in, leaning my crutches up against the island. Mal chose to remain standing across from me. Isabel got up, went over to a corner of the room, and dragged out a wheelchair.

"You won't be needing those crutches for a while tonight. This is your new mode of transportation."

"You want her to ride in a wheelchair?" Mal said.

"It was Duncan's idea. If anyone is watching for her, they'll be looking for the crutches." Her gaze moved toward my head. "And that signature red hair, so let's start with that."

Over the next hour, Isabel fitted me with a gray wig that was cut short, and then she made up my face, using pieces of latex and a variety of colors. Mal stood across the table from us, watching her work. Eddie had disappeared somewhere in the house.

When Isabel was done, she leaned back and looked at me with a critical eye. "Pretty good, if I do say so myself. What do you think, Mal?"

I turned and faced Mal, whose eyebrows shot up with surprise. "Wow," he said. "I've seen you do your magic before, but this is even better."

Isabel handed me a mirror and let me look. An old, wrinkled woman stared back at me, with sagging jowls, gray hair, and a timeworn face. "This is a bit disturbing," I said with a smile. "I hope this isn't a sign of things to come."

"Now we need to hide that cast," Isabel said. She walked over to a closet, and after rummaging around for a bit, she came out with a gray coat and a plaid blanket. She handed me the coat, which I donned, and then said, "Have a seat in the wheelchair."

I dutifully hobbled over and sat, and once I was settled, she spread the blanket over my legs and tucked it in around my feet. The cast was out of sight.

"I think we're good," she said, nodding approvingly. "Now you need to go meet Duncan." She looked over at Mal. "If you wheel her right up to the passenger-side door of your car and tuck the blanket around her once she's inside, no one will see that cast. Do the same thing getting out of the car."

Mal nodded his understanding, got behind the wheelchair, and steered it to the front door, Isabel trailing behind us.

I turned to Isabel and said, "Thank you for helping us with this."

"It's my pleasure," she said with a warm, genuine smile. "Duncan is like family to me, and I'd do anything for him." She opened the front door for us, and as I looked out, I realized we had one more hurdle to get over.

"What about the stairs?" I asked.

Isabel looked at Mal and said, "Can you carry her? I'll get the wheelchair."

Mal didn't hesitate. He came around to the side of the chair, slid one arm around my back, the other beneath my legs, and hoisted me out of the chair, cradling me against his chest. I wrapped an arm around his neck to steady myself and felt the heat of his body from beneath his coat radiating through mine. It made me see soothing waves of warm reds and sunny yellow. At the base of the stairs, Isabel locked the wheelchair, and Mal set me back down. I looked at him just before he let go of me, and our eyes locked for a few seconds. A tiny buzzing sensation zipped down my back, and I wasn't sure what had triggered it. The sight of him? His smell? Or the emotions I was feeling? I blushed beneath the intensity of his gaze and made myself look at Isabel.

"This chair is great for tonight," I said, "but I'm going to need my crutches later."

"Oh, right." She turned and headed back into the house.

Mal released the locks on the chair and wheeled me toward his car. Then we did as Isabel had instructed, a practice run for getting into and out of the chair. By the time I was settled in the front seat, Isabel had come out with the crutches. Mal opened the back door of the car and set the crutches on the floor. Then he went around to the trunk to load up the wheelchair.

"I'll get the wig, chair, and coat back to you as soon as I can," I told Isabel.

"No rush. And good luck."

"Thanks again." I shut the door and waited for Mal to get in on the driver's side.

As we pulled away, I looked back to wave at Isabel. She waved back and gave me a smile, but not before I saw the look of worry on her face.

Chapter 20

Mal headed for the impound lot, once again keeping a wary eye on the rearview mirror to look for any tails. There weren't any that he could see, and when we were about five minutes away, I called Duncan to let him know. He was waiting for us when we arrived. Mal parked in the street, and Duncan hurried over to Mal's window.

"I've been scoping the place out for anyone who might be watching," Duncan said. "I haven't seen anything." He shifted his gaze to me. "Wow. Isabel's talent is truly remarkable," he said, looking awestruck. "Is that really you, Mack?"

"It is," I said.

"Amazing." He took a few more seconds to appreciate my transformation before getting down to business. "There are video cameras in the lot, but I've been given permission to view Gary's car with someone I've listed as a potential witness. The cameras will show us entering the impound lot, but the car itself is not in view of the cameras. I gave them a phony name, so you shouldn't have anything to worry about, and when we're done, I'll tell them you said the car wasn't the right one."

Mal and I proceeded to get out of the car, using the wheelchair the way Isabel had instructed. As soon as I was settled in the chair, with the blanket tucked in around my legs, Mal wheeled me toward the lot's gate. Duncan punched in a numeric code on the lock mechanism, and with each beep, I saw a fleeting number appear before my eyes.

"Four, two, five, eight, six," I said, and Duncan turned to stare at me. "Those are the numbers I saw when I heard you push the buttons," I explained.

As the gate slid open, Duncan shook his head and said, "If the bar and this crime-solving stuff don't work out, you might have a career as a criminal, breaking and entering."

I tried to wiggle my eyebrows, but the makeup I had glued to my face made it difficult. Mal pushed me through the gate, and we followed Duncan across the lot and around the corner of a building to an older model Ford sedan.

"Sit for a moment and look at the outside of the car," Duncan said. "Let me know if anything strikes you."

I nodded and told Mal, "Wheel me around it slowly."

Mal did so, and I looked closely at the car's exterior, lowering the filters I typically had in place to shut out all my synesthetic reactions. I caught a faint whiff of gasoline, which made me hear the sound of rustling leaves, and the dark blue color of the car made me feel a dampness along my arms and hands. On the driver's side of the car, I saw that the window had a dark, thick stain on it, and I caught a whiff of blood, which made me grimace. As we continued around the car, I picked up on two other smells I recognized: rust and salt.

Gary's car was at least fifteen years old, and it had body rot in a number of places where the salted winter roads had eroded away the exterior finish. But neither of these smells told me anything useful.

When we were done circling the car, I told Duncan what I'd noted. "I don't think any of it is particularly helpful, though," I said when I was done.

Duncan nodded slowly. "Let's move on to the inside of the car, then," he said. "The evidence indicates that the shooter was in the passenger seat, so we'll approach it from that side. I have to warn you, the front of the car has a fair amount of dried blood in it, and while the interior has been thoroughly processed, there's a lingering odor. . . ." He didn't describe the smell; he didn't have to. "The techs also vacuumed the passenger seat and floor and dusted the interior for prints, so there will be some powder in there."

I nodded. Thanks to the investigations into my father's and Ginny's deaths, I knew what sort of reaction I'd get from the fingerprint powder. Hopefully, I'd be able to single it out from any other reactions I had. "Did the techs find anything useful?" I asked.

Duncan cocked his head to one side. "I'll answer that once we're done. I don't want to sway your reactions any."

I saw the wisdom of this and nodded again.

"I'm going to open the passenger-side door, and you can wheel up beside it and look in."

"Okay, but if there are any lingering smells other than what you mentioned, the longer the door is open, the greater the chance is that those smells will escape or diminish."

"I realize that, but the techs had the doors open for

a long time when they were processing the car, so I
think that ship has sailed."

"Too bad," I said.

Duncan opened the passenger-side door and, with
some help from Mal, I wheeled myself up as close to
it as I could get without touching anything.

The smell Duncan had referred to earlier was the
proverbial elephant in the room. It was a rank, rotten
odor that made me stifle a gag. The smell of blood typically generated a metallic sound, like two metal bars
clanking together. This old, fetid blood smell caused a
metallic sound, too, but it was duller, heavier, more of
a crunching metal noise. I'd had similar experiences
when I smelled meat that had gone bad, and once as a
child, when I and a couple of other kids came across a
raccoon carcass at the back of the school yard one day.

I catalogued my reaction to the rotten smell in my
head and then parsed it, trying to determine if I was
having any other smell reactions that didn't fit with it.
There were faint remnants of the gasoline, salt, and
rust smells, and there was another smell, which I recognized as a polish used to refurbish dashboards. My
father had used the stuff both on his car and on mine,
and I recalled the smooth, oily sensation on my fingers
that the smell of it always triggered.

As I sorted through these reactions, I became aware
of another smell, a very faint one that manifested as a
musical sound, like a note being played on a saxo-
phone. It was vaguely familiar—I knew I'd encountered
it before—but I couldn't place it.

"There are a couple of other smells in here apart
from the expected ones, like the gas, rust, salt, and . . .
decay smell. One is from some polish used on the
dashboard. But the other one I can't place. It's faint,

but I'm certain I've encountered it before. It must be one of those things that I've always suppressed or ignored."

"Is there any one area it seems to emanate from?" Duncan asked.

I leaned deeper into the car, but that made the smell and the sax music dissipate slightly. When I straightened back up, both of them grew a smidgen stronger. I leaned to my right, and they grew stronger still. Finally, I stuck my nose down by the armrest of the car door, and the musical sound crescendoed. "It's here," I said, pointing to the front of the armrest. "It's a faint odor. Something . . . spicy maybe? But I think it's also floral."

"Like an aftershave, perhaps?" Duncan suggested.

"Maybe. Like I said, I'm pretty sure I've smelled it before, but I can't place it."

"We can have Cora search her database later," Duncan said.

Cora, in conjunction with her other duties, had started a database of my synesthetic reactions, a virtual catalog of experiences, which she could search if I couldn't recall what triggered a particular reaction.

"It's worth a try," I said, staring at the armrest. I got a strong dirt taste in my mouth and recognized it. "Your tech people dusted this armrest for prints, but I don't detect any voids in the powder, so I'm guessing they didn't find anything."

Duncan said nothing, but I saw him give Mal a look. I scanned the other interior surfaces and experienced the same dirt taste, until I looked at the steering wheel and the gearshift lever. Here there were voids. I could tell because the dirt taste dissipated when I looked at certain spots.

"They found and lifted prints on the steering wheel and the gearshift lever. Gary's, I assume. But I don't think they found any fingerprints on the passenger side of the car at all."

"You are correct," Duncan said with a smile.

"That suggests your shooter was wearing gloves, which is not surprising given the time of year."

Mal, who was standing behind my chair, watching it all, said, "You're amazing."

I smiled but said nothing. What I was doing didn't feel amazing. It was just me. But I liked the praise, nonetheless. I went back to puzzling over that smell. I stared at the armrest, scouring it with my eyes, inch by inch. At one point the dirt taste intensified significantly, up near the front of the armrest, where the smell was the strongest.

"The spot where the smell seems to come from has a thicker layer of fingerprint dust than the rest of the armrest," I said. I closed my eyes then and imagined someone sitting in the passenger seat, their arm on the armrest.

I opened my eyes and looked over at Duncan. "I'd assume, given the time of year and the weather, that whoever was sitting here was wearing a coat, meaning the bulk of their arm was covered. If that smell was from the material in the coat, I would expect it to be along the entire armrest, but there's just this one spot along the front edge of the armrest." I pointed to the area. "It continues down the side of it a bit . . . here." I traced the area with my finger, getting close to it but not touching it.

Then I sat back in the wheelchair and reached down with my right hand into the pocket of the coat I was wearing. As I did so, the edge of my coat sleeve caught on the armrest of the chair and was dragged up. The sleeve of the sweater I had on beneath my coat moved along with it, and my skin came in contact with the armrest of the wheelchair.

"Though we can't be sure, odds are the shooter was right handed, correct?" I said.

"Correct," Duncan agreed.

"If they had something in their right pocket, like a gun, and they reached in there for it, their bare skin might have come in contact with the armrest in the car, the way my arm did here on the wheelchair just now. That may be how the residue of whatever it is I smell here was left behind. So maybe it's a lotion or a soap or a bath oil of some sort."

Duncan arched his brows and gave me a look of admiration. "Makes sense," he said. He leaned over the door and stared down at the armrest. "I suppose I could swab it and have the tech guys run it through the analyzer to see if they can find anything they can identify."

"You can try," I said, "but there's fingerprint powder mixed in with it. Won't that skew the results?"

"I think they can isolate the powder," Duncan said. He reached into his coat pocket and pulled out a small cardboard tube. From it he withdrew a cotton-tipped swab. "Show me the spot," he said, and when I pointed to the area, he swiped it and then placed the swab back in the tube. "Nice work, Mack," he said. "Anything else?"

I gave it another minute and shook my head. "I've had lots of reactions, but I don't think any of them are relevant or helpful."

"Okay," Duncan said. "Then let's call it a night."

Mal wheeled me back away from the car, and

Duncan closed the door. I stared at the car, realizing it had been Gary's tomb in a way, and a shudder ran through me.

"Are you cold?" Duncan asked.

"A little," I admitted. "More upset than cold, though. This damned letter writer is getting to me."

Duncan gave my shoulder a reassuring squeeze. "We got a break a little while ago on one of the cases I'm working, and I think I can sneak away later tonight. How about I take you over to my place and fix you dinner? You've fed me often enough. I think it's my turn. And if you're up for it, you can stay the night."

"That would be nice," I said. "But I don't feel comfortable leaving the bar for the entire night. As it is, I have my staff and Cora handling things, and I have a brand-new employee I hired last night. I need to go back."

Duncan scowled.

"Besides," I added, "how would I get back to the bar? You can't take me, because you might be seen."

He nodded grudgingly. "Well, then, I guess I'll have to sneak into the bar again, assuming I'm welcome."

"Of course you are."

Duncan looked past me to Mal. "Would you mind taking her back?"

"Happy to."

Duncan glanced at his watch. "I need to get this swab to the lab and finish off some paperwork on that case I mentioned. How about if I meet you at the back alley door at, say, eleven? That gives you a couple of hours to make sure everything is okay with the bar."

"You'll wear a disguise?"

"Of course," he said a bit impatiently. His scowl

deepened, and he looked at Mal again. "Would you mind waiting in the car? I want to talk with Mack alone for a few minutes."

"No problem," Mal said.

"Just push the green button on the panel by the gate, and it will open for you," Duncan said, and with that Mal headed back the way we'd come.

I looked at Duncan expectantly, waiting to hear what he had to say.

He watched Mal walk off, and once he was out of earshot, he looked back at me. "Mack, are we okay?"

"I don't know," I said honestly.

"Would you rather I didn't come by tonight?"

"That depends. Will you be there with me once you get there, or will your head be somewhere else all night?"

He arched a brow at me. "That's the pot calling the kettle black, isn't it? I offered to spend the entire evening with you away from all our other distractions, but you can't tear yourself from the bar long enough to do that."

I sighed. "I think the timing is off. All this sneaking around we're doing, and the demands we both have on us with our jobs . . . they make it impossible to carry on any sort of normal relationship."

"I never promised you normal," he said with half a grin. He looked away for a few seconds, back toward the gate. "Is it Mal? Is that the problem? Are you looking to dump me so you can hook up with him?"

I shook my head. "Mal is a great guy, and I admit, I've grown quite fond of him. But the feelings I have for him are different from the feelings I have for you. I just don't know if the feelings I have for you are enough with all this other stuff that's going on."

"Are they enough for you to hang in there until we can get to the bottom of this case? I know it's not easy, but I really care for you, Mack, and I want to see where we can go with this." He waved a finger back and forth between me and him. "With us."

"I can hang in for a while longer," I said with a smile.

"I promise you it will get better," he assured me. "I think our schedules will always be something of an obstacle, but once we catch this damned letter writer and we can stop all the sneaking around, I think it will make things a lot easier."

"Assuming we do catch whoever's behind it."

"We will. Have faith."

Have faith. There were those words again. Maybe it was a sign . . . the world or God or something telling me to be patient and trust that things would eventually work out.

"Okay. I'll try to be patient," I said with a pout. "See you later?"

"With bells on." His eyes lit up for a second, and he added, "You know, I could literally wear bells, or at least carry one."

"I don't follow."

"I think I have the perfect disguise. In fact, it's so good, you won't have to sneak me in the back door. But I might need a little help from Mal."

He had me puzzled but intrigued as he stepped around behind my wheelchair and started pushing me toward the gate. "What do you have in mind?"

And then he told me.

When we got back to the car, he wheeled me up to the door and held the chair as I climbed inside. Then he and Mal went around to the back of the car to load up the wheelchair. I heard the trunk slam closed and expected Mal to get in on the driver's side, but he didn't. Curious, I craned my head around to look out the back window. Duncan had hauled Mal some distance back from the car, and the two of them were huddled together in the cold night air, conversing. I rolled my window down, hoping to eavesdrop, but their voices were low and I couldn't make out what they were saying.

After a few minutes, Mal finally returned to the car and got in behind the wheel. "Ready to spread a little holiday cheer?" he said as he started the engine.

Though it seemed disrespectful, considering what we had just done, I was. After all, trying to find justice for the dead didn't mean the living couldn't be happy and celebrate once in a while.

Chapter 21

Just to be safe, Mal once again took a circuitous route back to the bar and looked for a tail. If there was one, he couldn't see it. As I went about removing the wig and makeup Isabel had applied, Mal and I discussed our trip to Forest Home Cemetery the next day.

"If anyone asks, we can say we're going to visit someone I know who's buried there," Mal said. "What time do you want to do it?"

"Why don't we plan to go around noon? That way I can get the bar open and running before we leave."

"Noon, it is."

I realized then that I had left my own coat at Isabel's house and would have to wear the one she'd given me for now. I hoped no one would notice that it wasn't the same coat I'd left in, and when we arrived back at the bar, I headed straight for my office to take it off. With that out of the way, I headed back out front, happy to see that everything appeared to be running smoothly.

Teddy was behind the bar with Billy, and I made my way over to the two of them, with Mal on my heels.

"How is my new protégé doing?" I asked, smiling at Teddy.

"I'm getting the hang of it," Teddy said.

"He's a natural," Billy said. "We had a couple of guys get into a squabble over a girl a bit ago, and it looked like the two of them were going to go at it. But as soon as Teddy walked over and asked them to leave, they did. One look at him and they were shaking in their boots."

"Solid work," I said to Teddy.

He shrugged and smiled. "I didn't have to do much. My size was enough."

Billy said, "The Capone Club members were asking when you were going to be back. They apparently have some news on this new case you're looking into."

"Good. I have some news for them, too."

"About that," Teddy said. "I did some asking around on that matter you mentioned to me last night."

I nodded, giving him an expectant look, and then he dashed my hopes.

"No one was aware of Tiffany Gallagher having any affairs of any sort after she and Ben started dating," he said.

I frowned with disappointment. "She must have been very secretive and careful, then. Because she had sex with someone other than Ben not long before she was killed."

"I did hear an interesting tidbit, though," Teddy went on. "Some of the folks who knew Tiff in her younger days said she disappeared from school during her senior year. When she came back, she told everyone that she was sent to a boarding school overseas to complete her education. There was a rumor going around that she had gotten pregnant and had gone somewhere to have the kid in secret, but no one knew of anyone who Tiffany was dating at the time."

"So there's no reason to believe the rumor," I said, not surprised that such juicy gossip was still in the minds of those with nothing better to do.

"I suppose not," Teddy said with a shrug, "but the rumor had more footing than some. It hung on for years. And Tiff's death resurrected it."

I had every intention of keeping my promise to Kelly Gallagher, so I said, "It's an interesting bit of gossip, but given that it happened more than six years ago, I doubt it has any relevance to the current situation. I'll keep it in mind, though." I gave Teddy a grateful smile. "Thanks for looking into it. Let me know if you hear anything else."

I turned to Billy. "Is Teddy here competent to man the bar for a bit? I'd like to talk to you in private for a few minutes."

"He's good to go," Billy said.

I led the way to my office, with Billy and Mal following. Once inside I told Billy what I needed, and we spent a few minutes making up a list.

"Not a problem," Billy said when we were done. "I'll get right on it. It's very sweet of you to do this."

"It's the least I can do," I said. "And one more thing." I handed him a folder. "Have Teddy fill out the employment paperwork in here tonight. He can shove it under my office door once it's done."

"Got it." Billy took the folder and the list and left the office.

Mal and I left right behind him and headed upstairs to the Capone Club. The usual group was there: Cora, Frank, Joe, Carter, Sam, Tad, Holly, and Alicia. Tyrese was there, too, along with Nick, both of them looking tired and sipping on cups of coffee. Also present were Stephen McGregor, the high school physics teacher, and Sonja West, the salon owner. And to my surprise, Clay Sanders was there. I hadn't expected him back until tomorrow.

"Hey, M and M," Carter greeted as we entered the room. M and M was the nickname Cora had given to Mal and me, and it had stuck with the group. "Where have you two been?"

"Out and about," I said vaguely. Then, to get the spotlight off of us, I said, "I hear you guys have something regarding the Middleton case."

"And we hear you have the same," Sam said. "How did the interview with Ben Middleton go?"

"It went well," I said, settling into an empty seat. Mal grabbed a chair and pulled it up beside me. "Ben Middleton seemed very sincere, and his story about what happened is believable."

"Did you ask him if he killed his wife?" Carter said.

"I did," I said with a nod. "He denied it, and he seemed to be telling the truth. He did lie to me once, about his and Tiffany's relationship, but he came clean as soon as I called him on it."

"So, I take it we're a go with the case, then?" Holly said.

"I think so, assuming all of you agree."

There was a series of nods around the room.

"Good. I have some other stuff to report, but first I want to hear what you guys have," I said.

Joe was the first one to speak. "Our friend Clay here got us some pictures of the inside of the Middleton car."

I blanched, wondering if the pictures included Tiffany's dead body, and remembering the horror of the car we'd just finished looking at. Cora must have read my mind.

"They show the blood evidence, but nothing else," she said.

Clay said, "I also brought a copy of the autopsy report on Tiffany."

"Anything of interest that we didn't know already?" I asked.

"Maybe," Cora said. "Our new friend Mr. McGregor here may have discovered something."

She slid some photos toward me, and I looked at them. They showed the front interior of a car, and there was a large bloodstain on the headrest on the passenger side, as well as a number of smaller spots that looked like blood scattered around the interior. These were circled in green, and the color made me think of the most recent letter.

Stephen McGregor explained. "If you look at the pattern of the blood in these photos, you can see an obvious void created by the victim's body. The void implies that she was sitting slightly sideways in the seat, with the right side of her back against the passenger door. The autopsy report says that the bullet entered the victim's head here." He pointed to a spot above his right eye. "And it came to rest in the back of her skull, on the left, meaning it crossed the midline."

I raised my hand, making him pause. "Ben said the gun fired twice. Where did the second bullet go?"

"It was embedded in the door on Tiffany's side of the car," Clay answered.

I nodded and signaled for Stephen to continue, which he did.

"For the bullet to have traveled the way it did, the

gun would have had to have been somewhere out in this area." He held a hand out in front of his face, waving it around in a small area. "Now, let's assume for a moment that Ben Middleton was alone and he made up the story about the carjacker. Look at this newspaper photo of Middleton during the trial, sitting at the table, pencil in hand. There's a tablet of paper in front of him, so presumably he was taking notes. Based on this, I think it's safe to assume that Middleton is right handed." Stephen got up from his chair and looked at Holly, who was seated nearby. "Holly, would you mind playing Tiffany this time?"

"Happy to," she said with a smile.

She rose from her seat, took the chair Stephen had just vacated, and assumed the position he'd said Tiffany was in. Stephen took her empty chair and set it beside her on her left, about a foot away. He sat facing forward in this chair, while Holly sat in hers with her head and body turned toward him.

"Imagine that I'm Ben Middleton," Stephen said. "I'm right handed, and I'm going to shoot my wife." He formed his right hand into a mock gun shape and aimed it at Holly's head. "In order for me to shoot her and have the bullet track the way it did, I'd have to have my hand out in front of me and bent backward." He demonstrated the position with his hand, which was obviously an awkward one, and then shifted his body. "As you can see, it doesn't work very well, even if I move in my seat and put my back against the driver's door." He dropped his right hand and made the mock gun with his left. "If I was left handed, it would make much more sense," he said, holding that hand out in front of him and aiming it toward Holly's head. "The angle might work then."

He straightened in his seat. "Now let's imagine there was a carjacker, and Middleton was struggling with the man, trying to wrestle the gun from him." He looked over at Carter. "Would you be our carjacker?"

Carter nodded, got up, and walked over to Stephen's left side, standing a foot or so away. Then he did the mock gun thing and thrust his hand toward Stephen's face.

"My first instinct," Stephen said, "would be to push the hand holding the gun or the gunman's arm away from my face." He did so, wrapping one hand around Carter's mock gun and grabbing Carter's wrist with the other. Then he pushed Carter's arm while Carter tried to bring the gun back toward Stephen's face. The two men struggled for several seconds, their arms waving about.

"As you can see," Stephen said, "this places the gun in roughly the same area it would have been in had Middleton been left handed. The carjacker would have been trying to aim the gun toward the back of the car, hoping to hit Ben. From this position, it would be easy for a bullet to track the way it did. Even if we consider a scenario where Middleton got out of the car with the window down and then leaned in to shoot Tiffany, the angles don't make sense if he's right handed."

Stephen relaxed his arms then and said thanks to Carter. Carter dropped his arms and went back to his seat. Stephen looked over at me with a smile. "So you see, the scenario that fits best with the evidence is exactly the one that Ben Middleton claimed."

"Unless Ben Middleton is ambidextrous," I said.

"Possible," Sam said, "but unlikely. Only one in one hundred people is truly ambidextrous, and the majority of them favor one hand over the other. Most often that's the right hand, a product of living in a right-handed world. And as we saw in the picture, Middleton writes with his right hand."

"So there *was* a third person there," I said.

Stephen nodded. "The physics suggest so, yes."

"Except there's a big fly in our ointment," Sam said with an apologetic smile. "Just because Ben didn't fire the bullet that killed Tiffany, it doesn't mean he didn't hire someone else to do it. And if that was the case, he was essentially telling the truth when he said he didn't kill her."

Mal leaned forward in his chair, frowning. "If he hired someone, there would be a money trail somewhere. Was there any mention during the trial of any unusual financial transactions?"

Clay shook his head. "They briefly covered the financials, because the prosecution was convinced money was behind Ben's motive. Tiffany had money in an account that Ben had no access to, and if there were any unusual transactions in that account, it wasn't mentioned. Ben's money all went into a joint account that both he and Tiffany were authorized to use. Occasionally, Tiffany would augment that account from her own funds, but everything that came out of that account was tracked and allocated to legitimate expenditures. The prosecution claimed that having his wife control the purse strings was what pushed Ben over the edge."

"Did Tiffany have sole discretion over her personal account?" I asked.

Clay shrugged. "I don't know. Why?"

"Just wondering if her parents had any control over what she spent."

Sam, not one to give in easily, said, "Just because there isn't any evidence that a shooter was paid doesn't mean one wasn't hired. Maybe Ben told whoever it was that they'd have to wait for the payment until things blew over and he got access to some of Tiff's money or the life insurance proceeds. Clearly, he wouldn't have been able to get at any of it, given how quickly he was arrested, but what's the shooter going to do? Complain that he wasn't paid for a murder? He wouldn't have much recourse."

Much as I hated to admit it, Sam had a point. But as I tried to visualize how it might have happened this way, the image kept falling into pieces like in a jigsaw puzzle where none of the edges matched up. "There are too many things that don't make sense," I said. "If Tiffany was the intended victim, why wouldn't the shooter go to her side of the car? Why risk reaching in and shooting her from the driver's side?"

"Maybe that's how Ben planned it, so that the car-jacker story would hold up," Sam suggested.

"But if he's that clever in his planning," I said, "why would he be stupid enough to buy the gun himself?"

There were lots of frowns and quizzical expressions in the room as everyone contemplated this question. No one came up with an answer.

"And the other thing that bothers me about this," I went on, "is why Tiffany didn't try to get out of the car and run. Why would she just sit there and not even shy away from it all? I asked Ben that question, and he said she had a history of panic attacks, but I would still think that having someone shove a gun in your face or your husband's face would make you want to get out of the way. And judging from the position she was in, in the car, she was shying away from something on the driver's side."

Several seconds of silence followed, and then Joe said, "Maybe she was drugged."

There were some tentative nods among the group, and then Mal said, "Or maybe we're looking at this all wrong. Consider this scenario. There's evidence that Tiffany was having an affair. Maybe the intended victim was Ben all along, and Tiffany was the master-mind. Maybe she wanted to get rid of him and didn't want to risk a nasty divorce, where she might have to share some of her money. Maybe the plan was for Ben to get out of the car when the carjacker demanded it and then get shot in the road. Then the carjacker could get into the car and drive off with Tiffany. Later she could say he took her at gunpoint and let her go at some point. In fact, if it was planned right, she could lay low some place and hide before going for help, giving the shooter a decent amount of time to get far away, ditch the car for a different one, and head for a hidey-hole and some future rendezvous."

It was an interesting theory, and when I flashed back on the dark, morbid nature of Tiffany's paint-ings, it wasn't hard to imagine her doing something like that.

Frank shook his head and said, "I don't see how this could have been a planned thing by either party. In order for a planned scenario to work, assuming it hap-pened the way Middleton said and some guy flagged them down, the planner would have needed a way to communicate with the shooter."

"Cell phone?" Holly suggested.

"According to Ben Middleton, there was no cell service where they were," I said.

"That's true," Clay said. "It was discussed at the trial, and again the prosecution twisted it around, saying that Ben planned it that way to make sure no one could come to Tiffany's aid."

"Except Middleton admitted that he drove into town earlier that day, and there was cell service available there," Mal pointed out. "He could have called someone then."

I frowned at this. "But he said they were planning to stay at the house at that point, so how would he have known they'd be on the road, headed home, later that day?"

"We're assuming Ben Middleton's version of the events is true," Mal offered. "Maybe it wasn't Tiffany who insisted they head home. Maybe it was Ben."

"I don't think so," I told the group. "I had a strong sense that Middleton was telling us the truth, and Tiffany's mother verified the fact that her daughter sometimes had episodes where she would get moody, withdrawn, and spooked. That fits with what Ben described."

"You talked to Tiffany's mother?" Frank said.

"I did. Clay was good enough to arrange a visit to their house earlier today, and I met the rest of the family, as well. But the only one I discussed the case with was Tiffany's mother, Kelly. She made it clear that Tiffany was a troubled young woman long before she met Middleton. And according to Middleton, Tiffany had been acting distant and withdrawn for months. She started sleeping in the guest room, she dropped the volunteer work she was doing at the animal shelter, and she didn't go out much."

"Maybe that was because she was having an affair," Holly suggested.

"Perhaps," I said, thinking. "Maybe we should try to talk to some of the folks at the animal shelter and see if Tiffany ever mentioned anything along those lines."

Sonja West perked up at that. "As luck would have it, a woman who volunteers at that same shelter is a regular client of mine. I know she worked with Tiffany, because she talked about her all the time back when the murder first happened. She comes in every other Monday for a mani-pedi, and shc's scheduled to come in tomorrow morning. I'll talk to her and see what she knows."

"That would be great," I said, once again amazed by and grateful for the diversity of this group. "One other thing I learned from Ben Middleton is that his father-in-law hired a private eye to dig up some info on him and tail him for several weeks." I looked over at Tyrese and Nick, both of whom had remained silent, listening. "Tyrese, Nick, any chance you guys would know who this was? Ben said he was quite distinctive looking—six-six, with a ruddy, pockmarked complexion and a large beaky nose."

"Doesn't ring a bell with me," Tyrese said. He grabbed a napkin, took a pen from his pocket, and scribbled down some notes.

Nick, his brow furrowed, said, "It sounds vaguely familiar to me, but I can't pull it out at the moment. Give me some time to think on it, and I'll ask around among some of the other guys, too."

"Thanks, guys," I said.

Nick beamed a smile back at me. "My pleasure," he said.

This generated a grunt from Tyrese, which I took to be his tired form of agreement.

I was about to switch the topic of conversation to Tiffany's morbidly dark artwork when someone new entered the room and everyone's attention shifted.

Chapter 22

"Ho, ho, ho!" Santa Claus bellowed from the doorway.

I looked over and smiled. The costume was perfect, with an authentic-looking wig, the red suit and black boots, an appropriately rounded belly, red, rosy cheeks, and sparkling brown eyes, which I recognized. Of course, I had the advantage of knowing ahead of time who Santa really was, but even so, it was hard to tell it was Duncan. He was carrying a big sack slung over one shoulder, and after entering the room, he set it down on the floor. Then he stood back, hands on his belly, and let out another string of ho-ho-hos, followed by a hearty "Merry Christmas!" His voice was well disguised, but even so, I experienced the rich chocolate taste that always came to me when I heard him speak. And I began to wonder if he had some theater background of his own, because the way he modulated and projected his voice hinted at some stage experience.

I watched with amusement as he unloaded a bunch of bottles of liquor, stuff I had agreed to donate to the cause. That was what Billy, Mal, and I had done in my office earlier, made a list of the drinks favored by everyone in the group. There was something for each person there: chardonnay for Cora, Kahlúa for Holly, gin for Carter, rum for Alicia, scotch for Tad, whiskey for Sam, vodka for Clay and Mal, brandy for Tyrese, and a six-pack each of assorted microbrewery beers for Joe and Frank. For the newcomers, I had to hope that what I had seen them drink so far was a favorite, and judging from the appreciative and somewhat surprised looks on their faces, I thought I got it right. Stephen McGregor got brandy, and Sonja West got a bottle of Amaretto.

I watched the group closely as Santa handed around the gifts. If anyone recognized that Santa was Duncan, they didn't let on. Since I hadn't known for sure who would be present, there were gifts for others in the group who weren't there at the moment: Tiny, whose work schedule had made him scarce lately; Dr. T; Tad; Kevin Baldwin; and Greg Nash, our Realtor newcomer. Duncan, aka Santa, set those gifts aside as he handed out the goodies. Then he tossed the extras back into the sack, wished everyone a happy holiday season, and left.

This was Mal's cue. With a mighty stretch and a faked yawn, he rose to his feet and said, "I'm wiped, so I think I better head home."

I rose, too—it would seem odd if I didn't escort him out of the room—and told the others I was going to call it a night, as well. Amid a chorus of good wishes, thank-yous, and good nights, we exited the Capone Club room and headed downstairs.

When we reached the main floor, we headed for the back hallway, down which was the door to my apartment. Anyone watching would assume we were headed upstairs, but also down that hallway were the bathrooms. When we were outside the men's room door, we did a quick check of the hallway to make sure no one saw us, and Mal ducked inside. I then went on to my apartment entrance and unlocked the door. With that done, I turned and hobbled back to the bar, where I made small talk with Billy and Teddy for several interminably long minutes.

Finally, I felt my cue—the vibration of my cell phone in my pants pocket, letting me know I had a text. I checked the message to make sure it was the one I was waiting for, and when I saw that it was, I excused myself and headed toward my apartment. Just as I reached the hallway, Santa emerged and hollered out, "Merry Christmas, everyone!" as he made his way to the front door. His exit was marked by a chorus of return greetings from the patrons and a series of toasts. Moments later Santa had left the building.

I crutched my way down the hall, and when I was outside of the men's bathroom, I looked to make sure no one was nearby. Then I knocked on the door three times. It whipped open so fast, it startled me, nearly making me lose my balance. Duncan dashed out, headed for my apartment door, and disappeared inside my apartment in a matter of seconds, leaving me behind in his dust.

We had managed the switch unnoticed, and as I headed for my apartment, I was feeling both happy and just a little bit smug. When I opened my apartment door and stepped into the small foyer, Duncan was waiting there. After I locked the door to ensure no surprise visits, he bent down and kissed me on the lips.

"I've missed you, Mack Dalton," he said in a low, husky voice that made me taste peppery chocolate.

"I saw you a little while ago," I said just before he kissed me again, longer this time.

"Not the same," he muttered against my lips.

We were both breathless when we finally parted, but Duncan clearly had some stamina left in him, because he swooped me off my feet and carried me up the stairs, one crutch jammed between me and his chest, the other banging on the stairs as he climbed them. I dropped the banging crutch as soon as we reached the top; the other one ended up in the bedroom with us.

And for the next hour or so, all my worries were cast aside.

Sometime later we were seated at my small kitchen table, eating cold chicken, cheese, and fruit, accompanied by a nice dry pinot. Duncan looked more relaxed and happy than I'd seen him in a long time. I was feeling pretty good myself, until he raised the topic that haunted me most.

"So where is this latest letter?"

I made a face, showing my disappointment.

"What? Did something happen to it?"

"No," I said, shaking my head. "It's not that. It's just that I was feeling so good about life . . . relaxed, happy, and content. And then you reminded me of my sword of Damocles."

"Sorry," he said, biting into a chunk of Gouda. "But I'm glad to know I left you feeling good for a little while at least." He flashed a wicked smile and winked at me.

"You left me feeling great," I said in a low, appreciative tone. "I guess I'm just disappointed that I couldn't bask in that glow a little longer."

"I can bring the glow back later if you like." As he said this, his eyes were dark as coals, like the entrance to a bottomless abyss, one I was more than willing to throw myself into.

"I *would* like," I said. Then, with a sigh, I got up from the table and headed into my father's office to fetch the letter and its contents.

"Here you go," I said when I returned, setting the letter, the aster, the weeping willow leaf, and the envelope on the table. All of them were inside the plastic Baggies we'd put them in earlier.

Duncan picked up the letter and read it through the Baggie, munching on some grapes as he did so. He frowned a little, scowled at one point, and then set the letter down.

Desperate to bring a little light into this cave of depression, I said, "Cora did some research on the recipients of the packages the letter writer sent, looking for any commonalities. She found one, though it might be a bit of a stretch. All the recipients have some connection to the university. Two of them are students, the art store guy carries books and supplies for many of the university art classes, and the spice shop lady sells her wares to several of the dorms and eateries on campus."

Duncan cocked his head to one side, looking contemplative. "Is that all she found?"

"So far, yes. But I was thinking about it earlier, and it might be a reasonable lead. Whoever delivered those packages had to have access to information about each of the recipients, things like addresses and schedules. And in the case of the art store and the spice shop, access to invoices would have supplied the necessary information. What if the letter writer is someone who works in a billing or financial capacity at the university? They would have access to financial records of the students, which I think would also give them access to their schedules and home addresses, maybe even their work history. And they would also know all the vendors that deal with the school on a regular basis."

Duncan considered this, and his expression lightened. "That's not a bad wrinkle," he said. "Definitely worth looking into. It will be interesting to see if your visit to the cemetery tomorrow turns up anything related to the university."

The reminder of tomorrow's agenda once again darkened my mood. A surge of anger swept through me, making me shudder. "When I get my hands on this damned letter writer, I'm going to . . . to . . . Argh!"

Duncan chuckled—not the reaction I was expecting. I gave him a curious look.

"Sorry," he said, swallowing whatever was in his mouth and taking a swig of wine to wash it down. "It's just that I love your spunk, your spirit. You have this fiery personality to go with your fiery hair."

"That's such a stereotype," I chastised.

"Most stereotypes exist because they have some basis in truth. Perhaps the genetic code for red hair is linked somehow to certain personality traits."

I opened my mouth to object, but he continued before I could get a word out.

"Or perhaps the way people treat those with red hair spurs those personality traits. Nurture or nature?" he said, his eyebrows raised, a smile on his face. He popped a grape in his mouth before he added, "Which do you think it is?"

"Neither," I said. "I think the whole stereotype is born out of a metaphor . . . red hair . . . fiery."

Duncan conceded the battle. "Fair enough. Let's switch topics. How did your visit with Ben Middleton go?"

Over the next hour I filled him in on the progress we'd made, some of the scenarios we'd tossed around, and where we were going next. He tried to poke holes in some of the theories I shared with him, but in the end he agreed Ben Middleton might be innocent. He admitted as much with a frown.

"Why do I sense that the prospect doesn't make you happy?" I asked him.

"Don't get me wrong," he said with a dismissive wave of his hand. "If the man is truly innocent, I'm all in favor of proving it and seeing that he goes free. But . . ."

I waited for him to finish, but all he did was deepen his frown.

"But it's not going to make me any friends down at the police station," I said, filling in words for him. "Is that what you're thinking?"

He nodded grimly. "Or with the DA's office. It won't make either of them look good if you discover they arrested and convicted an innocent man. The police in this country are under so much scrutiny these days as it is. Something like this is only going to reinforce the negative attitudes that seem so prevalent of late. It might have been better if you'd stuck to cold cases that haven't been solved yet. Figuring those out still makes the police look a tad incompetent, but not as bad as something like this will."

I knew he was right, but it didn't change my conviction to pursue the case, and I said so. "However," I noted, "maybe there's a way to do some damage control."

"How so?"

"If we can prove Ben Middleton is innocent, what if I go to the DA and your superiors, present them with the exonerating evidence, and then let them take the credit for looking into it? I'm more than willing to stay out of the limelight and let someone else have the glory."

Duncan shook his head and gave me a wistful look. "You're living in a fairy-tale land where morals and ethics rule, and good always wins out over evil. But that's naive thinking. There are a lot of politics involved here, and there are some folks who would rather see an innocent man rot in jail than risk their own reputation getting a smudge."

"That's horrible!"

"Perhaps, but that doesn't mean it isn't true."

His negativism irritated me. "Are you suggesting I let the case drop?"

"Not at all. I'm proud of you and what you're doing, Mack. But I'm also worried about you, about how you're going to hold up under all the fallout, and about how you'll deal with the inevitable disappointments and criticisms. There's bound to be some backlash, and I'm worried about how it might affect you."

"You should also worry about how it's going to affect you," I said. "You should probably distance yourself from me as much as possible."

"I can handle the flack," he said dismissively. "Don't worry about me. Besides, if you promise not to tell anyone where you heard it from, I'll tell you a little secret."

I was intrigued, and he knew it. I pantomimed locking my lips and tossing an imaginary key over my shoulder. Then I waited for what seemed like forever.

"The chief had a little chat with me about you," he said. "He's intrigued by what you've done, both with me and on your own, and he's interested in learning more about you. But that's his private view. Publicly, he needs to kowtow to the existing mayor and the DA to some extent, particularly since the mayor is up for reelection and reducing the crime rate is high on his political agenda. The chief is hoping to bring the mayor around at some point, but it's going to take some time, since they're still cleaning the egg off their faces from your past exploits."

I shook my head, dismayed. "This political crap is so annoying. Why can't people just say what they mean and be forthright and responsible? If you screw up, say so and apologize. All this media manipulation and the attempts to divert attention and shrug off the blame just make the public more suspicious. A little more honesty would be so refreshing."

"Honesty among politicians?" Duncan said, looking askance. "Surely you jest."

I sighed and blinked hard. "All this politicking talk is making me dizzy," I said, setting down my wineglass. "Or maybe it's the wine."

"Or maybe it's my awesome presence," Duncan said, only half sarcastic. "What do you say I take your mind off it all for a while?"

That made me smile, and without another word, I got up from my chair, grabbed my crutches, and headed for my bedroom. Duncan followed, and for the next several hours I was blissfully oblivious to the outside world and all the potential dangers, headaches, and pitfalls lurking within.

Chapter 23

Morning came all too soon. Duncan shook me awake around five, and I reluctantly let go of the idyllic dreamworld of my slumber.

"I need to leave while it's still dark," Duncan whispered in my ear. His breath was warm, his voice soothing, and the combination of the two made me taste sweet milk chocolate.

When I rolled over and blinked the sleep from my eyes, I was surprised to see that he was already dressed. He sat down on the bed beside me and brushed my hair back off my face. Then he kissed me.

"I wish I didn't have to go," he said.

"So do I." I threw back the covers, donned my robe, and then grabbed my crutches. I followed him out to the main area of the apartment, and from there down the stairs, a journey made in silence . . . if you didn't count the thumping of my crutches.

When we reached the bar's back hallway, he turned to me and said, "Are you still planning on going to the cemetery today?"

I nodded. "Mal is going with me."

"Good. I think," he said with a slightly troubled expression. "Be careful and call me if you need anything, okay?"

"I will."

He kissed me again, a little longer this time, and had the kiss lasted a second or two more, I don't think he would have made his escape in the dark. Not wanting him to see the disappointment on my face, I turned away and hobbled down the hall to my office, entered it, and disabled the back alley door alarm. I then headed back to the hallway, wondering if he would linger there until I returned for one last good-bye. But by the time I reached the hall, I could see the door closing and knew he was gone. My disappointment mounting, I went back into the office and turned the alarm back on.

I'd planned to return to bed, but by the time I hobbled back upstairs to my apartment, I knew that wasn't going to work. I felt wide awake and buzzed, so I made my way to the kitchen and fixed a pot of coffee. Then I dragged out my laptop, launched the browser, and read everything I could find about Forest Home Cemetery. It was a fascinating place, rich with Milwaukee history, and the pictures of the grounds I saw online depicted a serene and lovely place landscaped with magnificent old trees, a small lake, and a picturesque stone bridge. Of course, most of that would be barren, gone, or frozen for my visit today, since it was the dead of winter, and I felt a tug of disappointment. I spent some time reading up on the green burial process and the Prairie Rest section of the cemetery, which housed those who chose that form of interment. Though the topic was admittedly a bit morbid, I found the idea of our bodies being returned to the earth kind of refreshing and nice. A childhood ditty played in my head a few times—*the worms crawl in, the worms crawl out, the worms play pinochle on your snout*—and rather than being disturbed by it, I found it oddly humorous.

I became so absorbed in my research that the time passed by with startling speed. Before I knew it, it was time to shower, dress, and head downstairs to start prepping for my eleven o'clock opening. I abandoned the computer and headed for the shower after taping a plastic garbage bag over my cast. When I was done showering, I spent a good ten minutes debating what to wear, trying to decide what would be appropriate cemetery visitation garb and wondering if it really mattered. In the end I opted for black jeans, a turquoise sweater, and one sensible low-rider black boot. Over my casted foot I put on two pairs of my father's heavy black wool socks. After a quick fix to my hair, I headed downstairs just before ten thirty.

Debra and my daytime bartender, Pete, were already at the bar, setting things up, and my daytime cook, Jon, was in the kitchen. I crutched my way to the customer side of the bar, sidled onto a stool, and told Debra to pass me over some fruit, a cutting board, and a knife so I could help her with prepping the garnishments. She did so, and I went to work while she made coffee and helped Pete stock behind the bar.

The chopping duty was a monotonous task but one I typically enjoyed, because the mind-numbing tedium lessened my synesthetic reactions. I was intimately familiar with the sounds and sensations touched off by the citrus smell of the limes, lemons, and oranges, and I could easily suppress them. I'd been chopping this stuff on a daily basis for so many years that my hands functioned robotically, performing the necessary movements in a rote manner that was blissfully mindless.

With my mind thereby freed from outside distractions, I went back to pondering my visit to the cemetery. I was glad Mal was coming with me, but I also worried that having someone accompany me might, at some point, make the letter writer mad, assuming I was being watched. I'd dragged Mal along on my previous excursions, and since no mention of his presence had been made in the letters, I assumed that it was either considered okay or was not known by whoever was sending them. I knew it was risky to keep bringing Mal along, but I felt so much safer with him at my side, and I was willing to push the envelope a little more. Even as the envelope metaphor danced through my mind, I chuckled at how appropriate it was. I was so deep into my thoughts, it took me a few seconds to realize that Debra was talking to me.

"Mack? Are you in there?"

"Sorry," I said, looking at Debra with an apologetic smile. "My mind was wandering. What did you say?"

She made a pointed glance at her watch. "It's two minutes after eleven. Do you want me to unlock the front door?"

I blinked and glanced at the digital clock on the back wall of the bar and saw she was right. In front of me was a pile of cut-up fruit that would probably last through today and all of tomorrow. "I'll unlock it," I said.

I grabbed a nearby bar towel and wiped my hands the best I could; then I grabbed my crutches and headed for the door. When I got there, I saw Joe and Frank Signoriello coming up the walk—their arrival was never more than five minutes past my opening time—quickly threw the locks, and opened the door.

A frigid blast of cold morning air rushed in, and Joe and Frank tottered in behind it. Neither of them moved all that fast these days. They were fit men for their age, but they were both in their seventies, and the cold weather, combined with the ravages of Father Time, had stiffened their joints.

"Good morning, Mack," Joe said as the men shuffled their way to a table. Eventually, they would head upstairs to the Capone Club room, but for now they were content to rest from the several-block walk they'd already taken from their downtown apartment. "Perfect day for a couple of Irish coffees, I think. What do you say, Frank?"

"Sounds good to me. And I think we should have a couple of burgers to go with it."

"Coming right up," Debra said from behind the bar.

A moment later Cora came in, carrying her laptop. She greeted us all with a cheerful "Good morning!" and then headed for the Signoriello brothers' table.

"Your usual, Cora?" Debra asked.

"Yes, please. And I'll have one of Mack's famous BLTs, too, while I'm at it."

I settled into the fourth chair at the table and smiled at the trio. These three people were the closest thing I had to family these days. "What are you guys planning for today?"

Cora said, "I've been doing some searching on the Internet for Melanie Smithson, Tiffany's BFF. I've perused her social media and a few other sites and didn't come up with much."

She paused as Debra delivered the drinks and then

headed into the kitchen. After a glance at Pete, to make sure he wasn't eavesdropping on our conversation, Cora lowered her voice and leaned into the table. "I've also been searching to see if I can find any other commonalities among the recipients of the letter writer's packages. And I got nothing. They live in different neighborhoods, aren't from the same places, don't shop at the same stores or bank at the same banks . . . nothing. The only thing they all share in common is the university connection. I'm thinking that has to be it."

The Signoriello brothers weren't up to speed on this aspect of the investigation, so Cora and I quickly filled them in on Cora's theory, the contents of the latest letter, and my planned trip to Forest Home Cemetery later today.

When we were done, Frank said, "If that's the only thing they have in common, it makes sense to look into it. It might not lead to anything, but it would be dumb not to check it out."

"I agree," I said. "Keep looking, Cora, particularly at the financial office at the school. See if you can find any names that are familiar to us."

The front door opened, and Tad came in, bringing a blast of cold air and a few flakes of snow with him.

Frank shivered. "Got that fireplace upstairs fired up, Mack?" he asked.

"Not yet," I said, "but you guys can do it. Why don't you head up there, and I'll have Debra bring your food up when it's done."

Tad walked over to us, did the greeting thing, and asked if anyone was heading upstairs.

"We were just about to go there," Cora said, standing

and grabbing her laptop with one hand and her glass of chardonnay with the other.

The brothers got up, too, and followed Cora. Tad shucked his coat off and started to head upstairs with them, but I stopped him.

"Tad, I wonder if you might be able to help us out with something on this Middleton case."

"What?"

"Any chance you have financial info on the Gallagher family?"

"As a matter of fact, I do."

This made me happy, but I knew Tad was a conscientious businessman, and revealing private information about his clients was something he wouldn't do easily, if at all.

Hoping to appease his professional conscience, I said, "I don't need you to reveal any numbers to me, but I wonder if you might be able to look over things and let me know if you find any unusual transactions that occurred during the time that Tiffany and Ben were married, particularly right around the time of her death. I'm interested in Tiffany's money, of course, but also Colin Gallagher's. I'm mainly looking for any large chunks of money that might have been spent on some unknown cause. And I'd also like to know if Colin Gallagher had any control over Tiffany's purse strings."

Not surprisingly, Tad frowned at my request. "I can't betray my clients' trust by revealing private and personal information."

"I understand, and you don't need to give me specifics. Just let me know if you find any unusual transactions, and let me know the date they occurred and any other details you're comfortable revealing. Amounts would be helpful, but if you're not comfortable revealing that information, that's fine."

"Can you give me an idea of what specifically you're looking for?"

"Any monies that might have been a payment to a contract killer or used for an illegal gun purchase."

Tad considered what I'd said, his face a mask of consternation. "I'll take a look this afternoon, when I return to the office," he said finally. "If I find any unusual cash withdrawals, all I'll be able to give you is a date and an amount, and I'll give you that only if you promise not to reveal where the information came from."

"Not a problem."

His cell phone rang then, and when he glanced at it, he scowled. "It's Suzanne," he said with an impatient sigh. "She's really been on my case lately about all the time I'm spending in the office. I can only imagine how angry she'd be if she knew that half the time she thinks I'm in the office, I'm really here." He turned and walked off, answering the call with a cheery "Yes, dear. What do you need?"

The front door opened again, letting more of Old Man Winter inside, and I saw it was Mal. He walked over and hugged me, greeting me with a cheery "Good morning,"

Debra came out, carrying the food orders for the group upstairs, and I told her and Pete that Mal and I were heading out for a while. "I should be back in an hour or two," I told them.

To their credit, they didn't ask where we were going,

though I could tell from the look on Debra's face that she was curious.

After I donned my coat—I ended up wearing the same one I'd worn the night before on my excursion to the impound lot and made a mental note to get my own coat back—Mal and I headed out to go clue hunting in a cemetery.

Chapter 24

It was bitterly cold outside, and the air stung my exposed face. When we got to Mal's car, he started it up and turned the defroster on full blast. The windows were covered in a sheet of ice, but rather than scrape them, we sat in the car and let the warm air do its work.

"When we get there, let's stop in the office and ask about touring the grounds," I said as we huddled in the cold, waiting for the heat to warm us. "I know from their Web site that they welcome people who want to tour the grounds, but given the weather, we should probably come up with a reason for doing it. This isn't the time of year when many people visit the place for its aesthetic value. So I'm thinking I should ask about graves belonging to anyone with the last name Green. I can say I'm working on a family tree project or something like that. With any luck, that might be all we have to do to get a package handed over."

"And if that doesn't work?" Mal asked.

"Then we search. I think we should start with this Prairie Rest section, where the green burials are done. That's where the asters grow during the warmer weather."

My mention of the aster got me thinking. "You know, maybe we should have Cora look into the weeping willow leaf and the aster, which were included with the letter. It's wintertime. Where would someone find something like that during this time of the year?"

"Good question," Mal said, frowning thoughtfully.

I took out my cell phone, called Cora, and told her what we were thinking. When I was done, I disconnected the call and said to Mal, "Cora said asters are a common flower used by most florist shops, so that doesn't narrow things down much. She thought the leaf might be easier to follow up on, but it's still a long shot."

Mal nodded, his face still furrowed in thought. "What if our efforts today don't produce anything?"

I gave him a disheartened look. "Let's hope that doesn't happen. Because if it does, I don't know where to go next, and that means someone might die."

The windows had finally cleared enough to drive, and the interior climate was starting to feel survivable, so Mal pulled out and drove toward the cemetery, our last, morbid line of conversation hanging between us with a deadly, formidable weight. The roads were slick with patchy ice, and the traffic was crawling. Mal drove with great care and caution, my recent accident uppermost in both of our minds. When we arrived at the entrance to the cemetery, a shiver shook me. I wondered if it was the weather, the setting, or some combination of the two that had triggered it.

The transition from a bustling city street to a bucolic landscape was astonishing. Mal pulled into the

parking area near the office, and we headed inside
under an orange awning. The building had amazing
architectural details: stained-glass windows, wide var-
nished moldings, thick beams in the coffered ceiling,
and polished hardwood floors. The first room we entered had samples of headstones off to one side and
an empty counter straight ahead. There was another
room to our right, and there we saw a woman, who
looked to be in her late forties, sitting behind a desk.
She smiled at us as we approached—a smile that was
part greeting and part empathetic understanding. I
supposed that until she knew why we were there, she
needed this mixed message of an expression. A pin on
her blouse told us her name was Emma Cheevers.

"How may I be of service to you fine folks today?"
she asked.

"We'd like to explore the grounds," I said.

"I see," she said, her smile faltering a little. "Of
course, this isn't the best time of year to see our
grounds, but we still have many things I think you'll
find interesting." She slid a brochure across the
counter, and I took it. "Right here, next to the office,
is the Halls of History," she said, pointing off to the
right. "It's an indoor mausoleum that features a histor-
ical community education center on the lower level,
where you can learn about the history of Milwaukee
and how the cemetery ties into it. Many of Milwaukee's
most famous people are buried here, including politicians, beer barons, like Frederick Pabst and Joseph
Schlitz, newspaper publishers and editors, and many
of old Milwaukee's social elite.

"Across the road from the Halls of History is the
Landmark Chapel, an amazing Gothic structure built

using dark red sandstone from Lake Superior. Inside you'll find a peaceful environment that's ideal for quiet meditation, with leaded stained-glass windows and two large conservatories with decades-old tropical foliage."

I had the feeling Emma's rote spiel was going to continue nonstop if I didn't do something, so I jumped in and said, "I'm wondering if you have anyone buried here with the last name of Green? I'm doing one of those family tree things, and I'm looking for some lost relatives."

This request seemed to stymie her for a moment, but she recovered quickly after muttering, "Oh," and then "Um . . . ," and then "How nice." She shifted her focus from me to a computer and started tapping at the keys. "Oh, my," she said, giving me an apologetic look. "We have lots of Greens here. Is it Green with or without an *e* on the end?"

I had no idea, but I decided to keep it simple for now. "No *e*."

"That still leaves nearly sixty people. Can you give me some first names or dates?"

I couldn't, and there was no way we were going to visit sixty-some graves. So I tried a different tack. "I didn't realize there would be so many," I said. "I guess I'll need to do a little more homework. In the meantime, I've heard that you have an area called Prairie Rest that features . . . um . . . eco-friendly burials." On the heels of my inquiry about the name Green, I was hesitant to use the term *green burials*. "Can you show us where that is?"

"Certainly," she said, and she slid a booklet across

the counter. She opened it and folded out a map on the inside cover. Then she circled the area with a pen.

"Thank you," I said, taking the map. "I don't suppose anyone left or mailed a package to you to give to someone named Mackenzie Dalton."

The smile faltered again. "A package?" she said, looking bemused.

I could tell my question had made her wary, so I thought up a quick cover story. "I have an elderly cousin who has helped me with some of the family research, and she was supposed to mail me some documents. But I never got them. She knew I was coming here, and I just wondered if she might have mailed them here for some reason. She's a bit . . . eccentric." I gave her a vague smile.

"I see," Emma said, looking relieved. "No, I'm sorry, but we haven't received any packages addressed to anyone other than the people who work here."

"Okay. Thanks anyway."

We left and got back in the car, which thankfully had some remaining warmth, and after Mal started it up and turned up the fan, we consulted the map. Then we drove along narrow roads past snow-covered expanses filled with hundreds of grave markers, statues, and the occasional ostentatious mausoleum. We drove over a bridge that spanned a small frozen lake and eventually reached an open gate in the fence that surrounded the cemetery. Here we drove across a street and entered another section. Moments later we reached a cul-de-sac that bordered the Prairie Rest area. Mal parked the car, and we both got out and surveyed a large open field bordered on two sides by trees. About fifty feet across the field was a large wooden bench, and behind it was a collection of boulders. Negotiating the snow-covered terrain was a challenge for me, and Mal stuck close by my side. It was a good thing he did, because twice my crutches slipped on the snowy surface and I nearly fell.

When we reached the bench area, we saw that there were close to a hundred names carved into the flat surface of the two boulders in front—the names of those who were buried here. There were no other markers anywhere, and when I consulted the booklet Emma had given us, I read that the burial spots in this section could be located using GPS but were otherwise unmarked. I explained this to Mal, who was reading the names carved on one of the boulders.

"Any Greens there?" I asked him.

He shook his head.

Up a hill off to the right of the Prairie Rest area, the regular portion of the cemetery resumed. I scanned the gravestones, noting that some of them were decorated with Christmas wreaths, while others stood cold, empty, and barren. It was a sad sight either way, and I wondered about the families who had come out here to mark the graves of their loved ones, and about who was buried in the graves that had no adornments. A gust of wind came along, making me shiver, and I wished I could wrap my arms around myself in an effort to stay warm. I tried to envision the field filled with green grass and the deep blue of wild-growing asters, thinking that might warm me, but it didn't work. The bitter cold seeped through my coat and gloves, chapped my cheeks, and stung my eyes. My sock-covered foot felt like a block of ice.

I was about to suggest to Mal that we give up and

head back to the warmth of the car when he grabbed my arm and pointed. I looked where he indicated and saw it: on top of the hill, way off to the left, in front of the bordering oaks and maples, stood a huge weeping willow tree. Slowly, we made our way over to it, and when we were about twenty feet away, I stopped and said to Mal, "Look." To my right was a headstone, the closest one to the weeping willow. On it was carved the name Margaret Dunford Green, a birth date of August 21, 1993, and a death date of October 3, 2015.

"She was young when she died," I observed. "Only twenty-two."

Mal nodded but said nothing.

"So now what?" I asked him. "There's nothing here on her grave."

"Let's go have a closer look at the willow tree," he said.

I imagined the tree would look magnificent in the spring and summer. It was impressive even now, reaching at least forty feet into the air, the bare, pendulous branches hanging down like the tentacles beneath a jellyfish, swaying and dancing in the winter wind. At the center of this skeletal umbrella, the main trunk of the tree split off into five smaller trunks about five feet above the ground. This division created a platform of sorts, and something at the base of one of the subsections of trunk caught my eye. It was a tiny spark of light, the sun reflecting off of something metallic. I maneuvered closer and leaned in. There, tucked in behind that subsection of trunk, was a small metal box. It was the type often used to store cash or important documents, and for one dreadful moment, I was certain it would be locked. But it wasn't. Mal had seen it, too, and he reached up and took it down. It had a simple latch on it, and after Mal flipped it up, he opened the box. A small plain manila envelope was nestled inside. I started to take it out, but Mal stopped me.

"Most likely this envelope and box have been handled by the letter writer only, not by mail carriers or anonymous recipients like the others were," he said.

I got his point, but I was impatient to view the contents. Plus, we both had gloves on, so our prints wouldn't be on the box or its contents, and I felt certain the letter writer had been as careful with this delivery as with the others. I doubted we'd find any prints on any of it, but I knew Mal was right. On the off chance that the letter writer had slipped up this time, we had to be careful. I didn't want to jeopardize any chance we might have of figuring out who it was.

I nodded at Mal, though I did so with a frown of frustration, and he closed the box's lid and slipped the latch back down. Then he tucked the box under his arm, and we negotiated the snowy terrain back to the car.

Again, we sat for a while, letting the vehicle warm up. After a minute or so, I said, "I wonder if that Margaret Dunford Green has any connection to the university."

"Good question," Mal said. "I suppose we could Google the name."

"I have a better idea," I said, and then I shared it with him.

As we drove back to the office, I held the box in my lap, feeling the cold of the metal seep through my clothes to the skin below. The sensation triggered a brief aura, like a frost-rimmed window, around my field of vision.

Emma Cheevers looked a little surprised to see us again, but she quickly masked it, that ambiguous smile once again stamped on her face. "Done already?" she asked us.

"It's too cold to wander around much outside," I said, and she nodded, with an expression that suggested this should have been obvious to us from the get-go. "But I did run across a marker bordering the Prairie Rest area that I'd like more information about. It was for someone named Margaret Dunford Green. Can you tell me anything about her?"

"Let me see," she said, going back to her computer. She tapped away, and about thirty seconds later she said, "Ah, yes. Your Ms. Green is a relatively new guest here. She was interred last October." She paused and frowned. "A rather sad case, I'm afraid," she said next. "Ms. Green died at the age of twenty-two, the victim of a car accident."

"Does she have family in the area?" I didn't know if this particular grave had any significant meaning to the letter writer, but it was too much of a coincidence to ignore. I figured it was best to leave no stone unturned, both realistically and metaphorically speaking.

Emma tapped away again and a few seconds later said, "According to her obituary, she was from Colorado, and her only surviving relative was a great-aunt who lives in Florida. Her parents and a brother all predeceased her in a plane accident."

"That's odd," I said. "You'd think the aunt would have wanted to bury her closer to home and the other family members."

Emma shrugged. "Perhaps the area had some special meaning to Ms. Green. It does say in her obituary that she was a recent graduate from the U of Dub here in Milwaukee."

My heart skipped a beat. *There it is,* I thought. *A connection to the university.* Surely, it wasn't a coincidence.

"Perhaps so," I said. Then, eager to get back to the bar and examine the contents of the metal box, I added, "Thank you for your help."

With that, I turned and left the office as fast as my crutches could take me, with Mal close on my heels.

Chapter 25

I thought about calling Duncan right away but decided to wait until we got back to my apartment. I hoped we could get Cora to arrange another video-conference. When we arrived back at the bar, Mal parked, got out, and headed for the trunk. He was at my car door a moment later, holding an empty brown shopping bag.

"Slip the box in here," he said. "That way it won't attract any undue attention."

I did as he said, and he carried the bag as we walked the half block to the bar. As soon as we were inside, we headed straight to my apartment. I didn't bother to stop and chat with the staff or remove my coat. Once we were upstairs, with the door safely locked behind us, Mal took the metal box out of the bag and set it on my dining-room table.

I shucked off my coat and took a moment to catch my breath, staring at the box, wondering what sort of message the letter writer had for me this time.

"Coffee?" Mal asked.

I nodded, and he headed into my kitchen. I took out my cell phone and called Cora.

"Hey. What's up?" she answered.

"Mal and I are upstairs, in my apartment. Are you still here at the bar?"

"Where else would I be?"

"Can you come up here with your laptop? We struck gold at the cemetery."

"I'll be right there."

I disconnected the call and had Mal go downstairs to unlock the apartment door to let her in. It didn't take long. Despite having to excuse herself from the Capone Club group, negotiate the stairs, and then cross the entire length of the bar, Cora made it to my apartment in under three minutes. She practically ran up the stairs.

"I'm so glad the cemetery thing panned out," she said when she reached the top, Mal right behind her. "Was it awful?"

"To be honest, it's a nice place, for a cemetery. I think I'd like to go back in the summertime, when all the trees are in bloom. It was quite peaceful and serene. I imagine it's even more so when everything is growing and green."

Cora blinked several times very fast and stared at me like she thought I was crazy. Then she shrugged it off, set her laptop on the dining-room table, and said, "What did you find?"

I pointed at the metal box. "We opened it and saw an envelope inside but didn't take it out or open it, in case it contains any evidence. I was wondering if you could try to get Duncan on your computer using that video chat thing so he can watch us open it."

"Can do," she said. "Let me try to raise him."

She opened the laptop and started typing. While she did that, I went into the kitchen to grab some Baggies to use for evidence and then went into my father's office to get a sheet of plain white paper. I knew the drill by now.

"Duncan isn't responding," Cora said. "Can you call him and see if he can get to his computer?"

I nodded, took out my cell phone, and dialed his number. He answered on the third ring.

"Mack, is everything okay?"

"I'm fine," I told him. "We found something at the cemetery. Mal and Cora are here with me. Cora was trying to videoconference with you so we can open it."

"I'm not at the station," he said. "At the moment I'm in my car. Can you hold off for a bit? If you can give me a couple of hours, I can be there at the bar and open it with you."

I didn't want to wait, but I also didn't want to screw up any evidence that might be in or on the box. Given the deadlines imposed on me in the previous letters, I didn't think a couple of hours would make much difference. And the thought of getting to see Duncan would make the waiting a little easier.

"Okay. How do you want to sneak in this time?"

"Meet me at the back alley door at five."

"You got it. See you then."

I disconnected the call and filled Cora and Mal in on the plan. Cora eyed the box on the table the way a starving child might eye a sandwich.

"We have to wait?" she moaned.

I nodded, sympathetic to her angst. To distract her, I filled her in on the details of the person whose grave had been closest to the tree that had held the metal box. "It looks like you might be onto something with this university connection," I told her, and she seemed both pleased and placated for the moment. "We can kill some time by looking into this Margaret Dunford Green's background."

"And we can work on the Middleton case," she said. "Sandra Middleton dropped by and said she talked with Christine, Ben's lawyer. In fact, she was still upstairs in the Capone Club room when I came up here. She said Christine can put us in touch with the guy who supposedly sold Ben the gun used to kill Tiffany. The group thought it might be helpful if you had a chat with him, to see if he's telling the truth about the incident."

"That's a great idea," I said, nodding and thinking. "Any idea when she wants to do this?"

"I think she needs to know when you can do it, and then she'll set it up. Sandra also said that her parents are willing to talk to you if you want."

I thought about it and shook my head. "Maybe later. I'm not sure what good it will do at this point. I'd rather use my time talking to people who are more directly involved."

For the next half hour, we sat at the table while Cora dug up what she could find on Margaret Dunford Green. She found the obituary that Emma had consulted, and verified that Ms. Green's parents and brother had died in a plane crash. Cora dug up a news article on the crash, and it helped answer the question of why the great-aunt had opted to bury Margaret in Milwaukee. The plane carrying the rest of the Green family had burst into flames after hitting the side of a mountain. The occupants had to be identified through DNA extracted from bits of bone and teeth. There was nothing left of them to bury. It saddened me to think that this young woman, with her entire life ahead of her and a devastating past behind her, had come to such an untimely—and lonely—end. Then I realized that her life circumstances hadn't been that much different from mine. It was a sobering thought.

Cora found some of Margaret Green's social media entries, and I was happy to hear that hundreds of friends and classmates had posted on an Internet memorial page erected in her memory. As was the case with me, Margaret Green's family consisted of the people who were closest to her and a regular part of her life. She hadn't been alone, and she wouldn't be forgotten.

I hoped I would be so lucky.

Chapter 26

Once Cora had exhausted her research on Margaret Green, the three of us headed down to the bar and up to the Capone Club room. Thanks to the upcoming holiday, the bar was doing a brisk business, but the Capone Club room was surprisingly empty. It was mid-afternoon, and the lunch crowd regulars had all returned to work. That meant that Holly and Alicia were at the bank, Tad was in his office, Sam was doing a shift with his psych internship, and Clay was off doing whatever Clay did. Frank and Joe were present; since they were retired, the two men were practically fixtures at this point, always hugging up next to the fireplace. Nick was sitting off to one side, once again sipping what looked like plain old coffee, a scowl on his face. Carter was there, too. He'd cut back significantly on his waiter job hours recently so he could focus more on his writing. And, of course, Cora was with me. She, like the Signoriello brothers, was practically a permanent fixture these days.

Also present were Sonja West, Greg Nash, and

Sandra Middleton. Sandra was chatting with Carter when we walked in, while the others listened in. Whatever they were discussing was dropped as soon as we entered the room.

"Hey, Mack," the brothers said almost simultaneously.

The others all nodded at me, except for Sandra Middleton. She turned an eager, hopeful eye on me and rose out of her chair.

"Ms. Dalton," she said, "thank you so much for looking into my brother's case."

"No need to thank me," I said. "And please call me Mack."

Sandra nodded, still staring at me with that eager expression, like a dog waiting for a treat.

"I understand you can arrange for me to meet with this Harrington fellow who supposedly sold your brother the gun that was used to kill Tiffany," I remarked.

"Yes," she said, but her expression turned a bit more tentative. "Well, sort of. I can tell you how to find him, but if he knows why you want to talk to him, I doubt he'll say anything. I know because I've tried. If you can figure out a way to get him talking without him thinking you're connected to the case in any way, I'm sure you can get him to tell you what happened, or at least his version of what happened."

I frowned at this. From what Cora had said, I'd thought the man was going to be a willing participant. "Any idea how I'm supposed to broach the subject without making him suspicious?"

"He frequents a bar on the south side of the city. A friend of mine has a brother who works there, and he says John Harrington comes in there every day and talks about the trial, telling anyone who will listen how he helped crack the case." She shook her head in disgust. "Anyway, if you were to visit that bar when he was there, sit close enough to him, and start discussing the case, I'm betting he'd jump right in."

Her plan wasn't a bad one, sort of a surreptitious questioning of the man. It might be enough for me to tell if he was being honest about his version of the events, but getting any additional info out of him if I felt he was lying would be another story. Still, I figured there was little to lose in trying.

"Okay," I said.

Sandra clapped her hands together. "Great! Let me make some calls and see if he's at the bar now." With that, she got up and left the room, cell phone in hand.

Frank said, "Mack, Sonja has something to tell you."

I looked over at the woman and smiled. "What did you find out?"

"Like I told you guys last night, my client who came in this morning used to work with Tiffany at the animal shelter. So I brought up the subject and asked her if Tiffany had ever intimated that she was having an affair. She said no, and she also said that Tiffany was a very quiet, private kind of person. But Tiffany did share a story with this woman a couple of years back, after Tiffany arrived at the shelter one day all teary-eyed and sad. When my client asked Tiffany what was wrong, Tiffany told her that her dog had died. She said her father shot the dog because it had bit Tiffany's brother Rory. Apparently, it was a bad bite, and afterward, the dog got overly protective of Tiffany, growling at anyone who came near her, including all the family members. So her father put the animal down."

I reflected back on Rory Gallagher and his quiet, pensive demeanor, the way he had watched me from beneath hooded eyes, as if he was trying to hide something. I wondered if he had done something to the dog to make it bite him.

"Interesting story," Mal observed, "but I don't see how it impacts our case."

Sandra Middleton came back into the room then, her face flushed with excitement. "Harrington is at the bar now," she told us. "Any chance you can head over there?"

I didn't see why not. I still had time to kill before Duncan would arrive. "Sure," I said.

Sandra clapped her hands like she had before. "Great! He's easy to recognize because he always wears a Brewers baseball cap and he has a large scar on his left cheek, a half-moon-shaped thing."

I looked at Carter and said, "Want to come along? Your book would be the perfect cover story for our conversation."

"I'd love to." He got up from his table, flung on his coat, and grabbed his laptop, almost as ubiquitous an item for him as it was for Cora.

I leaned over and whispered in Mal's ear. "Do you mind waiting here, in case I get hung up and can't get back in time?" I didn't elaborate on what it was I had to get back for, knowing Mal would figure it out.

"No problem," he said.

"Thanks. And see if you can find out anything more about this dog story. Maybe Ben Middleton's lawyer can call him and ask him if Tiffany ever mentioned it."

Mal nodded.

Sandra then told us the name of the bar. I knew it and the owner—a cranky old guy in his sixties—and realized my familiarity with the place and the man could be a problem. I said as much to Carter. "Given all the publicity I've gotten lately, if this Harrington guy figures out who I am, he might clam up."

"Maybe the bar owner won't recognize you," Carter said. "Do you have a knit cap of some sort that you can wear to cover your hair? It's your most distinctive feature."

"I do, but I don't know if that will be enough."

"Even if it's not, I don't think it will be a problem," he said. "If this Harrington guy is as much of a publicity hound as Sandra says, he won't be able to resist puffing himself up and making himself the center of attention. I know the type well."

I didn't know if he was right, but since I had no better plan, I shrugged my acquiescence. Carter said he would get his car and pick me up out front. After stopping long enough to tell Debra and Pete that I was heading out again and that it would be okay to let Mal into my office if he asked, I went upstairs to my apartment. There I found a blue wool scarf and a matching knit hat that sufficiently hid my hair. By the time I made it back downstairs and out the front door, Carter was waiting for me.

"Think it's good enough?" I said, patting my hat once I had settled in the car.

He smiled and nodded. "But to be safe, I'm thinking we should come up with a different name for you. If I refer to you as Mackenzie or Mack, it might clue Harrington or the bar owner in to who you are."

I thought about it a moment, deciding that on this occasion an alternate name might be smart, since the bar owner knew me. "How about Rachel?" I said finally. "It was my mother's name."

"Works for me," Carter said.

The bar was twenty minutes away, and during the drive, Carter and I chatted about how we would play it once we got there. He dropped me off in front of the place, and I waited, propped up on my crutches, by the front door until he could find a parking spot and join me.

It took a few seconds for my eyes to adjust to the darkness inside the bar after the bright snow-lit day outside. As soon as they did, I noticed two things. One, the bar was nearly empty, with only a handful of patrons besides us. The location was one that didn't have the advantage of the holiday shopper traffic. Two, I saw that Sandra Middleton was right. Harrington was easy to recognize by his ball cap and the half-moon-shaped scar on his cheek. Unfortunately, he was seated at the bar, and manning that bar was Oskar Weber, the owner. I tugged my hat down low on my forehead and kept my face down as I followed Carter in.

He made his way to a table not far from where Harrington sat, and I followed and took a chair that put my back to the bar. As I shrugged off my coat and felt along the edges of my hat to make sure my hair was securely tucked inside, Carter asked me what I wanted to drink. I decided to take a cue from the Signoriello brothers and go for an Irish coffee. I reached into my pocket for my wallet, but Carter waved the gesture away.

"Let me treat you for once," he said.

I listened as he walked up to the bar and placed the order with Oskar.

"Coming right up." I knew the voice belonged to Oskar, because I'd heard—and tasted—it before. He had a deep, gravelly voice that made my mouth burst with a taste like salty popcorn.

Silence followed, and it took all my willpower not to turn around to see what was happening.

Finally, I heard Oskar say, "What brings you out on a cold day like today?"

"Doing a little research," Carter said, and I gave Oskar a mental kiss for providing us with the perfect opening. "I'm a writer, true crime stuff."

"Oh, yeah?" Oskar said. "Good for you."

Another brief silence followed, and I wondered why Carter wasn't offering up more information, like the fact that he was working on the Middleton case.

Then I heard a different male voice say, "What kind of true crime stuff are you working on? I know a little bit about a big one that you might be interested in."

Judging from the fact that the voice came from directly behind me and tasted like a marshmallow, I guessed that it was Harrington who asked the question. I realized then that Carter had been smart to wait and play it cool. His judgment of Harrington was correct. The guy was a publicity hound who couldn't resist a chance to interject himself into the topic of conversation.

Before Carter could respond, Oskar scoffed a laugh and said, "Yeah, John here fancies himself as some sort of antihero. He thinks he brought down one of Milwaukee's most infamous all by himself."

"How's that?" Carter asked.

"I'm sure you've heard of that Ben Middleton guy," Harrington said in a self-important voice that had me envisioning him puffing out his chest. "You know, the one who offed his rich wife and tried to make like it was a carjacking?"

"Of course," Carter said. "But that kind of story is as old as the hills. One spouse kills off another for money.

I'm looking for the kind of stories that are a bit more off the beaten path or for something with a big twist."

I wanted to turn around and give Carter a chastising look, convinced he was blowing our opportunity. Several more seconds of pensive silence ticked by while I steamed with impatience.

Then Harrington said, "What if there was a twist to the Middleton story?"

I could barely breathe as I waited to hear Carter's response. "What kind of twist?" he asked finally.

"Buy me a drink and I'll tell you," Harrington said cagily.

I heard a little *tsk*, which I was fairly certain came from Oskar, followed by the sound of drinks being slid across the bar.

"Okay," Carter said with a hint of suspicion in his voice. "I'll buy one for my new friend here, too."

Oskar mumbled, "You're wasting your money."

"Well, if nothing else, maybe I can get a plot idea for a novel out of it," Carter said cheerfully. The sound of another drink sliding followed.

Then Oskar said, "That'll be eleven-fifty."

I listened as Carter handed over his money, said, "Keep a fin for yourself," and then got his change. "What's your name?" Carter asked.

"John. John Harrington." He said his full name with a voice laced with innuendo. Clearly, he thought it would mean something to Carter.

"Well, John Harrington, why don't you come over to my table and tell me about your twist."

Harrington needed no more encouragement. Seconds later he was settling into the chair on my right with his drink, and I got my first good look at him. He was rail thin, buggy-eyed, and had long, shaggy brown hair. His nose looked like it had been broken a time or two, and his fingernails had dirt caked beneath them. He reeked of booze. He took a big swig of his drink—the smell and the subsequent sound I heard told me it was scotch on the rocks—before setting his glass on the table. He looked at me and narrowed his eyes. "You look familiar," he said, scrutinizing my face. "Do I know you?"

Before I could answer, Carter said, "This is Rachel, my assistant." He set my Irish coffee down in front of me and put his own drink, a screwdriver, in front of his seat. Then he slid his laptop across the table toward me. "She keeps my notes." Carter was good at distracting Harrington, because he quickly followed this with, "So tell me your story, Mr. John Harrington."

I opened the laptop, turned it on, and launched the word processing software that was on it as Harrington said, "Don't you recognize my name?"

Carter squinted and slowly shook his head. "Can't say that I do."

"I was the key witness in that Middleton case. I testified to the fact that I was the guy who sold Ben Middleton the gun he used."

Carter gave him a skeptical look. "Can't say I followed that case all that closely," he said. "But if what you're telling me is true, why aren't you in jail?"

"DA worked me a deal," he said. "No time and the charges dismissed if I told my story."

Carter nodded thoughtfully. "And what is that story?"

"That a guy I know told me about some rich man who wanted to buy a gun that couldn't be traced."

I typed as Harrington spoke, but what came out on the screen was gibberish, because I was busy focusing on the taste triggered by his voice rather than the keys. So far it hadn't changed.

"And you're saying you sold this man that gun?"

"I did."

"Where did you get the gun?"

Harrington shrugged. "If you know the right kind of people, it's easy to come by." There was a pompous, swaggering tone to his voice and a matching expression on his face. But the marshmallow taste didn't change.

"And you sold this gun to Ben Middleton?"

Harrington hesitated, leaned forward, and looked around. "Maybe," he said in a low voice. With this, the marshmallow flavor of his voice got a bit toasty.

Carter looked over at me with a tired expression. "I don't have time for games, Mr. Harrington. Like I told you before, I'm interested in stories that have some kind of punch or twist to them. Not some crackpot who might have told a lie to the cops to get some attention."

Harrington reared back, clearly offended. "I'm not some crackpot," he said. "I supplied the gun that was used in that crime."

We were back to plain old marshmallow, so I suspected this much was the truth. I was dying to ask Harrington again who he had sold it to, but I bit my lip. So far Carter was handling the man well, playing him like a fine-tuned instrument.

Carter stared at Harrington, who grabbed his drink and took another big gulp, draining the glass of all but the ice cubes. Apparently, he was trying to muster up his courage, because after setting down the empty glass, he looked around the bar, leaned in again, and said, "Being a writer and all, you're like reporters, right? You have to keep your sources confidential?"

"Sure," Carter said, and the taste of his voice changed, telling me this was a lie.

Harrington looked around again and lowered his voice even more. "Because if it gets out that I lied to the prosecutor, they'll send me to jail. There won't be no deal this time."

"Are you saying that your testimony in the case wasn't the truth?" Carter asked in an equally low voice.

"I sold someone that gun, all right," Harrington said. "But it wasn't Ben Middleton I sold it to."

The marshmallow taste didn't change. I barely dared to breathe, lest I upset the momentum Carter had going with the man.

"Who did you sell it to?" Carter asked.

"I don't know who the guy was," Harrington said, and both Carter and I let out exasperated breaths. "But I might recognize him if I saw him again," he added quickly, sensing our frustration.

Carter's lips narrowed to a thin white line. "Give me a verbal description."

Harrington looked toward the ceiling for a moment, then back at Carter. "My memory would probably work better if I had a little more of something to drink," he said slyly.

Carter shot me a look, and I shook my head. I knew from past experience that alcohol could tinge the subtle changes in a person's voice to the point where their lies became undetectable. Carter looked at Harrington and said, "You give me the description first, and then I'll get you the drink."

Harrington weighed the offer for all of two seconds. "Okay. Fine."

"Hold on a sec," Carter said.

He got up from his chair and approached the bar. Behind me I heard Oskar ask him if he wanted another round. "Not yet," Carter said. "I'm wondering if you could give me a piece of paper, something plain and white, like from a printer."

"I suppose," Oskar said with a world-weary sigh. Then I heard him walk away, muttering something under his breath. He returned a minute later and said, "Here you go."

Carter returned to the table, set the paper down in front of him, and took a pencil from his shirt pocket. "I'm going to try to draw this guy from your description," he said to Harrington. "Pay attention and tell me what looks right and what looks wrong. Let's start with what you can recall of the man's facial features. What shape was his face?"

Harrington looked intrigued. I didn't know if I looked intrigued, too, but I was. I had no idea Carter had any artistic talents.

"His face was kind of long and narrow," Harrington began. "He was a tall dude, tall and kind of lanky, you know?"

Carter quickly sketched the vague outline of a long, narrow face and said, "Describe his eyes for me."

"They were blue," Harrington said without hesitation. "And he had blond lashes and eyebrows. Heavy eyebrows."

Harrington and I both watched as Carter drew in two eyes and added some lashes and brows. "I assume his hair was blond?" Carter asked as he drew.

"What I could see of it was," Harrington said. "He had a long piece that hung down over his right eye. Other than that I don't know, because he was wearing a knit cap." He paused and looked over at me. "Kinda like what she's wearing, but his was black."

"Good, good," Carter muttered as he sketched away. He added the shock of hair and then sketched in the outline of a cap. "What about his nose? Was it big? Small? Wide? Narrow? Long? Pudgy? Upturned?"

Harrington looked up at the ceiling for a second. "It was long and narrow. But it was a bit hawkish, stuck out quite a bit." He demonstrated what he meant by outlining the nose in front of his own with his hand. Carter continued drawing, and for a bit, Harrington just watched.

"Any facial hair?" Carter asked after he finished the nose.

Harrington grimaced. "Don't know, because he was wearing a scarf wrapped around his lower face, like one of them muffler things, you know?"

"So you didn't see his mouth or chin?"

"That's right."

Carter drew in the scarf and added a few shading details. He then turned the picture around to Harrington. "How does this look?"

"That's good, real good . . . but not quite right." He pulled at his chin and studied the drawing. "His eyes were closer together."

Carter erased and redrew the eyes and eyebrows.

"That's it," Harrington said. "That's the guy."

Carter smiled. So did I, impressed with this newly discovered talent of his. Carter set the pencil down and slid the picture toward me. I studied it, saving it in my memory. Something about it seemed vaguely familiar and made me feel a sensation like cold water running over my feet.

"What was the guy wearing?" Carter asked.

"He was dressed kind of fancy," Harrington said. "Oh, he tried to hide it by wearing faded jeans and a ratty-looking old parka, but it didn't fool me. He forgot about his hands and feet. His boots were leather, expensive stuff, you know? And so were his gloves. I got a good eye for details like that."

Carter nodded. "Anything else you can recall?"

Harrington thought for a moment and then shook his head.

"Thanks, man," Carter said. "You've been a big help." Carter took out his wallet, removed a twenty, and handed it to Harrington.

Harrington's face lit up, but it didn't last. "You aren't going to tell anyone that I lied, are you?"

Carter gave Harrington an appraising look, which made the man squirm in his seat. "Your lie got an innocent man convicted," he said finally. "Doesn't that bother you?"

Harrington shrugged. "Who says the guy is innocent? Just because he didn't buy the gun doesn't mean he wasn't the one who used it."

"But it's looking like he wasn't," I said, irritated with the man. "Ben Middleton may well be innocent."

Harrington regarded me with an amused expression. "And just how do you know that?"

I stared back at him and didn't answer.

It took several seconds before dawning kicked in with him. "Wait a minute," he said. He looked over at Carter. "I thought you said you didn't know nothing about this case. If that's true, why would she say something like that?"

Carter smiled, but it wasn't a particularly friendly smile. "We might have lied a bit," he said.

Harrington clearly didn't like this. He got up from

his chair and stepped back from the table. "Everything I just told you was a lie," he said, and the taste of his voice changed instantly, taking on a blackened, burnt marshmallow flavor. "I made it all up."

"Did you?" I said. "And the picture? Was anything you told us about that true?"

Harrington's mental wheels turned surprisingly fast. "Made it all up," he said in a clipped tone. But that burnt taste remained. "Are you guys cops or something?"

Carter shook his head. "We're just interested parties who don't want to see an innocent man rotting in jail."

"You can't know the guy is innocent," Harrington said again, and the burnt taste disappeared. Clearly, he believed Ben Middleton was guilty, most likely because that was the only way he could justify his lies to himself.

"He might be," I said. Harrington looked like he was about to turn and run out the front door. The last thing I wanted was for him to disappear. We might need his testimony down the road, though I had doubts as to whether or not he'd be willing to give it and incriminate himself. So I tried to reassure him. "We have other evidence that suggests he might be innocent," I said. "So you can relax. We don't need your statement. We just wanted your help in verifying what we already suspected so we can get a lead on the real killer."

Harrington weighed this for several seconds, looking back and forth between me and Carter.

"Can I ask you one more question, Mr. Harrington?" I said. I was fairly certain he was done cooperating with us, but figured it couldn't hurt to try. I didn't give him time to answer. "How much did the man in the picture pay you for the gun?"

He stared at me for several seconds and then said, "Five hundred." His voice tasted all burnt again.

"That's a lie," I said with a smile and saw Harrington's eyes widen. "It was more than that, wasn't it? You can tell us. We're not going to turn you in to the IRS or anything." He didn't look convinced, so I upped the ante. "If you don't tell us the truth, we *will* turn you in to the cops."

Harrington ran a nervous hand through his shaggy hair. "Fine," he said irritably. "It was a grand. And the guy handed me a photo and told me that if anyone questioned me about the gun, I was supposed to say that the man in the picture was the one who bought it. He said if it came to that and I did what he said, he'd pay me another grand."

That piqued Carter's interest. "How was he going to pay you?"

"Hell if I know," Harrington grumbled. "I ain't seen it, and I ain't seen the guy again, neither. That's one reason why I decided to tell the truth. He told me he'd find me after the deed was done, but he never did." He let out a little puff of disgust. "That guy . . . ," he said, pointing to the picture, "went back on his deal, so I figure my end of the bargain is done, too."

The plain marshmallow taste flavored everything he'd just said, so I believed him. I looked over at Carter and said, "I think we have enough."

He nodded, and the two of us shrugged back into our coats in preparation for leaving. Harrington watched us with a wary eye.

"You sure you aren't going to turn me in?" he said.

I looked at him hard. "Not if we don't have to," I said finally. "But I hope this has been a lesson for you."

"Yes, ma'am, it has been," he said, suddenly all

polite. "I really didn't think I was doing anything wrong." This last statement was flavored with burnt marshmallow.

I grabbed my crutches and got up from my chair, shooting Harrington a look of skepticism. Carter folded his drawing and tucked it into an inside pocket of his coat. Then he grabbed the laptop.

"Good day, Mr. Harrington," he said as we took our leave.

Despite the reassurances we'd given him, I had a strong feeling John Harrington would disappear, just in case we reneged on our promise. Hopefully, with the information he'd just provided, we'd be able to find the proof we needed some other way.

Chapter 27

"I had no idea you could draw like that, Carter," I said once we were outside.

He shrugged. "I got myself through college by drawing portraits of people. At one time I thought I might try to make a living with my art, but I'm not very good at coming up with anything original. And my writing muse sang a more alluring song."

"You could get a job as a police sketch artist," I said. "I'm sure it has to pay more than waiting tables."

"I looked into it, but the demand isn't as great as you'd think, especially these days, when everything seems to be caught on camera and done with computers. Neither is the pay." We had reached the end of the block, and he nodded to our right. "The car is just another block over. Want to wait while I get it, or can you make it okay?"

"I'm good," I said. "As long as I take it slow. The sidewalks here are relatively clear."

He nodded, and we waited for the light to change so we could cross the street.

"I have to say, I'm impressed by all your hidden talents," I said as we stood there.

"*All* my hidden talents?" Carter said with a quizzical smile.

"The way you handled Harrington back there. I thought you were blowing it a couple of times, but you psyched him out perfectly. You played the man right into our hands."

"Oh, that," he said. The light changed, and we headed across the street. "You can thank Sam for that. I've picked up a lot of psych stuff helping him study over the years." His mention of Sam reminded me of Tiffany's paintings. I wanted to chat with Sam to see what he thought about them. "What was your take on the stuff Harrington told us?" Carter asked.

"I think he was telling us the truth. I picked up on the lie about the money because it made the flavor of his voice change dramatically. And it changed again when he told us that he'd made everything up and none of it was true. So I think your picture is good to go. Now all we have to do is find out who really bought that gun."

"And just how are we going to do that?"

"I think we need to dig a little deeper into Tiffany Gallagher's life."

We arrived back at the bar at 4:35 P.M., and I saw that Mal was seated at the bar. I sent Carter upstairs to the Capone Club room, telling him I'd join the group a bit later and claiming I had some bar business to tend to. In the meantime, he could share the information we'd gleaned from Harrington with the others.

I walked over and said hi to Mal, who kissed me on

the lips. It wasn't a long or particularly romantic kiss, but it warmed me down to my toes, nonetheless. Maintaining this little subterfuge about the two of us dating was getting more dangerous with each passing day.

I checked in at the bar—Billy and Teddy were both on duty—and things seemed to be moving along well. Then I invited Mal to join me in my office. He followed me there, and once I was inside, I took off my hat and coat and filled him in on our visit with Harrington. "Did you come up with anything?" I asked him when I was done.

"I did. I got ahold of Ben's attorney, and she was able to call the prison and talk to him. He told her that Tiffany had mentioned the dog thing once, saying how much it had upset her. The story she told him was the same one Sonja's client relayed, that the dog was a family pet but had always favored Tiffany, and that for some reason, it bit her brother Rory one day. Then Colin shot and killed it."

"Interesting," I said. "Rory is a bit of a strange duck, so maybe he did something to provoke the dog."

"It's an interesting bit of insight into the family's dynamics, but I don't see how it helps us."

"No, I don't, either." I glanced at my watch and saw that it was three minutes before five. "I need to disengage the alarm. Duncan will be here in a few minutes." I walked over to the alarm control panel and flipped off the switch for the alley door. I looked back at Mal. "Can you do sentinel duty in the hallway for me while I let Duncan in?"

"Sure."

We left the office and went down the hall toward both the back alley door and the entry to my apartment. The hallway was empty at that moment, so I unlocked the door to my apartment. I was about to open the alley door when two women entered the hallway from the other end, heading for the bathroom. Caught nearly red-handed, I knew I looked guilty. But Mal covered by stepping in front of me and effectively blocking the girls' view.

He placed both of his hands on the back door, leaned in close to me, and whispered, "Kiss me, or they might think we're up to something."

He lowered his face to mine, and our lips met. I heard the tittering of the women down the hall, and a moment later I heard the bathroom door open. The receding sound of their voices accompanied the closing of the door.

Mal pulled away quickly. "Sorry about that," he said. "I didn't know what else to do."

"That's okay," I said, a little more breathless than I liked. I peered past him down the hallway. It was empty. "Let's do it."

I turned around and opened the alley door, hoping Duncan would be there waiting. He was, and as soon as the door was open, he stepped inside and sidled into the foyer area leading up to my apartment. He was wearing the same bulky parka he'd worn on a previous visit, and he also had on a fake beard, a mustache, and a wool cap that was pulled down low over his ears and forehead.

Mal and I stepped into the foyer, and I locked the door behind us.

"Good disguise," Mal said to Duncan.

"Thanks," Duncan said. "But I may have to come up with a different one. This damned beard and mustache itch like crazy."

We made our way upstairs, the two men sandwiching

me in the middle, with Duncan in the lead and Mal bringing up the rear. Once we reached the dining room, I pointed to the box.

"There it is," I said. "We handled it with gloves on the entire time, so if there are any prints on it, they won't be ours."

Duncan shrugged his coat off and draped it over the back of one of the chairs. "I brought a fingerprint kit with me," he said. "I'll dust it before we do anything, and if there are any prints, I'll take them in and get them run."

"With a cover story, I assume."

Duncan gave me a patient, somewhat patronizing smile. "Yes, with a cover story. The same one I used last time, that someone is stalking my sister."

"Can't we open the box and get the letter out first so we can read it?" I asked. "The suspense is killing me, and if history holds true, there will be another deadline. Every minute counts."

Duncan looked at me and then at Mal, who shrugged.

"As long as we wear gloves, it shouldn't make a difference," Mal said. "Besides, there probably aren't any prints on the thing. So far this letter writer has been exquisitely careful not to leave any incriminating evidence behind."

I pointed to the boxes of gloves—two different sizes—sitting on the table. "They're right there," I said in a hopeful voice.

"Okay. Fine," Duncan said in good humor. I'd feared he might be annoyed, so I was pleasantly surprised by his rapid and agreeable capitulation.

After we all donned gloves, Duncan opened the metal box and removed the envelope. He flipped it

over, revealing a folding metal clasp on the other side.
The edges of the envelope flap were raised slightly, in-
dicating that it hadn't been glued down. Duncan pried
up the metal tabs and opened the flap. The piece of
plain white paper was still on the table from earlier, and
he carefully reached into the envelope and removed
the contents, holding everything over the paper.

Like many of the letters before it, this one was a
single sheet of plain white paper folded in thirds.
Duncan carefully unfolded it and held it up for all of
us to see. It was written in a calligraphic style with black
ink. The smell of it was essentially the same as that of
the ink used in the other letters I'd received.

> *Dear Ms. Dalton,*
>
> *If you are reading this, then you have succeeded
> once again in interpreting my clues. Kudos to you,
> though perhaps I made the last one too easy. Still,
> your success has ensured that your friends will all
> live to see another day. How lucky! I'd wager you are
> breathing a sigh of relief right now, though it will be
> short-lived.*
>
> *Are you enjoying our little game so far? I bet you
> are, though you probably won't admit it. Life is better
> with a bit of risk in it, don't you think? Consider our
> little game your final adventure in life, a way to
> experience an adrenaline rush. And remember the
> rules. You are not allowed to have any contact with,
> or get any help from, the police, particularly Detective
> Albright. If you do, I will consider it a foul, and
> I'll come after you so fast, you'll feel like you are in
> the middle of a buffalo stampede. You have until
> 9:00 p.m. on Wednesday, December 23, for this one.*

I hope you are as clever as you think you are,
because you are allowed one more miss. After that,
your friends will all be safe. You, however, won't be.

Sincerely,
A skeptical fan

"Damn it!" Duncan said when we'd finished reading the letter. "Now this bastard is threatening you."

Mal said, "This is getting to be a bit much. I think the writer is tiring of the game and Mack's success with it."

Duncan nodded his agreement. He set the letter down on top of the sheet of blank paper, and we all stared at it in silence. "What does this one mean?" He looked over at me. "Mack? Do you sense anything?"

I did sense something odd about it, something in the words themselves. "The ink used in this letter smells like the ink in the first letter . . . mostly, anyway. But there is some subtle difference, a hint of something else."

"Meaning what exactly?" Duncan asked.

I kept staring at the letter, my vision blurring a little so that I was focused more on the overall look of the letter, as opposed to the individual words. Then I saw it . . . and smelled it. "Some of the lettering is a slightly different color," I said. "It's very subtle, just different shades of black, but it's there." I reached over and pointed to a word. "Some of the words are different, like this one. They're a smidgen lighter in color." I moved my finger and pointed at another word. "And this one." I moved my finger again. "And these." I pointed out several more words.

Mal looked at Duncan, then at me with a big smile.

"You just pointed out the words *lucky, wager, game, bet, risk,* and *buffalo stampede.*"

"Gambling," Duncan said. "Except for the buffalo stampede part, all those words imply gambling."

"The casino," Mal said. "It must be the Potawatomi Casino."

"Maybe, but how do the words *buffalo stampede* play into it?" I asked.

"Early Native Americans hunted buffalo," Mal said. "And they own the casino."

I thought that made some sense, though it felt like a bit of a stretch. "If you're right, what am I supposed to do once I get there? I've been to that casino before for conventions and meetings. It's huge."

Duncan said, "Given the words you see as different— a difference I don't see, by the way—I think it means you need to play a game of some sort."

"You mean I'm supposed to gamble? I've never done that. The only card games I know how to play are War, Hearts, Old Maid, and Go Fish, because I played them with my father when I was little."

"It may not be a card game," Duncan said. "It could be bingo, craps, baccarat, roulette, or a slot machine."

"None of which I've ever done," I said. "And how am I supposed to know which one I'm supposed to play?"

The two men thought for a moment, and then Duncan said, "Look at the letter again. Are you sure the words you already pointed out are the only ones that are different?"

I refocused on the letter, this time blurring out the individual words and focusing only on the letters. And I saw that there *were* other variations, but with individual letters, not entire words. I explained this to Duncan and Mal, and then added, "Maybe whoever wrote this made two batches of ink and went over some of the words and letters. Maybe I'm reading more into this than there is."

Mal shook his head. "It's no coincidence that the only whole words that are different are all related to gambling or a casino." He looked over at Duncan. "Do you carry a notebook?"

"Of course." Duncan reached into an inside pocket of his parka and removed a small flip notebook and a pen. He handed both to Mal, who flipped the notebook open and clicked the pen.

"Give us the letters that look different," Mal said.

I looked at the page and read out each letter that was in the slightly lighter shade of black. "*C, a, s, t, m, e, o, h, n, i,* and *l.* That's it."

Mal had scribbled the letters in Duncan's notebook, and he set it on the table for the three of us to consider. "Maybe they spell something," he said.

As I stared at the letters, they began to assume colors, shifting and changing through the spectrum until four of the letters settled on blue and the rest were red. I motioned for Mal to hand me the pen, and beneath the letters he had written, I rewrote them, putting the *c, a, m, e, h, n,* and *i* on one line and *s, t, o,* and *l* on another.

"Why did you divvy them up like that?" Duncan asked.

I shrugged. "I don't know. It's just the way my brain works. The letters all have colors, and the colors go together this way. I think it's two words." I mentally re-arranged the four-letter word first, coming up with *lost* and *lots* initially. Then another word leaped out at me.

Getting that word gave me the other one. "This is *slot*," I said excitedly. "And this word is *machine*."

Duncan and Mal both looked at me like I had turned green and had four eyes and antennae sticking out of my head.

"Remind me never to play Scrabble with you," Mal said.

My excitement ebbed quickly. "Still, even if we know what type of game I'm supposed to play, there must be a thousand slot machines in that place."

"Closer to three thousand," Duncan muttered.

"How am I going to figure out which one to play?"

"Maybe you don't have to play," Mal said. He tapped the letter with a gloved finger. "Presumably, this is supposed to lead you to the next clue. It could be that an employee there will see you and give you something, or maybe there is an envelope taped beneath a machine somewhere."

I sighed, feeling irritated. "I'm tired of getting yanked around by this nut all the time. I've got more important things to do with my time."

"Not now you don't," Duncan said. "Until we can get a line on who's behind this, you have to play the game. If you don't, someone will die. And, as this letter makes clear, that someone might be you."

Chapter 28

"So when do we go on a date to the casino?" Mal said with a smile.

Duncan frowned at this, but then said, "I suppose that makes sense. So far, the letter writer hasn't objected to your presence, assuming Mack is being watched."

Since this echoed my own feelings, I wasn't about to object. But something else was bothering me. "Why is this letter writer so against you, Duncan?" I said. "I get why I've been singled out, but why you?"

Duncan shrugged. "I imagine it's because you and I were connected in the press, and this letter writer wants to test your abilities without any police investigatory aids."

"I've been out and about with other cops—Tyrese, mainly—while investigating the Capone Club's cases, and so far the letter writer hasn't called foul. It seems that you are as much of a target as I am."

Mal looked over at Duncan. "She has a point, man," he said. "Granted, I'm operating undercover, but Mack has spent a fair amount of public time with other cops, just not while she's following up on the letter writer's clues. If the motive behind these letters is to test Mack's abilities and ensure she isn't getting police help, how does the letter writer know Mack isn't hitting Ty up for assistance? Who's to say she hasn't involved the whole police department and they're not helping her on the sly?"

Duncan looked perplexed.

"Unless the letter writer somehow knows I haven't," I suggested, seeing an in for raising my concerns about Duncan's partner, Jimmy. "What if it's someone in the police department?"

Both men looked skeptical at this, and I felt my hopes sink.

"I think it's more likely that it's someone who is familiar with you and the bar, and possibly the Capone Club," Duncan said.

"Perhaps, but at least consider the possibility," I said. "Maybe you could look into who at the PD has connections to the university."

Duncan nodded, but he didn't look convinced. "I'll see what I can dig up without seeming too obvious, but I think it's a long shot."

"In the meantime," Mal said, "when should we hit up the casino?"

"We have until Wednesday, and I've got some things I want to look into on the Middleton case," I said. "How about tomorrow?"

"That works for me," Mal said. "What time?"

"Around noon? That will give me time to get the bar open and running and check in with the lunchtime Capone Club group."

"Sounds good. I think I'll head out and give you guys some time alone."

Duncan held up a hand and said, "I can't stay. I'm on call this evening, and as soon as I dust this stuff for prints, I need to get back to the station. Maybe you can help Mack with whatever she has going on with the Middleton case." He looked at me then. "Do you still think this Middleton guy might be innocent?"

"I do." I then I told him about Carter's and my rendezvous with John Harrington and what the man had confessed, along with the blood splatter evidence and other things we'd uncovered. "Without Harrington's support, we won't be able to prove anything yet, but I think we'll get there." Duncan looked doubtful and worried. "You don't look very pleased about it," I observed.

"I admit my feelings are mixed. I'm happy that you might be able to exonerate an innocent man, but if he's innocent, it means there's a killer still out there, a desperate one. You need to be careful, Mack."

"I will be."

Duncan switched his gaze to Mal. "Thank you for looking after her for me."

"My pleasure," Mal said, and I smiled at the irony.

An uncomfortable silence followed, and I had to admit I admired Duncan's unwavering trust in Mal. He knew Mal had feelings for me, and yet he kept allowing the two of us to spend so much time together. It couldn't be easy, and I marveled at the level of trust and friendship they shared. I hoped I wouldn't be the cause of some future estrangement between them.

"One other thing," Duncan said, shifting his attention back to me. "If you get to a point where you can prove Ben Middleton is innocent, we need to discuss a way to present the information so it doesn't make the police department and the DA's office look bad."

"They arrested and prosecuted an innocent man," I said. "They're going to look bad no matter how the information is presented."

"To a degree, yes," Duncan said. "But that can be spun and mitigated. If you cooperate with them in that effort, it will smooth over a lot of things for you. Plus, given what this idiot is doing"—he pointed to the letter on the table—"I think the less publicity you get, the better it will be."

I didn't argue the point. I hated the publicity. I hated the letter writer, the danger it put me and my friends in, and the hoops I was being forced to jump through. But I also saw the wisdom in what Duncan had said. Handle things right, and theoretically everyone would end up happy.

"What or who are you following up on this evening?" Mal asked.

"I'd like to try to have a chat with Melanie Smithson, Tiffany's closest friend, assuming I can track her down. I want to see if she knows anything about Tiffany having an affair and, if so, who it might have been with. If anyone would know about an affair Tiffany was having, it would be her. I also want to have a chat with Sam about Tiffany's paintings. I feel like there's a clue to her somewhere in them. And I learned that Colin Gallagher hired a PI to follow Ben at some point. I'd like to find him and see what, if anything, he might have to offer on Ben's lifestyle and any secrets the guy might have been hiding. I've got Nick and Tyrese trying to track the PI down. Based on Ben Middleton's description of the man, it shouldn't be too hard."

"Sounds like a busy agenda," Duncan said. "Wish I could help." He glanced at this watch, reached into another pocket of his parka, and pulled out a couple of small jars and a cloth bag. Inside the bag were three brushes, each one with a slightly different type of bristle on the end. "In the meantime, I want to see if I can find a print on this anywhere." He gestured toward the metal box, the envelope, and the letter. "Mack, any chance you have some clear packing tape up here anywhere?"

"As a matter of fact, I do." As I headed into my father's office to grab the roll of tape, Duncan hollered after me.

"Grab a couple more sheets of paper, too, please."

By the time I returned to the dining table, Duncan had opened up one of the small jars, which contained a fine black powder, and he was using a brush with very fine splayed bristles to dust the metal box. He held the brush a smidgen over the surface and twirled the brush between his fingers, flinging the powder onto the box, my table, and his gloved hand. After covering both the outside and the inside of the box, he frowned and shook his head. "Nothing."

"Maybe the envelope or letter will have something," I said with halfhearted hope. No one agreed with me. We all knew the odds of that happening were miniscule.

"I'll need to take the envelope and letter with me," Duncan said. "Getting fingerprints off those requires a different process."

I nodded, but I didn't want to have the letter completely gone, in case I wanted to look at it again. "Let me take a picture of it first," I said, and I snapped a photo of it with my phone. Then I watched as Duncan put both it and the envelope inside the plastic Baggies I'd fetched when Cora was here. Then he placed them back in the metal box and slipped that into the large shopping bag Mal had used. As he reached for his parka, his cell phone rang. Mal and I both stood by as he took the call.

"Hey. What have you got for me?" he said. Whatever the person on the other end said made him frown. Finally, he said, "Okay. Thanks," and then he disconnected the call.

Duncan stared at the two of us with a curious thoughtful expression. "Was Gary Gunderson dating anyone around the time he was killed?"

I shrugged. "Not that I know of, but I don't know if I would have been privy to that info if he was. Billy or Debra might know. Why?"

"Remember that swab I took from the armrest of Gary's car?"

I nodded, sensing that he was about to reveal something big. My mouth was dry, and I licked my lips in anticipation of his answer.

"The techs found something on it," he said. "A perfume. Specifically, Opium perfume by Yves Saint Laurent. So if Gary wasn't dating anyone, then . . ."

He let us come to the conclusion on our own.

Chapter 29

"The killer might be a woman," I said. I stood a moment, letting the possibility sink in and searching my memory banks for any woman I had met who was wearing Opium. But I couldn't recall ever documenting a reaction to that specific perfume. I might have smelled it before and not realized it. I needed to get my hands on a sample.

"There's no way to know for sure if the perfume came from the killer," Duncan cautioned. "It could have been left by some woman he had riding in his car on or around the day he was killed."

"I'll ask Billy and Debra right away," I said.

"Even if they don't know anything, it doesn't mean Gary wasn't seeing someone," Mal said. "He was an ex-con. Those guys tend to be kind of private."

Duncan nodded his agreement, and as he did so, his phone buzzed with a text message. He looked at it, said, "I have to go," and finished putting on his coat. Then he looked at Mal and said, "Can you go downstairs and hang on the other side of the door for a minute or so? I'll be right there. I'll knock before opening it, and you can knock back if the coast is clear."

I looked at Mal, too. "You can check the alley, too, while you're there. I left the alarm off."

Mal nodded and headed downstairs.

I looked at Duncan, my head cocked to one side. "Wish you could stay," I said.

"Me too." He leaned down and gave me a kiss, a nice long kiss that made my toes curl and sparked all kinds of other sensations. The fake mustache and beard tickled my face. "You be careful," he said when he finally pulled back.

"I will. You do the same."

With that, he pulled on his knit cap and lowered it so that the front came to just above his eyebrows. He picked up his bag of goodies, and I followed him down to the small foyer, where he lightly rapped on the door. A second later Mal knocked back. Duncan turned and gave me one more kiss, this one on the cheek. Then he opened the door.

I was still relishing all the synesthetic sensations when I realized he was gone.

"You okay?" Mal asked me.

I nodded and hobbled out into the hallway, letting the apartment door close behind me. I locked it and then headed for my office, where I reengaged the alarm for the alley door. Mal followed me in silence, and as I turned to leave the office, he stepped in front of me.

"I know this is hard for you and Duncan," he said, "but it will get better. Have patience."

I looked up at him and smiled. "Do you always have to be so nice and understanding?"

He gave me a rakish smile in return. "Hey, I can't help being what I am."

"You don't make this any easier for me, you know."

His smile faded. "Do you want me to back off and not hang around so much? I can watch you from more of a distance if my presence makes you uncomfortable."

I shook my head and smiled again. "It's just the opposite," I said. "Your presence makes me very comfortable. I've enjoyed having you around, and you've been so patient and understanding about all of this. I feel a little guilty taking you away from your life. Anytime you want to move on, just let me know."

His smile returned, and I felt relieved. I liked his smile. "I'm having fun," he said. "Besides, I had no life prior to this, other than my undercover work. Eat, sleep, work. That was my life. At least with you I've gotten to do some fun stuff. And I promised Duncan I'd look out for you. So that's what I'm going to do until one of you kicks me to the curb."

"But what about your social life? You should be out dating for real, instead of pretending with me."

"Yeah, the women are just flocking around me," he said with great sarcasm.

"I'm sure they would be if they thought you were available." I arched an eyebrow at him.

He smiled hard and blushed a little, looking away from me. "Thanks," he said. When his gaze returned to mine, his smile turned melancholy, wistful. Our eyes locked for several seconds, until he sighed and turned to open the door.

My heart ached for him. And for a moment I wondered if I was making a mistake, letting my hormones rule my head while a great man got away.

It was a thought I tucked away for a later time, because I had other things to tend to for now.

We left the office and headed for the bar. Billy was behind it, and Debra stood at one end of it, waiting on a drink order.

I hobbled over to them. "Hey, guys," I said. "Do either of you know if Gary was seeing or dating anyone when he was killed?"

Billy shrugged, but Debra shook her head. "No, he wasn't," she said. "I know because I had a discussion with him the day before it happened. He asked me if I knew anyone I could fix him up with."

"And did you?"

"As a matter of fact, I did. My sons have a friend whose mother is single, and she did some time a few years ago for drugs. But she straightened up, and she's been clean for four years now."

"Did you give him her info?"

Debra shook her head. "I wanted to ask her first if it was okay." Her expression turned sad. "But I never did."

"Why are you asking?" Billy said.

I couldn't tell them the real reason, so I made one up. "I was just wondering if there might have been someone in his life, someone who, well . . . you know."

They both nodded solemnly, and I quickly changed the subject.

"Everything going okay?" I asked.

"Right as rain," Billy said.

Debra nodded and smiled, confirming his answer.

"I'm going to head upstairs to the Capone Club, then," I told them. I looked back at Mal, who had been standing quietly behind me the whole time. "Do you want a drink or something to eat?"

"I am kind of hungry," he said, rubbing his stomach.

We decided to order some burgers, and then Billy mixed us a couple of drinks, which Mal carried upstairs.

The group had fleshed out. Sam, Carter, Holly Alicia, Tad, Dr. T, Cora, and the brothers were all present, along with Sonja West and Stephen McGregor. Tyrese and Nick were there, too. After a general greeting, Mal and I settled in.

"What are you guys up to?" I asked.

"We were discussing the Middleton case," Carter said. "But we keep hitting dead ends. The biggest stumbling blocks are the location and the timing. Unless the carjacking was a random event by someone who was stranded on that road, we can't figure out how anyone would have known when Ben and Tiffany were going to be there. We've been tossing around the theory that Ben might have hired someone to kill Tiffany. Maybe he set something up while he was in town earlier that day. Clay here showed us transcripts from the trial that prove he did go into town, like he said. There were witnesses who said they saw him. Plus, he had receipts for the stuff he bought."

"Are you sure Middleton's version of the events was the truth?" Holly asked me.

"As sure as I can be."

"Then there's Harrington's story that the guy he sold the gun to wasn't Ben Middleton," Carter added.

Debra appeared with the burgers for me and Mal, and the conversation stopped while she set them on the table for us. As soon as she was gone, Sam said, "Maybe this Harrington guy made that up as a way to get more attention."

I made a face and shook my head. My mouth was full of burger, so it took me a few seconds before I was able to speak. "I don't think so," I told the group once I had swallowed. "At the end he tried to take back everything he had told us, and his voice changed when he did that. I'm convinced that what he told the police was a lie."

"Back to square one," Carter said with a sigh of frustration. "Where do we go from here?"

"I want to run something by Sam," I said. I then described for him and the others the paintings I'd seen in Tiffany's workshop. "I feel like she was trying to tell the world something. I mean, that's generally the purpose behind most art, but I had a sense that she was revealing something personal about herself, about her life. Any insight?"

Sam nodded thoughtfully, pulling at his chin. "Well, the depiction of the flower, the poppy, is typically a symbol of remembrance, to honor the dead. It's a popular symbol used to honor soldiers who die in battle and dates back to World War I. But these days it's often used for other forms of remembrance and consolation."

"Interesting," I said between bites. Had the pregnancy in her senior year and the subsequent loss of the child been behind those paintings? It was a thought I had to keep to myself, thanks to my promise to Kelly Gallagher. I wondered about the mystery man behind that pregnancy. Granted, it had happened years ago, but maybe the man had resurfaced in her life. More than ever, now I wanted to talk to Tiffany's high school friend Melanie Smithson.

Holly piped up and said, "I called and chatted with three of Ben Middleton's ex-coworkers today. It sounds like he was kind of a tight-lipped loner. He didn't talk much about himself, his marriage, or any other part of his private life. But the third guy I spoke to did say that he got an interesting comment from Ben one day about a month before the carjacking, when one of the women in the office came by with her one-month-old baby. This guy asked Ben if he and Tiffany had any plans to start a family. Ben's answer was that he had thought they did, but then he'd discovered that Tiffany was still taking her birth control pills on the sly."

"That had to hurt," Carter said.

"I'm surprised Ben didn't tell us that," I said. "Did this guy you talked to say whether or not Ben was angry about it?"

"On the contrary," Holly said. "He said that Ben seemed concerned but resigned. He said something along the lines of how he feared he'd pushed too hard, too fast, because Tiffany wasn't ready yet."

"Any talk of Ben having an affair with anyone?" Nick asked.

Holly shook her head. "All three of the guys I talked to agreed that he wasn't a flirter and seemed devoted to Tiffany."

"Sounds like that's a dead end, too," I said. I turned to Clay. "Any luck tracking down Melanie Smithson?"

"I need to talk to you about that," he said cryptically. "Maybe out in the hall?"

"Okay. Just a sec." I turned to Tyrese. "Any luck tracking down our PI?"

"Yes and no," he said, glancing over at Nick with a half smile. "Nick figured out who he was, but the guy is deceased." Tyrese saw my panicked look and held up a hand. "Nothing nefarious. He died of a heart attack six months ago."

Nick leaned forward, his elbows on his knees, chin in his hands. "I was hoping we might be able to get the case files and glean some information that way. The guy's widow sold off his PI business to someone, and I thought maybe the files went with the business. But then she told me she had shredded all the closed case files."

"Bummer," I said, and several people in the room nodded.

"Hey, I tried," Nick said with a frown. He flashed me an apologetic smile.

"It was good idea," I told him. "Just not a viable one, unfortunately." I shifted my attention. "Carter, did anyone have any ideas about your drawing?"

"Which was amazing, by the way," Cora piped up.

Carter smiled, blushed a little, and shook his head. "Nope. Nothing so far. I think the picture is too vague with the lower half of the face missing."

Joe said, "Maybe we should experiment a little with adding in features, play around with the drawing and see what we come up with."

"Not a bad idea," I said. "You can make copies of the original and block out the part that includes the scarf. Then you can draw in some lower facial features."

Carter perked up, liking the idea.

Cora said, "Hand me the picture, and I'll go make some copies in Mack's office."

Carter dug the drawing out of his laptop case and handed it to her. I gave Cora my keys, and she headed downstairs, carrying her laptop with her. I ate the last bite of my burger and then turned to Clay, nodding toward the door. He grabbed his coat and followed me out into the hallway.

"Tell me about Melanie Smithson," I said.

"I found a way to get ahold of her, but it wasn't easy. She dropped out of grad school last year and moved out of the Milwaukee area. So I had Cora do an online search. She told me her company does computer security work for the IRS and she might be able to find me something by tapping into their confidential files. She threatened my manhood if I breathed a word of what she was doing. That woman is amazing, by the way," he added, his eyes wide. "And scary."

"Tell me about it."

"Anyway, she came up with a cell phone number and told me that Smithson is currently hanging out in Washington State somewhere. I called Smithson about an hour ago and asked if some folks looking into Tiffany's murder could talk with her, but she said no. Then she asked me why anyone was looking into it, since Ben had already been convicted."

"What did you tell her?"

"That we thought he might have been wrongly convicted. That made her gasp."

"Really? I wonder why."

"I don't know, but she sounded spooked. She wanted to know how I'd found her. I made up some story about hiring a PI and said that all he found was a phone number. I promised her I wouldn't share the number with anyone, but she still said she didn't want to talk. I asked her why she'd quit grad school and dropped out of sight, but all she told me was that she'd needed some time away from the grind." He paused and frowned.

"What?" I said, sensing there was more.

"I don't know," Clay said, pulling at his chin. "I got the sense that she did want to talk to me, even though she said she didn't. She could have hung up on me several times, yet she didn't. She kept skirting around the issue and asking me why people were looking into Ben's case." His frown deepened, and he scratched his head. "My reporter instincts kept telling me there was a story there, but maybe I was reading more into it than there was."

I pondered his information for a few seconds. "Think she might talk to me?"

"I doubt it. But I can give you the number if you want to try."

"I do," I said.

He reached into his shirt pocket and pulled out one of my bar napkins with a phone number written on it. "Here you go," he said: "Good luck."

I took the number, stuffed it in my pocket, and thanked him.

"I have to go finish an article for tomorrow's paper," he said. "Let me know how it goes."

He donned his coat and headed downstairs.

I took a moment to think about Melanie Smithson and how to approach her. If Clay was right, the woman was scared of something. But what?

While I was thinking, Cora came up the stairs, carrying a stack of papers and her laptop.

"Hey, Cora. Do you happen to recall whether or not we've recorded my reaction to the smell of Opium perfume?"

She squinted in thought and shook her head. "I don't think so. Why?"

"Duncan had me take a look at Gary's car last night, and I detected a smell on the passenger armrest. Duncan had it analyzed, and it came back as Opium perfume."

Cora's eyes grew big. "Does that mean the killer is a woman?"

"Possibly. I want to know the specific reaction I have to that perfume, because there were other smells there, too, and that complicated things."

"I'll check the database, but I'm pretty sure we haven't logged that particular one. I can order some for you if you want."

"That would be great. Thanks. I'll reimburse you for the cost."

"Did you open that box from the cemetery yet?"

"We did." I filled her in on the contents of the box and our interpretation of them. "Mal and I are going to hit up the casino tomorrow and see what we can find."

"Be careful," she said. "It sounds like this letter writer is ramping things up." She handed me back my office keys. "Did Clay have any luck with the Smithson girl?"

"He was able to talk to her, but she didn't tell him anything. He said she sounded scared."

Cora nodded, looking thoughtful.

"I'm surprised you trusted Clay enough to tell him you were accessing confidential IRS files to find a number for Smithson," I said. "What if he prints that information?"

Cora gave me a sly smile. "That wasn't exactly the truth. It was a test of sorts. I don't do any work for the IRS, but I do handle security for some banking networks. I was able to dig up Smithson's credit card info and saw that she had purchased several burner phones over the past year. I gave him the number for the most recent one she bought, and told him that she was living out in Washington State somewhere. That was a lie. She pays her credit card bills online, and I was able to trace her ISP to somewhere in Pennsylvania."

"I should have known you'd be smart enough to cover your tracks," I said with a smile.

"Did he give you the number?"

I nodded.

"Are you going to call her?"

I nodded again.

"Well, good luck with it. I'm going to go hand over these drawing copies and see what the group comes up with."

"Good luck to you, too. Tell Mal I'm headed for my office. He can join me if he wants."

She nodded, and we parted company. Cora returned to the Capone Club room, while I made my way down to my office.

Chapter 30

By the time I reached my office door, Mal had caught up to me. "What are you up to?" he asked.

I told him about Clay's talk with Melanie Smithson and my intent to call her.

"Mind if I sit in?"

"Not at all."

We went into the office and locked the door behind us. I settled in behind my desk, and Mal sat across from me. I took out my cell phone and started to make the call but stopped. I set the cell aside and picked up my landline desk phone instead.

"If the woman is paranoid about people finding her and discussing this case, it might be better if I call her from a number with a caller ID that she can verify," I said as Mal gave me a curious look.

He made no comment, and I dialed the number. Then I switched over to speakerphone. We listened as the phone on the other end rang several times, and I felt my hopes flag. Just as I was about to disconnect the call, someone answered.

"Hello?" said a tentative female voice. Melanie's

voice manifested with a visual reaction rather than a taste, something that sometimes happened with women's voices. I saw falling flower petals.

"Is this Melanie Smithson?" I asked.

"Who is this?"

"My name is Mackenzie Dalton. I own a bar in Milwaukee called Mack's Bar. You can look it up and call me back at the listed number if you want."

Silence.

"I'm calling you about Ben Middleton."

She let out a perturbed sigh. I waited, expecting her to hang up, but she didn't.

"Melanie, I work with a group of people who look into cold cases and adjudicated cases where we think an injustice may have been done. We have reason to believe that Ben Middleton is innocent. I'd like to talk to you about his wife, Tiffany, specifically about her life from several years back."

More silence. No, that wasn't quite true. I heard a faint tapping sound in the background, and it made me smile and give Mal a thumbs-up. I recognized the sound as the tapping of computer keys, but Mal gave me a confused look, making me wonder if he was able to hear the sound.

"Something happened to Tiffany when she was in high school, something that affected her deeply," I said. "I'm trying to determine what that might have been, and I understand that you and she were close. Do you know anything about it?"

More silence ensued, as the tapping sound had stopped.

After a few seconds I said, "Melanie? Are you still there?"

"You're passing yourself off as some kind of mind reader?" she said finally.

I looked at Mal and saw that he finally understood. "You must have found some of the news articles about me," I said. "They aren't totally accurate. I don't read minds, but I do have a disorder that gives me a different perspective on things. It's complicated. Suffice it to say that I can pick up on things others can't."

"I can't help you," she said, and I felt my spirits tank. "Please leave me alone."

"Melanie, I promise you I won't tell anyone we spoke. I don't know what or who you're hiding from, but your secret will stay safe with me. I promise you that. Please think it over. If you decide you want to talk to me, call me back. You can call on my landline here at the bar. You can find the number online. I live above the bar, and the phone rings there, too. If you call after two A.M. and before ten A.M., I should be the only one here. Or if you want, you can call me anytime on my cell." I gave her the cell number and then said, "I hope you'll talk to me. If you really were a friend to Tiffany, don't let her death be for naught."

I closed my eyes and waited, listening. I heard her breathing for several seconds, and then the sound was gone. I waited a little longer and then heard a sound that told me our call had been disconnected.

"Damn," I muttered, punching the speaker button. "She knows something. I can feel it."

"Even *I* can feel it, and I don't have your sensitive . . . talents."

"I guess I'll just have to wait and see if she calls back."

A knock came on my office door, and Mal got up and opened it. It was Tad.

"Oh, sorry," he said, looking at Mal. "I was hoping to have a chat with Mack."

"Come on in, Tad," I said. Mal stepped aside and waved Tad in.

"I have some information for you," he said, and then he slid his eyes toward his left shoulder, toward where Mal was standing. I got the message.

"Mal, would you mind letting me talk to Tad privately for a few minutes?"

"Not at all," Mal said. He stepped out of the office and shut the door behind him.

"What have you got for me?" I gestured toward the chair Mal had just vacated.

"I don't need to sit," he said. "I don't have much to tell you. I looked over the finances of the Gallagher family, and I can't pinpoint any unusual large expenditures, *large* being a relative term here, given their wealth. But Colin Gallagher pulls cash out of his accounts all the time. There's no way for me to know what he does with it. As for Tiffany, her trust account had some transfers of money from time to time, out of her account and into the joint account she and Ben shared, but I saw nothing there to raise any eyebrows. And for what it's worth, her father did have control over that account. His electronic or real signature was required for any money transactions. Ben pulled down a decent salary on his own, but—"

His cell phone rang, and after a little hiss of annoyance, he pulled it from his pocket and looked at it. "Sorry," he said, rolling his eyes again. "It's Suzanne. I have to take it."

"Go ahead. Want me to step out?"

"No need." He answered the call with, "Hey, Suze. What's up?" I watched as he closed his eyes and grimaced. The muscles in his cheeks twitched with annoyance, and after a few seconds he took a deep, bracing breath, then blew it out through pursed lips. "Yes, dear," he said in a tone that belied his impatient expression. "I understand. I just have a few more things here in the office to finish up." He listened some more and then said, "You know I don't answer the office phone after hours. I've told you that." He shot me a guilty look. "Give me an hour or so and I should be done. See you soon." More listening. "I love you, too." He disconnected the call and dropped the phone into his shirt pocket. Then he raked a hand through his hair. "Suzanne has been on me a lot lately about not coming home earlier."

"Why are you lying to her?"

"She's worried that I'm having an affair. I keep assuring her that's not the case, but I think she knows I'm not in the office sometimes when I say I am."

"So tell her where you are."

"I can't. I mentioned the bar once weeks ago and told her about the Capone Club thing and how much I enjoyed it. She had a meltdown, told me that the kind of publicity this place has gotten is bad for my reputation and hers. She said if I kept it up, I'd end up losing clients. I think she might have hired someone to follow me. That's why I haven't been here as often in the evenings. I feel safe coming here for lunch, but not so much in the evening."

"I'm sorry, Tad. You don't think you can talk her into some sort of compromise?"

He laughed at that. "Have you met my wife? The word *compromise* is not in her dictionary. She expects me to be at her beck and call all the time, and she drags me around to all these social events that are so boring, they make me want to kill myself."

With those words, an idea popped into my head. "What were you going to tell me right before Suzanne called?"

"Just that Colin Gallagher wielded a lot of control over Tiffany and her money. The house she and Ben lived in was owned by him, and while Tiffany's name was on the deed, Ben's was not. Same thing with the boat Ben and Tiffany had, and Tiffany's car."

I thought about Tiffany and whatever demons had haunted her. Had the girl been so depressed and controlled that she wanted to kill herself? Was that why she hadn't tried to get out of the car when Ben was wrestling with the gunman? It was a sad, dark thought, one that made me ache for the girl. Her life didn't sound like a very happy one, which just went to show that money couldn't buy happiness.

Tad glanced at his watch and said, "I really should go. I still need to run by the store and pick up some perfume for Suzanne for Christmas. But before I do, tell me if you guys have made any progress on the case."

I updated him on what I knew, and then, curious, I asked him what type of perfume he planned to get for Suzanne.

"Opium," he said. "It's the only thing she wears."

Chapter 31

After Tad left, I sat in my office, trying to decide what to do about what Tad had just told me. Suzanne Collier wore Opium perfume. But then, hundreds, maybe thousands of women in and around Milwaukee probably wore it, as well. What possible motive would a rich woman like Suzanne have for taunting me? Then I recalled Tad saying that Suzanne suspected him of having an affair. Did she think I was Tad's mistress? But that didn't make any sense, either. If she was having Tad followed, she would know that he and I rarely saw one another. Plus, I'd been plenty visible courting around with Mal lately.

I convinced myself that Suzanne's choice of perfume was nothing more than a coincidence, and left my office. Business had picked up, and the bar was bustling. Billy looked a little frazzled, something I almost never saw, so I chipped in for the next few hours and helped out, propping myself up on my crutches and mixing drinks behind the bar. Mal settled in on one of the barstools and watched for a while, and then he headed upstairs to the Capone

Club room. The customers were all hepped up on holiday cheer, and a group of people in the dance floor room started singing Christmas carols. More folks joined in, and at one point nearly the entire first floor was singing. It should have lifted my soul and put me in the holiday spirit, but I had too much on my mind.

By one o'clock things had slowed down enough that I was able to head upstairs to the Capone Club room. The group had dwindled some. The Signoriello brothers had gone home, and Holly and Alicia had left, too. The remaining group was huddled around some tables that had been pushed together, and on top of the tables were dozens of papers with Carter's drawing on the top half and different lower facial features drawn on the bottom half.

"Hey, Mack," Carter said. "We've been playing around with the facial characteristics, and it's interesting, but we're all a little confused as to just what it is we're supposed to be looking for."

"I don't know," I admitted. "I thought maybe you'd get lucky and come up with something that looked familiar."

"We haven't," he said.

"Well, save them all. I'll show them to Clay later and see if any of them resemble anyone he might have seen at the trial." Thinking about Tiffany's mystery lover from her senior year in high school, I decided I should probably show them to Teddy Bear, too. He knew a lot of the same people Tiffany would have known, and maybe he'd recognize someone.

Tyrese said, "You might even take them up to the prison and run them by Ben Middleton. See if he can identify the shooter."

"Good idea."

Carter gathered up all the sheets and handed them to Mal. "Why don't you guys hang on to these for now. I'm going to call it a night."

"Me too," Sam said. And then, as if by some unspoken agreement, everyone in the room got up, gathered up their belongings, bid one another good night, and headed out.

"I think I'm going to head home, too," Mal said. He held up the drawings in his hand. "I'll walk you downstairs and drop these in your office."

Half an hour later, I was upstairs in my apartment. Mal had gone home, and Billy was closing up shop for me downstairs. I readied myself for bed and climbed in, feeling exhausted and certain I'd fall asleep quickly and easily. But I kept staring at the phone beside my bed, willing it to ring, hoping that Melanie Smithson would rethink her willingness to talk.

It was well past four before I finally drifted off, and my phone remained silent throughout the night.

I awoke at ten the next morning, and after a quick shower I went downstairs. Pete was in already, readying the bar for the eleven o'clock opening time, and Jon arrived at ten thirty and fired up the kitchen. Debra and Teddy both came in shortly after Jon, and Missy showed up just prior to opening time. I unlocked the door at eleven, and Cora, Frank, and Joe all arrived minutes later. Other customers quickly followed, so I invited Cora and the brothers upstairs to the Capone Club room and filled the brothers in on the latest letter and my planned trip to the casino today. I barely had time to tell them everything before other members of the group began arriving.

I went downstairs to wait for Mal, who arrived at quarter to twelve. I told Pete and Debra we were heading out to do some shopping for a few hours, and without further ado, we left.

It had snowed some during the night—not a lot, but enough that everything outside was covered with a fresh, clean layer of white. The sun was out, and the new snow sparkled in its light. With only two more shopping days left until Christmas, the downtown traffic was heavy and the sidewalks were crowded. That plus the newly fallen snow made maneuvering with my crutches that much more difficult. Mal held my arm as we walked to his car, and then he helped me get inside.

"I don't suppose our gal called you last night," he said as soon as we were under way.

I shook my head. "I fear that's a dead end. When we get back from the casino, I want to take those drawings Carter did last night and run them by Clay and Teddy, to see if either of them recognizes anyone."

Mal shot me a questioning look. "Why Teddy?"

The burden of my promise to Kelly was a heavy one, and I desperately wanted someone to help me shoulder it. After giving it a millisecond of thought, I decided I could trust Mal to keep the secret along with me. I told him about Tiffany's senior year, the pregnancy, and the mystery man. "I can't help but wonder if whoever got her pregnant might have come back into her life around the time was killed," I concluded. "And if so, there's a good chance he's someone who hung with that social circle. Since Teddy knew the same group, I'm thinking it's worth a shot to have him look at the pictures and see if he recognizes anyone."

"Wow. That poor girl had a time of it, didn't she?" Mal said.

"Yes, she did," I agreed. "It makes me wonder if the reason she didn't try to escape from the car was that she didn't care if she died."

We fell silent for the rest of the trip, and I imagined Mal was thinking along the same lines as I was, about how tragic, lonely, and desperate Tiffany Gallagher's life might have been. It made me grateful for what I had, and determined not to lose any of it.

That was a good mind-set for our arrival at the casino, but as soon as we were inside, I felt myself resenting my synesthesia. We were surrounded by flashing lights of all types and colors; loud noises that roared, rang, banged, clanged, wheedled, and whistled; the smell of people, food, booze, and cigarette smoke. The place was a cavernous open room with a high raftered ceiling, and there were gaming tables and slot machines as far as the eye could see. My brain went into a synesthetic overload similar to what I often experienced when I went to a mall or to the Public Market, but this was ten times worse than anything I'd ever experienced. I couldn't help but wonder if the letter writer had planned it that way in an attempt to throw me off.

"I need a minute," I told Mal. "This is overwhelming."

Mal nodded, and we stepped off to one side. I closed my eyes and focused on trying to shut down the synesthetic side of my brain, parsing through the things I could still smell and hear, relegating each one to real or synesthetic. As soon as I felt I had those senses under control, I opened my eyes and tried to do the same with the smells and sensations triggered by all the colorful flashing lights, which were everywhere I looked. When I felt as if I could function normally, I examined our surroundings more closely.

"I have no idea where to even begin," I told Mal. "This place is huge."

"Let's just survey it for now, walk around it all. Maybe something will come to us."

We did so, meandering our way past large card tables and down aisles that ran between rows of slot machines. It was a busy place, which made maneuvering on my crutches that much more difficult.

"I'm surprised this place is so packed," I told Mal at one point. "You'd think with the holidays coming, people would have better things to do."

"Don't underestimate the lure of Lady Luck," he said.

After traipsing up and down dozens of aisles without seeing anything that might be a clue, Mal stopped and said, "You have a picture of the last letter on your phone, don't you?"

"I do."

He gestured toward a seating area and a coffee shop near the front entrance. "Let's sit for a few minutes and take another look at it. Maybe there's a clue in there that we overlooked."

We wandered into the coffee shop, ordered up some drinks, and settled in at a table. I took out my phone, pulled up the picture of the letter, and then set my phone on the table between us. We huddled together, both of us reading.

"Tell me again which words were written in the different-colored ink," Mal said after a few minutes.

I didn't need to look at the letter to answer him.

"The key words were *lucky, wager, game, bet, risk,* and *buffalo stampede.*"

Mal looked thoughtful for a moment, and then his face lit up. "All those words are general gambling terms except for the words *buffalo stampede.* I thought at first it was a reference to the Native American casino ownership, but what if it means something else?"

"Like what?"

He turned on his stool and studied our immediate surroundings. "Look at these slot machines," he said. "They all have themes of some sort. What if buffalo stampede is the name of a particular game?"

I considered this, and it made as much sense as our first interpretation. "Let's give it a whirl."

We slid off our stools and continued our meandering, weaving between rows of slot machines and tables filled with card players. It was a constant and somewhat exhausting effort to shut out all the synesthetic reactions; there was a never-ending stream of sounds, tastes, smells, and visual manifestations. My head throbbed, and I wasn't sure if it was a headache from the strain of trying to deal with all the sensory input, or a synesthetic reaction of some kind. Either way, I wished it would go away.

After another fifteen minutes or so, we had made our way to the opposite end of the casino and an exit that led out onto Canal Street. My frustration level was through the roof, both from the irritating environment and my anger over our lack of success. My spirits tanked, and as I turned to ask Mal what he thought we should do next, I felt his hand grip my arm. He was staring off to my right, and when I looked that way, I saw what he saw: a bank of slot machines along the wall. There were ten machines all together, and six of them were called Buffalo Stampede. All of them had someone seated in front of them, playing.

Mal and I walked over to the area and stood behind the players, scanning the machines for any envelopes or packages that were lying around. All I saw were plastic drink cups and several ashtrays crammed into the narrow spaces between the machines.

"Do you think we need to play one of them?" I asked Mal.

Mal leaned close to my ear and spoke in a low voice, though how anyone could overhear what we said amid all that clamor was beyond me. "I don't think you can rig one of these machines that easily, and even if you could, how would the letter writer know when we'd be here or when we'd play it? There's the same problem if it's been set up so that someone who works here is supposed to look for you playing this machine. This place is open twenty-four hours a day, seven days a week. There would have to be several shifts of workers looking for you." He paused and shook his head. "It makes no sense. I think we need to check out the area around the machines more thoroughly."

The slots sat atop a credenza-type structure that was flush with the carpeted floor. That eliminated anything getting stashed beneath them. There was a small amount of space between each machine—eight inches or so—but it was easy to see into each of these spaces all the way back to the wall. However, the Buffalo Stampede slots were made in such a way that the face of each machine extended out beyond the main body, creating a small hidden spot along the top and around the perimeter of each one, behind the bright neon edge. It wasn't a large enough space to hide a full-size envelope, though, and since the main body of the machines was black, a white, gold, or manila envelope would be painfully obvious. Still, I sidled my way down the bank of players, scanning what I could see around and on top of each machine. I saw nothing and said as much to Mal.

"I suppose there could be something taped beneath the seats," he said, "though that would be risky since they can easily be moved." He looked above us and then scanned the room. "This place is monitored all the time, so if there is something attached behind the face of any of these machines, it would have to be small and not easily seen."

Just then, a woman playing one of the Buffalo Stampede machines got up from her seat. Mal quickly moved in and motioned for me to sit down. He fished out his wallet and handed me a twenty-dollar bill.

"Here. Play it," he said.

"I don't know how."

"Stick the money in here." He pointed to a slot, and I slid the twenty in until the machine sucked it up. "Now push this button labeled MAX BET."

"Max bet? Isn't that a bit reckless?"

"It's a penny slot," he said. "The max bet isn't that much."

I put my finger on the button Mal had indicated and pushed it. Things on the screen in front of me spun and shifted, triggering a cacophony of synesthetic smells. The sounds of bells, whistles, snorting buffalo, and Lord knew what else made my mouth burst with fleeting tastes. I had no idea what I was doing, so I just kept hitting the button. Mal sidled up next to me on my right—it wasn't easy, because the person at the next machine was mere inches away—and ran his hand around the back side of the front flange on my machine. Then he switched sides and did the same thing on my left. When that produced nothing, he turned his back to me and faked a stumble, using it as an excuse to run his hand around the back side of the flange of the machine to my left.

I hit the button for the umpteenth time, and the machine started clanging away, triggering a metallic taste in my mouth. "What happened?" I said, staring at the screen. Strobes were flashing, highlighting card faces, cartoonish wolves and eagles, and lines that crisscrossed the screen.

"You just won two hundred bucks, that's what happened," Mal said with a smile.

The woman on my left glowered at my machine and muttered a cussword under her breath. Then she hit a button, took the paper receipt the machine spat out, and got up. "Come on, Fred," she said to the man beside her. "These machines are a waste of time." The man cashed out, as well, and followed her.

Mal quickly moved in on the machines, settled in the farthest seat, and patted the one next to me. "Cash out and switch over here," he said.

"Cash out?" I stared at the machine's flashing screen. Mal stood and hit a button in front of me. A paper receipt spat out.

"Grab that and move over here to play. Slide it in the same slot where you put the twenty earlier."

I did what he said, and as soon as I was settled in front of the new machine, I slid my paper receipt in the appropriate slot and started hitting the MAX BET button Mal had shown me before. Mal, in the meantime, checked out the hidden space on the left side of my machine and on both sides of the one he sat at. I knew from the look on his face that he'd struck out.

Now I was the one cursing under my breath. I'd hoped my little win on the other machine was a sign of good luck for us. Maybe it was, and I'd used it all up.

Undaunted, Mal got up, turned to the woman on his left, and started chatting with her about how the machines were rigged and what terrible luck he had. As he talked, his hand ran around the back side of the flange on her machine. When I saw his hand stop near the top, I held my breath. A moment later he turned to me, his right hand cupped around something. He slid it into his pocket.

"Let's get out of here while you're ahead," he said. "Cash out."

I pushed the button I had watched him push when he cashed me out on the first machine, and a moment later the machine spat out a paper receipt. I glanced at it, shocked to see that it was for just over 230 dollars. I handed it to Mal and then followed him to a cash machine so we could redeem it. Ten minutes later I was standing out in front of the casino, propped on my crutches, waiting for Mal to bring the car around to pick me up. My curiosity was killing me. When he finally pulled up, I nearly leapt into the front seat and almost hit Mal with my crutches as I tried to toss them behind me.

"Show me," I said.

He stuck his hand in his pocket, and when he pulled it out and opened it, I saw a small black envelope—the size a hotel keycard would come in—sitting in his palm. Its flap was sealed, and stuck to the outside of it was a small piece of Velcro.

"It was stuck to another piece of Velcro, which was glued to the back side of the front flange on the machine," he said. "I tried to peel that other piece off, thinking it might contain some DNA evidence, but it must have been applied using some sort of industrial-strength glue, rather than the adhesive these things typically come with, because it wouldn't budge."

I eyed the tiny envelope and then gave Mal a questioning look.

He smiled at me but shook his head. "We should take it back to your place to open it." He ran his thumb over the top surface of it and added, "Though I can tell you there's a key in it."

"A key? You mean like a house key or a car key?"

"Smaller than that. We'll get a better idea once we open it." He raised his hand closer to his face and scrutinized the tiny envelope. "Smart," he said. "I was thinking that a black envelope this small might be hard to find and therefore easy to trace. But the envelope was white to start with. It looks like it's been colored over with a felt-tipped marker."

"Maybe not so smart," I said, and Mal shot me a curious look. "Let's get back to the bar and open this thing. Then I'll tell you why you're wrong."

Chapter 32

I wasn't going to wait on Duncan this time and told Mal so as we drove back to the bar.

"Give him a call. See if he's free. If not, we'll go ahead and open it," Mal said.

I took out my cell phone and dialed Duncan's number. It rang several times, and just when I thought the call was going to flip over to voice mail, he finally answered.

"Yeah?" His voice sounded tired, and the chocolate taste I got was both fizzy from hearing it over the phone and diluted, like weak chocolate milk.

"Duncan, it's Mack. Did I wake you?"

"Yeah, but that's okay. I need to get up and moving, anyway. What's up?"

"Mal and I found another clue at the casino." I described it for him—what it looked like, how we'd found it, and what Mal thought it contained. "I don't want to wait to open it. We were wondering if you could meet us somewhere."

"I can spare an hour, give or take," he said. "Give me fifteen minutes to get showered, and another fifteen to get to the bar. Can you have a cup of coffee ready for me?"

"Absolutely."

"I'll be at the back door, as usual. Three knocks, a pause, and then one knock."

"Got it."

I disconnected the call, glanced at my watch, and calculated the time of his arrival. It was nearly two thirty, which should put him at the bar around three, and I filled Mal in on the plan.

"What? No packages?" Debra said when we arrived back at the bar ten minutes later.

Thinking fast, I said, "I'm having some stuff wrapped. I have to go pick it up later."

The place was crowded with mid-afternoon, last-minute holiday shoppers. Every table in the main area was full, and shopping bags littered the floor.

"You guys managing okay?" I asked.

"We're doing fine," Debra said. "It got a little crazy an hour or so ago, but we got through it."

Mal and I headed for my office, where I took off my coat and gloves. Mal did the same. Then I walked over and turned off the alarm to the back door. By now, this process was old hat to us.

"Tell me what I said that was wrong," Mal said.

"Let's wait until Duncan gets here, so I can tell you both at the same time. I'm going to go upstairs and get a pot of coffee brewing. Would you mind staying down here and manning the door? I'll leave the apartment entrance unlocked."

He nodded, and I headed upstairs. I started a pot of coffee brewing and then went into the bathroom to fix myself up a little. I was putting on a touch of mascara when I heard my cell phone ring. I reached into my pocket, fearing it would be Duncan calling to say he couldn't make it, after all, but I never found out who the caller was. As I pulled the phone from my pocket, it fell out of my hand and landed in the toilet.

I reached down and grabbed it, uttering a cussword or two. It had stopped ringing. As I looked at it, I realized it had stopped doing everything. The face of it was dark. I tried turning it on, but nothing happened.

I heard male voices coming from beyond the bathroom door, so I grabbed a hand towel, wrapped the phone in it, gave my hands a quick washing, and headed out to greet them. I headed straight for Duncan, who was wearing the same bulky parka and knit cap pulled down low, but this time he had a scarf draped over his shoulders. I gave him a kiss. It wasn't a long one—with Mal standing there watching the two of us, that would have been too awkward—but it was enough to get my innards sparking.

"We can do this quick, and I can leave so you two can have some time alone," Mal said.

Duncan smiled at him. "Thanks, pal. I'd take you up on it if I could, but I can't stay long. I have to get back to the station." He looked at me then and added, "I can come back later tonight, though."

"That would be nice," I said.

"It might be kind of late. I'll call you when I know."

That reminded me of what I held in my hand. "You might not be able to. I just dropped my phone in the toilet, and now it's not working. Did either of you just try to call me?"

They both shook their heads.

Duncan said, "Stick it in a bowl with some uncooked rice and leave it there for a while. The rice will suck the moisture out of it. It might work after that, or it might not."

"In the meantime, I have a burner phone you can borrow," Mal said. "I keep a couple in my car all the time. They come in handy with the undercover work."

"Thanks," I said. "That would be helpful."

"I'll run back to my car and grab it now, while you put that one on rice."

As Mal headed downstairs, Duncan slipped off his coat and hat, while I went into my kitchen and started rummaging through the cupboards in search of some rice. I found some and dumped the bag into a bowl. It was just enough for me to fit my phone in and cover it. As I scooped the rice over the phone, Duncan came up behind me, snaked an arm around my waist, and pulled me back against him.

"No beard or mustache disguise today?" I said.

"I didn't have time to put them on. I wrapped the scarf around my face instead. Besides, they itch and make it hard to do this." I felt his breath warm on my ear, then his lips soft on my neck.

I stopped what I was doing, closed my eyes, and leaned back against him, relishing the sensations, both real and synesthetic.

"We ought to do this more often, Mack," he whispered against my neck.

"Wish we could." I abandoned the rice, pivoted on my good foot, threw my arms over his shoulders, and gave him the kiss I'd wanted to give him earlier.

By the time we heard Mal returning with the burner phone, both of our faces were flushed. So was most of my body. Reluctantly, I released my hold on Duncan, grabbed my crutches from where they were propped up against the kitchen counter, and headed for the dining room. "The coffee is ready," I said over my shoulder. "Help yourself."

I met Mal in the dining room, and he showed me the basics of using the phone. Duncan joined us after a couple of minutes, and both he and Mal entered the number for the burner phone into their own phones. As they were doing so, I thought about who might have been calling when I dropped the phone in the toilet. Had it been Melanie Smithson? I wondered if I should try to call her again, to give her a different cell number, but then I thought that might make her suspicious. Besides, I no longer had her number. I'd tossed the cocktail napkin Clay had written it on, burying it deep in the bar trash so no one else could find it. I knew Cora could get it for me again, and made a mental note to ask her later. Besides, if Melanie was trying to hide from someone, chances were she had ditched the cell I'd called her on earlier and replaced it with a new burner phone.

Once we had the swapping of phone numbers done, we turned our attention to the envelope. It sat on the dining-room table, looking innocuous, but I could feel the weight of it bearing down on me, nonetheless. What ill-conceived surprises did the letter writer have in store for me now?

We went through the usual routine of donning gloves and fetching a clean piece of white paper to place on the table. Then Duncan picked up the tiny envelope and studied it.

"It's been colored black with something," he said.

"Felt marker?" Mal suggested.

"That's where you were wrong," I told him. "That's the same black ink that was used to write the letters. I can tell from the way it smells."

Mal gave me a grudging nod.

"Think that means anything?" Duncan asked.

"That it came from the letter writer," I said. "Other than that . . ." I shrugged.

He slid the point of the letter opener under one edge of the flap and then sliced the envelope open. He squeezed the edges of it together and peered inside. Then he tipped it over above the paper.

A tiny silver key fell out. Duncan once again looked inside the envelope, this time reaching in with two fingers. He pulled out a small piece of folded paper, and holding it over the paper on the table, he unfolded it.

Like two of the letters before it, this one contained no cryptic words, no prophetic warnings. All that was written on it, in tiny calligraphic letters, was a date and a time: *December 26, 4:00 p.m.*

Duncan held it up for me. "Anything about it jump out at you?"

I examined the individual letters carefully. They were consistent in color, and the ink used to create them smelled the same as the other inks had, but there was an underlying additional smell, too. I shifted my focus to the paper. At first glance it appeared to be the same ubiquitous white printer paper used for all the other letters, but then I sensed something different: the texture and the color had both been altered slightly.

"The paper is off," I said. "I think it might have been sprayed with or soaked in something, like that previous letter we got." I wiggled my fingers in a "give it to me" gesture, and Duncan handed it over. I held it up closer to my face and breathed in through my nose. I heard the deep bass notes of a cello and recognized the smell instantly. "It's beer," I said. "I can't tell you what brand of beer, but I'm certain this paper had beer on it at one time."

I handed the paper back to Duncan and picked up the key. "Look," I said, showing them the side of the key that had been down on the table. The two men stared at the key, then at me with questioning looks. "You don't see it?" I said.

The two of them looked again.

Finally, Duncan said, "I'm not sure what you're seeing, Mack."

I rubbed my gloved hand over the broad, round end of the key, the part one would hold. There was a hole at the end of it, but in the middle of that round-ness there was something else, a slight rise in the surface. "There's something on here," I said, setting the key down and pointing. "Something clear."

Duncan bent down until he was eye level with the key. "Wow," he said. "I'll have to take your word for it. I don't see it."

Mal picked the key up and brought it close to his face, turning it first one way, then the other in the light overhead. "I can see a faint shine," he said. He put the key back on the table and looked at me. "Any idea what it is?"

"I think it's nail polish," I said. "Clear nail polish, like you'd use for a top coat. I recognize the faint smell of it and a sound like rustling taffeta."

"Interesting," Duncan said. "So does the polish itself mean something, or is there some sort of design drawn on the key?"

"It might be both," I said. The nail polish made me think of our idea that the letter writer might be a woman, and that prompted the thought that had been niggling at the back of my mind since last night. "There's something else I need to tell you guys. I was talking to Tad last evening, and he happened to mention as he was leaving that he had to go shopping for some perfume for his wife, Suzanne. Want to guess what kind she wears?"

"Opium," they said in unison.

I nodded. "I didn't put too much stock in it at first, because there must be hundreds of women who wear that perfume. But it's been nagging at me. And Tad told me Suzanne has been giving him a lot of grief about all the time he spends here at the bar with the Capone Club. She seems to feel that his association with the group could cast both him and her in a negative light. You don't suppose she would go so far as to kill people to stop him, do you?"

I waited, breath held, expecting them both to dismiss the idea immediately. But neither of them did.

"She certainly has the money to do something like that," Duncan said, frowning. "And I've heard rumors about her, that she's a ruthless, cunning businesswoman who has no compunctions about leaving figurative bodies in her wake. It may not be a big leap from that to the literal version."

Mal said, "We should look into her connections to the university."

I nodded and took out my cell to call Cora and tell her to start investigating that line of thought, but then I remembered that I didn't have her number. "Can one of you call Cora and ask her to come up here? I don't know her number, and I'd like to get her to start looking into Suzanne Collier a little deeper."

"I got it," Duncan said, taking out his phone. "I'll

try to do a little digging myself when I get back to the station, see what I can find without raising any alarms."

Mal and I stood by, listening as Duncan placed the call and asked Cora to come up to the apartment with her laptop.

When he was done, Mal went down to the bottom of the stairs to let Cora in. I picked up the key again and studied the shiny area.

"I think there is something drawn on here with the nail polish. It doesn't cover the whole surface." I looked over at Duncan. "You don't still have that fingerprint powder with you, do you?"

Duncan's eyes grew wide. "That's bloody brilliant!" he said. "And no, I don't. But we can make some right here."

"Make some?" Now it was my turn to look puzzled.

"All I need is a pencil and a makeup brush. Have you got those? In fact, if you have some facial powder or powdered eye shadow, we can use that instead of the pencil."

I went into the bathroom and brought out my makeup bag, which contained what little I used: some mascara, some facial powder, and a tube of lipstick. "Will this do?" I said, handing Duncan the powder and the brush I used to apply it.

"It will." He took both items, then set the brush down. Then he opened the powder compact and scraped along its surface with his thumbnail until he had accumulated a small pile of fine powder in the center. After picking up the brush, he dipped it in the powder and then held it over the key. He didn't touch the brush to the key; instead, he spun the brush between his fingers, letting the powder drift down.

As I watched, we heard a commotion from the

bottom of the stairs, and a moment later a breathless Cora arrived, with Mal on her heels. Though I could tell Cora was practically bursting with curiosity, when she saw what Duncan was doing, she set her laptop on the table and watched him without saying a word.

Once the surface of the key was covered with the powder, Duncan picked the key up, tapped it a few times, and then carefully brushed over the surface. Then he eyed the end result.

"That looks like a pound sign," he said, pointing to a tiny figure on the left. "And this on the right . . ." He tilted the key in the light, studying the revealed figure. "It looks like the number one." He handed the key off to me, and I saw what he saw: a pound sign followed by the numeral one. I handed the key to Mal, who examined it, with Cora peering over his shoulder.

"What does it mean?" I asked. "Number one?"

"It could be a hashtag," Cora said. "People use it online, on Twitter," she explained.

Mal handed the key back to Duncan, who took out his phone and snapped several pictures of it, playing with different lays of the overhead light to see which angle showed it best.

Cora went on with her explanation. "Folks who use Twitter use the hashtags to highlight keywords or trending topics. It makes it easier for other people to find all the tweets on any given topic."

"Twitter and tweets?" I said, shaking my head. "What is the world coming to?"

"It's the wave of the future," Cora said.

"So do we have to go on Twitter and search for this hashtag with a one after it?" I asked.

Cora frowned. "I don't know. It seems a bit too

generic, too vague, though I suppose it can't hurt to try."

"Okay. Then how do we do it?" Mal asked.

"It just so happens, I have a Twitter account," Cora said.

"Of course you do," I said with a smile.

Cora took a seat, opened her laptop, and started tapping away at the keys. "By the way," she said as she typed, "I ordered a bottle of Opium through my Amazon Prime account. It should be here tomorrow."

"And that leads right into the main reason we called you up here," I said. We then filled Cora in on the Opium connection to Suzanne Collier, Tad's comments, and what we wanted her to do. She became so enthralled by our story that she momentarily forgot what she was doing on the computer.

"I can tell you of one connection I know about without doing any searching," she said when we were done. She looked excited. "The Collier family is a huge sponsor of Boerner Botanical Gardens. I know because it's a spot I visit often whenever I need to escape somewhere and meditate. It came up in a discussion once, and Tad mentioned that Suzanne is very involved with the place. I imagine it would be easy for her to get her hands on an aster or a willow leaf given that."

We all exchanged looks, but no one said anything. I thought we were all letting the idea of Suzanne being the letter writer ferment in our minds. And that got me to wondering about Tad. Was he involved somehow, too? Or was he an innocent bystander in it all?

I didn't know about the others, but I was starting to feel like I couldn't trust anyone anymore.

Chapter 33

"Okay," Cora said, returning to tapping her keys. "I'll do some more digging as soon as we get done investigating this hashtag thing."

Mal was already standing over Cora's shoulder, staring down at her screen. Duncan and I moved around the table to do the same.

"I don't know," Cora said after a moment, looking grimly at her screen. "A hashtag with just the number one after it is going to bring up all kinds of crap. It's too simple, too common. And Twitter doesn't like searches for hashtags that have only numbers in them." She pointed at her screen. "This is exactly what I feared," she said. "There are thousands of things that come up when you search for a hashtag and the number one. It could take days to wade through all of this."

"What about if you type out the number one as a word instead of using the numeral?" Mal asked.

Cora did so, but the results were equally voluminous and, to my eye, confusing.

"Is there a way you can look for things having to do

with keys or with beer?" I asked. "Maybe that will help narrow it down."

"Beer?" Cora asked, sounding confused.

I explained to her that the paper that was inside the small envelope with the key had been treated with beer.

"I can try," Cora said with a sideways grudging nod. "But don't get your hopes up. I think I'm going to need something a little more unique and specific to narrow down the search."

"Do what you can," Duncan said.

Cora didn't look hopeful.

Duncan went into my kitchen, grabbed some Baggies, and packaged up the evidence. As I watched him drop the key in a Baggie, I bit my lip.

"Are you sure you should take that?" I asked. "What if I have some kind of brainstorm and need that key to try to open something?"

"Like what? A key this small can't be for a lock on anything much bigger than a diary or a box like the one you found at the cemetery. If you find something like that, you should be able to break it open in an emergency. And if need be, I can get the key back to you at any time."

I caved, but I wasn't happy about it. My gut was telling me to hang on to that key.

"I have to go," Duncan said, "but I'll call you later to let you know what time I'll be back."

"Don't forget to call the new phone."

"New phone?" Cora asked.

"Yeah. Mine got wet," I told her.

"Put it in rice," she said.

"Already did."

"Give it twenty-four hours, and if that doesn't fix it,

let my guys take a run at it. And give me the number of your temporary phone in the meantime."

I gave Cora the new number, and she entered it into her phone. Then I asked her to give me Melanie Smithson's number again. A few key taps later, she had it, and I entered it into the burner cell. I dialed the number right away, but my hopes sagged when I got a message informing me the number was no longer in service.

"It looks like she ditched the phone," I told the others when I was done.

"You'll just have to wait and see if she calls back on your landline," Mal said.

Cora said, "I'll see if I can find another transaction for a new phone for her, but it might take a day or two for the charge to show up on her card, assuming she uses it again. In the meantime, I'll play with this stuff on Twitter for a while and see if anything comes up that looks like it might pertain. But don't hold your breath."

We all pulled off our gloves and Mal collected them, tossing them into the kitchen trash. Duncan put his coat and hat back on, pulling the hat down low over his forehead. Then he wrapped the scarf around his lower face. The sight of him, with just his eyes and nose showing, reminded me of the drawing Carter had done based on Harrington's description. Something niggled at the back of my mind, but I couldn't quite figure out what it was.

Mal, Cora, and I followed him downstairs, and once we determined the coast was clear, he exited out the alley door. Cora headed upstairs to the Capone Club room, where she would likely be bent over that laptop for the rest of the day. Mal and I went into my office, where I turned the alarm back on.

"What's next on your agenda?" he asked.

I looked at the stack of drawings on my desk with all the lower faces that Carter had drawn the night before. "I want to run these by Teddy to see if he recognizes anyone." I shuffled through the sheets of paper until I got to the original drawing Carter had done. I stared at it, and that same niggling sensation came back to me, but then a knock came on my office door, and whatever thought had been trying to surface went back into hiding.

Mal opened the door to Debra. "Sorry to bother you, Mack," she said, stepping over the threshold. "But Pete is sick. He just ran into the bathroom and upchucked. He needs to go home. Plus, that new waitress, Linda, just called in to say she can't work today, because her mother is in the hospital. And we're slammed out here."

"I'll be right out."

With that, Debra returned to the bar.

I looked at Mal and shrugged. "I guess my agenda for today has changed."

"I'd help out if I could," he said, "but I don't know anything about bartending or waiting tables."

"Thanks. We'll manage. Why don't you take some time for yourself?"

"I think I will," he said. "I've got some shopping I need to do. I'll check back in with you later."

We left the office, and I went behind the bar, where a pale, shaky-looking Pete was struggling to mix some drinks. "I got this," I said to him, taking the glass he had in his hand. "You go home."

"Thanks, Mack. Sorry."

I waved away his apology. "Not a problem. Go home and get better."

Mal waved good-bye and headed out. Pete followed closely on his heels. Teddy was helping Debra wait on tables, and when he came up to the bar, I told him to keep at it. I could manage behind the bar fine on my own, even with my crutches.

For the next several hours, we stayed crazy busy. Billy came in at five and joined me to help. I was woefully inadequate when it came to carrying a drink tray with my crutches, so I kept making drinks and had Teddy continue to wait on tables. Duncan called around five thirty to say he was going to be held up at work, thanks to a gang shooting, and he didn't know when, or even if, he'd be able to come by. Normally, I would have been disappointed, but given that I was also being held up at work, I told him it was fine. He said he would call later if he could come by at all, but that it would likely be very late if he did.

The dinner service was equally busy, and the evening hours flew by. Somewhere around ten o'clock we finally got a break and things slowed down. My leg was aching, my arms were throbbing, and my head was pounding from working on my feet—or rather foot—for so many hours. I told Billy I was going to take a short break and went into my office, where I downed a handful of ibuprofen. I sat down at my desk after dragging the spare chair around so I could prop my casted foot on it. And then I just sat for a while, letting my mind wander.

I nearly fell asleep, but a knock on the office door a short time later brought me back to attention. I got up and maneuvered my way to the door, where I found Clay Sanders.

"I hope it's okay that I knocked," he said. "Your staff said you were in here."

"Of course. Come on in."

I headed back to my seat, and Clay stood across the desk from me. "You look beat," he said.

"I am. It was a busy day. And getting around with these things"—I pointed to the crutches, which were propped off to one side—"makes it doubly hard. What's up?"

"I was wondering if you'd had any luck with Melanie Smithson."

"I don't know," I told him. Then I replayed the essence of my initial conversation with Melanie to him. "You're right. She sounds like she's afraid of something. And to make matters worse, my cell phone is dead." I told him what had happened and that someone had called me just as I dropped the phone into the toilet. "Maybe it was her," I said. "If it was, I may never know. Even if I could figure out who called by looking at my bill, she apparently deactivated the number we have. I tried to call it again a little while ago and got a message saying it was no longer in service."

"Bummer," Clay said. He was looking down at my desk, at the stack of drawings. "What are these?"

I explained to him how the group had spent last evening playing around with the faces in the drawings to see if any of the results looked familiar.

Clay started shuffling the papers around. At the fourth or fifth one, he stopped, cocked his head to the side, and took a step back.

"What is it?" I said.

He picked up the drawing and turned it so that I could see it right side up. "Does this look like anybody you know?" he asked me.

I stared at the picture, and that niggling thought that had been hiding out at the back of my mind leaped to the forefront. The lower face featured a narrow, weak chin and thin, pale lips. The face was instantly familiar. "It looks like Rory Gallagher!"

Clay nodded, his mouth set in a grim line. "Yes, it does." He set the papers down and walked over to the couch. He sat, placed his elbows on his knees, chin in his hands, and stared at the floor, saying nothing. He looked troubled.

"It could be a coincidence," I said. "We have no way of knowing what the man Harrington met with looked like underneath that scarf."

Clay shook his head and gave me a grim smile. "Maybe, but it makes a weird kind of sense. Rory has always been a strange, moody kind of fellow, and as far as I know, he's never dated anyone for very long. And there's the incident of the family dog that was so dedicated to Tiffany and bit Rory." Clay looked at me briefly, then tore his gaze away. I could see his thoughts were churning.

"Where are you going with this, Clay?" I had an idea, but it was so disturbing, I didn't want to voice it.

He made a face like he felt ill. "Ben told us that Tiffany seemed upset, that she got into one of her moods after they attended a family gathering, remember? And Rory might have known where Ben and Tiffany were staying when they went to Door County." His expression made it obvious that whatever he was thinking, he found it distasteful, and I felt certain he'd made the same leap I had.

I had a mental image of puzzle pieces floating around me. Slowly, they started coming together, fitting snug and tight. The idea that Rory was behind it all did answer some questions and fill several holes. It could explain why Tiffany suddenly grew so sullen and withdrawn in her teenage years. It could explain why she started cutting herself, and why she wouldn't reveal who the father was when she got pregnant during her senior year in high school. The puzzle pieces fell into place one by one, until only a couple remained floating. But the ones that had fit together provided enough. The picture they formed was of Rory Gallagher's face.

I thought I knew how to make those last pieces drop into place. I recalled my promise to Kelly Gallagher. At the time I'd had every intention of keeping it, and I'd already broken that promise by telling Mal. But this . . . this changed things, didn't it?

Except what if we were wrong? What if I told Clay what I knew and none of what we were surmising proved to be true? Would he leak it somehow, print a scandalous story about it? Could I trust him? I didn't know if I could, but maybe if I made him promise he wouldn't take it any further, I'd be able to tell if he meant it by listening to his voice and looking for changes. Except here I was reneging on a promise that would have rung truthful when I first made it to Kelly Gallagher. Clay might make promises to me that he intended to keep, but there were no guarantees he wouldn't change his mind down the road for some reason, the same way I had.

The puzzle pieces flapped and fluttered as they floated, insistent, demanding. It felt like the right move was to say something, and I prayed that I wouldn't live to regret what I was about to do.

"Clay, Kelly Gallagher confided something to me when we were looking at Tiffany's paintings, something

I think might be relevant to our discussion. But I promised her I wouldn't tell anyone."

Clay looked at me with angst-filled eyes. "Was it about Tiffany getting pregnant during her senior year?" My stunned expression gave him his answer. "I already know about it," he said. "Aidan spilled the beans one night when we were at a party. He was very drunk. He made me promise not to tell anyone."

"And did you keep that promise?" I asked, wondering about the rumors that had circulated about Tiffany's absence that year.

"Until now I did," he said, and based on the taste of his voice, he was telling the truth. "Colin Gallagher's preference of Aidan over Rory is painfully obvious, even during the few times I've seen the family together. What if it's because he knows Rory is twisted? What if he knew about him and Tiffany all along and tried to cover it up? He couldn't let a scandal like that get out."

The idea that Tiffany might have had an incestuous relationship with her brother was bad enough. The thought that her father had known and done nothing about it was even worse. My heart ached more than ever for that poor girl. Had Kelly known? I didn't think so. But I thought she might have suspected.

"What about the semen they found in Tiffany?" I asked him. "There was no sperm."

"Maybe Colin forced Rory to have a vasectomy, knowing that his proclivities might get him into trouble again down the road."

"How can we find that out?"

Clay's forehead wrinkled with thought, and he ran a hand over his head. "I don't know. Getting medical information these days is like trying to push a wall.

It was easier before all the facilities went to these electronic medical records. Back in the day I could get someone to sneak a peek into a medical file for me anytime. But now if they do that, it can be tracked. No one is willing anymore. They're afraid they'll get fired or, worse, prosecuted."

"Didn't the trial files say that they were able to determine a blood type from the semen? Isn't that how they knew it wasn't Ben who'd had sex with Tiffany?"

Clay nodded, looking thoughtful. He got up from the couch and said, "Give me until tomorrow and let me see if I can come up with something. And let's keep this between us for now."

I nodded, and as I watched him leave my office with his shoulders slumped, his step almost dragging, I knew that if what we suspected was true, it was going to devastate a lot of lives.

Chapter 34

After Clay left, I came out of the office and saw Mal sitting at the bar.

"How did your shopping go?"

"Well enough. I bought, wrapped, and shipped all my gifts back home. They'll be late, but then my family expects that of me." He winked. "What were you and Clay talking about in there?"

"I was updating him on my call to Melanie Smithson," I said. And I left it at that.

There was a lot of cleanup to do, so I busied myself helping Missy and Billy get things tidied up and chatted with Mal as I worked. Everyone was tired but in a good mood. I knew my staff would be eager to head home for the Christmas holiday, so I let them all go when I closed up at two. Mal hung for a few minutes and offered to help me finish the cleanup, but I told him to go home. I wanted some time to think through things without any other distractions.

I still hadn't heard from Duncan and figured that meant his work stuff had kept him longer than expected and I wouldn't be seeing him tonight. I took my time with the rest of the cleanup and closing duties, toddling along as best I could with my crutches, my mind thinking about Tiffany, Ben, and the Gallagher family. At around two thirty in the morning my phone rang.

"Hello?"

"Hey, Mack. It's Duncan. Wasn't sure if you'd still be up."

"I am and will be for a bit. We had a very busy day, and Pete had to go home sick. One of my other waitresses called in, too, so I've got a bit of cleanup to do yet."

"Want some help?"

I smiled at the unexpected surprise. "I'd love some."

"I can be there in fifteen minutes. The usual knock."

"Got it."

I disconnected the call and headed for my office to disable the door alarm. But I'd gone only a few steps when I heard someone knocking at the front door. I switched directions, and when I got to the front door and looked out, I saw Clay Sanders standing outside. Beside him was Aidan Gallagher. I hesitated, wondering why Clay was here with Aidan. Sensing my reluctance, Clay hollered through the door.

"Mack, can you let us in? We need to talk. I tried to call you, but I forgot about your phone problem."

I cursed, remembering that I hadn't given Clay the new number. I unlocked and opened the door.

Clay rushed in, Aidan on his heels. "I got the evidence we need," Clay said.

I shut the door and turned to look at him. "What do you mean?"

"I couldn't get anyone to tap into medical records

for me, so I thought about it and decided to give
Aidan a call. We've been talking, and while it took
some convincing, I've managed to sway him to our line
of thinking. He just came back from his house, where
he went through Rory's wallet. Rory donates blood,
and he carries a card in his wallet with his blood type
on it. The blood type of the semen found in Tiffany
was A-positive, and Ben is O-negative. That's how they
knew he couldn't have been the donor. Want to guess
what type Rory is?"

"A-positive?"

"You got it. What's more, Aidan said Rory had
some kind of surgical procedure done after his first
summer home from college. It was all very hush-hush.
Aidan doesn't know what was done, and he said his
mother doesn't know, either. But after I shared our
theory with him, he had a guess."

"A vasectomy," I said, feeling my excitement grow.

Aidan shook his head sadly, looking abashed. "I
knew my brother had issues, but I never would have
guessed he was this messed up."

Clay, looking excited, said, "Aidan is willing to go
with us to the DA's office to see if we can compel them
to look into the case again."

I looked at Aidan, surprised. "Are you sure?" I asked
him. "This is bound to destroy your family."

"My family is already destroyed," he said, looking
morose. "It's the right thing to do."

"Okay. How—" My bar phone rang then, and my
first impulse was to ignore it. But then I thought it
might be Duncan. "Excuse me," I said. "I need to get
that." I crutched around behind the bar and grabbed
the handset. "Hello?"

"Is this Mackenzie Dalton?" a female voice asked.

I recognized who it was right away: Melanie Smithson. "It is."

"I tried to call you earlier on your cell phone, but no one answered."

"I'm sorry about that," I said. "I dropped it in . . . in some water, and it's not working at the moment. I tried to call you to let you know, but it said the number was no longer in service."

There was a pause, and when I looked over at Clay and Aidan, Clay mimed the pouring of a drink and gave me a questioning look. I nodded, waved a hand at the bottles behind me, and then moved from behind the bar. Aidan walked up and settled on a stool, while Clay came around behind the bar and started mixing drinks for the two of them.

"I thought long and hard about whether or not I should call you," Melanie said. "You have to promise me that you won't tell anyone. He's threatened me several times. He said he would kill me if I ever said anything."

I looked over at Clay as he set a drink down in front of Aidan and gave him a thumbs-up, getting a curious look in return. I mouthed the name Melanie Smithson to him and pointed at the phone. I started to tell Melanie that it was okay, that we already knew Rory was the culprit, but she went on in a rapid-fire, panicked voice before I could get a word out.

"He is . . . was," Melanie went on, correcting herself in a sad tone, "infatuated with her, you know. And he's not right in the head. He raped her when we were in high school, and he kept after her all those years, showing up at unexpected times, strong-arming her into having sex with him, threatening to kill her if she didn't, and later threatening to kill Ben. He tried his damnedest to break those two up, and when he couldn't, it made him furious. Tiffany told me she was afraid he would go through with it and kill Ben." She paused, sucked in a quivering breath, and then said, "I think he finally did, or at least he tried." She sucked in a quick, ragged breath and rambled on. "You can't tell anyone. And you have to find a way to get him put away. If he finds out I told you about him, he'll kill me. I know he will." The fear was evident in her voice, and I could tell she was one heartbeat away from having a full-blown panic attack.

"It's okay," I said. "We already figured it out on our own. In fact, we're putting together a plan right now to go to the DA and ask them to look into the murder again."

"That won't happen," she said. "That family has too much money, too much influence. They'll buy their way out of it somehow." She hiccuped back a sob. "Oh, God, I shouldn't have said anything."

"Maybe you need to say more," I said. "Would you be willing to talk to the DA if I go with you?"

"Are you crazy?" she screeched. "The minute I set foot back in Milwaukee, that family will have some hired killer do away with me."

Aidan and Clay were both watching me closely, hanging on my every word. I felt bad for Aidan, and a little awkward, given that I was trying to convince someone to help me crucify his brother. His sad, hang-dog expression tore at me. I hobbled around on my crutches, angling myself away from the men's stares.

"I know a lot of cops," I told Melanie in a low voice. "I can see to it that you're safe if you come back."

"Sorry, but I can't do it," she sobbed.

"The only way we'll ever be able to put Rory away is if we gather enough evidence so that the DA can't ignore it. With your help—"

"Rory?" she said, her voice shrill. "Not Rory, lady. It's Aidan."

"What?" I shot back. My voice reverberated in the phone like a gunshot. I felt my blood run cold. Literally. The hair on the back of my neck rose, and my body began to tremble. My ears suddenly became hypersensitive, and I heard noises, sounds coming from behind me. And another noise, more distant. And then I felt the cold, hard steel at my neck.

"Hang up the phone, Ms. Dalton," Aidan said in a cold, dead voice. I knew he was right behind me, not only because of how close his voice was, but because I could feel the warmth of his breath on the back of my neck mingling with the coldness of what I knew from the smell was a gun.

"Aidan, what the hell?" Clay said.

"Hang up the phone *now*," Aidan said, jabbing the gun into my neck.

"I have to go," I said to Melanie. "Thanks for calling." As I took the phone from my ear and went to press the disconnect button, I heard her gasp.

"Turn around," Aidan said. "Slowly."

I didn't have much choice other than to do it slowly, thanks to my crutches. Carefully, I twisted around until I was facing him. I glanced over at Clay, who was standing behind the bar, looking confused and bewildered.

"It was you," I said to Aidan. "You were the one who raped Tiffany. You were the one who tried to kill Ben." I looked over at Clay. "It makes sense," I said to him. "Aidan and Rory look alike, have the same eyes, nose, and hair. If we had put Aidan's lower facial features on that drawing instead of Rory's . . ." I left the rest for him to glean, knowing he'd figure it out.

He did, and when he shifted his gaze to Aidan, there was no doubt he understood, based on the expression of betrayal I saw on his face. Despite that, he said, "She's wrong about you, Aidan, isn't she?"

"Shut up, Clay," Aidan snapped. His voice was loud enough that it made me jump, but not so loud that I couldn't hear something else. "Go sit down," Aidan said to me, gesturing toward one of the barstools. "I need to think."

I started for the stool he'd indicated, my mind racing, trying to think of a way to keep him talking. But Clay beat me to it.

"Damn it, Aidan," he said, running a hand over his head. "You did this, didn't you?"

Aidan didn't answer. He was watching me sidle up onto the barstool.

"This has to end now," Clay said. He set his drink glass on the bar and started walking toward us.

Aidan moved so fast, I barely had time to register what was happening. A deafening sound exploded near my head, and my ears started to ring. The smell of gunpowder filled my nostrils. A second later the faint smell of blood followed. A host of synesthetic reactions came, too, triggered not only by all the sensory input, but also by the hopelessness and fear I felt. I heard Clay groan behind me and then slump heavily to the floor. I wanted to look, to go to him and try to help him, but I stayed frozen, afraid to move so much as a hair, lest I be the next victim. Even so, part of me knew that my bullet was likely only seconds away, anyway. Now that Aidan had shot Clay, he was committed to seeing it through. There would be no turning back.

I hung onto the phone, hoping that the sounds I'd heard meant what I thought they did. I hadn't disconnected the call when Aidan told me to. Instead of hitting the hang-up button, I'd hit one of the number buttons. I was pretty sure Melanie had heard Aidan's voice in the background—that was why she had gasped—and I prayed she was still on the line, listening. At least that way my death wouldn't go unsolved and, hopefully, unpunished.

In the periphery of my vision I saw Aidan swing his gun arm back my way, and I closed my eyes, bracing for the bullet. I heard a faint click, and my heart skipped a beat. I prayed it would be swift and painless, a head shot, so I wouldn't have to hear it, wouldn't feel the pain. Instantaneous death.

But I did hear the shot, loud and clear. It was painfully loud, and immediately afterward I felt a warmth spreading over my face. The smell of blood was powerful and overwhelming, and I felt the heat of it marking a path as it trickled down my cheeks. I waited for the pain—the real pain—to register. But it never came.

"Jesus, Mack, are you okay?"

It sounded like Duncan's voice, but it seemed to be coming from far away. I opened my eyes, convinced that I'd see nothing but darkness or maybe an approaching light, but instead I saw a red haze. And then I felt a hand grasp my arm.

I heard other sounds then: sirens, someone yelling for an ambulance, feet scuffling, a moan. Something soft swiped at my face, over my eyes, and when it was gone, so was the red haze. Instead, I saw Duncan, his face in front of mine, his expression one of panic and worry.

"Are you okay?" he asked again.

I took a quick self-inventory. Nothing hurt. Over Duncan's shoulder I could see the front door of my bar and the cops who were streaming through it. I lifted up my hand, saw the phone still in it, and put it to my ear.

"Melanie? Are you still there?"

"Oh, thank God you're okay!" I heard her say through the phone.

And with that, I set the phone on the bar and began to sob.

Chapter 35

Christmas Day dawned bright and sunny. The city was blanketed in six inches of fresh snow. The downtown streets were quiet and empty, for the most part, as families gathered together to celebrate within the confines of their homes. Most of my customers would be doing the same, including the bulk of the Capone Club, though I suspected most of them would find their way to the bar later in the day, once I opened. We had more than just the holiday to celebrate.

I awoke a little after nine, relishing the fact that I didn't have to get up right away. I rolled over in bed, smiled at the sleeping man beside me, and curled up to spoon his back. I stayed that way for a while, flitting in and out of sleep, trying to embrace the moment.

I knew the peace and serenity couldn't last. My sword of Damocles was still hanging over my head.

Eventually, I sensed something different in Duncan and knew he was awake. "Coffee?" I whispered.

"Of course, but let me make it." He rolled over, kissed me on my nose, and got out of bed. He pulled on his boxers and jeans, said, "Merry Christmas!" and then shuffled out to the kitchen.

I stayed in bed, lying on my back, staring up at the ceiling. My mind was whirring a hundred miles an hour, flipping back and forth between the events of the past few days and the last letter writer clue, which we had yet to figure out. When Duncan returned to the bedroom with two steaming mugs of coffee on a tray and some coffee cake I'd made the day before, I sat up and leaned my back against the headboard.

He joined me in the bed, and the two of us sat there sipping and eating for several minutes, not a word spoken between us. It was a comfortable silence, despite the discomfort I felt inside. We had yet to talk about what had happened with Aidan, though I'd gone over it several times with other cops. I decided now was the time.

"Thanks again for your excellent timing the other night," I said to him after we'd finished eating our cake. "I honestly thought I was done for."

"You very nearly were," he said. "I knocked on the back door three times, and when I got no answer, I knew something was off. I went around to the front of the bar and looked through the window. I saw Aidan standing there, holding a gun on you as you were getting onto the stool. I called right then for backup." He paused and gave me a sheepish smile. "I was trying to figure out how I was going to get inside when it occurred to me to check and see if the door was locked. I can't tell you how relieved I was when I pushed down on the thumb latch and felt it click."

"I shut it after I let Clay and Aidan in, but I was so distracted by what Clay was telling me that I forgot to lock it."

"Good thing. I wasn't sure what was going on, just that Aidan Gallagher was aiming a gun at you. I didn't know if Clay was with him and in on it or a victim like you. When I saw Clay start to come from behind the bar, I was about to burst through the door, thinking he was going after you. Then Aidan shot him, and I switched my focus."

"I never saw you come into the bar, because Aidan was blocking my view." I took in a deep breath, trying to settle myself, as the memory of that night jangled my nerves. "Hitting him in the shoulder the way you did was smart. It disabled his gun arm. But when the blood splatter from his shoulder hit me in the face, I thought it was my own blood. I thought he'd shot me and I was dead." I looked at him and shuddered. "In another few seconds I would have been if you hadn't shot him when you did. Thank goodness your aim is good."

Duncan draped an arm over my shoulders and pulled me to him, hugging me tight. It felt safe, warm, reassuring. He held me like that for several seconds and then said, "I was aiming for his head."

It took a moment for the words to register, and when they did, I started to laugh. I pushed away from him and looked him straight in the eye, still sniggering. "You're making that up," I said.

"Sorry, lass, but I'm not."

"Oh, my." My laughter crescendoed until it bordered on something close to hysterical as the realization of how close I'd come to death washed over me like ice-cold water.

"Mack," Duncan said, taking my hand and squeezing it. "You're okay. It's over." He leaned in close to my face and looked me straight in the eye. "Take a deep breath."

I did, then exhaled it with another shudder. Finally sobering, I said, "Well, whatever you were aiming at, you saved my life. Thank you."

He leaned back against the headboard and eyed me with a serious expression. "I'm so sorry for all the darkness I've brought into your life, Mack. I can't help but feel that none of this would have happened to you if it wasn't for me. Promise me you won't let any of this erase the goodness and happiness inside you."

I cocked my head to the side and gave him a feeble smile. "I promise I'll try," I said, "but I'm getting very pissed off about this letter writer. And scared. Cora hasn't found anything on Twitter, and I have no idea what the beer means. We have only today and tomorrow to figure it out. What if we don't?"

I expected him to feed me some platitude about not worrying or a reassurance that we'd get there, but instead he sighed, ran a hand through his hair, and said, "I don't know."

On that somber note, I pushed my worries down deep and locked them away for later. Today I wanted to escape from all the death and cruelty and darkness in the world, if only for a little while.

A short time later we got up and went downstairs to make ready for the group of "family" that would be joining us for the afternoon. I was planning a holiday meal with all the trimmings: roast turkey, mashed potatoes, gravy, an assortment of veggies, and a variety of pies for dessert. While I busied myself getting the turkey in the oven and peeling potatoes, Duncan worked alongside me, whipping up a traditional Scottish Christmas pudding, a fruit-filled concoction with rum sauce as the topping. He also made up a batch of his grandmother's hot buttered rum, a hot, sweet, creamy drink that seemed perfect on a cold winter's day.

I had told our guests they should plan on eating around two, but that they were welcome to come earlier if they liked, any time after eleven. Joe and Frank Signoriello arrived first, coming at their traditional time of a few minutes past eleven. They settled in at a table, and I served them each a bottled beer at their request. For this occasion, all drinks were on the house.

Mal arrived a few minutes after that, and Cora showed up twenty minutes later with Tiny in tow. She assured me that Tiny understood the need to keep Duncan's presence a secret, and despite the fact that Tiny's loose lips were a big reason all the press headaches had descended upon me in the first place, I felt he could be trusted at this point. His original slip had been made out of ignorance, and at this point he was so grateful to us for solving the murder of his sister, I knew he would never do anything to hurt me or the group.

Since Tiny hadn't been around much lately, much of our conversation revolved around what the Capone Club had been up to and the evolution of the Middleton case. Everyone had brought small gifts, which we would exchange at some point, but the biggest gift any of us would give this season was the one we got for Ben Middleton. He was still in prison—the wheels of justice turn painfully slow, particularly when the players are forced to backpedal—but his innocence was now obvious.

Not only had Melanie Smithson stayed on the line

during my phone conversation with her the other night, but she'd also recorded the entire thing. She'd brought a small handheld recorder with her when she'd gone on the run, and any phone calls she got from an unknown number were put on speaker and recorded. Her motivation for this was her fear of the Gallaghers and what they might do to try to find her and silence her. She had decided to record her phone call to me, as well, and when she heard Aidan Gallagher's voice in the background, she'd had the wits to keep the line open and the recorder running.

Duncan told us that once Melanie knew the Gallagher family secret had been exposed, she had expressed a willingness to return home and testify against Aidan. Her testimony and the recording of what had happened in my bar the other night would likely be more than enough to put Aidan away. But we had plenty more. It had turned out that Aidan's blood type was the same as Rory's.

Once the truth about Aidan and Tiffany was known, secrets started spilling out of the Gallagher family like blood from a deep wound. And it turned out the Gallaghers had a lot of wounds, some of them festering. Several stunning revelations had come to light over the past day and a half, not the least of which was the real reason behind Colin Gallagher's dislike of his son Rory. Not only was Aidan the golden child in Colin's eyes—the firstborn, as well as the more handsome, successful, and charismatic son—but he was also the only son Colin actually had. Kelly revealed that she'd had an affair years ago, during which she found out she was pregnant. She'd had no way of knowing if the child was Colin's or her lover's, so she had hidden the truth from Colin and broken off the affair, intending to pass the child off as Colin's no matter what. Since both of the boys favored their mother, and Rory bore enough of a resemblance to Aidan to quell any suspicions Colin might have had, the patriarch had been none the wiser, though in retrospect I couldn't help but wonder if he'd sensed all along that something was off.

And speaking of off, Colin had eventually figured out that his eldest son had some sexual proclivities that were outside the norm. He caught Aidan and Tiffany together during the family gathering Ben had mentioned, the one that had gotten Tiffany so upset. When Colin later confronted Tiffany, she admitted to her father that Aidan had been sexually assaulting her for years and that he was the one who had gotten her pregnant the summer before her senior year in high school. By this time, Colin was grooming Aidan to take over the family business, and he'd already bought the silence of two girls Aidan had raped while he was in college, one of whom had ended up pregnant and subsequently had an abortion. So Colin hauled Aidan off to a counselor in New York City, hiding the sessions under the guise of business trips. The counseling didn't work, and during one of these "business trips," Colin forced his son to have a vasectomy, before his activities resulted in a passel of kids with a future claim on the family fortunes. It wasn't Rory who had had some secret procedure done, as Aidan had said. It was Aidan himself.

Aidan's fixation on his sister never subsided. If anything, it grew stronger. The dog bite incident happened during one of Aidan's attacks on Tiffany while the two of them were home alone. Tiffany had tried to fend Aidan off that time, and during the struggle Rory

came home unexpectedly. He heard the sounds of a
struggle coming from his sister's bedroom and opened
the door to her room. When he saw Aidan slap Tiffany,
he ran into the room, grabbed his brother's arm, and
yanked him back. The two boys started grappling,
and Tiffany got knocked down at one point when
Aidan shoved Rory and he fell into her. The dog had
entered the room by then, and when Tiffany went
down, the dog rose to her defense, biting Rory in the
process. It was enough to stop the fight, but the dog
ended up paying the ultimate price for his devotion to
his mistress.

Rory never knew what the fight between Tiffany
and Aidan had been about, but he began to suspect
that his brother wasn't right. That suspicion grew
stronger when Ben came into the picture. Rory could
tell Aidan hated the guy, though he couldn't figure
out why. And when Tiffany became engaged to Ben,
Aidan's fixation on the two of them intensified. He was
constantly tailing his sister, wanting to know where she
was and what she was doing. He tried several times to
drive a wedge between the couple by telling lies about
Ben to both Tiffany and his father, prompting Colin
to hire the PI. When those efforts failed to break the
couple up, Aidan grew desperate.

It was Aidan who had bought the gun from Harrington, but when it came time to actually kill Ben,
he hired someone else to do the job. He knew Tiffany
and Ben were heading for the house in Door County
and where the house was located, because the couple
had shared the information with Kelly, who had written it down and left it hanging on the fridge. Aidan
hired an old down-on-his-luck college buddy named
Jack Cartwright to rent a house two miles away and buy

both a four-wheel-drive vehicle and a snowmobile. Aidan paid for the items, though he told Cartwright he would be allowed to keep them as part of his payment. Aidan and Cartwright then went to the rented house the day after Ben and Tiffany left, and Aidan spied on the couple numerous times during their stay, walking to their rental house before the heavy snowfalls came, then using the snowmobile.

On the day of Tiffany's death, Aidan watched as Ben headed into town for supplies. Then he paid a visit to Tiffany, forcing himself on her yet again and threatening to kill Ben if she ever told anyone. After leaving the house, he hung around outside long enough to see Ben return. He listened outside a window, heard Tiffany insist that they head home before the storm, and then saw Ben start packing up the car. At that point he hurried back to Cartwright and put his murder plan into action. The two men snowmobiled to a point several miles down from the house where Ben and Tiffany were staying, and got ready. Aidan stayed off in the woods with the snowmobile, while Cartwright went out to the road to wait for Ben and Tiffany's car.

Aidan was so angry that Tiffany had been killed and Ben hadn't that he killed Cartwright. Though Duncan said Aidan denied it, there was a commonly held belief that killing Cartwright had been part of Aidan's plan all along. Cartwright's body had not been found, and if what Aidan had told the cops was true, it never would be. Aidan said he had disposed of it in the wood chipper that came with the house they were staying in.

Aidan was arrested, and once he was released from the hospital after the treatment of his shoulder wound, he was taken down to the station and questioned. In a blazing display of his psychotic thought processes and his unmitigated arrogance, he confessed to everything. He declared himself a free entity, a member of his own ruling government, and as such, he insisted that he was not subject to the laws of the state or the country. He claimed that it didn't matter what he told the cops, because he was one of the wealthy elite and was therefore untouchable. He told them they could lock him up for now if they wanted, but eventually, he would buy his freedom and make all of them pay.

Listening to Duncan tell us about Aidan's behavior was surreal. The man had hidden his psychosis well, but once it came out, it came out with a vengeance. It was a grim, sad, and yet oddly satisfying tale that proved money wasn't the secret to happiness. I could only imagine what things would be like inside that magnificent house on the lake in the days to come. No doubt this Christmas would be one that none of the Gallaghers would forget for a long time to come, if ever.

"What's going to happen to Aidan?" Cora asked once we had finished bringing Tiny up to date on the story.

Duncan's lips compressed into a thin line. "He's being held pending a psych evaluation. Based on what I observed, I'd say the odds are good he'll be declared insane and locked up in a mental institution somewhere."

"And how is Clay doing?" Joe asked.

"He's doing well," I told them. "He came through his surgery fine. He'll be eating through a straw for a few days and out of commission for a week or two, but he'll recover. And the nurses told me he's already sitting up in his bed, typing out an article about the case."

"I hope it's not going to lambaste you again," Frank said.

"I don't think so," I said. "Cora visited him yesterday, and they had a little chat."

Everyone looked over at Cora, curious.

"It's true," she said with an enigmatic smile. "I think Clay Sanders has seen the wisdom of having Mack on his side. I'm not sure the police department or the DA's office will fare so well, however."

"I'm working on that," Duncan said cryptically.

With that, I got up to fetch the brothers another round of beers, and Tiny excused himself to go to the men's room.

"I have some other news," Cora said when I returned with the brothers' beers. "It's about the letter writer, and it's important, but before I tell you, I'd like to ask that we let Tiny in on what's going on. He already knows Duncan is still coming by, and I feel confident he'll keep mum about anything that we tell him has to stay secret. And besides, he's pretty busy with work right now and won't be around much for a while."

I frowned, uncertain about bringing anyone else in on the case, and gave a questioning look to the others.

Joe and Frank both shrugged.

Mal pursed his lips in thought for a second and then said, "I think we can trust him."

I turned to Duncan, my eyebrows raised expectantly.

"I don't know," he said, shaking his head slowly. "I'm not keen on bringing anyone else into it, but I imagine it has to be hard for Cora to keep a secret like that from someone she's close to. And I agree with

Mal. I think Tiny is trustworthy. So I'll leave it up to you, Mack."

I looked over at Cora. "You're sure he won't let something slip at some point?"

"Positive," Cora said without hesitation. "Tiny might come across as a big, dumb oaf at times, but he's actually quite intelligent." She sighed and flashed me an apologetic smile. "And to be honest, he's already figured out that I'm working on something for you, something that's very hush-hush. He's asked me twice already, and I've been stalling him, but I think it's only a matter of time before he figures out some or all of it on his own."

"Okay then," I said. "Let's bring him in on it."

As if on cue, we heard the squeak of the men's room door opening and Tiny's heavy, clumping footsteps as he headed back to the table.

"Tiny," I said once he had resumed his seat. "There's something we need to tell you."

Over the next ten minutes or so, we brought Tiny up to speed on the letter writer case, including our suspicion that Suzanne Collier might be behind it and why.

"Cora ordered a bottle of Opium perfume for me, and it came yesterday," I told him and the brothers, since they didn't know this part yet, either. "The smell of that perfume is definitely the same smell I picked up on in Gary's car. That doesn't prove it was Suzanne who was in there, because I'm sure there are hundreds, maybe thousands of other women in the Milwaukee area who wear that perfume, but it certainly points another finger in her direction."

"And I've uncovered several more fingers that point that way," Cora said. "Quite damningly, in fact." She leaned over and reached into the laptop bag she had brought with her, though in an amazing display of holiday spirit and ardent restraint, she hadn't taken the machine out since her arrival. She still didn't take it out. What she removed instead was a notebook. She opened it and then went on, glancing at the items she had written down. "To start with, the Collier family has established a fund that awards several scholarships a year to students at the U of W. Suzanne Collier is the family representative on the board that reviews the applicants' files and makes the final decision on who gets the money. And it just so happens that both the girl who worked at the zoo and the young man who worked at the Miller plant were recipients."

"Of course," Mal said with a snap of his fingers. "Those scholarship applications would have given her access to their financial information, their names and addresses, their areas of study, their employment . . . all of it. It would have been easy for her to deliver the packages to both of them."

"And that's not all," Cora said. "Remember the art store you went to for the very first clue?"

I nodded.

"The guy who owns it was about to go bankrupt two years ago, but he was able to secure a loan to keep the store afloat. Guess who gave him that loan," Cora went on.

"Suzanne Collier?" Joe said, unnecessarily. We'd all made the appropriate leap in logic.

Cora nodded and then looked at me apologetically. "Do you remember the name of that store?"

I thought back, and then my eyes widened in amazement. "Oh, my goodness," I said, slapping myself on the side of my head. "It was Collier Art Supply!"

Cora nodded. "I don't know how we all managed to miss that connection. But when I was going back over some notes I had on the case, it suddenly leaped out at me. So I did some digging. It turns out the owner is a distant cousin of some sort to the Collier family."

Everyone at the table exchanged sheepish looks of disbelief, all of us stymied by the fact that we hadn't made the connection sooner.

"If Suzanne owns that store," I said, "she'd have unlimited access to the ink that was used in those letters."

"Not only that," Cora said, looking a bit smug. "I had a chat yesterday with one of my clients, a very wealthy lady here in the city who hangs out in many of the same circles that Suzanne does. I had to talk to her about something related to some computer security work my company is doing for her with regard to the printing businesses her family owns, and given what I'd already uncovered about Suzanne, I purposely steered the conversation around to the topic of modern-day printing doing away with certain endearing but old-fashioned skills, like calligraphy. She insisted that the old way of doing things would always linger on. I disagreed and asked her if she knew even one person who does hand calligraphy anymore. I'm sure you can guess whose name she mentioned."

"Suzanne's," the brothers said in unison.

"And there's more still," Cora said, licking her lips and looking like the cat that had just eaten the canary. "That spice shop at the Public Market? They have several business arrangements with entities in the city, including the one with the university that we know about. That connection, which I'm not sure Suzanne knew about, may well have been a lucky coincidence because it put us on the right track. But the one I'm betting she does know about is the contract the shop has with an upscale restaurant in town called Toby's."

"I've heard of it, but I've never eaten there," I said.

"Neither have I," Cora said. "It's a bit pricey for my tastes. But the interesting thing about it is who owns it—the Collier family. Toby Collier is Suzanne's grandfather. Want to guess who does the books for the place?"

"Tad?" I said, feeling my heart sink.

Cora nodded.

"Oh, God," I said, squeezing my eyes closed for a moment as the ramifications of this sank in. "Do you think Tad is in on it?"

Cora cocked her head and made a tentative face. "I don't know, but my gut tells me no. My gut isn't proof, however."

"He wouldn't necessarily have to be a part of it," Frank said. I suspected that he, like me, didn't want to believe that Tad had been fooling all of us all this time. "If Tad does the books for the restaurant, Suzanne might have access to the spice store's account info. That's all she would have needed. Right?" Frank looked at the rest of us with a hopeful expression. There were some tentative nods in the group, but I knew that for now, everyone would be very wary of Tad.

"Is that everything?" Duncan asked, looking solemn.

Cora shook her head. "No. I have one more connection. The Collier family owns a series of plots at Forest Home Cemetery. Several of Suzanne's ancestors are buried there. And those plots are on the hill very near to the Prairie Rest area where Mack found that clue in the willow tree. Plus, we've already established

Suzanne's possible connection to the aster and the willow leaf that came in the letter that led Mack there."

"What about the casino?" Mal asked. "Any connections there?"

"Not that I've been able to find," Cora said, shaking her head. "But it's a public enough place that I'm not sure there needs to be one."

There was a period of silence as we all sat, digesting the huge course of information Cora had just fed us.

It was Duncan who finally broke the silence. "If we're on the right track and Suzanne Collier is the one behind all of this, it's not going to be easy to prove. What you've told us is very damning, but none of it is evidence that would hold up in court. And given Suzanne Collier's reputation, and the money and power resources she has at her fingertips, it won't be easy to convince anyone that she's behind it. In fact, I find it hard to believe that the woman is twisted enough to actually kill people over this."

"Well, there is one more thing," Cora said a bit cryptically. She reached into her laptop bag again and pulled out a sheet of paper, which she laid in the center of the table. We all leaned forward to look at it.

"This is a printout of an article from last year from one of those paparazzi-driven gab rags that like to stalk the rich and the famous. It says that Suzanne Collier was observed on three different occasions exiting the office of a shrink who caters to high-society types. It's not much, but it might suggest that Suzanne has some issues we don't know about."

Cora was right that it wasn't much, and the entity that had printed the article was well known for circling the truth with their use of innuendo and suggestion.

After giving us all a few moments to read the brief

article, which came with a fuzzy picture that might or might not have been of Suzanne Collier, Cora then threw a wrench into the works.

"I hate to burst this nice bubble I've created for all of you," she said with a guarded, cautious tone, "but despite all these connections to Suzanne, there is a big problem."

Everyone averted their gaze from the article on the table to Cora.

On cue, Cora reached into her laptop bag yet again and withdrew another piece of paper. She set it atop the first article, and everyone's attention shifted to it. This one was a printout of a news article from the *Journal*, and in a large, very clear picture at the top was Suzanne Collier.

"This is from last week," Cora explained. "It's a story about how Suzanne visited some orphanage in Mexico and donated a bunch of money to help feed and clothe the kids there. Look at the date in the article."

I scanned the text to find what she was referring to. At first, I didn't understand the point she was trying to make, but then I made the connection.

So did Duncan. "She was there when Lewis Carmichael was killed," he said.

Cora nodded grimly.

"So that means she couldn't have killed him," I said, leaning back in my seat and sighing with frustration. I felt my hopes go up in smoke like a magician's flash paper.

"To be honest, I was thinking she couldn't have done it, anyway," Duncan said. I and the others gave him an inquisitive look. "Lewis was stabbed to death," he explained. "But he was also beaten pretty badly. It would be very difficult for a woman, especially one

Suzanne's size, to do that. Perhaps not impossible, but certainly unlikely. And given this"—he tapped the article on the table—"I'd say it's safe to assume she didn't do it."

The disappointment everyone felt over this revelation was palpable. And then Mal made it worse.

"But I imagine Tad could have done it."

The pain of that suggestion was like a knife in my back. Judging from the horrified expressions on the faces of everyone else at the table, I wasn't alone.

But then Cora took on the rolé of the cavalry. "Tad couldn't have done it, either," she said. "He was here with us, upstairs in the Capone Club room, at the time Lewis was killed."

"That's right!" Joe said, slapping his knee and sounding excited.

There was a collective sigh of relief around the table, and I could sense a lifting of the oppressive melancholy that hung over the group.

"Okay," Duncan said. "So Tad is in the clear, at least in Lewis's death, but we still have the other issues at hand. And I think Mal may have been on the right track. Suzanne Collier may well be our suspect. In fact, given all the stuff that Cora has dug up, I'm inclined to think she is. But she didn't do it alone. I think she had an accomplice."

This made perfect sense to me. "Of course," I said. "With her money, it would be easy to hire someone to do her dirty work, or at least some of it."

Frank leaned forward, his eyes big. "That would be the smart way to do it," he said. "Either hire someone or find someone with a motive that meshes with hers. If they split the nastiness between them but connect all the murders with the letters, it gives both parties alibis for at least some of the murders. Kind of like that movie *Strangers on a Train.*"

Mal shot Duncan a look. Based on the expression on their faces, I knew they were both thinking the same thing, and whatever it was, it didn't bode well.

"What?" I said, staring down the two of them. "What are you two thinking?"

Neither of them answered at first, but after Mal stared Duncan down for several seconds, I saw Duncan's shoulders sag. He gave Mal an almost imperceptible nod.

Mal looked at me, his expression grim. "Duncan and I have discussed these letters and the lack of any usable evidence to go with them. I think we have to consider the possibility that whoever is involved has some solid knowledge of forensics and police procedures. Would Suzanne Collier have that kind of knowledge?"

Looks were exchanged, and after a few seconds of silence, Cora said, "I don't know."

My thoughts immediately leapt to Duncan's partner, Jimmy, but that was water I had to tread carefully.

"Anyone who participates in the Capone Club will have that kind of knowledge," Mal noted. There were several solemn nods around the table.

"There's one thing we're forgetting," I said. "I can buy a certain amount of coincidence, but there seems to be enough connections to Suzanne Collier for me to believe she's involved in some way. If we assume her motive is to disband the Capone Club so Tad doesn't spend so much time here—a motive that sounds a bit flimsy to me, but we can talk more about that later—then why target Duncan in the letters? Why allow the

Capone Club to continue to go on and target me and Duncan?"

"Well, the two of you are the heart of the Capone Club," Cora said. "Eliminate the two of you from the mix and the club will likely disband, particularly if several members end up dead."

My mind was reeling with the possibilities, and I felt a stab of anger—literally, as it manifested itself as a sharp pain in my side—that our holiday had been tainted with these morbid thoughts.

"Enough," I said, determined to shift the mood to a lighter topic. "Let's table the discussion for now and come back to it at a later date. I want to focus on the holiday. Who wants to give me a hand in the kitchen?"

An hour later we were all sitting around our pushed-together tables, stuffed, sated, and content.

"Anyone want coffee?" I asked.

There were some sleepy-eyed nods from the group, so I got up and went behind the bar to start a pot brewing. Once I got it going, I stood a moment and watched the others laughing, talking, and enjoying themselves, and it made me smile. It was an odd, misfit group of friends I had, this substitute family of mine, and given that I'd always felt like a bit of a misfit myself, I found it apropos. Watching them, I prayed that no harm would come to any of them in this cruel game I was forced to play with the letter writer.

I felt fiercely protective of all of them suddenly, and this imbued me with a new sense of determination. Somehow I had to beat this letter writer. I was going to win this game, no matter what it took. I imagined myself in a horse race, riding a white stallion who was surging ahead from the back of the pack. I saw myself overtake a ghostly image riding a black beast of a horse, which snorted and stomped in anger as I crossed the finish line a nose ahead of it. And then I envisioned my friends, my makeshift family, running to my side and congratulating me, showering me with flowers and a giant first-place ribbon.

Just like that, I figured out part of the meaning behind the key that was the latest clue.

"Cora," I said, painfully aware that I was about to violate my own edict to stay away from the grim topic of the letter writer, "do me a favor and fire up your laptop."

She did so as the others all watched, curiosity stamped on their faces. Something in my voice must have told them that the chase was back on.

"Ready," Cora said.

"See what you can find out about the Pabst Mansion and any connections Suzanne Collier might have to it."

Cora stared at me curiously for a moment before smiling. "Of course!" she said, starting to tap at her keys.

The others were staring at me with confusion, so I explained. "That number one sign on the key and the beer on the paper. I think it means Pabst Blue Ribbon."

Since both Duncan and Mal were relatively new to the city and might not know the history, Cora summarized her findings even as she kept searching. "The Pabst Mansion served as home to Captain Frederick Pabst—the founder of the Pabst Brewing Company—and his family back at the turn of the twentieth century. The opulent structure later passed into the hands of the Archdiocese of Milwaukee, and it served as home to priests and nuns for the next sixty-plus years. Back in the seventies it was nearly demolished, but a historic preservation group stepped up and saved it. After some painstaking restoration, it now stands surrounded by modern-day buildings in downtown Milwaukee and is open to the public for tours." Cora paused with her typing and looked up at the others. "Their Christmas decorations and tours are quite famous and popular." She went back to her keyboard and started tapping again, her eyes scanning her screen.

"So you think that key might have something to do with this mansion?" Duncan asked.

"I do," I said, hoping I was right. The deadline was rapidly approaching.

For the next minute or two, the room was silent, except for the light tapping sound of Cora hitting her keys. Everyone looked pensive and hopeful, but warily so.

Finally, Cora leaned back in her seat and said, "Bingo! Suzanne Collier sits on the board of directors for the historic preservation group responsible for maintaining the Pabst Mansion."

Duncan sighed and shook his head, a hapless look on his face. "Mack is right. That's too much coincidence for anybody. But now that we know who we need to go after, we have to figure out how. All we have so far is supposition and circumstantial evidence, none of which would be enough to make an arrest, much less get a conviction. Plus, we don't know if she's working alone. Based on the facts so far, I'd say it's a good bet she isn't. And as was pointed out before, someone with that kind of financial clout won't be easy to catch."

He was right, of course, and I knew that my problems were far from over. But at least now I knew who the enemy was, one of them, anyway. Suzanne Collier had just been demoted from hunter to prey, and for the first time in days, I felt hope again for the future.

To be continued . . .

Look for the next Mack's Bar Mystery
in August 2017!

Shot Recipes

THE ALMOND JOY SHOT

Yield: 1 serving

½ ounce brown crème de cacao
½ ounce Amaretto
½ ounce coconut-flavored rum
½ ounce cream or half-and-half

Pour all the ingredients into a two-ounce shot glass, stir, and serve at once.

THE PUMPKIN PIE SHOT

Yield: 1 serving

½ ounce coffee liqueur
½ ounce Original Baileys Irish Cream
¼ ounce cinnamon schnapps

Pour all the ingredients into a two-ounce shot glass, stir, and serve at once.

THE SANTA CLAUS SHOT

Yield: 1 serving

½ ounce grenadine
½ ounce green crème de menthe
½ ounce peppermint schnapps

Pour the grenadine into a two-ounce shot glass. Next, add the green crème de menthe by pouring it in slowly over the back of a spoon so that it creates its own layer in the shot glass. Then add the peppermint schnapps in the same way. The end result will taste like a candy cane and will have three pretty layers of red, green, and clear liquid. Serve at once.

THE APPLE PIE SHOT

Yield: 1 serving

   ½ ounce vodka
   ¼ ounce sour apple schnapps
   ¼ ounce cinnamon schnapps
   1 tiny dollop whipped cream

Pour the vodka, the sour apple schnapps, and the cinnamon schnapps into a one-ounce shot glass and stir. Top with the dollop of whipped cream and serve at once.

THE PINEAPPLE UPSIDE-DOWN CAKE SHOT

Yield: 1 serving

   1 ounce vanilla vodka (or plain vodka mixed with
      a few drops of vanilla extract)
   1 ounce pineapple juice
   ¼ ounce grenadine

Pour all the ingredients into a three-ounce shot glass, stir, and serve.

THE BUTTERNUT SHOT

Yield: 1 serving

   1 ounce Frangelico
   1 ounce butterscotch schnapps

Combine the Frangelico and the schnapps in a two-ounce shot glass, stir, and serve.

THE CHEESECAKE SHOT

Yield: 1 serving

   ½ ounce Baileys Irish Cream
   ½ ounce pineapple juice
   ¼ ounce grenadine

Combine all the ingredients in a two-ounce shot glass, stir, and serve.

THE CHOCOLATE BOMB
PUDDING SHOT

Yield: 8 servings

   1 small (3.5- to 3.9-ounce) package instant
     chocolate pudding
   ¾ cup coffee-flavored liqueur
   ¾ cup coconut-flavored rum
   4 ounces Cool Whip

Whisk the instant pudding and the coffee liqueur together in a medium bowl until thick, about 1 to 2 minutes. Add the rum and whisk until all the lumps are gone. Then whisk in the Cool Whip. Spoon the mixture into two-ounce plastic shot cups, cover with plastic wrap or seal them in a container with a lid, and put them in the freezer. Let them set for several hours or overnight. Serve the shots with a teaspoon or a wooden ice cream spoon.